White Blood

White Blood

Angela Holder

Deore Press
Houston, Texas

For everyone who has nursed or tried to nurse a baby, especially the seven women who founded La Leche League.

One

maryn snuggled Frilan against her body and guided her breast into his mouth. His hungry wails cut off, replaced by eager sucking. Maryn bent her head until the silky strands of her son's hair tickled her nose and cheeks and breathed the musky scent she found so irresistible.

The straw mattress crackled as Edrich rolled over and curled around her. Maryn pressed her back into his solid warmth. "I'm sorry we woke you."

"I don't mind." He reached over her to stroke the curve of Frilan's shoulder. "I'll need to be up soon, anyway. I've got to get working on the tapestry at first light, if it's going to be done in time."

She twisted around as much as she could without disturbing Frilan's nursing. It must be close to dawn; she could make out the familiar profile of her husband's beaked nose and bushy eyebrows. "I thought you had plenty of time. Princess Voerell isn't due for weeks yet. And won't it be three months after the prince is born before the heirship ceremony?"

Edrich shrugged. "The town council's been pressuring me. They sent another messenger yesterday, asking how soon it would be ready." He was quiet for a moment. "And I have to redo the section with the tower again. I can't seem to get it right."

Maryn bit back an impatient rebuke. The woven tower had looked fine to her each of the three previous times Edrich had ripped it out. But she knew better than to argue. His perfectionism was what made him such a gifted craftsman.

When the tapestry was finished and presented as the town's gift to the prince who would soon be born, all of Milecha would recognize Edrich's talent. Orders would pour in from nobles and wealthy merchants. She wouldn't be able to spin enough yarn to keep up with the demand. Coins would pour into their coffer, until they could laugh and wonder how they had ever scraped by on the small and rapidly dwindling amount it now contained.

She sighed. "I was hoping you could watch Frilan for an hour or two, while I take the wash down to the river. We're almost out of clean diapers." Frilan released her breast and rooted for more. She scooped him onto her chest and rolled them both over. The baby nestled between Maryn and Edrich as she helped him find her other nipple.

"I don't think I can spare the time. Unless you want to go now? It's earlier than I thought. It will be at least two hours before the light's good enough."

Maryn hated the thought of leaving their warm bed and venturing into the chill spring dawn. None of the other women would be at the washing place so early, and she would miss the friendly chatter that made the work go quickly. But it was much easier without Frilan. The older women handled the task easily with their latest babes slung on their backs, but in the six weeks since Frilan's birth Maryn had not yet learned that knack.

"All right. As soon as he goes back to sleep."

Maryn twined her fingers with Edrich's and

closed her eyes. She nearly drowsed off again before Frilan's sucks slowed and her nipple slid from his slack mouth.

Edrich's deep slow breaths indicated he was asleep as well. Maryn tucked his hand around Frilan and slid out from under the covers as quietly as she could.

In the darkness she pulled on her skirts and laced her bodice over her shift. She scooped up the basket piled high with dirty diapers and backed down the narrow ladder from the sleeping loft. Pausing by the hearth, she lit a candle at the banked coals and placed it in the lantern, then headed for the door.

She had to stop, though, to hold up the lantern and admire the tapestry. Only the top few inches, with the sky and the palace that was giving Edrich so much trouble, remained to be woven. The main scene was complete, and she caught her breath as always at the magnificence of Edrich's vision.

In the foreground stood Lord Hoenech, ancestor of the expected prince. His hands were raised in a magical gesture, brilliant scarlet blood fountaining from a gash across one palm. Azure bolts of sorcerous energy radiated in every direction. Victims of the plague, their skin blotched with purple boils, crowded around him. Their gaunt faces were just beginning to transform from despair to incredulous joy, as they felt the effects of the healing magic that would cure them at the cost of Lord Hoenech's life.

Because of Lord Hoenech's sacrifice, his son was acclaimed as king, for the former dynasty had all perished in the plague. King Froethych could not fail to be pleased with this reminder of how his family had come to the throne, and consider it a fitting gift for his grandson.

Maryn's thoughts faltered. The Royal Sorcerer had worked scrying magic, and proclaimed that Princess Voerell's child would be a boy. But what if he was wrong? Under the law of Milecha, a girl could not be made heir. The heirship ceremony would be canceled. The painstakingly prepared gifts would be stored away against the hope that someday Princess Voerell or one of her brothers would produce a boy child. All the months of work Edrich had invested in this tapestry would be wasted. It had been a great honor for him to be chosen over all the other weavers in Ralo to make the town's gift, but the town council had not offered payment. He and Maryn would have to scramble to make and sell more of the rugs, blankets and simple tapestries that had previously provided their livelihood before their meager savings ran out.

She shrugged off that worry. Of course the scrying was correct. Even the smallest drop of blood contained powerful magic, and the Royal Sorcerer was deeply learned in the spells required to safely control it and turn it to useful purposes. He would not make a mistake in so important a matter.

Maryn resettled the laundry basket on her hip and slipped out the door. The air was crisp enough to make her shiver, although it would likely be hot by afternoon. Or maybe her shiver was for the dark emptiness of the narrow cobblestone streets. She couldn't help but imagine what might lurk in the deep shadows that made the familiar way seem sinister. She told herself not to be silly. But when she opened the little postern gate in the town wall and set off down the path that led to the river, her fears were harder to dismiss. Everyone knew the trees and tangled undergrowth that lined both sides of the river were home to all manner of wild beasts, to say nothing of the specters and ghouls that favored such places. Maryn traced the sign of the noose around her neck for protection.

The birds were just starting to twitter when Maryn reached the washing place. She would need to hurry if she wanted to get back before Edrich and Frilan woke. She sat down on one of the scattered boulders to pull off her shoes and stockings, tucked up her skirts, and waded out into the cold shallow water with her first armful of diapers.

By the time she rinsed out the last large linen square and spread it on a convenient branch, the light was bright enough to sparkle on the rippling water. Maryn began to gather the damp diapers into the basket. She'd hang them up in the little yard at home to finish drying, and to let the sun bleach out the last stubborn stains.

Pain lanced up from the sole of her foot. Maryn cried out and hopped to sit on the closest boulder. Bright droplets of blood stained the sharp rock she'd stepped on and splashed on the ground. She snatched a clean diaper and pressed the damp cloth to the wound.

The slice wasn't deep, but all that blood would have to be dealt with quickly. Out here specters would soon catch the scent and flock to make a meal of it—and her, too, if she wasn't careful.

Maryn took a deep breath and called to mind the familiar words. She used them frequently, whenever she needed to clean up after some minor mishap like this, as well as when she had cleansed her monthly blood before she became pregnant with Frilan. Only in the past few days had she stopped needing them to cleanse the flow of blood that had followed his birth. But the spell the Holy One had given for his people's protection was powerful, and holy, and not to be spoken lightly.

Once she was sure her mind was suitably composed, Maryn began the chant. The words were in the ancient language, but she knew roughly what they meant. The first section was a prayer to the Holy One, praising him and asking for his protection. After that came the words that released the blood's power, burning it up harmlessly so it couldn't be used for any evil purpose.

As Maryn recited the crucial words, she spread the crimson-smeared cloth across her lap. A vibration began deep in her bones and traveled through her body, until her teeth rattled and a buzz like swarming bees filled her ears. At the climax of the spell, each patch of blood—on the cloth, on her foot, and on the ground—erupted into a blaze of sparks. For a moment they swarmed in the air like blue fireflies. Then they died away, until all that was left were a few smudges of sticky, powerless residue.

The cut on her foot no longer bled. It only hurt a little as Maryn rinsed her foot and the diaper in the river and pulled on her stockings and shoes. The sun was well up. Edrich would be impatiently waiting for her so he could get to work. Frilan would be getting fussy, ready for another nursing.

At the thought, a warm rush flooded her breasts. Maryn pressed her forearms firmly across her chest to ease the sensation and prevent her milk from leaking. She'd soaked her shift and bodice several times before Siwell, her midwife, had shown her that trick. When the feeling passed, she gathered up the basket, piled the last of the diapers into it, balanced the lantern on top, and set off toward home.

On her way up the path, Maryn smelled smoke.

She smiled at the warm, homey scent. Her arms were still cold from the frigid river water. It would feel good to build up the fire in the hearth and warm herself. She'd put on a pot of porridge to cook and she and Edrich would enjoy breakfast together before he lost himself in the demands of his weaving.

The smell kept getting stronger. Odd. It wasn't so cold that everyone in Ralo should be stoking their hearthfires high. And there was a strange, bitter note underlying the familiar scent. The voices beyond the gate were louder than they should be. Maryn shaded her eyes from the glare of the risen sun and peered through the trees. Beyond the wall, over the town's rooftops, a thick black cloud billowed into the sky.

The postern gate flew open, and a man carrying a bucket burst through. He rushed past Maryn without a glance, down the path toward the river. Maryn started forward, but more townspeople crowded through the narrow gate and shoved her aside. She tried to fight her way through, but someone knocked her arm, and the basket of diapers flew from her hands.

The bells from the church tower jerked into life, clanging in wild discordant peals. Maryn scrambled to retrieve the scattered cloths, as men and women, many carrying buckets or tubs, pushed past her.

A large woman grabbed Maryn by the shoulder. "Forget your wash; what will it matter if the whole town burns?" She thrust a bucket into Maryn's hands and gestured urgently toward the river.

Maryn's heart raced. "What's happening? Is there a fire?"

"Is there—Of course there's a fire, girl, wake up! Half the south quarter is burning!"

"The south quarter?" A sick, hollow feeling lurched in Maryn's stomach. "That's where I live."

"You'd better pray your home escapes. Not many will, I fear."

Maryn stepped back, the bucket falling from her numb fingers. The woman cursed and lunged to grab it. "I've got to go home! I left my husband there, my baby..."

"By the Rope and Gallows, girl, you can't help them now. Save by—" She tried to press the bucket on Maryn again, but relented when Maryn could only stare at her, horror-stricken, her clenched fists pressed to her mouth. "Look, child," she said, her voice a trifle softer, though still harsh. "We're all doing the best we can. They'll send for a sorcerer; maybe we'll be lucky and one will get here in time. Or maybe Priest Vinhor will be able to do something. Until then, all we can do is bring up water. Get to it, girl, for your loved ones' sakes."

Maryn gaped at her. She turned and gazed in the direction of her home, past where a line of townspeople was forming, passing full buckets from hand to hand. A thick haze hung in the air, and she heard a dim roar like distant drenching rain. Maryn shook, her thoughts fragmented, whirling in every direction. She had to get home, scoop up Frilan from the bed and run...

She pushed past the woman, ignoring her angry shouts, and fought her way through the gate and into the crowded streets. When packed bodies blocked her way, she kicked shins and dug her elbows into sides until her path cleared. The smoke grew thicker, choking her, and heat beat against her face, but she didn't stop until she rounded a corner and came in sight of the fire.

Buildings blazed, orange flames leapt high into the sky, black billows poured forth. Even so she tried to press on, but one of the structures that leaned out over the street collapsed in an explosion of sparks and ashes, blocking her way.

Maryn ducked into a side alley and ran, trying to find a path around, but every street she tried ended in a wall of fire. Finally she found a spot that seemed passable. Townsfolk with buckets had quenched the worst of the flames, reducing them to a ruin of ash and shimmering coals. Maryn put her arm over her face and plowed forward. But even weakened, the fire was far stronger than she. Fumes seared her throat and burned in her eyes. Sobbing, she surrendered to the driving waves of heat and stumbled back. A gust of wind swirled around her and whipped the blaze to ravenous new life.

Voices shouted. Hands grabbed her and dragged her away from the conflagration. A man hurled the contents of a bucket into the flames, the splash of water vanishing instantly in a hiss of steam. He thrust the empty bucket at Maryn and turned to seize another from the woman next to him. The woman snatched the bucket from Maryn's hands and sent it back down the straggling line of townspeople.

Maryn wanted to keep running, to search until she found some miraculous passage through or around the raging furnace to her home. But she knew it was hopeless. Only one small means to defy the fire was open to her.

She fell into line, accepting a heavy filled tub from the woman. She staggered under its weight. Water sloshed out and soaked the front of her shift and bodice. She barely managed to pass it on to the man without dropping it. He cast its contents into the heart of the blaze.

After that, Maryn's world narrowed to a needle-sharp focus. Take the full vessel from the woman on the left, turn, pass it to the man on the right. Take the empty container from the man, pass it to the woman. Keep the water level, don't let it spill. Keep the rhythm going, don't let it falter.

She labored for hours, with only rare brief pauses to wipe sweat from her brow and blink stinging smoke from her eyes. Her arms grew heavy and her back cried out in pain. Water drenched her clothes and soot blackened them. Several times the heat of the approaching flames drove her and the others back, but they always reformed their line and kept the buckets moving.

Someone made their way down the line, passing out loaves of bread and hunks of cheese. Maryn stuffed the offered food into her mouth. She must keep up her strength. She snatched a drink of the murky river water as it passed, grimacing at the foul taste. But nothing mattered except the battle against the ravening beast that devoured Ralo's buildings with licking yellow tongues and jagged orange teeth.

The muscles in Maryn's arms screamed as she accepted yet another heavy tub. She staggered under its weight and turned to pass it on. But the man next to her was frozen, staring into the sky. Maryn jammed the tub into his back. "Take it!"

The man accepted it and set it down at his feet. He waved a quelling hand at Maryn. "Hush. Look. Something's happening."

"No! We've got to keep—" But then Maryn saw.

High above, the black pall of smoke swirled, blown by a wind sprung from nowhere. Other than smoke, the sky had been cloudless all day, the merciless sun beating down, augmenting the heat of the fire. Now a towering thunderhead began to build, growing in minutes from a mere wisp to an enormous dome looming overhead. Blue lightning flickered around its edges, but no thunder sounded. A buzz started in Maryn's heels and ascended to the base of her skull, intensifying until she felt as if all her teeth would fall out and her skull would crack open.

The cloud grew dark. The light took on a green cast. A drop of rain smacked Maryn in the nose. Another struck her outstretched palm. The heavens opened and sheets of water plummeted down, streaming through Maryn's bedraggled braids and sluicing into her eyes and down the back of her neck. She reveled in the flood, raising her hands in thanksgiving, until she had to duck her head again to keep from choking and drowning.

"Sorcery!" the man cried, the excitement in his voice tinged with fear. Maryn understood his apprehension. It must have taken a huge quantity of blood to fuel so tremendous a spell. Far more than any sorcerer could spare of his own.

But the man shook off his doubt, as rain poured down and the fire roared and billowed mountains of white steam. "Ralo is saved!"

Someone flung her arms around Maryn, laughing and sobbing. The woman spun away, but Maryn grabbed a stranger in turn and embraced him. Everyone clung to one another in a riot of celebration and release.

The deluge continued, cold and relentless. The crowd pressed forward, eager to see the fire swallowed up by the magic rain. Maryn went with them, down the street that led toward her home.

The flames subsided beneath the pounding water, though in places they still flared, defying the downpour. Skeletons of buildings tilted at crazy angles or lay collapsed in steaming, hissing piles of rubble. Scorched plaster walls stood, empty shells encasing ash. The whole south quarter of Ralo was a black, sodden ruin stretching as far as Maryn could see.

Maryn's steps slowed until she halted, cold and soaked. She began to shiver. She could not seem to control her body; it shook in ragged waves that seized her more strongly every moment. She sank to the ground. Water flowed in the street. It pooled around her, muddy and foul, but she couldn't bring herself to care.

She didn't know how long she huddled there. Others came and went around her. She heard screaming, and shouting, and agitated voices. At length the rain slackened, and stopped as suddenly as it had begun.

Someone tugged at her sleeve. "Girl, come. They've opened up the church to shelter those who've lost their homes. You can get dry there, and warm."

She shook the kindly stranger off. "No. I haven't lost my home. I'm sure it's fine. It's not in the part of town that burned. It's not!"

"If you're sure." He still sounded concerned, but Maryn stared at his feet until he left.

She had to get home. She had to find Edrich. Frilan would be so hungry. Her breasts hurt, hot and heavy with the milk that should have gone to feed his greedy appetite. Siwell would scold her. The midwife had warned her not to go too long without nursing; that she would risk clogging up her breasts with blockages or developing a fever. Maybe that's what was happening now. Maybe that's why she felt so odd and disoriented.

Maryn struggled to her feet. She needed to nurse

Frilan. That would heal the ache in her breasts and clear the fog from her mind. Once she held him in her arms, everything would be fine again.

Many obstructions blocked her path, where beams or stones or whole walls had fallen into the street, but she picked her way around them. A number of people were making their way through the devastated area, but she ignored those who called out to her. She climbed over the smoldering remains of an ox-cart. The corpses of the oxen smelled like the great public roasting pits on a feast day. The landmarks that usually guided her through the maze of narrow, twisting streets were altered almost beyond recognition. The sign for the free public privies at the dyer's hung askew by one nail, the dyer's wall half fallen in. But enough remained for her to find her way.

Her street was all wrong, though. She was sure their house was around here somewhere. It should be on the east side of the street, but all the buildings there were empty, smoking shells, doors and windows gaping like eye sockets in a row of skulls.

Maryn stood looking blankly at an empty doorframe that was at once familiar and horribly strange. She started as a voice hailed her. "Miss?"

She turned to see a soldier. By his uniform he was one of the garrison the king kept at the small fortress in the northern wall. "Miss, I'm sorry, but you've got to leave. We've got orders to clear everyone out. There's looters abroad. Not that there's much left for them to steal."

Maryn shook her head. "I've got to find my house. I must have got turned around; I thought it was here, but this can't be…"

The soldier hesitated. "I'm not supposed to—Oh, here, where was it?"

"Nedry Street."

"This is Nedry." He poked with the butt of his spear at the rubble in the doorway. "Do you recognize anything?"

Maryn shook her head. "I've got to find my husband. He was asleep when I left, with my son. Maybe that's my house over there." She pointed far to the north, where untouched structures were just visible in the failing light.

"No, Nedry doesn't go that way. I think you found the right place. The sleeping loft was in the back?" He peered into the cavernous shell of the building. "It's all collapsed back there." He looked at Maryn's stricken face, and his voice softened a little. "Lots of people were trapped. No one had any warning; it spread blocks before the first bell sounded."

He worked his way into the ruins. Maryn was drawn to the doorway but could not bring herself to step through. She watched as the soldier poked through the scorched, sodden piles. "This is no good. I tell you, miss, you're going to have to—Wait. Here's something. Do you recognize this?"

He pulled a limp scrap of fabric from under a fallen beam and picked back through the rubble toward Maryn, holding it out. She took it, unthinking, and spread out the crumpled folds.

A face stared up at her, blotched by the plague, mouth open in a soundless cry for mercy. Across the raveled edge of the scrap ran a woven spatter of blood, still dull red in places though most of it was charred and blackened.

Maryn stared at it. "No..." she whispered. She crumpled the fragment of tapestry in her fist. "No!" She flung it away from her. "I've never seen it before. It's not his; it's completely different. You're wrong, this isn't my house. I've got to find Edrich. Frilan will be crying for me..."

Her legs buckled underneath her and she sank into a huddle. The soldier put his hand on her shoulder in rough sympathy. "I'm sorry, miss. But this is the place. If they were here, they must be—"

Maryn clamped her hands over her ears and screamed, trying in vain to block out the soldier's words.

Two

Once Maryn started screaming, she couldn't stop. She resisted the gentle pressure of the soldier's hands on her shoulders, and curled into a tighter ball. But he was persistent, and at length her shrieks subsided to ragged sobs. She kept her head bowed and her eyes squeezed shut, but allowed him to lift her to her feet and lead her away.

She heard his voice, a dull rumble. "I found this one in the ruins. Poor girl, she lost her family; she's out of her wits with grief. What should I do with her?"

Another voice, weary and gruff. "Take her to the church. Nothing else we can do."

Maryn shrieked again to drown them out, but her throat hurt too much to keep it up for long. None of this was real. It couldn't be. Any minute now she would wake up from the nightmare.

After a while there was a smooth stone floor, and candlelight, and a blanket around her shoulders. They let her stop walking. She sank to the floor, wrapped her arms around her knees, and buried her head.

"This one's not hurt, but all she does is scream."

"Leave her alone. She'll get over it. We've got much worse to deal with."

After that there was merciful peace. People came and went all around, but they ignored Maryn, and she ignored them. She scooted over to where a wall met the floor and curled up with a wad of blanket under her head. Sleep was good. If she slept, she could wake up, and Edrich would tease her that she'd let a silly dream upset her...

"Maryn? Maryn, dear, is that you? Wake up, child. I'm sure I can find you a warmer spot somewhere." The voice was familiar and comforting.

Maryn stirred and cracked her bleary eyes. "Siwell?"

The midwife crouched beside her and helped her sit up. Her arm brushed Maryn's breast; Maryn cried out in pain.

"By the Holy Orphan, child." Her experienced hands exploring Maryn's hard, swollen breasts were gentle, but agonizing. "Where's your little one? How long has it been since you nursed him?"

"I don't know!" Maryn slumped into Siwell's arms. "I left Frilan with Edrich, in bed. I couldn't find them; everything was burned. They tried to tell me that was my house, but I know they're wrong. That wasn't Edrich's tapestry. They're lying to me, trying to make me think Edrich and Frilan—"

Maryn broke into frenzied sobs. Siwell held her close and rocked, humming and stroking her hair.

At length Maryn's wails quieted to shaky breaths, broken by hiccups. Siwell gave her a few minutes more before speaking. "I'd let you rest, but we must do something about those breasts. I won't let you come down with milk fever if we can help it. Have you taken milk from your breasts by hand before?"

"A little. And I've milked cows and goats plenty of times."

"It's not quite the same, but close enough. Let me go find a container you can use." Siwell hurried away.

Maryn put her arms around her knees again and rocked. Agony hovered around the edges of her mind. It threatened to pounce on her and rend her apart, like a pack of stray dogs tearing the last shreds of meat from a bone.

To hold them at bay, she focused on the soaring panels of stained glass that adorned the church's high walls. The colors were jewel bright; Edrich would have bargained with the Vulture himself to obtain dyes so vivid. The story of the Holy One's life was told in a series of scenes that ringed the building. Directly opposite her was the depiction of one of her favorite episodes, when he had transformed a single drop of blood from his finger into a feast for a hungry crowd.

Siwell dropped to her side with one of the wooden bowls the healers used to capture blood. It was polished to a glossy shine and ornately carved with sacred symbols. She pressed it into Maryn's hands.

Maryn drew back. "I couldn't. Wouldn't it be sacrilege?"

Siwell shrugged. "Just don't let the priests see. I don't think it's inappropriate. Milk's a lot like blood. White blood, some call it. It has its own power. Now, let me show you what you need to do."

Though Maryn's shift was stiff with the milk that had leaked from her overfull breasts, it wasn't easy to coax more out. But Siwell was a patient instructor. She showed Maryn how to position her fingers well back from her nipple, behind the edge where darker skin met fair, and first push back in toward her chest, then roll down and out. Maryn doubted at first that the awkward motions could work, but after a few attempts she managed to produce a dozen thin white streams, and felt the relief of eased pressure.

Siwell kept her under a watchful eye until she was sure Maryn had mastered the technique. "I suppose you should drink it. I don't think milk attracts specters, but no use taking chances, and you're too tired to work the releasing ritual safely. Besides, you'll be lucky if you get much decent to drink for a few days."

Maryn nodded her understanding. The bowl was nearly full already. She raised it to her lips and sipped. It was sweeter and lighter than the milk from cow or goat. The taste took her back to her own childhood, when she had climbed into her mother's lap and drunk deeply of the rich warm liquid. Whatever scrape or bruise or fit of temper troubled her was forgotten as she snuggled safe, and all was again right with the world. Tears came to her eyes at the memory, and she had to struggle to swallow the last few mouthfuls.

Siwell delicately probed Maryn's breast. "That's much better. Get the other side as well, now." She hesitated. "No need to take much; just until you're comfortable. You'll need to cut back a little at a time, as a weaning child does, to let it dry up gradually."

Maryn wanted to protest, to exclaim that of course she couldn't let her milk dry up. Frilan needed it. But she was so tired. No matter how hard she tried to keep believing this was all a horrible dream, she couldn't anymore. Everything was too real. Her breasts hurt, the floor was hard and cold beneath her, the air reeked of smoke, and the sobs of her fellow refugees rang in her ears. The truth was still too terrible to face, but she knew. Frilan would never need her milk again.

She grunted and went on drawing the milk from her breast in long, rhythmic strokes, trying to get the maximum amount with each effort, before repositioning her fingers and pressing again.

"No, wait. I just had a thought." Maryn glanced up, startled by the change in the midwife's voice. Siwell gave her a searching look. "Go ahead and get as much out as you can, for now. There will be time enough later to cut back. But there's something you might be interested in..." She rose. "I must go help the other healers. Until I get back, don't nurse any other babies, if someone should offer, or ask for help."

That was an odd instruction. Surely there were babies orphaned by this disaster, or separated from their mothers. Why wouldn't Siwell want her to help them? Not that Maryn wanted to. Under normal circumstances she'd be glad to nurse any child in need, but right now she couldn't even think of letting some other child take Frilan's place.

Once she had drained both breasts, she drank the last of it, set the bowl aside, and did up the tie of her shift. She set her back against the wall and stuck her legs out in front of her. All around were other refugees from the devastation. Some of them huddled together in tight little groups, but many, like Maryn, sought solitude for their distress. Near the altar where Siwell had gone healers moved among the wounded. Blue sparks flared often, and a nearly constant dim echo of the buzzing emanations of magic came up through the polished stone of the floor.

She closed her eyes and tried to think about nothing. Eventually the numb emptiness that had gripped her earlier returned. Later she sank into fitful sleep.

When she woke, the noon bells were ringing. Robed brothers and sisters of the abbey moved among the refugees, offering coarse brown bread trenchers with meager scoops of lentil pottage. The fare was a significant step down from even the modest meals she was used to, but she was so hungry she didn't care. She made the food last as long as she could, breaking off tiny bits of bread and chewing until nothing was left but the gritty residue of the millstones.

With her energy restored by rest and food, it was much harder to steer her mind away from dangerous thoughts. She jumped to her feet and went in search of some task to occupy her attention.

The healers were too deeply absorbed in their work to notice her. She stood for a moment, watching them. Victims of the fire lay everywhere. Maryn had to avert her eyes from their raw burned flesh. A healer chanted as he untied a blood-soaked bandage from around a deep cut on one woman's arm. The blood erupted into a fountain of blue fire, and the woman's moans subsided as the gaping edges of her wound drew together and began to scab over.

Two brothers pushed past Maryn, bearing on a stretcher the still form of a large, well-muscled man. One side of his face was a blackened ruin. Though he wore the leather apron of a smith, something about the dead man's heavy build and the lank blond strands of his soot-streaked hair reminded her suddenly and forcefully of Edrich. She had to sink her teeth into her lower lip to keep from screaming.

She snatched at a passing sister. "Please, give me something to do. Anything, I don't care, I just have to stay busy…"

The sister patted her hand. "There, there, dear. You don't need to fuss. We've got things well under control. You go lie down and rest, and stay out of the way."

Maryn grabbed the sister's arms and shook her. "No! Give me something to do! I don't want to lie around and—I want to help! You have to let me do something!"

The woman stared at her, shocked, and tried to pull free. Maryn clung to her arms. The sister raised a frightened voice. "Brother Ohwich, help!"

A large, stern brother was at their side in an instant. "What's the matter? Girl, step back and settle down. We'll have to put you out of the church if you don't—"

Siwell hurried up. "Maryn, child, I heard you shouting. It's all right, Brother, I know her."

Maryn dropped the sister's arms and stepped back, the looming dark wave of her pain threatening to crash over her. "Siwell, I just want to help…"

"Of course you do." Siwell turned to the sister. "Can't you find the girl some useful task?"

After a good deal more chiding from Siwell, a brother brought Maryn a mop and a bucket of water. She seized them and set about zealously scrubbing every exposed inch of beautifully inlaid floor. Some of the refugees cursed at her as she pushed them out of her way or dripped water onto their precious blankets. The healers were more welcoming of her presence, shifting cots and tables out of her way so she could remove the frighteningly large quantities of power-emptied blood residue and other less palatable body fluids. Maryn didn't care how noxious the task was; it felt good to scrub the filth away and leave behind glistening clean floors.

Near sunset she was going over the stretch of floor nearest the altar for the third time, certain there were still a few spatters of mud and soot she had missed, when Siwell came to fetch her. She took the mop from

Maryn's hand as she tried to push past to reach one more dirty spot. "Maryn, that's enough. Stop now. Come, they're bringing around dinner; I'll sit with you while we eat."

Reluctantly, Maryn complied. Siwell frowned as they walked toward the spot by the wall where Maryn's blanket lay. "Have you taken care of your breasts since this morning?"

Maryn ducked her head. She had ignored the gradually increasing need. Her breasts felt full and sore again. "No."

"Do it now. You have to keep your supply up."

Maryn gulped and looked away. "What…what does it matter?" She rushed on, trying to keep ahead of the flood of misery that crashed in through the opened gate. "If Frilan…if I don't need to nurse him, what's the use? I might as well let them dry up. I'll never…never…" She swallowed hard.

"Sit down." Siwell put her back to the wall and slid down with a sigh. She kept her gaze fixed on Maryn until she sank to the floor as well.

Siwell leaned her head against the stone and closed her eyes for a moment. "Have you given any thought yet to what you're going to do next?"

Maryn stared at her. Next? What did that mean, anyway, besides the next spot of dirt on the floor, the next task she could beg them to assign her? Once she had thought effortlessly, without fear, about days and years to come, when they had stretched in peaceful happy abundance far into the hazy future. Now it was difficult to consider what even the next sunrise might bring. Only more misery, and greater danger of being overwhelmed by the fierce grief she must constantly struggle to control.

Maybe she should just give up. If she stopped

fighting the pain, would it destroy her? Would it drive her so far into madness she could lose all thought and feeling? Would it kill her, so her soul would be free to seek out Edrich and Frilan in the courts of the Holy One? Perhaps that was the best she could hope for. She couldn't imagine that she might ever come out on the far side of this endless night of grief to anything resembling her former innocent contentment.

Siwell looked at her, waiting for an answer. Maryn turned away. "No. Not really." She tried, tentatively, to consider the practicalities, at least. Her home was lost. She yanked her thoughts back from the image of the scorched pile of rubble that seared the back of her eyelids. Was there anyone she could stay with? One of her friends, perhaps? The women she knew had been her neighbors, or the wives of Edrich's Weaver's Guild colleagues. Most of them also dwelt in the south quarter. They would be in the same straits she was, if any survived.

The midwife still waited, but Maryn could think of nothing to say. She shook her head.

Siwell sighed. "Will you go back to your father's house?"

"I could." She hated the thought, but what other choice did she have? Her marriage to Edrich had let her escape the hard life of endless drudgery that was a serf's lot. Mother and Father had been so pleased. Their whole family's labor in Lord Negian's fields earned them only a tiny strip of land. It had produced barely enough to feed them in years past, even before her younger brothers had grown into hungry youths. "I guess I'll have to."

"Maybe not, if you find a way to take care of yourself."

"Take care of myself?" Despair weighed heavy as

the lead that sealed a coffin in Maryn's heart. "How can I do that? I have nothing. Everything was in our house. My spinning wheel, my wool...it's all gone." No, she still couldn't let her thoughts venture so close to where the ashes of the sleeping loft lay buried under wreckage. "I even lost the basket of diapers. Maybe I could find them." The thought of scouring the woods for the pitiful little pile of cloths was so funny she broke into giggles.

"Maryn." Siwell's sharp voice shook her back to sobriety. "Listen. I'm aware of an opportunity that could prove very valuable to you, if you choose to pursue it." Her voice gentled. "I know nothing can come close to replacing what you've lost, but this could at least allow you to remain a freewoman, and independent."

"What do you mean?"

Siwell picked up the carved bowl from where it lay forgotten among the folds of the blanket. "Here. We can talk while you take care of this. Your breasts must feel miserable."

They did, though not nearly as bad as they had that morning. Maybe her milk was already starting to go away. Maryn untied the drawstring of her shift and lifted her breast free. She fumbled for a moment, but quickly remembered how to go about it. She let the rhythm of her motions and the hiss of the milk spraying into the bowl calm her as she listened to Siwell's words.

"A few days ago I received a message from the head of my order in Loempno. The stewardess of the royal household seeks a wet nurse for Princess Voerell's coming child. Ideally she would like a woman between twenty and twenty-five, who gave birth less than a month ago, and has an ample supply of milk. But most important, she needs someone who has no ties to land or family to bind her."

Maryn blinked. "Are you suggesting I might—But I don't fit that. I'm only eighteen. And Frilan is... was..." She had to stop and swallow, and search for words she could say. "Frilan was born more than six weeks ago."

"Yes, but that's not too far off. And the other factors matter more. It's rare to find a woman anywhere close to those criteria who's free to give the full commitment they're looking for." Siwell looked gravely at Maryn. "I'm going to be blunt with you Maryn, because I believe you're strong enough to handle it. The Royal Stewardess is looking for a woman whose baby is dead. Recently, so her milk is still abundant. And no husband, though the church would frown on one who conceived out of wedlock. But a widow is perfect."

Dead. Widow. The stark words stabbed into Maryn's heart, releasing a gush of anguish. She squeezed her eyes shut against tears, and her hands trembled until her milk almost spilled and she had to put the bowl down. Siwell was quiet while she scrubbed at her wet cheeks and drew deep breaths, trying to regain her composure.

Calm came more quickly than she would have thought possible. It was almost a relief to have the words out in the open. Their truth settled on Maryn, cold and empty and final.

She picked up the bowl and concentrated on sending a few more jets of milk streaming into it, until she was sure her voice would not fail her. "I see."

"Have you ever nursed another child? A sister's, a friend's? One you were minding for pay?"

"No. There was one neighbor, we had planned,

after hers was born, that we might help each other sometimes, but she's..." Most likely lost, along with so many others.

"You're quite sure? Not even once, not even a drop?"

"Yes, I'm sure. Why? What does it matter?"

Siwell dropped her voice. "I mean to imply no slander, but I must ask...have any men tasted your milk? You can be honest with me; it would go no further."

Maryn's face flushed hot. "No! Of course not." She ducked her head, and blushed a little deeper. "Only... Only Edrich," she muttered.

"Thank you, dear. Obviously your husband, that's to be expected. And...he's not a problem."

"Why? Why should they care?"

Siwell gestured to the bowl of milk in her hands. "Milk creates kinship bonds. If two children nurse from the same woman, they become siblings. So for instance, a boy and a girl, even if they have no other relationship, cannot later marry."

"Oh. That's right. One of my aunts has a milk-sister that her mother took in when a friend died. She's always been a part of our family."

Siwell nodded. "Under the law of Milecha, as well as the laws of nature and magic, they are in fact sisters, with all the legal rights and responsibilities that go with that status. So if any other person drinks of your milk, and the new heir also, that person would have a claim of kinship to the prince. You can see why they would want to avoid such entanglements."

Maryn shrugged. "I suppose. But it's not like anyone would ever know if I had nursed some neighbor's baby once or twice."

"They would find out. There is sorcery that can reveal kinship ties. They will settle for a woman with such a history if they have no other choice, and pay off any potential milk-siblings, but they would prefer not to take the risk. It's enough of a burden that they must extend kinship to whichever wet nurse they choose. For of course, as milk-mother to the child, the same laws will apply to her. Not that they ever do more for the woman than the bare minimum, but still…Do you see why I think this could be such a good opportunity for you?"

"I guess." Maryn could understand the objective, logical reasons why she should leap to seize this chance. But her heart rebelled. She hated the idea of going to some strange city, of dwelling among people far above her in rank, who would look down on her as a lowborn and a burden, of permitting some other woman's child the intimacy of her body that only her own deserved. Her anger flared. "Why doesn't Princess Voerell nurse her own child? Wouldn't that avoid any of those 'entanglements' they're so worried about? Can she not be bothered?"

"Maryn, a highborn woman is not free to do as she pleases. As the third child of the king, with two elder brothers between any child she might bear and the throne, Princess Voerell is not as constrained by her duties as many. But since neither of her brothers has yet produced an heir, she is still expected to contribute as much as she can to increase the royal family. If she were to nurse this child, it would delay the time until she could conceive again, perhaps as much as a year or two. She will not be permitted that option."

Maryn felt a pang of sympathy for the princess, but pushed it away. What need had that august personage for her pity? She possessed more wealth and power than Maryn could imagine. She enjoyed admiration and adulation from everyone around her, servants to tend her least need or whim, rich food and fine wine and jewel-encrusted gowns. She would undoubtedly be perfectly happy to send the child away with its nurse, free of any obligation to put her own pleasures aside to tend the baby's needs.

She pulled her blanket around her shoulders and turned away from Siwell. "Even if I wanted to, I can't. Loempno is miles away. I have nothing, not even other clothes to wear while I wash these." She brushed futilely at the sooty, muddy wreck of her skirts. "If I went before the Royal Stewardess like this she'd think a beggar had wandered in off the streets."

"I could help you. I have a little set aside that I could use to buy you what you would need. You could pay me back after you begin to receive your wages."

Maryn blinked. "You would do that for me? Why?"

"I like you, Maryn. I always hate to see a good person fall victim to the whims of fate, and I try to do what I can to redress the balance a little. You deserve another chance at life, and I'm willing to go out of my way to make it happen. I haven't fulfilled my Obligation of Charity yet for the year; I expect the priests will rule this qualifies."

"I can't possibly ask you to do this—"

"I insist." Siwell dusted her hands on her skirt and rose. "If you still want work to keep you busy, the healers are going to be moving our patients. Captain Tennelan has granted us permission to use a spare barracks at the fortress. The priests are anxious to get us moved out before the Sabbath. They're going to be sending all the refugees away as well. If you like, I would welcome you in my home until we can send word to the Royal Stewardess and get you prepared for your journey."

Maryn nodded and scrambled to her feet, glad of the chance to lose herself again in hard physical labor. She still didn't know how she felt about Siwell's proposal. It wouldn't be so terrible to go back to her father's farm. But though she loved her family, she did not want to burden them, nor strain their meager resources. She had grown accustomed in the last year to being considered an adult, the mistress of her own household. It would be good to continue to provide for her own welfare.

Still, the whole thing seemed ridiculous. She, Maryn Loesella, a poor serf girl, wife to a minor craftsman, living in the royal palace? Meeting, even if only as a servant, the princess, maybe even the king? Caring for the new prince? What if he were to become king someday? Nobles had been known to lavish great largesse on their nurses, the women who functioned in all ways but blood as their mothers. She couldn't imagine herself in that role.

But her options were so limited, and Siwell's offer so generous, Maryn did not see that she had any other choice.

Three

The next morning dawned grey and leaden, matching Maryn's mood. There was not even a moment of blessed forgetfulness as she emerged from sleep; the knowledge of her loss weighed heavy in her heart with her first awareness. She picked at the breakfast Siwell offered and followed the midwife's every suggestion with dull compliance.

They spent the morning doing errands. Siwell purchased new clothes for Maryn, sent a message by post to the Royal Stewardess, and arranged for Maryn's passage to Loempno. Maryn watched with increasing dismay as Siwell handed over more and more coins. When she had accepted Siwell's offer, she hadn't fully realized how much it would cost. She felt greedy, taking so much advantage of Siwell's generosity.

"Siwell, is there anything I can do to repay you?" Maryn asked, as they emerged into the street from the cobbler's shop where Siwell had bought Maryn new shoes. "You're giving me so much. It doesn't seem right."

Siwell brushed aside Maryn's protest with a dismissive gesture. "You'll have plenty of opportunity to repay me later."

"But I want to do something now."

Siwell tilted her head and regarded Maryn. "I

have a few clients to visit this afternoon. You could
come and help with any little tasks I might need."

The thought of seeing round pregnant bellies and
hearing the mewling cries of newborns gave Maryn a
hollow feeling in the pit of her stomach. She
swallowed.

"No, what am I thinking?" Siwell took Maryn's arm
in a firm grasp and steered her toward the midwife's
home. "You need to rest. If you must do something,
you can sweep the floor and put supper on."

Maryn threw herself into the work. By the time
Siwell returned, the house was spotless, and stew
simmered in a pot over the coals. She even managed a
semblance of welcoming cheer when she greeted
Siwell at the door and fixed her a cup of tea.

Siwell regarded Maryn thoughtfully as she sipped.
"I know you're not ready for this yet, but it won't get
any easier. While I was out I heard talk that they're
letting people into the burned zone. There are a
couple hours of daylight left, if you want to try to
salvage anything from your house."

Every fiber of Maryn's being rebelled at the idea.
She felt as if she might vomit. But she hated the feeling
of being in Siwell's debt. Even if she were far more
fortunate than she had any right to expect, and was
actually chosen as the prince's nurse, it would be many
long weeks before she would accumulate enough to
pay the midwife back for what she had spent on
Maryn's behalf today. She and Edrich had kept their
savings in a little coffer under their mattress. The
coins should have survived the fire. Maybe.

"All right," she muttered.

Siwell studied her doubtfully for a moment. But
when she finished her tea, she rose and led the way
out.

Barriers blocked the road where it entered the burned section of the south quarter, and a cordon of soldiers guarded the boundary. A line of people waited to be allowed through. Soldiers escorted parties in and out of the wreckage.

Maryn and Siwell fell into line. It moved quickly; the soldiers managed the task with ruthless efficiency. When they reached the head of the line, one approached them, bored and gruff, obviously repeating words he had spoken many times already. "Your escort will take you to your residence. Any bodies will be collected by a cart for transport to the churchyard. Get in, get what you want, and get out. After sunset tomorrow, the Town Council has decreed that the quarter will be closed. Crews will start clearing it so rebuilding can start. Anything left will be forfeited to the town. If we find out you're taking stuff that's not yours, you'll be tossed in the gaol. Understand?"

Maryn nodded dumbly. The stink of wet ash was undercut by a note of burnt meat. She felt faint. Bitter gorge rose in the back of her throat.

Siwell peered at her. "Maybe this wasn't such a good idea. We can come back tomorrow, or I can go in alone, if you'd rather."

Maryn swallowed hard and shook her head. Tomorrow would only be worse. Better to get it over with. "No. Now."

Siwell frowned. "If you're sure."

The soldier waved them over to another who was waiting, having ushered his last party out past the barricade. This soldier was young, not much older than Maryn, and stout. His face was pale and his shoulders drooped.

"You holding up, Tior?" the first soldier asked. "I can relieve you if you need a break."

He straightened. "No, sir. I can manage."

His superior grinned. "We'll make a soldier of you yet."

Tior led them down the street. In places whole buildings had fallen, and lay in piles of broken plaster and charred beams, but most still stood, blackened walls open to the sky. A thick layer of ash covered the ruins, and swirled into choking clouds with every gust of wind. The worst of the rubble had been pushed to the side of the street, but there were many places where Maryn had to watch her step carefully.

Tior glanced back. "Where are you going?"

Maryn tried to respond, but she couldn't force her mouth to form the words. After a pause, Siwell said, "Nedry Street."

"This way."

It wasn't far. Everything was so different that Maryn quickly became disoriented, but when Tior stopped she recognized the soot-stained, gutted shell that had once been her home. She balled her hands into fists and halted, frozen, before what remained of her doorway.

Tior peered past her. "Do you expect to find any bodies?"

Maryn's legs felt wobbly and her head swam. She shouldn't have come. She had thought she would be able to face what she must, but she couldn't. She took deep breaths, trying to ignore the stench, and fought the urge to flee.

Siwell pulled Tior aside. She kept her voice low, but Maryn could still hear. "There was a sleeping loft in the back. We have reason to believe a man and a baby were there."

Tior gulped, and his round face blanched a shade paler. "All right. I'll signal the cart and take care of them for you." He took a horn from his belt and blew a blast back in the direction they had come. He pulled a length of blue cloth from a belt pouch and tied it to a projecting beam. "You two stay well back. I've been clearing bodies all day; it's not a fit sight for a woman."

"Nor a man, either," Siwell said sympathetically.

Tior shuddered. "You have no idea. But I've got to show the captain I can take it."

They entered the building. Only the outer, plastered walls still stood. The wooden walls within, the sleeping loft, and the thatched roof above had burned away or collapsed. The remains covered much of the floor in broken, ashy heaps. Tior picked his way though the rubble toward the back, and began heaving beams and charred boards out of the way.

Siwell put a hand on Maryn's arm. "Maryn, where would anything of value that might have survived be? Maryn? Maryn, look at me."

Maryn swallowed and shook her head. She had to get control of herself, or Siwell would despise her as a coward and weakling. "What?"

"I shouldn't have brought you here. Come, let me take you home."

"No!" Maryn pulled away and forced herself to concentrate. "I'm fine. Let me think. We kept our money in a coffer under our mattress. The fire wouldn't have hurt coins, would it?"

"I wouldn't think so. I'll ask Tior to search for it."

"I can do it myself." Maryn steeled herself and pushed past Siwell. Tior was at the big mound of wreckage that had been the loft, hauling half-burned boards from the pile. Maryn tried to go join him, but her feet faltered and slowed to a stop before she'd gone more than a few steps.

Siwell caught up to her and pulled her aside. "No.

You are not going back there. At least not until Tior is finished and everything is decently dealt with. What else can we look for?"

Maryn focused on Siwell's face. It was easier to think when she wasn't looking at the devastation. "I don't know. We didn't have much that wouldn't have burned. Everything we had went into Edrich's tapestry, and I know that..." She couldn't finish. Instead she went over to the pile where the other soldier had found the fragment of cloth, and began to shove aside chunks of debris.

Siwell came to help her. Together they uncovered the remains of Edrich's loom and tapestry. The fire hadn't burned it completely before the magically summoned rain had drenched it, but large sections had been reduced to ash, and the rest was ruined, barely recognizable as the masterpiece it had been. The biggest remaining fragment tore beneath Maryn's hands as she attempted to spread it out. She straightened and rubbed her smarting eyes with the back of her hand. "It's useless. There's nothing here worth salvaging." She kicked at the sodden mess.

Siwell sighed. "No."

Maryn turned her back on the ruined tapestry and destroyed loom. "My wheel was over here. I'm sure the fire got it, too."

It had, but there were a few metal fittings that she carefully picked free of the splinters of charred wood. A wheelwright would be able to make use of them. She could sell them, or save them for a time she might be able to afford to have a new wheel made.

Creaking and rumbling drew Maryn's attention to the door. Outside, an ox cart rolled to a stop. The driver swung down, along with several other workers. They crowded into the building, ignoring the women. One bore a roll of canvas, the others shovels. "Found them yet?" the driver called to Tior.

Tior was standing, hands clenched into fists at his sides, face turned away from the cleared space at his feet. He parted his pinched lips and took a shallow breath. "Over here—"

His voice cracked, and he stumbled a few steps to a corner, where he doubled over and retched. Maryn's stomach lurched in response, and she had to fight to suppress the nausea. She couldn't see what Tior had found. She didn't want to see, yet she couldn't tear her eyes away from the spot.

The driver laughed. "Come on, Tior, you've been at this all day. Are you going to puke every time?"

Tior rose. His face was nearly white, but he forced a composed expression. "I'm all right. Over here; there's two of them."

Maryn backed away. She bumped into Siwell, and didn't protest when the midwife's arms went around her. They stood together, pressed against the farthest wall.

The workers were fast and efficient. They spread out a length of canvas and went to work with their tools. Maryn watched until she caught a glimpse of the blackened form they uncovered. Then she twisted around and buried her face in Siwell's shoulder. But she couldn't escape the sickening smell that wafted stronger as they disturbed the corpses, like the rancid ashes of a cooking fire where fat had dripped.

After she heard the men pass on their way to the door, she dared a peek. Several of them carried a long, canvas wrapped bundle out the door toward the cart. Once they were gone she raised her head and swallowed, trying to settle her stomach.

Another worker brushed by her. Without thinking,

Maryn looked. In his arms he bore a second, much smaller bundle.

Maryn's head swam, and her guts churned. Dropping to her knees, she vomited, heaving until her stomach had no more contents to empty.

Siwell knelt beside her and murmured soothing words into her ear, though her voice shook. Tior came to stand beside them. He waited until she finished and sat back on her heels, struggling to catch her breath.

He extended a water skin to her. "I've lost count of how many times it's happened to me today. Here, rinse out your mouth; it will help a little. Just be careful how much you swallow."

The watered ale was warm and flat, but it served to clear most of the foul taste from Maryn's mouth. She struggled to her feet and handed the skin back to Tior.

One of the men from the ox-cart came back in. He was dressed in the brown robes of a lay employee of the church. "Miss, would you come out here a moment? I have a few questions for you."

Maryn pulled free of Siwell's supporting hands and followed him. He took out a quill and bottle of ink, uncorked the bottle, and balanced it on the seat of the wagon. Maryn very carefully did not look into the open bed. The man opened a small bound book and turned to a blank page. "Their names and ages?"

Maryn drew a deep breath. Her voice was not too shaky. "Edrich Loesella. Um, his birthday was just after the thaw, so that would make him twenty-four. And Frilan Loesella. He was born six weeks ago." She forced herself to focus only on the cold facts the man wanted.

"Do you have the exact dates?"

She had to wrack her brain to remember Edrich's, but she thought she got it right. And of course the date of Frilan's birth was engraved in her mind.

"Are you going to be able to pay for individual graves for them, and markers? Or should I put them down for burial in the mass grave? Priest Vinhor said to assure you it's all holy ground, and their souls will rest safe no matter which. But it does show a great deal more respect to the memory of your loved ones to give them their own space."

"I...How much?"

He named a price; it was far more than Maryn could possibly scrape together, even if she managed to salvage all the coins she knew had been in the coffer. She gulped, her stomach threatening to rebel again, as she thought of Edrich and Frilan tossed in among a jumble of other bodies, nothing to mark the place where they rested but a single stark stone. There was one in the north corner of the churchyard, engraved simply, "The Victims of the Great Plague."

Siwell, her face white with anger, dug into her belt pouch and slapped a handful of coins into the man's palm. "There. That should cover graves and markers for both of them, even at your ridiculous price."

"Siwell, no, I can't accept—"

"Just because Priest Vinhor is trying to make a profit from what should be every citizen's by right doesn't mean you should have to see your dear ones' bodies dumped in a pit." She tossed another two coins at the man; he caught them deftly. "And there's the payment for prayers at the next Sabbath service, for the repose of their souls."

The man's eyes brightened as he tucked the coins away. "For only a little more you could have candles, and the amount for prayers every week for a year is quite reasonable..."

"Take your money and go. And if I hear of you treating these two with anything but the utmost respect, I will take the complaint all the way to the Prelate."

The man narrowed his eyes as he snapped the book closed. "The king granted Prelate Kiellan his office, and he can take it away, if another rises higher in his favor."

"Are you suggesting he would consider Priest Vinhor? Not unless he were the only servant of the Holy One left in the kingdom!"

The vehemence of Siwell's words surprised Maryn. Why was she so upset? The amount was high, but it must be a fair price if the Church said so. She had seen Priest Vinhor leading the Sabbath services. He was tall, elegant, dignified—everything a priest should be.

The man shook the excess ink from his quill. Some of the drops landed on the hem of Siwell's skirt. "Don't think you're immune to his enmity, just because you know a few healing spells. Priest Vinhor will be very interested when I tell him about your opinion of him."

"I'm not afraid of your master. Tell him what you wish." Siwell stepped back, and the driver yelled for the clerk to climb aboard. He scowled as he did. The wagon rumbled off toward the church.

"What was that about?" Tior asked in a low voice. "If you think you might need protection, I can speak to my captain. He has no love for Priest Vinhor."

"No, it's not a problem. That clerk is all bluster with nothing to back it up." She shook herself. "Now that the back is clear, maybe you can help us search there. Maryn's looking for a small coffer with some coins in it; she says it was under their mattress."

"If you're sure you don't—" Tior shrugged. "I found the place where the bed fell, when the loft collapsed. We can look there."

"Good."

Tior went back into the building. Maryn longed to turn and run, far away from the mutilated remnants of the place that had been so dear to her. But she set her mouth into a grim line and started to follow him.

Siwell put a hand on her arm. "Wait."

Maryn had never seen the midwife look so uncertain. She stopped. "What is it?"

"I don't know if I should tell you." Siwell stepped closer and lowered her voice. "But Priest Vinhor might succeed in making it to the capital someday, and if he should learn I recommended you...He has a long memory for a grudge. Stay away from him, Maryn. He's dangerous."

"But he's a priest. Surely he wouldn't do anything to harm me?"

"I hope not. But he might, if he thought he could strike at me through you." She considered for a moment longer, then spoke low and rapidly. "Listen. The rain that stopped the fire...that was Vinhor's doing. I went to the church, as soon as I heard that's where they were taking the victims, to offer what healing skills I have. Priest Vinhor was there, consulting with the chief healers. The first few they brought in died before they got to us, or soon after. Vinhor took the bodies and began collecting their blood. But most of them were burned so badly little was left he could use.

"Then they brought in a woman who was still alive. She was screaming. Her burns were severe, but I'm nearly certain we would have been able to heal her. But Vinhor took one look at her and declared that she was beyond aid, and that he would grant her the Holy One's mercy. I spoke up against him, but why should he listen to a mere midwife?"

Siwell's voice faltered. "He cut her throat, and caught her blood. That gave him enough. He went outside and used the blood to call up the storm."

Maryn remembered the towering cloud wreathed in blue lightning. "You must have been mistaken about her. Surely a servant of the Holy One would never…And the fire could have destroyed the whole town, without the rain."

"I hope you're right. But I fear Vinhor's ambition. When the king hears how his sorcery stopped the fire, he's bound to be impressed. And he's rumored to be displeased with Prelate Kiellan." Siwell shook her head. "I should have kept my mouth shut with that clerk."

Maryn frowned at Siwell. The midwife's story seemed incredible. But Siwell would never lie to her, so she must believe it was the truth.

Tior called from within, "Can you come in here? I think I found it. But there's a beam I'm going to need help moving."

Siwell stepped between Maryn and the door. "I'll get it. You don't have to—"

But Maryn pushed by her and went inside. She was sick of this place. All she wanted was to find what she had come for and get away. She stomped over to the pile of rubble, grabbed a random beam, and began to heave.

Tior hurried to direct her to the appropriate spot. With Tior, Siwell, and Maryn all working together, they managed to lift the beam and throw it aside.

Maryn spotted the corner of the coffer. She dropped to her hands and knees and scrabbled in the ashes, unearthing it. The iron-banded wood was deeply scorched, but intact.

"Edrich always kept the key. I suppose it would

have been in his belt pouch. He usually left it hanging with his clothes, over there…" She twisted around, trying to orient herself.

"We'll never find it. Here, let me." Tior drew a knife, slid the point into the crack where the lid met the body of the box, and levered. With only a little pressure, the hinges broke away from the charred wood and the coffer popped open.

Maryn picked it up and dumped the contents into her lap. The coins were dark with soot, but appeared undamaged. She picked one up and rubbed it with a fold of her skirt. Copper gleamed at her.

"There you go." Tior jumped to his feet. "I'll go get a few pots I saw that looked worth keeping, and we can leave."

"Thank you." Maryn scooped the pile from her skirt into her pouch. "You've been so kind, helping us."

Tior shrugged. "It's no more than my duty."

The three of them gathered up Maryn's salvaged belongings and headed out of the building. Maryn looked back once as they made their way down the street. The life she and Edrich had shared there, that she had thought would be hers forever, had vanished into the flames. Siwell had offered her the chance for another life, and Maryn had agreed to take it. She couldn't help but feel, though, that anything that happened to her from this point on was artificial, unreal. Her life should have ended back there, with her husband and child, and she should lie beside them now in their graves.

Four

The grand front entrance of the palace rose before
Maryn, tall and splendid. She clutched her
precious letter of introduction and stared
through the iron bars of the gate. Beyond a stretch of
lush green lawn and gardens bright with flowers,
white stone gleamed in the morning sun. Carvings of
beasts and birds and twining vines lavishly decorated
the arches and turrets, bright with gilding. Troops of
soldiers stood at rigid attention. A banner bearing a
stylized gold stag and red splash of blood floated
above the highest tower. She had thought the church
in Ralo rich and beautiful, but compared to the
splendor of the palace it seemed little more than a
country chapel. The idea that she was about to ask
admittance within those imposing walls seemed even
more ridiculously presumptuous than it had when
Siwell first proposed it.

She almost surrendered to the impulse to flee back
to the inn where she had spent the night. She could
leave for Ralo in the morning. Even retracing all those
weary miles of walking seemed preferable to
completing the last few steps of her journey.

But she couldn't turn back now. Hadn't she been
just as afraid yesterday, when the caravan arrived in
Loempno and all the other travelers went their

various ways, leaving her lost and alone in the huge city? She had dealt with her fear then, and made her way through the bustling streets. She had forced herself to remain calm and asked directions until she found the King's Inn. The Royal Stewardess couldn't be worse than all those brusque strangers. At least she knew Maryn was coming, assuming Siwell's message had arrived safely.

Maryn turned away from the front gate, and walked through the city streets, around the palace wall. It was a long way, for the wings of the palace sprawled over many acres. Finally she came to the servant's entrance, where Siwell had instructed her to present herself.

The high wall blocked the view of all but the tallest peaks of the palace. A heavy iron gate stood open. Servants in formal blue livery hurried in and out.

Guards flanked the entrance. She approached one, her pulse pounding so loud in her ears she almost couldn't hear herself speak. "Excuse me? I'm here to see the Royal Stewardess; she's expecting me. My name is Maryn Loesella. Here's my letter of introduction." She was proud that she neither stammered nor rushed. Her voice sounded calm and professional, at odds with the shaky, terrified uncertainty she felt. Her hand didn't even tremble as she extended the folded document.

The guard took the letter and examined the seal. "Wait here." He stepped into a small guardhouse beside the gate. After a few minutes he returned. "Stand aside, please, Miss. Madam Coewyn will send word when she's ready."

Maryn obediently moved away from the gate and pressed herself against the wall. Traffic flowed in and out the gate: servants, tradesmen in wagons piled high with goods, and once a troop of men-at-arms. The guards stared straight ahead when they weren't dealing with others seeking entrance. Maryn waited as the sun crept higher in the sky. She longed to go to one of the vendor's stalls she had passed and buy a mug of ale to moisten her dry tongue, but she didn't dare venture away from the gate lest she miss her summons. How long would she have to wait? What if something had gone wrong, and the Royal Stewardess never sent for her? Or worse, told her to go away? Maybe the position was already filled. Or maybe, despite Siwell's reassurances, she would consider Maryn unworthy of consideration.

Finally, well after the bells had rung the fourth hour, a boy of perhaps thirteen years, in a bright blue uniform with a plumed velvet hat crooked on his head, ran up from within the palace grounds. He jerked to attention before the guard. "Madame Coewyn says to send her in, sir."

"Very good." The guard turned. "Miss—Oh, there you are." He frowned at Maryn, and she fell back a step from where she had crowded eagerly close. "This page will escort you to the Royal Stewardess."

"Thank you," Maryn managed to get out, almost faint with relief. The page saluted and dashed off at nearly as rapid a pace as he had come. The guard cleared his throat, and the page halted, sheepishly waiting for Maryn to catch up before setting out again, slow enough for her to keep up this time.

They passed through a busy courtyard and entered a wing of the palace. The page led her through long corridors until they reached a door that opened to a spacious office. Shelves lined one wall all the way up to the ceiling; they were stuffed full of bound volumes and loose sheaves of paper. Wide windows in another wall admitted generous light. In front of them stood a large, imposing desk, its surface covered with neat stacks of documents. Behind it, a woman dipped a quill in a pot of ink, blotted it, and made a few precise strokes. She was perhaps fifty years old, with steel gray hair fixed in a tight bun at the nape of her neck, all her movements sure and controlled.

Maryn's guide said, "Madame Coewyn? Here she is."

"Ah, good." The Royal Stewardess set down her pen and regarded Maryn. "Come in; sit down. Boy, go find the Royal Sorcerer and ask him to attend me."

The page nodded and left, banging the door shut behind him. Maryn perched on the edge of one of the chairs that faced the desk. Madame Coewyn picked up and unfolded a sheet of paper Maryn recognized as her letter of introduction.

"Midwife Siwell Narila has recommended you for the position of wet nurse to Princess Voerell's child. I've read over your history. You do have several qualities in your favor. I am impressed that you seem to be entirely free of entanglements. All of the other women I am considering have impediments of some sort. We can deal with milk-ties if we have no other choice, but it is much preferable if that is not necessary." She held Siwell's letter up to catch the light, adjusted its distance from her eyes, and squinted. "She says your baby died in a fire?"

Maryn flinched, and struggled to suppress the memories roused by the stark words. She tried to make her voice steady, but it came out a squeaky whisper. "Yes, ma'am."

Coewyn looked at her sharply. "There can be no

question your milk was at fault, then. He was healthy and thriving up to the time he was killed?"

This time Maryn did not trust her voice. She nodded.

"Hmm." Coewyn pursed her lips. "The midwife explained to you the significance of the fact that you have nursed no other living child? Nor shared your milk with any other? I must stress that your honesty in this matter is non-negotiable. If you are lying, we will find out, before the prince tastes one drop of your milk, and you will be punished."

Maryn stared at her clasped hands. "I understand, ma'am. I'm telling the truth."

"Good." Coewyn set the paper down briskly. She opened a drawer in her desk and drew out a small round mirror. She passed it across the desk to Maryn. "Let's see what you have to offer."

Maryn took the mirror and blinked at it stupidly. It filled her palm. The glass was smooth and clear, reflecting her face sharply. She was startled to see how young she looked. She didn't feel young.

"Go ahead." Coewyn scowled at her.

"I'm sorry. I don't understand what I'm supposed to do."

Coewyn gave a gusty sigh. "Your milk, girl. I need to test your milk. Squirt a bit onto that mirror."

"Oh." Maryn groped at the tie of her shift. At least after all her practice of the past few days it was a simple matter to spray a generous splash onto the smooth surface of the mirror. She pulled her shift up and passed the mirror back to Coewyn, watching the Stewardess in surreptitious fascination while she retied her drawstring.

Coewyn tilted the mirror, studying the droplets of milk as they rolled across the surface. "Nice white color, clear, no spottiness or cloudiness." She ran the tip of one finger through the middle of the puddle, intently observing the clear streak left behind. "A tad thin, but it will do."

Her actions reminded Maryn of a herdsman evaluating whether he should purchase a dairy goat. The thought made her feel small and insignificant, but she shrugged aside the discomfort. That's what the Royal Stewardess was doing, wasn't it?

Coewyn set the mirror down on her desk. She took a cloth from the desk drawer, meticulously wiped the trace of milk from her finger, and murmured a brief phrase Maryn recognized from the blood-cleansing ceremony. The towel sparked faintly and Maryn felt a tiny buzz of power. Coewyn leaned back, set her elbows on the arms of her chair, and steepled her fingers. "Now, tell me about yourself, Maryn." Maryn thought her tone sounded positive, even pleased.

Maryn obediently began a recitation of the basic facts of her life. Coewyn interrupted often with questions. She probed deeply into the most intimate aspects of Maryn's experience, until Maryn found herself describing her physical symptoms upon her first flow of blood, and the fleeting attractions she had felt for various neighbor boys before her marriage. She blushed and stammered, but forced herself to answer as truthfully as she could manage.

"And your husband? Tell me how you met." Coewyn looked at her expectantly.

Maryn's voice faltered. She had barely spoken of Edrich since the fire. But if she was to have any hope of being chosen, she would have to answer, no matter how painful she found it. She forced the words past reluctant lips. "I was sixteen. Every day I would bring our family's tithe of eggs to Lord Negian's manor.

One day Edrich was there, negotiating to buy fleeces from Lord Negian's flocks. He saw me, and stopped the steward in the middle of their haggling to ask who I was..." The words flowed more easily as she went deeper into the dear memory. She found herself cherishing every tiny detail she could recall about Edrich, from the way his thick blond hair had fallen over his forehead, to the way he had clenched his hands behind his back so tight the fingers whitened when he finally worked up the nerve to approach her father. Coewyn listened with a little half-smile as Maryn rambled on about their courtship and wedding, almost forgetting that her words were being judged.

Coewyn leaned forward a bit. "So you came a virgin to your husband's bed?"

The intrusive question shocked Maryn out of her momentary reverie. If anyone else had asked, she would have refused to dignify the question with an answer, but the Royal Stewardess held Maryn's fate in her hands. "I—Yes, of course. But I don't see what that has to do with my suitability to be the prince's nurse."

Coewyn frowned. "It has everything to do with your suitability. Don't you know that the character of the nurse is transmitted to the child through her milk? I am charged to choose only someone of the highest moral fiber, the most impeccable reputation. So far nothing of what you have told me casts any doubt on your qualifications in that regard. Though if you are in the habit of indulging in such rude outbursts, I might have to reconsider that judgment. It will not do for the prince to acquire a defiant temperament."

Maryn gulped. "I'm sorry, Madam Coewyn. I'll tell you anything you want. I promise, I'm not rude or defiant. Of course you know best what to ask; I won't question you again."

Coewyn leaned back, satisfied. "Remember that. Now, tell me more about your relationship with your husband. How soon after you were wed did you conceive?"

Maryn was about to launch into a detailed account, desperate to give Coewyn whatever she might want, when the door opened. The page poked his head in. "Madam Coewyn, the Royal Sorcerer is here."

"Ah, yes. Send him in." She rose and beckoned for Maryn to do the same.

The Royal Sorcerer strode into the office. He was a tall man, and his rich burgundy robes swirled about him dramatically. He nodded graciously at the Stewardess. "What can I do for you, Coewyn?"

She returned his nod. "One more wet nurse candidate, Rogelan. I hope I haven't put too much of a burden on you, with so many. But I do think this should be the last, as long as the scrying doesn't show anything unexpected."

Did that mean the Stewardess favored her? Hope caught at Maryn's breath and set her heart racing. But there still remained whatever mysterious test the sorcerer was going to perform. Maryn eyed him warily. She knew she had nothing to hide, but magic was dangerous and unpredictable, and she had always viewed those who wielded it with awe and fear.

"Not at all. I'm always happy to assist you. May I use your desk again?"

"Certainly. Here's the sample." She indicated the mirror on her desk and came to stand by Maryn.

Rogelan settled into Coewyn's seat. After fussing for a moment with the exact position of the chair and the mirror, he drew a knife from a sheath at his belt. It was smaller than the common knives everyone carried to cut their food. The blade was polished to a brilliant shine, the hilt gold and set with precious gems. Rogelan laid it crossways on the desk, between him and the mirror that held Maryn's milk.

The sorcerer set both his hands flat on the desk, to either side of the knife and mirror. He drew a deep breath. Taking up the knife in his right hand, he extended his left over the mirror, and began to chant in the ancient language of sorcery.

His rich bass voice intoned the invocation used at the beginning of every working. He pricked the ball of his left thumb with the point of the knife. A drop of blood welled out; he twitched his hand and it fell onto the surface of the mirror. The scarlet spread and mingled into the white puddle of Maryn's milk.

The buzzing sensation of magic vibrated in Maryn's bones. Setting the knife down, Rogelan picked up the mirror and swirled it, further mixing the blood and milk. He continued to chant; his incantation reached the end of the words Maryn knew and continued in unfamiliar cadences.

The liquid on the surface of the mirror began to steam, like water boiling in a kettle, though no bubbles disturbed it. More and more vapor poured from its surface and swirled into a dense cloud, shot through with a network of faint blue sparks. Rogelan set down the mirror and put out both hands. The cloud stayed confined between them, thickening. Maryn began to catch glimpses of shapes forming within. Vague and indistinct at first, they gradually resolved. Her own face first, just as it had appeared in the mirror, though drained of all color in the white mist. Then, fainter, and wavering a little even when they reached full resolution, two other faces. Maryn caught her breath and bit back a cry. There were Edrich's beloved smile and bushy eyebrows. And there were Frilan's plump baby cheeks and long lashes, and the unbearable sweetness of his bow-shaped lips.

Coewyn scowled at her, and Maryn choked down her sobs. She fixed all her attention on the cloud, to feast her eyes on the dear faces as long as possible.

Rogelan's chanting went on. The faces in the mist held steady, nothing else appearing. Too soon for Maryn, the sorcerer lowered his hands. The shapes faded into indistinctness, and the mist began to disperse. When it was fully gone, Rogelan's chanting shifted, and Maryn began to recognize some of the phrases again. The remnants of the pool of blood and milk burst into a fountain of blue sparks. The buzz, which had subsided into a background drone, crescendoed to a teeth-rattling throb before ceasing. The sparks died, until all that remained was the mirror, smudged with residue. Rogelan brought his spell to a close with a reverent intonation of the closing words, and fell silent.

Coewyn broke the silence first. "Well, girl, it seems you spoke the truth." She turned to the sorcerer. "I only saw the three. Did I miss any faint traces?"

Rogelan examined the tip of his knife. There was a bit of blood residue, but he apparently detected no power left in it, for he wiped the blade on a cloth at his belt and sheathed it. "No, no traces. Just the three, and the two clearly passed into the next world. She's free of kin-ties."

Coewyn sighed, and for the first time since Maryn had entered her office seemed to relax. "That's a relief. I'd been worried we were going to have to settle for that woman from Whito and pay off the friend to take her son out of the country. But there would always have been the possibility of something like what happened with that milk-sister of Marolan's, and you remember what a mess *that* was."

"Indeed." Rogelan rose and moved out from behind the desk. "This girl will serve much better. Good work finding her."

Joy and terror churned together in Maryn's gut. It was going to happen. They were going to give her the job. She hadn't believed it was possible, not really. In the back of her mind she had never stopped rehearsing the gracious words she would use to accept rejection and thank the Stewardess for her consideration. She had plotted the route from the palace to the merchants' guildhouse; the coins to pay for her passage back to Ralo were safe in her purse. Becoming the prince's wet nurse was only a dream. She had to go through the steps so she could say she had tried everything, before accepting her fate and going back to the miserable but familiar life of a serf. But now, impossibly, the dream was becoming real. What had she gotten herself into?

Coewyn ushered Rogelan to the door. "Thank you again for your aid."

"It's no more than my duty. Don't hesitate to call whenever you have need." He swept from the room.

Coewyn turned back to Maryn. "Well, Maryn, my choice is clear. The position is yours. Now let us discuss the terms of your contract."

Maryn fought an impulse to stammer a refusal and flee. She would not throw this chance away, not after she had worked so hard and come so far. She drew a deep, shaky breath. "Thank you, Madam Coewyn."

"Thank me after the prince is safely born and your place is secure." The Stewardess sat down at her desk and pulled a cloth from the drawer. She picked up the mirror, rubbed off the sticky film of blood and milk residue, and tucked cloth and mirror away. "With any luck this will see much use in the next few years, with Princess Voerell married, and Prince Marolan's bride arriving in the fall. Now, if only Prince Carlich will leave off his wild ways and settle down, King Froethych might finally be able to rest easy."

The Stewardess rummaged through the papers on her desk and produced a sheet of finely written text. "This contract spells out your responsibilities and obligations. It's the standard agreement, save for a few provisions unique to the royal family. You will note, in particular, that instead of the typical five-year term, you will be bound to abide by certain conditions for life. Under no circumstances are you permitted to engage in any sexual relationship, licit or illicit, until after the prince is fully weaned, on pain of immediate dismissal. If at any point after that you wish to marry, your prospective spouse must be approved by my office." Coewyn looked sharply over the paper at Maryn. "You will receive a generous payment each year you refrain from producing a milk-sibling for the prince."

Maryn blushed and looked down at her lap. While she knew intellectually that someday she might wish to wed again, her grief was still so fresh she couldn't imagine wanting another man. Certainly not before the prince weaned. That might be as soon as two years, although some children nursed much longer. But even if the prince was one of those who didn't wean until he was five or six, Maryn didn't anticipate the prohibition would pose any difficulty. "I understand."

Coewyn studied her a moment, and nodded. "If you fulfill all your duties adequately, you will remain in the employ of the palace after your charge weans, continuing to serve as his attendant and servant. When the prince reaches the age of twelve, he will become a page, and you will be assigned other duties." She went on for a good while longer, enumerating all the details of the contract in complicated language Maryn found difficult to understand. Eventually she quit trying and just nodded whenever Madam Coewyn paused for breath.

Finally the Stewardess stopped speaking and looked at Maryn. "I trust you find all these terms satisfactory?"

Maryn had no standing to negotiate them, even if she didn't. "Yes, ma'am."

Coewyn pushed the paper across the desk to Maryn, and thrust a quill pen into her hand. "Good. Sign there."

"Excuse me, Madame Coewyn?" Maryn clutched the pen and stared at the marks on the paper. "I don't read or write."

Coewyn narrowed her eyes. "That's right; you were a serf. Didn't you learn, after you moved to the town?"

"Only a little." Edrich had made a few half-hearted attempts to teach her, but he didn't have the temperament for it, and it had not gone well. Truthfully, she had not been particularly interested. She was quite willing to allow Edrich to keep the family's accounts, and there was little other practical use for the skill.

Coewyn sighed. "Just make whatever mark you can; it will have to do."

Maryn poked the pen into the pot of ink and

dragged it across the paper at the indicated spot. The ink blotched and smeared, but she managed to produce a wobbly approximation of the first letter of her name, the one symbol she had successfully committed to memory.

The Royal Stewardess set the contract aside. She picked up another piece of paper, frowned at it, and set it down. "I suppose this won't do you any good. It's a list of the rules of protocol you are required to follow. I was going to instruct you to study it." She glanced at Maryn's contract as if she wished she might rescind it, but set her mouth and went on. "You'll just have to listen while I explain." She sat back in her chair and fixed Maryn with a stern gaze. "As wet nurse, you rank quite high. Beneath Princess Voerell's ladies-in-waiting, who are all daughters of noble houses, but above her personal servants. Be sure to note, however, that the Under-Stewardess in charge of the Royal Nursery will have final say over the prince's education, and you will be expected to conduct yourself accordingly.

"Of course, Madam Coewyn."

"You must at all times observe the proper etiquette in your interactions with your superiors and inferiors. You will find life in the palace very different from the provincial town you come from. I will assign someone to instruct you in the full details, but for now you must at least understand the basics." She launched into a description of the types of servants, employees, officials, dignitaries, and nobles that Maryn might encounter.

Maryn listened as carefully as she could, but she soon became aware of growing discomfort. At length she had no choice but to interrupt. She chose her moment carefully, waiting until Coewyn paused between topics. Even so she spoke over the beginning of Coewyn's next sentence, and the Stewardess glared at her. "Excuse me. But I must express my milk soon, if I'm to maintain a good supply until the prince is born. And if there's a privy I might use…"

Coewyn rolled her eyes. "I suppose you must. I'll have one of my aides get you settled in your rooms, and show you to the garderobe." She rose and led Maryn toward the door.

Before they could reach it, the door flew open and a page burst into the room. "Madam Coewyn, the Royal Midwife sent me. She's certain Princess Voerell is really in labor this time. She thinks the prince might be born in only a few hours!"

Coewyn raised her eyebrows. "Tell the Royal Midwife I am on my way. And you can inform her I have secured a suitable nurse, and will present her to the princess shortly." She turned to Maryn. "Take care of your business quickly. I will come to your room in half an hour to collect you. With any luck, you will begin your service before nightfall."

Five

A low moan sounded beyond the ornate door. As Madam Coewyn conferred with the guards that flanked the entrance to Princess Voerell's quarters, it escalated into a shriek.

Maryn caught her breath. The sound brought back a vivid memory of her labor with Frilan, the way the pain had wrapped around her body, squeezing tighter and tighter until she feared she might break in half. The same cry had burst from her own lips as the pain climaxed. She had fallen quiet as the pressure eased, as the voice beyond the door did now.

The guards swung the door open and Coewyn entered, Maryn at her heels. No one noticed. The spacious room held many female servants, and a number of well-dressed ladies clustered to one side, but everyone focused on the two women by the hearth.

A tall young woman, her loose silk dressing gown draped over the swell of her belly, leaned on a plump older woman. "Gallows, Litholl, you didn't tell me it would be this bad! I can't take this much longer. Not if it gets worse."

The midwife brushed back a strand of sweaty hair that had escaped the laboring woman's braids. "Remember what I told you, your Highness.

Surrender to the sensation, don't fight it. Accept it, allow it to sweep over you and do its work."

The princess glared at the midwife. "Surrender? Would you counsel one of my brothers to surrender to the foe that drove a sword into his gut? Don't say that again."

The midwife remained unruffled. "As you wish, your Highness. You must choose your own way to deal with your trial. Come, walk with me a bit more. It will help your child descend and hasten the birth."

"Anything to get this over with," the princess growled. She pushed Litholl away and drew herself upright.

Madam Coewyn stepped forward. "Excuse me, your Highness. I'm sorry to interrupt, but you asked me to inform you when I had chosen a wet nurse. This is Maryn Loesella of Ralo. Maryn, Princess Voerell."

Maryn sank into a deep curtsy. She wasn't sure what she had expected of the princess, but she knew she hadn't pictured anything like the fierce, angry woman in front of her. Although perhaps she was judging her unfairly. Labor could bring out strange sides of a woman. Her own mother, when Maryn had been present at her siblings' births, would grow tearful and afraid as her labor progressed, quite unlike her usual stoic, confident self. Maryn hoped the princess was just experiencing a similar temporary shift in mood. Otherwise, working for her could be most unpleasant.

Voerell's eyes brushed over Maryn without focusing. "It took you long enough. But you made it in time. Barely. Gallows, I hope it's barely! Oh, curse it, Litholl, here comes another one." She turned back to the midwife, fear in her eyes and voice.

"You're doing wonderfully, your Highness. Relax and breathe." Litholl demonstrated, inhaling slowly and sighing the breath out. Voerell tried to follow suit, but her face twisted into a grimace, and she let out a stream of profanity.

Coewyn took Maryn's arm and pulled her to the side, where a velvet-upholstered bench stood on scrolled gilt feet. "Wait here until you're needed. It won't be long, if the midwife is right. I hope so. The way Voerell carries on, you'd think she fancies herself the first woman to feel a little pain giving birth." She bustled off toward the ladies-in-waiting. The group of young noblewomen clung to each other, watching the princess with fearful eyes. "Come, come, make yourselves useful. Her Highness will be fine. You and you, go help the midwife. And you, have the servants build up the fire. We can't have the prince taking a chill."

Maryn sank down onto the bench. Voerell trudged in a slow circle around the room, pausing occasionally to lean on one of her ladies and give loud voice to her discomfort. Maryn wished there were something she could do to help ease the princess's misery. During her labor with Frilan, Siwell had given her much the same advice. Maryn had found that when she was able to induce her taut muscles to go limp it really had made the pain more bearable. But Maryn was sure that if Voerell resisted listening to her midwife she would never pay heed to a lowborn stranger.

She had been so innocent back then. Just like the princess, she had been overwhelmed by the agony of her body. Now she knew far worse pain existed. Pain that no relaxing would ease, that would not fade away if only she endured long enough. She longed to go back to that day, when all she had to suffer were the simple pangs of labor.

The hours wore on. Voerell lay down on the bed for a time, but grew restless and rose again to resume her heavy shuffle on Litholl's arm. The fire blazed high in the hearth, warming the room until the heat was stifling and Maryn could hardly breathe. Large wet patches blotched the princess's silk robe, and beads of sweat formed on Litholl's forehead.

Maryn shifted on the bench and stretched her stiff back. Her breasts were beginning to feel full again. Soon she would have to seek permission from Coewyn to go back to her new quarters and get her bowl. Voerell's cries were duller now, edging toward exhaustion. The midwife still appeared unworried, but fear stirred in Maryn's gut. What would happen to her if the birth did not go well? If the baby, or Holy One forbid, Voerell herself, did not survive? She tried to remember what Coewyn had read from the contract. Maybe they would at least pay her way back to Ralo.

Voerell halted in front of Maryn and bent over, moaning. Maryn noticed a different quality in her voice. Interspersed with her moans were low, throaty grunts. Litholl looked closely at Voerell's face, while the two ladies-in-waiting exchanged anxious glances.

When the contraction passed, Voerell pulled herself up and frowned at Litholl. "I felt something different that time. I had to push; I couldn't stop. Is that all right?"

"Yes, your Highness." A new brightness tinged Litholl's voice, though her calm assurance never wavered. "It won't be long now."

Voerell nodded. Her voice held a note of steely determination. "Good. Let's get this done."

She braced her feet and stood panting until the

next pain. As her ladies clung to her arms, Voerell bent her knees into a squat. She put her head down, and her face twisted into a grimace of effort.

"Gently, your Highness," Litholl cautioned. "Let your womb do the work; it's quite capable. You'll only wear yourself out trying to make it go faster."

"I'll do as I please," Voerell said, her eyes closed, breathing hard.

"Yes, your Highness. Whatever you say. Would you like me to get my birthing stool? Or perhaps you'd be more comfortable lying down."

"No! Just be quiet and catch the thing when it comes out."

"Yes, your Highness." Litholl gestured for the servants to bring fresh straw and spread it at Voerell's feet. She crouched and pushed the hem of Voerell's robe aside to examine her. With a nod, she settled on her heels to wait for the next contraction.

Before long it came. Voerell squatted again, giving a series of fierce, angry grunts. Maryn scooted to the end of her bench and leaned over to see past the ladies-in-waiting who crowded close, eager to catch the first glimpse of the new prince. She hadn't expected to care so much. Voerell's labor aroused intense memories of Frilan's birth. Painful as they were, she found she treasured them. And the excitement of the imminent birth caught her up, just as it always had when she'd been present for her siblings' births. She waited, as breathless as all the other women in the room, for the miraculous moment when new life would enter the world.

Litholl watched Voerell, hands loose in her lap. When the princess subsided into exhausted gasps, she spoke quietly. "Your bag of waters is bulging, and I could see the top of your baby's head. All is well."

Voerell nodded, her eyes closed. She slumped against her lady-in-waiting, who supported her mistress stoutly despite her look of dismay. It's all right, Maryn wanted to assure her. The midwife said all was well. Maryn well remembered the feeling graven on Voerell's face, of dazed and weary numbness. She had been sure, between contractions, that the task was impossible, that there was no way she would be able to muster the strength for one more push. And yet, when the waves of need came, they overpowered all her fear and exhaustion. She had thrust with all her might, over and over, as long as it took, until Frilan slid into the midwife's waiting hands and Siwell placed him in her arms.

Voerell drew a deep breath and sank into her squat. Her face flushed red, and she opened her mouth in a wordless cry. Litholl leaned forward. A burst of fluid splashed into the straw at Voerell's feet, and Maryn caught a glimpse of a dark round shape between Voerell's legs.

"Just one more should do it," Litholl said. "Here, your Highness, you can put your hand down and touch his head if you like."

Voerell shook her head. She kept her eyes scrunched closed, and breathed in great ragged gasps. Her arms clung tight around the necks of the ladies-in-waiting on either side, until Maryn feared she might strangle the poor girls.

After a long moment of waiting, the contraction came. This time Voerell was silent. She pressed her lips together in a fierce line and bore down until she went white. Litholl reached up, and a small wet form slid from Voerell's body into the midwife's waiting hands.

Voerell sagged into her ladies' arms, shaking.

Servants hurried to bring Litholl clean soft cloths. The midwife wiped the baby's face. The small mouth opened and gave a thin wail. Dark eyes blinked and tiny fists waved.

Litholl smiled and displayed the child to Voerell. "Look, princess, you have a son. Milecha has a new heir."

Voerell opened her eyes just long enough to scan her child and see that Litholl's words were true. Then she turned away. "Give him to the nurse," she ordered hoarsely. "Help me over to the bed. I want to lie down."

Litholl's brow creased. "Wait, your Highness. I must cut his cord, first, and you must deliver the afterbirth. Are you sure you don't want to hold him for a moment?"

"I'm sure. Do what you must quickly."

Litholl frowned, but she nodded, and looked around. "Where's the wet nurse?"

Maryn was so caught up in watching events unfold that it took a moment before she realized they were talking about her. She jumped to her feet and rushed to the midwife's side. "Here I am."

Madam Coewyn appeared at her elbow. "You must be extremely careful with the prince," she cautioned. "Let Madam Litholl wrap him up first, and hand him to you."

An offended retort, that she knew very well how to hold a baby safely, sprang to Maryn's lips, but she bit it off. Litholl intervened. "She won't drop him, Coewyn. Yes, I'll wrap him, though you've got it so warm in here he's more likely to overheat than take a chill." Litholl deftly swaddled the crying baby in a length of soft white fabric.

She beckoned Maryn to approach within the span

of the cord that still bound mother and child. Maryn had to crowd close to Voerell's side, though she shrank back to avoid touching the princess more than necessary. Voerell kept her eyes closed and her face turned aside. Without ceremony, Litholl deposited the babe in Maryn's arms.

The warm soft weight roused intense, painful memories. Just so had Frilan felt, when Siwell set him in Maryn's arms. Just so had his cries ceased as he nestled against her chest, curious eyes opening to survey the world. Just so had his head turned, lips moving in eager search.

Maryn froze, caught between longing and revulsion. This child felt so much like Frilan. But Frilan was dead, and a part of Maryn had died with him. This alien babe sought to force it back to agonized life. He wanted to usurp the place that would always, only, ever belong to Maryn's own lost child. She ached both to gather him close to her body and hurl him violently away.

Instead she held him stiffly, as Litholl pushed aside the folds of cloth to gain access to the place where the thick, whitish-purple cord sprang from his belly. The midwife's expert fingers bound a short string around the cord near his body. Litholl's ceremonial knife was plain undecorated steel. She used it to sever the cord; a spatter of dark blood drops flew out and splashed over the baby's wrapping and Maryn's sleeve.

"I'll take care of that in a moment. Don't go anywhere until I've made sure you're both thoroughly cleansed." Litholl turned back to Voerell. "Your Highness, do you feel any more contractions yet? The afterbirth should be ready to pass soon."

Maryn stepped back from her uncomfortable

proximity to the princess, who continued to steadfastly ignore both her and the child. The baby squirmed in Maryn's arms. Reflexively she gathered him close, but she could not seem to think clearly enough to understand what to do next. Coewyn fixed her with a hard stare. "Well, girl? The poor thing's hungry; nurse him."

No! Maryn wanted to shout. *He's not mine! I don't want him!* For a moment she felt a tremendous urge to dump the babe in Coewyn's arms and run, out of the palace, out of Loempno, back home where she belonged.

But her home no longer existed. There was nowhere she belonged. She had come all this long way for just this purpose, and she found her pride would not let her fail now, not before Coewyn's coldly judging eyes.

Maryn clutched the prince close and walked back to her bench. She angled her body away from Coewyn's gaze and pulled down her shift. Drawing a deep breath, she forced herself to look fully at the baby in her arms, as she had not yet quite dared to do.

He wasn't much like Frilan, after all. He was nearly bald, only a few short wisps of fuzzy blond gracing his head, in contrast to Frilan's thick shock of dark hair. He was stockier, his face much rounder and his limbs thicker. His skin had flushed bright pink, though his lips were still a dusky shade of purple. They opened in soundless groping, and his hand came up to open and close in front of his face. It clenched into a fist, and found its way to his mouth. He sucked fiercely for a moment before his arm twitched and tore his hand away. He burst into a heartbroken wail.

A warm flood rushed into Maryn's breasts. A few

drops of milk leaked from the exposed side. She closed her eyes, swept by fresh grief, but also an overwhelming desire to put this lost, helpless infant to her breast and nurture him.

It would be all right. She could do this. He wasn't Frilan, but he needed her. Maryn shifted the prince into the crook of her arm and maneuvered his mouth toward her nipple.

He took a while to catch on. At first he wouldn't open his mouth wide enough, and his hands kept getting in the way. Maryn knew Coewyn was watching them, and felt flustered and rushed, but she did her best to ignore it. Finally she managed to get her breast into the prince's mouth. His sucking was painful, but she could deal with that for the moment. Later, when they were alone, Maryn would work harder to get him latched correctly. Right now she was just happy he was nursing. Coewyn would see that she could do this job, after all. She looked up and met the Stewardess's gaze, jutting her chin out.

Coewyn nodded curtly. "Very good. See that he gets plenty." She watched for a few more minutes, nodded again, and went off to speak with Litholl and Voerell.

Maryn's nipple stung, and she shifted around, trying to find a more comfortable position. It had hurt in the early days with Frilan, too, she remembered. She didn't think it had been quite so bad, but maybe she had just forgotten. The prince must be getting milk; she could hear the little gulps as he swallowed. It felt surreal to have a strange child there instead of Frilan's familiar face.

To distract herself from the pain and her confused emotions, she watched Litholl. The midwife finished seeing to Voerell and tucked her into bed. She went around the room, located each place blood had splashed or dripped, and cleansed it. Blue sparks bloomed, and buzzing rattled in Maryn's teeth.

When she finished with the pile of straw heaped in the place Voerell had given birth, Litholl came to stand before Maryn. She gazed at the nursing prince. The midwife looked weary, but she glowed with warm satisfaction, and to Maryn's eyes seemed remarkably little affected by her hours of hard work. Just the effort of cleansing all that blood would have exhausted Maryn several times over.

"Is all well? He seems to have taken to you nicely." Litholl sank to the bench next to Maryn with a sigh.

"Oh, yes. He's very eager."

"No undue discomfort?"

"No," Maryn lied. She didn't want to admit any weakness, when the other woman was so strong and skilled. She shifted the baby in her arms and tried not to wince as his mouth pinched.

Litholl nodded. "If any problems develop, feel free to send for me." She heaved herself to her feet. "Let me go ahead and cleanse the two of you."

She launched into the words of the ritual. The vibrations of the magic thrummed in Maryn's bones. Blue sparks haloed the prince's skin where the blood of birth had smeared it, and erupted from every spot where droplets had splattered or Maryn's milk had leaked. He squirmed and broke away from Maryn's breast with a squall of discomfort, before seizing her nipple again with renewed and painful vigor. Litholl brought the spell to a close, and the fire died. "There. All safe now. You'll want to bathe him after a bit, but let him get his fill first."

Madam Coewyn bustled up. "Are you finished,

Litholl? The princess is asking for her husband. If everything is taken care of I'll send for him."

Litholl glanced around. "Yes, I think so. Go ahead. And I'm sure the king will wish to greet his grandson and heir as well."

"Of course." Coewyn nodded frostily to the midwife and strode off toward the door to confer with a page.

Only a few minutes later the doors swung open again to admit a tall, dark-haired man. He hurried to Voerell's bedside. "Are you all right?"

Voerell pushed herself up from the pillows and threw her arms around him. "I'm fine, Whirter. We did it. We have a son."

"You did it, dearest." Whirter held her close a moment more, then released her. "Where is he? May I see him?"

"Of course. Nurse, bring him here."

Maryn jumped to her feet. The prince came off her breast and wailed. She tugged her shift up and moved him to her shoulder. Coewyn scowled and reached for the baby, but Maryn bounced him and patted his back, and he quieted. She carried the baby over and held him out toward Voerell. "Here he is, your Highness."

Voerell looked away. "You take him, Whirter."

Her husband eagerly accepted the small wrapped form into his arms. "He's so small." He stroked the baby's pale downy fuzz of hair with the tip of one finger. "He's beautiful."

The baby peered at his father. His face scrunched and reddened, and he wailed. Whirter pulled his hand back, an anxious frown creasing his brow. "What did I do?"

"Nothing. Babies cry. Even princes." Voerell

waved at Maryn. "Take him back and quiet him. But stay close; my father and brothers are on their way."

Whirter reluctantly surrendered the child to Maryn. She tried to rock him against her shoulder, but nothing would soothe him. At length she put him to her breast again, trying the other side this time. He seized her nipple and sucked urgently. It hurt, even more than before, but she dared not take him off to disturb the princess and her husband with his complaints. She stood by the bed, cradling the baby's slight weight in her arms, and focused on Voerell and Whirter.

"Are you sure everything went well? You seem upset." Whirter sat on the edge of the bed and took Voerell's hand in his.

"Yes, yes, it was fine. It was harder than I expected, is all."

"Not so hard you don't want to do it again, I hope? You've always been so eager for children. Just think, next time it might be a daughter for you to pamper and coddle and teach to be a princess."

"Instead of a son for you to train as a soldier and take off to war?" Voerell waved Whirter's protest silent. "No, you know I'm proud to see the men I love stand strong to defend Milecha's borders. I will do my duty to the kingdom and the Sompirla dynasty, and bear as many children as I am able. But better sons, I think. I would not wish a daughter to have to go through this—"

Voerell's voice broke and she turned away. Whirter gathered her into his arms, and after a moment of resistance, Voerell buried her face in his chest. She shook with muffled sobs while Whirter stroked her braids. "Shh. It's all right. I'm sorry, what was I thinking, rushing you to think about another so soon. We'll take as long as you need. I didn't realize it was so terrible for you."

Voerell pushed back and scrubbed her eyes with the sleeve of her robe. "No, it's not that—"

She broke off as a commotion sounded outside the door. "Gallows, it's Father. Quick, Whirter, how do I look? I don't believe I let myself get all weepy. Are my eyes red? Coewyn, grab the robe there, and help me put it on. I suppose I don't have time to fix my hair."

She struggled into the heavy embroidered robe and arranged herself more gracefully on the pillows. Whirter chuckled and patted her hand. "You're perfect, dear. They won't be looking at you, anyway."

Instead of calming, Voerell scowled deeper and turned on Maryn. "Isn't he full yet? My father will want to hold him, and I won't have him acting the squalling brat for the king."

In fact, the prince had slowed his nursing to an occasional light suck, and came off Maryn's breast easily. He regarded her with quizzical dark eyes as she shifted him to the crook of one arm and did up the tie of her shift with trembling fingers. The king! Coming here! Of course he would want to greet his grandson, but Maryn had not quite registered until now the fact that she would be standing in the presence of her monarch in just a few moments. She brushed at the skirt of her crisp blue servant's uniform and adjusted the swaddling fabric around the prince.

The door swung open. Guards stationed themselves to either side.

The face of the man who entered was familiar to Maryn from the profile imprinted on every coin, though it was considerably older and rounder than the handsome young ruler portrayed there. King

Froethych was tall and broad, with thick shoulders that had once been muscular but now had softened. He was dressed in resplendent layers of velvet and satin, closely embroidered with gold and silver threads. On his thinning hair rested the crown of Milecha, its distinctive hammered gold curve rising above his brows. He strode across the room and spread his arms wide in greeting. Voerell bowed her head, and Whirter sank to one knee.

All the servants and ladies-in-waiting, along with Coewyn and Litholl, also knelt. Maryn dropped to her knees just quickly enough to avoid being caught the only one standing. She ducked her head over the baby in her arms and looked sideways to see what was happening.

"My dear, I heard the wonderful news." Froethych flung his arms around Voerell. She returned the embrace, a little breathless, until he released her and turned to draw Whirter to his feet. "Rise, rise! My good duke, what a marvelous day!" He clasped Whirter's hand and thumped him on the back. "Rise, all of you. Where's my grandson? Let me see him!"

A rustle of skirts filled the room as everyone rose. Maryn scrambled to her feet, trying not to jostle the prince, and stumbled forward, shaking. She shrank back as she offered the baby to the king, but Froethych never looked at her. All his attention was fixed on the child he scooped up and held triumphantly before him. "A grand big boy! You'll be a worthy warrior someday, won't you?"

The prince stiffened and flung his arms wide, and seemed on the verge of breaking into frightened wails. Froethych shifted him into the crook of one arm and the baby settled. The king turned to display the baby to the two young men who trailed him, as proud as if he had personally created each wispy strand of hair and dainty finger. "Look at your nephew! Was ever a king blessed by the Holy One with three such heirs?"

The elder of the two, tall and slender, with cropped hair and a neat short beard and mustache, nodded to Froethych and stroked the baby's head. "Congratulations, Father."

The younger was a bit shorter and more solidly built, with a thick fall of wavy blond locks and light blue eyes. He grinned at his brother. "You're congratulating the wrong person, Marolan." He stepped around the king, giving the baby a quick tickle on the cheek as he went, and bent to hug Voerell. "Congratulations, Voerell. He's beautiful. Good work."

She squeezed his shoulders. "Thanks, Carlich. Let Father have his fun. I don't mind."

Froethych seated himself on the edge of the bed, his big hands nearly engulfing the baby as he shifted him into his lap. "What are you going to name him?"

Voerell glanced at Whirter; he quirked an eyebrow at her and she nodded. Whirter inclined his head to the king. "We had thought to call him Barilan, your Majesty, after my ancestor who stood by Lord Hoenech's side, and was named duke by King Fridollan. In honor of the bonds of friendship and loyalty that have always joined the houses of Sompirla and Rottolla."

"A proud name! And a proud history. I knew when I chose you for Voerell that you would honor our family and our kingdom." Froethych beamed. "Ah, is there anything so good as a grandson? I wonder when I shall be granted more such blessings?" He flashed a teasing grin at his sons.

Marolan inclined his head. "I count the days until my marriage, Father. You saw fit to betroth me to Dolia, so you have no one to blame but yourself that you must wait until she comes of age, as I must."

"True, true. But the alliance with Wonora will reward our patience many times over." Froethych turned a sharper glance on Carlich. "What of you? When are you going to leave off this nonsense of refusing every match I try to make? Is there no woman in Milecha or among our allies that will please you?"

"Many women please me, Father. Perhaps someday I'll find one who can entice me away from all the others." Carlich kept his tone light and joking, but Maryn still sensed a bite in his words.

Voerell snorted. "I pity her, if you ever find her. The Holy One knows I wouldn't put up with you if it was anything less than blood-ties that bound us."

Carlich grinned, unruffled. "I love you, too, little sister. Truly, Father, between Voerell and Marolan you'll end up with so many heirs the kingdom won't have room for them all. Why should I add to the number of princes who'll never see a crown?"

Marolan frowned. "We never know what might chance. Look at Father; he was Grandfather's fourth son. All of us must be ready to step forward if fate calls us to serve. There's no reason for you to be so resentful—"

"Perhaps, but you must admit some of *us* have a better chance than others of *us*—"

Froethych raised his hands. "Boys! Now is not the time for your bickering! If you cannot be respectful of your sister's happiness, you may leave." The baby in his lap stirred, wrinkled his face, and broke into a thin wail. "Now see what you've done. You've made

Barilan cry." Froethych scooped up Barilan and set him on his shoulder. Maryn held her breath lest Barilan spit up and mar the rich velvet of the king's robe, but the baby only subsided into muffled whimpers. Froethych glared at his sons.

Marolan inclined his head with every indication of respect. Carlich, too, nodded in submission, but he shot a covert glower at his brother.

Froethych spent a good deal longer exchanging pleasantries with Voerell and Whirter, laced with many admiring comments on Barilan's appearance, size, health, and heritage. At length Barilan fell asleep against the king's shoulder.

Maryn shifted. Her feet were still sore from her journey, and she was deeply weary, but she wasn't allowed to move until the king left or dismissed her. All the rest of the servants stood in respectful stillness. Most of them wore bored, resigned expressions that told Maryn she couldn't expect the king to have any consideration for their comfort.

At long last Froethych ran out of things to say. He patted Barilan and moved to pass him to Voerell. The princess glanced at Maryn, but set her mouth in a grim line and accepted her son into her arms. She remained stiff, even when the sleeping baby snuggled into her chest with a little sigh.

Froethych rose. "Come, Marolan, Carlich, let us leave them to their rest. Join me in the main hall tonight; we'll feast to celebrate Barilan's arrival. Whirter, you're invited, too, if you can tear yourself away from your wife and son."

He swept from the room. Marolan followed him. Carlich bent to give Voerell a quick parting embrace and Barilan a pat before he trailed after.

All around the room came an exhalation and a

rustle of skirts as everyone relaxed from their frozen attitudes of deference and returned to their duties. Servants bustled about. Coewyn went to confer with Litholl. The ladies-in-waiting clustered around the bed, oohing and ahhing over the baby.

Voerell put up with their attentions for a few minutes, responding to their compliments and delighted comments with a strained smile and clipped words. The moment Barilan stirred, only a slight shifting in his sleep, she shooed them away. "Come, nurse. Take him away. I want to rest."

Maryn moved quickly to comply. Barilan's warm weight felt good back in her arms. He snuggled in close to her body, and she wrapped her arms around him. She didn't know why Voerell acted so coldly toward her son, or remained so unmoved by his newborn sweetness, but it distressed her. Perhaps that was the way all highborn women treated their children. No wonder they gave them to wet nurses. As Maryn trailed Madam Coewyn toward the nursery, she silently promised Barilan that she would do her best to shower him with all the affection and tenderness his mother could not, or would not, give him.

Six

maryn pressed her lips together, but she wasn't able to entirely smother a gasp of pain as Barilan's eager mouth clamped around her nipple. She glanced across the nursery to see if Madame Semprell had noticed, but the Under-Stewardess was much too busy looking over the array of gowns laid out on the table to pay any attention to Maryn.

Semprell frowned, and fingered the linen of one sleeve. "This is much too rough. Nothing so coarse can be allowed to touch Prince Barilan's skin." She scowled at the servant assisting her, and the woman whisked the offending garment away into the growing pile of rejects.

Under-Stewardess Semprell was fairly young, only a few years older than Maryn, but her manner often belied her age. She idolized Royal Stewardess Coewyn and copied many of the older woman's mannerisms. But the erect posture and haughty stares that gave Coewyn her natural authority seemed mere pretentious bossiness when Semprell affected them.

Semprell moved on to the next gown. "This one is better, though the embroidery is uninspired. Still, it's competent. Hang it up; it will do for daily wear." She continued down the row, finding fault with some, accepting others.

Maryn breathed deeply and blinked back tears. Semprell must not be allowed to see her distress. Barilan's mouth on her breast felt like fire, every suck scraping across her raw nipple like a whetstone across a blade. Cracks broke her tender skin; they barely scabbed over before another nursing session tore them open to bleed again. Blood stained the dribbles of milk at the corners of Barilan's mouth pink; she writhed inside with worry that so much uncleansed blood must surely harm the prince somehow.

But to all appearances he was thriving. He had grown so much in the six weeks since his birth that already he required larger gowns. His skin glowed; his arms and legs were plump and dimpled; his eyes were bright and alert. He filled his diaper regularly and generously. By all these signs Maryn knew he must be receiving a sufficient quantity of her milk. But this required many long hours of nursing each day, every minute a trial for Maryn. Something must be terribly wrong. Nursing Frilan had never hurt like this. She didn't know how much longer she could endure the torture.

But she must. If Semprell or Coewyn ever found out how badly she was failing at the task for which she'd been hired, she would be dismissed from her position immediately. Some other woman would be chosen to replace her, perhaps not so desirably free of entangling ties, but at least able to put the prince to her breast without wanting to scream. On particularly bad nights, when Barilan insisted on staying latched on for hours and Maryn was unable to snatch even a brief stretch of sleep, the thought of being freed from her miserable duty seemed a welcome relief, and she resolved to confess all to Semprell in the morning. But always, so far, when dawn came she sealed her lips and schooled her face into stoic calm.

Except for this one thing, her life in the palace was everything she had hoped. Her surroundings were luxurious, the food was rich and plentiful, her position in the hierarchy of palace servants was privileged. She spent her days in relative leisure, her only duty to feed and tend the prince. She would have enjoyed that task, if not for the nearly constant pain.

And Barilan needed her. She was the only one he ever seemed truly happy with. When Semprell took him for an hour each morning, to manipulate his limbs in the series of exercises that were supposed to strengthen his arms and legs and coax them to grow long and straight, Barilan would wail and thrash. In the afternoons he repeated the performance while the Under-Stewardess tried to recite long passages in the ancient language into his ear. Finally Semprell agreed, scowling, to conduct the lessons while Barilan nestled content in Maryn's arms.

Semprell had such odd notions of how an infant should be treated. She ascribed religiously to a treatise penned by Letwillan, an ancient Wonoran scholar that Semprell revered as an expert in all matters of child-rearing. Some of his pronouncements were harmless enough, Maryn supposed. She didn't see that the morning exercise sessions could do much harm, though she doubted they would do any good, either; serf children grew fine without all that fuss and bother. The afternoon language lessons might actually be helpful when it came time for Barilan to learn sorcery.

Others of Letwillan's strictures, however, were

more troubling. Semprell constantly badgered Maryn to hold Barilan less, and put him down more often in his cradle by the fire. This wouldn't have bothered Maryn if Barilan had been content, as Frilan had often been, to play with his toes or gaze at the flickering shadows on the wall. But Barilan would almost always shriek in protest the moment Maryn released him. She didn't mind holding him as much as he wanted; everyone knew some babies needed more holding than others. But Semprell frowned whenever Maryn picked him up.

The Under-Stewardess didn't like listening to Barilan scream either, so she had not yet pressed the point, but as the prince grew older Maryn feared she would. If Maryn was dismissed, whoever replaced her might be less willing to defy Semprell. Or she might even share the same views. The thought of Barilan wailing for long hours, alone and uncomforted, steeled Maryn to endure many miserable nursing sessions when otherwise she would have been glad to hand over her difficult charge to some other nurse.

Full at last, Barilan's sucking slowed, and he came off Maryn's breast. Her whole body unclenched with a shudder at the relief from pain. Quickly she tucked in place the folded cloth she used to keep blood from staining her shift and fastened her drawstring before Semprell had a chance to glimpse the raw red mess of her nipple.

Semprell glanced at Barilan. "Is he finished at last? Hurry up and play with him. We've still got to get him dressed before we can go. Princess Voerell has no patience for tardiness."

Letwillan prescribed a session of "playful interaction" between baby and nurse after every feeding. Maryn found this pronouncement somewhat less objectionable than his others. Of course playtime was important, even if trying to force it into such a rigid schedule was ridiculous. When Semprell was absent from the nursery, she ignored the timetable and played with Barilan whenever he seemed in the mood. Now, though, with Semprell hovering nearby, she had to at least pretend to comply.

Maryn patted Barilan's back until he released a hearty belch. "There, that's better." She shifted him from her shoulder to her lap. His eyes were bright and alert, watching her inquisitively. Good, this time she wouldn't have to fight to keep him awake.

She caught his waving hands in hers, brought them together rhythmically, and crooned a rhyme she'd learned from her mother. "Clappa clappa handikins, clappa clappa do..." Out of the corner of her eye she saw Semprell turn back to the gowns. She pressed Barilan's hands first to her cheeks, then to his own. "Clappa for me and clappa for you..."

Maryn let her thoughts wander as she continued to go through the motions of the song. Litholl was coming to the palace today to check on Voerell and Barilan. The other times she had come Maryn hadn't dared asked her for help with her damaged nipples, not with Coewyn and Semprell right there. But they had gotten much worse since the midwife's last visit. Maybe she could find some way to speak with Litholl privately. If she couldn't, she feared it was only a matter of time until the pain increased so much she wouldn't be able to force herself to endure it any more.

She released Barilan's hands and grabbed his feet. "Clappa clappa footikins, all the way to town. Clappa too close and I'll gobble you down!" She made a great show of munching on his wiggly bare toes, tucking her lips over her teeth to cushion the mock bites. Barilan's legs flexed, pulling against her grip, his arms waved in excitement, and his mouth split open in a broad gummy smile.

Maryn caught her breath. "Look Semprell, he's smiling!" Once or twice before she'd though she'd caught the hint of a real smile from him, but this was unmistakable. She couldn't help but laugh in response to the way his whole face lit up with unrestrained delight. After a moment his expression fell back into its normal eager watchfulness. Maryn attacked his toes again with even greater pretend ferociousness, and was rewarded by a squeal and another excited grin.

"Very good," Semprell said, her voice approving. Maryn glanced up to find the Under-Stewardess beaming proudly at Barilan. "Letwillan says that smiling in the sixth week is a sure sign that his program is proceeding successfully. I must record this immediately." She hustled off to find the book in which she meticulously noted every little detail of Barilan's growth.

Maryn made a face at Barilan as soon as she was sure Semprell wouldn't see. She kept her voice conspiratorially soft. "We know it has nothing to do with her precious Letwillan. Frilan started smiling when he was six weeks old without any..." She trailed off as her throat tightened. She turned away from Barilan and closed her eyes as the inevitable grief rolled over her. She could see Frilan's smile, just as wide and carefree as Barilan's was now. How much more would she have treasured those fleeting grins, if she had known how few there would be?

She had to find a way to get Litholl to help her

nurse Barilan without so much pain. He was all she had, now. She couldn't let him be taken from her, too.

After Maryn dressed Barilan in the finest of the new gowns, Semprell led the way to Voerell's quarters. Maryn had only been there a few times since Barilan's birth. Voerell evinced little interest in her child. Occasionally when the king visited her she would summon Barilan, but would invariably hold him as little as possible and send him away again as soon as Froethych left.

Maryn didn't understand how Voerell could bear to have so little contact with her son. Didn't the princess realize what a precious gift a child was, and how easily lost? Sometimes Maryn's cheeks grew hot with rage when she thought about it. Maryn would give anything, her life, her soul, to have Frilan back in her arms again. And here Voerell was, casually throwing away the chance to spend time with her son like so much worthless garbage.

It was just as well Barilan didn't have to be exposed to his mother very often, if that's the way she felt about him. Far better for him to spend his days in Maryn's company. She might not be his kin by blood, but at least she knew how to give him attention and affection.

They entered to find Litholl tucking Princess Voerell back into her bed. "Everything is well healed, your Highness. I see no reason why you should not attempt to conceive again as soon as you wish. I'll be happy to take the last of your cloths and cleanse them for you. Unless you'd rather take care of the matter yourself."

Voerell waved a dismissive hand. "I've already dealt with them. You didn't think I'd leave them lying around asking to draw specters, did you? I may not be the sorcerer Carlich is, but I can certainly manage to cleanse my own—"

She broke off, seeing Semprell and Maryn. "Thank you, Litholl. You'll excuse me if I don't join you while you examine Barilan. I didn't sleep well last night; I think I shall take a nap." She beckoned to a servant, who began to draw the heavy curtains around the bed. "Perhaps you should take him into the solar."

Litholl nodded as Voerell rolled away and pulled the covers up to her chin. "If that's what you wish, your Highness. It's important that you get your rest."

Maryn suppressed a disdainful sniff. The princess had done little but lie abed in the weeks since the birth. It must be nice to have that luxury. Maryn had been back to all her usual work of spinning, cooking and cleaning within a week of Frilan's birth.

The servant tugged the last curtain closed, shutting Voerell in. Litholl led Semprell and Maryn across the bedroom and through a set of heavy wooden doors. The room beyond was brightly lit by wide windows that gave a pleasant view of the palace gardens and furnished with comfortable upholstered chairs and settees. Maryn breathed a little easier when the stout doors closed behind them, releasing her from the subtle tension she always felt in Voerell's presence.

"Come here, Prince Barilan, let me see how you're doing." Maryn surrendered Barilan into Litholl's arms. His face clouded, but Litholl caught his eye and stuck her tongue out. Barilan forgot his distress, staring in fascination. She hefted him. "My goodness, I believe you're twice as heavy as when I last held you. Your nurse must be feeding you well." She smiled at Maryn, who blushed and dropped her eyes. "So, how are things going, my dear?"

Maryn shot a glance at Semprell. The Under-

Stewardess was still paying close attention. Maryn shrugged. "Everything's fine. He started smiling today."

"How wonderful! Such a happy boy you are." Litholl seated herself, laid Barilan in her lap, and continued examining him. She offered him her finger, and tested the strength of his grasp when he seized it. "I see he's holding his head up."

"Yes," Semprell jumped in, before Maryn could say anything. "It's clear how efficacious Letwillan's exercises have been. We have adhered rigorously to the prescribed schedule. At least for the most part." Semprell frowned briefly at Barilan.

"I see. Tell me about what you've done." Litholl listened closely as Semprell launched into a detailed account of her work with Barilan. At first the Under-Stewardess skimmed over her dissatisfaction with Barilan's fussiness, but in response to Litholl's earnest attention and obvious sympathy she eventually gave a full airing of all her complaints.

Maryn shifted from foot to foot. Why was Litholl so patient with Semprell's whining? The midwife must realize how ridiculous Letwillan's teachings were. But Litholl continued to nod and murmur in commiseration. Maryn kept an anxious eye on Barilan. For once he seemed content enough, so she remained quiet.

At last Semprell wound down. Litholl shook her head. "That must be terribly frustrating. I'm impressed by how devoted you are, and how determined to persist in the face of such obstacles." Semprell beamed at the praise.

Litholl turned back to Maryn. "Tell me more about how often he nurses, and for how long. Does he wake at night?"

Maryn was hesitant at first, but Litholl's attention proved quite as effective at drawing her out as it had with Semprell. At last, someone to talk to who cared what she had to say. Maryn found herself describing Barilan's nursing patterns in greater and greater detail. She kept her voice bright and positive, doing her best not to betray by word or expression how miserable every feeding had become for her. But she watched for any chance to speak more openly.

At last her opportunity came. Semprell's attention wandered as Maryn spun out the minutiae of her account as much as she could. The Under-Stewardess drifted over to the window to gaze at the riot of flowers below. Maryn dared to lean close to Litholl and drop her voice. "Please, if I could speak with you alone, I can't tell you everything while Madam Semprell is listening—"

Semprell turned back from the window. Maryn broke off. Litholl's eyes widened a bit, but she only nodded gravely. "I see. If you could tell me a bit more about—Excuse me, Semprell. I need to get a few more details from Maryn, but you've managed to intrigue me about Letwillan's work. You've had such good results. I must admit I haven't read the full treatise. If you have a copy I might borrow...?"

"Of course." Semprell brightened. "I'd be happy to fetch mine for you."

"Oh, no, I wouldn't want to take your own copy; you must need it often. But if the palace library has an extra, or if you could arrange for a scribe to prepare one for me, I'd be happy to purchase it."

"No, no. I'm sure King Froethych would be glad to provide it for you. I'll go see about making the arrangements right now." Semprell hurried away with a bouncy step.

As the doors closed behind her, Litholl turned back to Maryn. She disentangled Barilan's hand from the wad of her sleeve he had dragged to his mouth and gummed until it was drenched, and gave him her little finger to suck instead. "Now, child, what's troubling you?"

Maryn dropped her eyes. "Barilan really does nurse the way I told you. But I couldn't let Madam Semprell know how badly it hurts. I don't know what's wrong with me, but there must be something, because my nipples are so sore. It was never like this with Frilan." She struggled to hold back tears.

"Let me see," Litholl said. Maryn glanced up, afraid to see condemnation in the midwife's face, but Litholl wore only an expression of concern and interest. Maryn undid the ties of her shift and pulled it down to display her cracked and bloody nipples for Litholl's examination.

"Oh, my dear," Litholl exclaimed. She tutted to herself as she looked closely at Maryn's damaged nipples. "I had no idea! How long have they been like this?"

Tears choked Maryn's throat. "All along, really. It's always hurt when Barilan nursed, right from the first day. I kept trying different ways to hold him, and nursing him less, or more, but nothing I did made it any better. I couldn't let anyone know..." She scrubbed at her eyes with her sleeve.

"I'm so sorry you've had to endure this, Maryn. I wish you had come to me earlier. I could have helped you fix the problem before it became so severe." Maryn squirmed in shame, but Litholl put a hand on her arm. "Never mind. Let's see what we can do now. Here, take Barilan back and offer him your breast, so I can see what's going on."

Maryn accepted Barilan into her arms, wincing in anticipation. Barilan was almost always happy to nurse when offered the opportunity; he seized her nipple now with his usual enthusiasm. Pain shot through Maryn's breast, but she ignored it as best she could, focusing on Litholl as the midwife studied them. Litholl moved around and leaned over to get a better view of the place where Barilan's mouth met Maryn's breast.

"Yes, it's just as I thought. See how his mouth is hardly open, and his lower lip is tucked under? No wonder you're in such pain. He's got too little of your breast in his mouth; all his sucking is right down on the tip of your nipple. I'm only surprised he's managed to get as much milk as he obviously has, to grow so well."

Maryn gulped. "I'm sorry. I knew he didn't open his mouth as wide as Frilan always did, but I didn't think it would make such a difference. I should have done something about it; I should have known I was doing it wrong—"

"By the Holy One, Maryn, it's not your fault. If anyone's to blame it's me, for not checking on you sooner. Now let's put aside regrets for what might have been and concentrate on solving the problem. Here, take him off before he does any more damage."

"Can you? Solve the problem, I mean? You're not going to tell Madam Coewyn to find another nurse for Barilan? You don't think my nipples are hurt too much to fix? I don't see how they can ever heal, if he keeps nursing on them and breaking the cracks open." Maryn slipped her finger into the corner of Barilan's mouth and broke the seal of his lips on her skin. The suction released and her nipple slid from his mouth, granting blessed relief from her pain. Barilan squalled in complaint.

"You'd be surprised. If we can get him latching correctly, the cracks will heal well enough. I think we can fix the problem, yes, though it won't be easy. He's had a long time to get used to doing it the way he likes; he won't want to change. You'll have to be stubborn and insist that he do it your way."

"Whatever it takes." The thought of being able to nurse Barilan with the same relaxed ease she'd felt with Frilan seemed an impossibly enticing dream. "But how can I get him to change the way he nurses?"

"Here, let me show you." Litholl gestured for Maryn to sit, and moved around behind her. "Hold him the way you do when you're beginning to nurse him. Yes, like that. Now, instead of letting him lie on his back, with his head turned to the side, turn his body so his belly faces yours. See, now he can look straight ahead at your breast; that will allow him to open his mouth much wider."

Litholl put her arms around Maryn and adjusted the set of her hands on Barilan's body. Maryn struggled to comply, though the new position felt awkward and unnatural.

"Now move him this way a little, and support your breast with your free hand. Instead of aiming your nipple at the center of his mouth, hold him so it points towards his nose."

"His nose!" Maryn almost laughed. Barilan squirmed, struggling to get back into his comfortable accustomed position. Maryn couldn't manage to aim her nipple anywhere, let alone the way Litholl wanted her to. Her hands slipped, and Barilan almost slid from her lap. She scrambled to get a better grip and repositioned him, feeling clumsy and self-conscious.

But Litholl remained patient, waiting until Maryn had returned Barilan close enough to the correct position. "Yes. He's been keeping his chin tucked down into his chest. If your nipple is near his nose when you move him toward your breast, that forces him to tilt his head back to reach for it, and that will allow his mouth to open wider. Try it, bring him in."

Maryn attempted to pull Barilan in close. He kicked, and fought, and her breast mashed into his cheek, nowhere near his mouth. Thoroughly upset now, Barilan began to wail in earnest. Maryn felt perilously close to doing the same.

"It's all right. Try again."

For a moment Litholl's continued calm infuriated Maryn. What the midwife was asking was impossible; her ridiculous instructions would never accomplish anything, but only make Maryn appear incompetent and subject her to further humiliation. Nothing could ever allow Maryn to nurse Barilan properly. She might as well give up now, confess her failure to Semprell, and run as far and as fast as she could away from this miserable place.

No. Maryn drew a deep breath. She would not surrender. Nothing was wrong with her breasts; they had nursed Frilan perfectly well without pain. Barilan would just have to bend to her will and learn to latch the right way, even if she had to fight him for every suck.

Maryn shifted Barilan to her shoulder until he calmed. When he seemed amenable, she slid him down into position, careful to keep his belly turned in as Litholl had shown her, and tried again to do as the midwife had instructed.

This time it worked for an instant. Barilan's head tilted back, and he grabbed for her nipple. It went deep into his mouth, and when his lips closed around her breast she felt very little pain, only strong warm sucking. But then he squirmed, and pulled his head back, and her nipple slid down to its accustomed place, accompanied by the familiar scraping agony.

"No, that's no good, take him off again." Litholl gestured for Maryn to once again break the suction of Barilan's mouth and pull him away, and she complied.

Barilan began to scream, overwhelmed and angry that Maryn would not let him nurse undisturbed. Maryn turned to Litholl. "It worked! For a moment it didn't hurt at all. Just for a second, then he moved, but it really did work!"

Litholl smiled, encouraging. "Good. That's what we're looking for. When he's on right, you can tell. If it hurts, take him off and try again."

With renewed hope Maryn patted Barilan's back and shifted him down for another attempt. She had to hold on determinedly to the memory of that brief pain-free instant, for it took at least another dozen tries before once again she managed to get everything to work as it was supposed to and her breast went deep into Barilan's mouth. This time it lasted a little longer. He was so frustrated by this point that he was willing to accept the odd sensation on his lips and tongue and suck a few times. It amazed Maryn how different it felt. There was still a little residual soreness from the cracks, but so much less she hardly noticed it.

She looked up at Litholl, nearly overcome with relief. "He's got it! I don't believe it. It feels so much better. Do you think he'll—Ow!" Her concentration on keeping Barilan in place lapsed, and he slid back down her nipple again.

Litholl put a hand on Maryn's shoulder as Maryn hastened to remove Barilan from her breast. "Now you know what it feels like when it's right." The midwife gave Maryn a smile of weary commiseration. "You just have to insist he do it right every time. Don't ever settle for less. You deserve to be comfortable nursing him, and he's quite capable of learning. He'll get more milk more easily this way, as well, so it shouldn't take long before he comes to see the advantages and becomes more cooperative. Go ahead and try the other side for a while, to make sure you've got it there, too."

Either Barilan was tired of fighting her, or he was beginning to get the hang of it, for this time it only took a few tries before Maryn got him to latch in the new way, and he stayed that way for several long minutes while Maryn marveled. This was what nursing Frilan had felt like, she recalled now, as easy and comfortable as breathing, none of the fear that tensed her shoulders and tightened her jaw, none of the misery that flooded her heart with resentment and guilt. This was how it should be, and she could only berate herself that she had waited so long to get the help she needed.

Barilan squirmed and slipped down, but once Maryn took him off and repositioned him, he latched correctly again. Much more quickly than she was used to, he grew content, his sucks slowed, and he drifted off to sleep.

Litholl pulled up a chair beside Maryn's and sat down, leaning over to look at Barilan's limp form as Maryn eased her nipple from his slack mouth. "I have an ointment I can give you to put on your nipples, to help them heal a bit quicker. I'll fetch some and bring it by the nursery later. But the best thing for them is to always keep a good latch. Will you be able to manage that on your own from now on?"

"I think so." Maryn sighed. "I should be getting back to the nursery. Madam Semprell will wonder if she comes back and finds me still with you."

"Yes." Litholl glanced at the door to the bedroom. "I wonder if Voerell is asleep yet, or if she'd like to visit a moment with Barilan before you leave."

Maryn ducked her head over the sleeping Barilan and stirred his blond wisps of hair with her fingers. Though she and Litholl were alone in the solar, she dropped her voice almost to a whisper. "She won't. Even if she's awake. She never looks at Barilan any more than she has to. I don't know why she hates him so much. I guess it's different when you're a princess. I guess your children don't matter to you the same way they do for everyone else, not as babies, not as people. Just as heirs, a way to fulfill your duty, to secure your family's power."

Litholl frowned at Maryn, her brow creasing. "Do you believe so? I think you'd be surprised if you could learn what is in Voerell's heart. She would never confess to me, or anyone, but I've seen the same thing often enough among highborn women to have a fairly good idea. I would venture to guess that Voerell loves her son deeply. She longs to do what any serf or servant woman thinks nothing of, and gather her child close, and nurse him, and give him all her devotion. But the constraints of her position prevent her from indulging her desires to their full extent, and Voerell is not one to do anything by half measures. So she withdraws even from the small amount of contact she might have, in order to shield herself from the pain of having to give over the one she loves into another woman's arms."

Maryn frowned. "That doesn't make sense. If she cared about him at all, wouldn't she want to spend as much time with him as she could? At least hold him occasionally. She acts like she can't stand having him around."

The midwife smiled wryly and shook her head. "When does the heart ever make sense? Just believe me, Voerell must endure her own pain at her son's touch. Not as physical as yours, perhaps, but real enough. And I'm afraid there is no ease for her trouble as straightforward as correcting a misplaced latch. She would do well to learn from your willingness to endure pain, in order to give Barilan what he needs." She sighed. "I'll speak with her. No, of course I won't tell her you said anything. But this state of affairs is not healthy for anyone."

Litholl subsided into silence. Maryn was just as glad she had dropped the subject. It still seemed obvious to her that Voerell cared very little for Barilan, no matter what Litholl said.

She eased Barilan into her lap and tied the drawstring of her shift. Life would be so much better now, if the new latching technique continued to work, and her nipples healed as Litholl had promised they would. She gathered Barilan into her arms and rose, giving the midwife a quick impulsive embrace. "Thank you so much."

"Call for me if you need anything else." Litholl led Maryn out of the solar and through the bedroom to the main entrance of the princess's suite. Quietly, they bid each other farewell.

As Maryn nodded to the guards and eased the heavy wooden door closed behind her, out of the corner of her eye she thought she saw the curtains of the bed ripple, and a pale flash as of a hand withdrawing. But when she looked again, all was still, and she was sure she must have been mistaken.

Seven

Voerell stopped in the hallway outside her brother's quarters and swept a last critical gaze over her family. Duke Whirter passed her inspection, but her lips pinched when Maryn turned Barilan out to face her. "It's still not right. Why won't it sit straight?" Voerell tugged at Barilan's lace-edged cap. She sighed. "That's a little better, at least."

Maryn could see that the princess's intervention had pulled the cap down over one of Barilan's ears, which had gotten folded under the crisp fabric. He batted at the offending garment. Maryn scowled at the back of Voerell's head as the princess turned away. She attempted to get Barilan's ear unstuck as unobtrusively as she could. The cap ended up more crooked than before. Maryn hoped Voerell wouldn't notice.

Litholl must have spoken to Voerell as she had promised, for in the month since the midwife's visit the princess had made sporadic attempts to interact with her son and participate in his care. More often than not the efforts proved clumsy and intrusive. Sometimes Maryn wished Voerell would resume her former distance and leave Barilan to those who knew what they were doing.

Tonight, for instance, she'd have been much

happier if she and Barilan were spending a quiet evening in the nursery as usual, instead of accompanying Voerell and her husband to a private dinner with Prince Carlich. But the princess had insisted on taking Barilan with her. Maryn had no choice but to follow her orders, even though it meant upsetting Barilan's routine. At two and a half months, he was finally settled into a predictable pattern of eating and sleeping. This late night would disrupt his rhythm so much it might take days for Maryn to get him back to normal.

But Voerell was trying, and Maryn did her best to view her efforts as charitably as she could. Even when they made her own job harder.

Whirter smiled at Barilan and put a hand on his wife's arm. "He looks fine. Don't fret so. Your brother won't notice what he's wearing."

"Carlich notices everything." Voerell tugged at her close-fitting bodice and smoothed her skirt. "I should have known better than to try to wear this yet. My belly is still round; everyone will be saying I'm pregnant again."

"Let them. Perhaps by the time it makes a difference, it will be true."

"Perhaps." Voerell fussed with her skirt again, patted her braids, and gave a final glance at Barilan. She squared her shoulders and took a breath. "Very well. I'm ready."

After a brief conference between their guards and the ones at the entry to Prince Carlich's private quarters, the doors swung open and their party was formally announced. Carlich waited to greet them, all smiles and enthusiasm for his sister and her family. "Come in, come in, have a seat. You look lovely, Voerell. And can this possibly be Barilan? Look how much he's grown! You'd better watch out, Whirter; he's going to be as big as Father by the time he's a page."

Carlich ushered Voerell and Whirter into his sitting room. Maryn trailed behind. She was accustomed enough now to life in the palace that being in the presence of royalty no longer intimidated her the way it had at first. She still got nervous, but as her fear faded it was replaced with curiosity. Who were these people, so far above her, yet to whom she was inextricably bound through her attachment to their youngest member? Were they truly a breed apart, as she'd always believed, specially blessed by the Holy One and set above common humanity? Or, as seemed more credible the longer she was around them, were they simply folk like any others, just richer and more powerful?

She took up a position behind the elegant couch where Voerell settled. Her duty was to remain unobtrusively nearby, keeping Barilan happy and quiet, ready to present him the instant his royal mother, father or uncle expressed a desire to interact with him.

For the moment Barilan was content, looking at the strange surroundings with wide eyes, and Maryn's task was easy and tedious. Carlich, Voerell and Whirter settled into a pleasantly trivial discussion of palace gossip and the latest news of city and realm. Servants bustled about, offering wine. Maryn let her gaze wander around Carlich's quarters. The room was as casually elegant as the prince himself. All the furnishings were extremely well made, but without excessive ornamentation. A starburst of swords and daggers decorated one creamy yellow wall. Forest green drapes framed wide windows that looked out over the city, where the golden glow of sunset had faded to streaks of orange and purple across the sky.

"Are you sure?" Carlich's voice wasn't loud, but his sharp tone drew Maryn's attention.

"Quite sure," Whirter said. "King Froethych confirmed it to me this afternoon so I could get to work on the security arrangements. He'll make the formal announcement tomorrow."

Voerell shook her head ruefully. "Marolan will be delighted. He'd resigned himself to not meeting Dolia until just before the wedding. Now he'll have a whole month to get to know her."

Maryn's interest stirred. All the palace servants gossiped ceaselessly about the upcoming wedding and the arrival of the Wonoran princess. The news that she would be arriving earlier than expected would be received with excitement. The information might even be enough to buy Maryn a measure of acceptance into their ranks. She listened attentively, hoping she might hear more that she could share.

Carlich sat back in his chair, sipping at his goblet. "You're right. Marolan will be beside himself with joy. He might even smile."

Voerell laughed. "Oh, Carlich, don't be so hard on Marolan. How would you like it if you'd been betrothed since you were nine to a girl you'd never met? I think he's handling the matter far better than I'd be able to. I was nervous enough before my wedding, even though Whirter and I had known each other for years."

Whirter grinned at her. "What? I thought you told me you'd been pining for me since you were Dolia's age, and begged your father to make the match."

"You know what I mean." Voerell gave him a

playful swat before sobering. "But she is only sixteen. I hope they'll be able to be happy together, or at least not too miserable. And I hope the treaty with Wonora will make it all worthwhile."

Whirter nodded. "Those new trade provisions are going to bring great wealth to Milecha. What, Carlich, don't you agree?"

Carlich leaned forward in his chair and fixed Whirter with a calculating stare. The intensity of his reaction struck Maryn as odd. Whirter had done no more than echo the common wisdom she'd heard voiced by everyone from the youngest pages to Voerell's highborn ladies-in-waiting. "In fact, I do have reservations about the treaty. That's one of the reasons I invited you to dine with me tonight; I hoped we might discuss them."

"I'm willing to discuss whatever you like." Whirter shrugged. "But you'll have to work hard if you hope to persuade me there's anything wrong."

Barilan chose that moment to grab at Maryn's ear with a cheerful babble, and she missed Carlich's next words as she disentangled his fingers from the strands of hair he'd pulled loose from her braids. She offered the baby a knuckle to gnaw on, trying to catch what Carlich was saying. None of the chambermaids or kitchen girls would care about details of the treaty, but tales of discord within the royal family would be worthy of their notice.

"—listen with an open mind." Carlich turned to Voerell. "I'll need both of your support if I hope to have any chance of persuading Father and Marolan to hear me."

"You know you can always count on me, Carlich. But whatever you think you've found must be troubling, indeed, if you think you can get Father and

Marolan to consider the treaty as anything other than a gift from the Holy One himself."

"From the Vulture, more likely," Carlich muttered. At Voerell and Whirter's quizzical looks, he put on an expression of determined cheerfulness and waved away their concern. "But that's much too weighty a subject to tackle before we've eaten. If you're ready, let's move to the table and enjoy our repast. Afterwards I'll share my thoughts with you."

He rose, and ushered Voerell and Whirter into the next room, where servants bustled around a long table spread with many silver dishes. Maryn followed, shifting Barilan to her other shoulder and stretching her tired arms as unobtrusively as possible.

Steam rose from platters, and the smell of roasted meat and rich spices drifted in the air. Maryn breathed the delicious scents wistfully. Semprell had warned her to eat earlier, so she wasn't hungry. But her meal had been the plain fare provided for the servants, while the banquet spread before her was surely the same food that graced the king's table.

Barilan squirmed and made fretful noises. Maryn bounced him and patted his back as she took her position behind Voerell's chair. It quieted him momentarily, but she could tell he wouldn't stay happy for long. As soon as the nobles were absorbed in their meal, she unfastened her shift and positioned Barilan to nurse.

She paid close attention as he latched on. The first time was too shallow, so she detached him and tried again. Better, but still not quite right. Maryn treasured the sensation of nursing without pain too much to let herself get lazy and allow Barilan to use anything except perfect technique. Finally, the third time, her nipple went deep enough into his mouth. Maryn relaxed. Now that her nipples had healed as Litholl had promised they would, nursing Barilan was a pleasure. Her life as his nurse was all she could ask for. She was almost happy. As happy as it was possible for her to be, after—

The pain of her loss, never far away, swept over her. She closed her eyes and breathed deeply as images of Edrich and Frilan filled her mind. It was the only way she'd found to cope on the frequent occasions when some stray thought triggered a fresh outbreak of grief. Surrender to it without fighting, the way Siwell had taught her to respond to the pains of labor. Like those, after a time this pain eased, and she could focus again on her surroundings.

Voerell and the others continued to ignore her and Barilan as they ate. Maryn's feet grew sore and her back stiff, and her arms ached with Barilan's weight. Why had Voerell even bothered to bring her son along? To show off her perfect little family to her brother, Maryn supposed, though Carlich had so far given no sign that he was any more interested in the baby than Voerell was. Only Whirter occasionally glanced at Barilan in Maryn's arms and smiled.

It felt to Maryn as if many hours passed, although the peals of church bells across the city drifted in through the windows only once. Finally the last of the frothy confection of creamed berries vanished from the crystal bowls and the feasters settled back in their chairs with sighs of replete pleasure. Voerell sipped a cup of steaming tea, while Carlich shared a bottle of spirits with Whirter.

"All right, Carlich." Voerell set down her cup and crossed her arms. "You've kept us in suspense all through the meal, though I must say it was a pleasant distraction. Now tell us what terrible secrets you've discovered in Marolan's marriage treaty."

Carlich swirled his glass, his eyes fixed on the amber liquid. "I suppose I must. All I ask is that you don't dismiss my concerns out of hand. Give everything I say due consideration before you make up your mind."

"Of course. Gallows, you make it sound so ominous! I scarcely think anything in the treaty can be that bad. To hear you, you'd think Father had signed away Milecha's sovereignty along with Marolan's hand."

"He may have." Carlich met Voerell and Whirter's startled looks squarely. "I've had the scribes prepare a copy, so you can see for yourselves. I'll have it brought to the other room; we might as well get comfortable while we talk."

Carlich summoned a servant and spoke to him in a low voice. Maryn trailed after Voerell, back to the sitting room. She felt just as curious as the princess and her husband looked, but she kept her eyes downcast. Barilan, full and happy, wiggled in her arms and made cheerful noisy comments to the room at large.

Whirter came and reached for his son. "I'd like to hold him for a while."

"Yes, my lord." Barilan stretched eager arms to his father as Maryn passed him over.

Whirter settled on a soft couch and balanced Barilan on his knees. Voerell seated herself stiffly next to them, while Carlich took a sheaf of closely written parchment from his servant and perched on the edge of a large upholstered chair at right angles to the princess and duke. Maryn took her usual position behind Voerell, but she edged to the side enough that she could see everything that was happening.

Carlich riffled the pages in his hands. "I suppose I first began to have concerns about three years ago. We had just beaten back the Hampsian incursions across the border. Whirter, you remember."

Whirter nodded. "A costly battle." He toyed with Barilan's grabbing fingers.

They must be talking about the summer Maryn had turned fifteen. Fearful rumors had swept the land then, how the warlords of Hampsia, the large and powerful country to the northeast, would conquer them, slaughtering any who resisted and enslaving the rest to their pagan gods. Lord Negian had answered the king's call to defend Milecha, taking Maryn's father along among his levies. Father had been gone until the first snows, leaving the rest of the family to bring in what meager harvest they could without his labor. He'd returned with a limp and an angry red scar across his thigh.

Carlich nodded. "It was my first command. My men acquitted themselves well; Father rewarded me by allowing me to accompany him and Marolan in the negotiations to end hostilities. I was supposed to be quiet and observe, but of course there were a few matters I couldn't help but express my opinion about."

"Of course," Voerell agreed wryly.

"In particular I was deeply impressed by some of the feats of sorcery I'd seen the Hampsians perform on the field. They accomplished things with gestures unlike anything we could do with incantations. I was eager to learn their techniques. I tried to persuade Father to offer to send me for a year to the Hampsian court, as a gesture of goodwill. But he wouldn't hear of it; wouldn't even put the offer on the table. We could have won some valuable concessions in exchange, too.

"I was furious, and I insisted on knowing why he was so opposed to the idea. He tried to put me off with a lot of nonsense about how I was needed in Loempno, how he didn't want me influenced by Hampsia's pagan ways. But finally, when I kept badgering him, he looked at me." Carlich drew back his shoulders, puffed out his chest, and made his voice a fair imitation of King Froethych's round tones. "He said, 'Son, you should be looking west, not east. In a few years when your brother marries the Wonoran princess, there will be no place in Milecha for the kind of sorcery they practice in Hampsia.'"

Whirter frowned. Voerell started to speak, but stopped, shaking her head. Carlich raised his eyebrows at them. "I stormed off, and the negotiations were concluded without me. Once back in Loempno I hired a Hampsian sorcerer to teach me gestural magic. And I started reading a copy of the treaty with Wonora. I wanted to know what other restrictions on my freedom I could expect when Marolan married Dolia. I found much to trouble me."

He flipped through the pages. "For instance, right here, in the section on trade. Father talks a lot about how Wonora will drop all tariffs on our goods, while we'll still receive payments for theirs, and be free to set our own policy in regards to trade with other kingdoms. But did you know that only holds true for twenty years? After that, over a period of five years we've contracted to drop all tariffs on goods from Wonora, and bring the rest of our tariffs in line with Wonora's. Including, though it's not spelled out in so many words, the ridiculously high charge on Hampsian linen."

Voerell frowned. "But half of Milecha wears

Hampsian linen, at least when we're at peace. Nothing we grow compares to it."

"That's just my point. Wonora wants to force us to buy their linen, though it's far inferior quality. It will take a few years for their plan to come to fruition, but the king of Wonora is patient, unlike Father."

All this talk of tariffs and trade policy confused Maryn. But it certainly didn't sound good for Milecha. And she'd spun both Hampsian and Wonoran linen, as well as that grown in Milecha, and she agreed with Voerell's assessment of their relative qualities. It would be a shame indeed to have no more access to the smooth, strong strands of the flax that grew in the colder lands to the northeast, and have to make do with the weaker, rougher southwestern variety.

Voerell looked troubled. "I don't like it. Still, that's only one provision. Milecha gains so much in return, surely it's worth it."

Carlich dug further through the pages of the treaty, passing several to his sister. "I might agree, if it were just the one. But there are many others. Look at this, for instance. We grant Wonora freedom to move their troops across our lands. Invaluable for us if it comes to war with Hampsia again. But there's no limit on how many, or how long they can stay. I'm not implying they intend an actual invasion, but how strongly will we dare to disagree with them on any matter if their forces are all over our kingdom? And we've agreed to eventually raise the tax rates to match theirs, without regard to whether or not our people can support such high payments."

Maryn's attention began to wander. She couldn't follow all the technical details Carlich was explaining, though Voerell listened intently and frequently interrupted him with questions or objections. Barilan was still happy with Whirter. He played with his father's fingers as Whirter quietly listened, only occasionally making a comment.

Maryn was wondering if she might persuade Semprell to allow her to take Barilan for a walk in the garden tomorrow if the weather was fair, when Barilan's name called her attention back to Carlich's words.

"—puts Barilan at risk, and me as well."

Maryn stiffened. What in the treaty could put Barilan at risk? She strained to catch every word.

"I must have read it a dozen times without realizing what it meant." Carlich held up a sheet of paper. "But once I thought about it, I understood the danger. And I realized I must stop the treaty from going into effect."

Voerell accepted the paper from Carlich and studied it, her brow furrowed. Whirter shifted Barilan to his shoulder and bent close. Maryn held herself very still, lest any of them notice she was listening.

"Everyone knows that Marolan and Dolia will each keep their separate inheritance, with him becoming king of Milecha upon Father's death, and she reigning as queen of Wonora when her father passes. And that their first son will become heir to Milecha, while their second"—Carlich quirked a wry smile at the word—"will inherit the crown of Wonora."

"Of course." Voerell shifted impatiently.

"But do you know what will happen if Marolan and Dolia do not produce two male heirs?"

Whirter cocked his head. "Doesn't it say that if they have no issue after ten years, the marriage will be dissolved, and both will be free to wed again?"

"Yes, and that was a point Father had to fight hard for, because the Wonoran laws on divorce are so strict. I have no problem with that provision; in fact it might be the best possible outcome. But say they have one son, and a whole palace full of daughters."

"Well, then, I suppose the eldest girl would inherit Wonora. Since the law there allows for women to take the crown if there are no male heirs." Voerell's voice was bitter.

"That's just what the treaty specifies. But here's the trick. What if they have no boys, only girls?"

Whirter leaned in. "I think I see your point. That would be fine for Wonora, for their daughter could become queen. But Milechan law never allows a woman to wear the crown in her own right."

Carlich nodded. "If Marolan should die without a son, the Kingship would pass first to me, then to any sons I might have, then to Barilan and any brothers you give him. But what if we were out of the picture, and there was no Sompirla heir available?"

Voerell frowned. "I suppose it would be the same as when the plague killed off all the last dynasty. The magic of the Kingship would be loosed, and it would fall to the people to acclaim a new king. The way they chose Great-Grandfather Fridollan, because of his father's sacrifice."

Carlich stabbed his finger at the paper. "That's the way it should be. But do you know what the treaty says would happen? Not just in this generation, but if ever again in the future Milecha is without a male heir?"

Voerell creased her brow. "No, I don't think I ever heard what it specifies in that case."

"It's hidden far down in an obscure paragraph, couched in confusing language, but if you read it you'll see there's only one possible interpretation. If either country ever finds itself without a suitable heir, rule will revert to the sovereign of the other kingdom. Forever. And I ask you, with Milecha's more restrictive laws, which land is more likely to be heirless?"

Voerell sat back, eyes wide. "Milecha would be no more."

Maryn's heart raced. Her homeland, destroyed? But she swallowed and shook off her reflexive horror. It couldn't be as bad as Carlich said. If Milecha no longer had its own royalty and was ruled by the king of Wonora, would it even matter to most people? Serfs didn't care which king their lord owed fealty to, as long as he didn't go to war too often. And townsfolk didn't care which treasury their taxes filled, as long as the laws that governed their lives weren't unduly restrictive.

Whirter pulled his hand away from Barilan's grasp and took the page of the treaty. He scanned it. "Even if you're right, how likely is that to happen? As you pointed out, you and Barilan are Marolan's heirs."

"What would our lives be worth?" Carlich's voice was low and urgent. "With Wonora's history of conspiracy and assassination? They've hungered to swallow Milecha for generations. It wouldn't be hard to make it look accidental. If Marolan and I go off to war, we might very well not come back. And children's lives are fragile; no one would question if Barilan were to conveniently sicken and die."

Fear twisted Maryn's gut and rushed in her ears. She had to clench her hands together to keep from reaching to snatch Barilan from his father's arms. Suddenly he seemed so vulnerable. She'd never considered before that his position as heir might make him a target for Milecha's enemies. But of course Carlich was right. Maryn ached to gather Barilan to her breast and shelter him from danger. But what good could she do, powerless as she was?

Carlich turned to Voerell, who met his gaze squarely, only a slight quickening of her breath betraying that his words had affected her. "I'm willing to wager that if this treaty goes forward as written, Milecha's Kingship will be lost within three generations, and we will become one small province of Wonora."

Whirter's arms tightened around Barilan. "Have you told the king about this?"

Carlich slumped back in his chair and rubbed at his temple. "Of course I have. I went to him as soon as I realized. But he refused to take me seriously. Father is so ridiculously proud of that treaty; he sees it as the greatest accomplishment of his reign. He won't hear a word against it."

Whirter sank back in his seat. Barilan squirmed; Maryn stepped forward, but Whirter shook his head. He stood the baby in his lap and supported him under the arms while he bounced.

Voerell chewed her lower lip. "What can we do, if Father refuses to listen?"

"Maybe if we went to him together...but you know Father. Once he sets his mind on a course, nothing can sway him."

"You're right." Voerell glanced at her husband and son. "But if Barilan is in danger..." Her face grew hard.

"I fear he is." Carlich spread his hands.

Voerell nodded, fixing Carlich with steady eyes. "You have to figure out some way to stop it."

Carlich shook his head, looking down at the papers. "I don't know. I have spies in Wonora; they tell me some factions oppose the treaty. There are those who reject the idea of any but one of pure Wonoran blood on the throne." He hesitated, and licked his lips. His gaze flicked up to meet Voerell's. "There are even rumors that the princess herself shares those sentiments."

"Dolia?" Voerell's brow wrinkled. "That hardly seems likely."

Carlich shrugged. "Nevertheless, that's what my spies report. Perhaps she can be persuaded to appeal to her father to end the betrothal. Supposedly he gives her whatever she asks; if he thought she didn't want this marriage, he might be willing to cancel the treaty."

Voerell looked troubled. "That would break Marolan's heart."

"He'd get over it." Carlich did not seem worried by the prospect. "Or, if that approach bears no fruit, there are those in Hampsia who might be willing to aid us—"

Whirter jerked his head up. "You would conspire with our enemies?"

"No, of course not. And they're not our enemies at the moment. We'd just ask for help in pressuring Father to renegotiate the treaty. Or Marolan, in due course. Even after the wedding it might be done."

Whirter still looked doubtful, but he did not renew his objection. Voerell twisted her hands in her lap. "I suppose Marolan sides with Father?"

"In this, as in all things."

"If he ever finds out we've been talking about this, he'll be furious."

"That's because he cares more about himself and

his position than the welfare of Milecha." Carlich grimaced. "If only our laws weren't so idiotic. Either you or I would make a far better ruler than Marolan, yet because of some ancient decree, neither of us will get the opportunity. Did you know the king of Hampsia chooses among his sons which one will succeed him, without regard to their order of birth?"

"That wouldn't help you. Father would never choose you over Marolan." Voerell shrugged. "And it would still leave me out. I agree you'd make a better king than Marolan, but unless something happens to him, Holy One forbid, you're out of luck. Our way is written into the magic of the Kingship."

"Holy One forbid anything should happen to Marolan," Carlich echoed, irony in his tone. He shot Voerell a sideways glance. "Sorcery created the Kingship, and a good enough sorcerer could modify it. Perhaps someday one of us will get the chance."

She laughed. "You know I'm not a tenth the sorcerer you are."

"You could be, if you cared enough to study." Carlich waved his hand in a grandiose gesture. "I promise, if the Kingship ever comes to me, I'll change it so that only the best possible candidate can inherit, be that younger son or daughter, general or merchant or beggar in the street."

"Hah! If the Kingship ever came to you I'd wager you'd never let it slip from your fingers, even to your own son. You're so stubborn you'd contrive a way never to die. Or else work some spell to let you continue to rule from your grave."

Carlich raised an eyebrow and grinned at her. "I'll have to look into that." He sobered. "In all seriousness, though, if I discover some way to keep the treaty from going into effect, can I count on your support?" He leaned forward, searching Voerell's face.

Voerell glanced at Barilan in Whirter's lap. She met Carlich's eyes. "I'll want to study the treaty for myself. But if I find you are correct, and there is danger to Barilan in its provisions, I will support you."

Maryn breathed a little easier. Surely Barilan's mother and uncle together would be able to keep him safe.

"Thank you." Carlich settled back in his seat, his tense shoulders relaxing.

Whirter looked back and forth between his wife and her brother, frowning. Maryn could tell Barilan was growing impatient with his father's distraction. He bounced insistently; when that was ignored he grabbed at Whirter's beard, his pudgy fingers catching in the strands and yanking them. Whirter turned back to his son and forced his features into a silly grimace. Barilan crowed in laughter.

Carlich rose, went over and reached for Barilan. "Here, let me hold my nephew for a bit."

For a moment Barilan looked apprehensive, but Carlich grinned at him and swung him up over his head. Mixed emotions played across the baby's face, but pleasure won, and he laughed. Carlich swung him down, then up again, eliciting more excited squeals.

"Be careful!" Voerell half-frowned, half-laughed at Carlich's antics. Maryn bit her lip to keep from echoing her sentiments.

"He's fine. Look, he loves it." Barilan's eyes were bright and his mouth open in excitement.

At length Carlich tired of the game and collapsed with an exaggerated sigh into his chair. Barilan wiggled and squirmed in his lap. After a few moments, when no more entertainment was forthcoming, he burst into wails.

"Look what you've done. Give him to me." Voerell snatched Barilan from Carlich and tried unsuccessfully to quiet him. She glanced over her shoulder at Maryn. "Nurse—"

Maryn stepped forward, reaching for the baby, but Carlich waved her away.

"He's not hungry, just disappointed I stopped playing with him. Here, Barilan, watch this." Carlich pulled a jewel-encrusted ceremonial knife from his belt and nicked his finger. With a quick gesture, blue fire erupted in his hand, fountaining up in a shower of sparks. Maryn jumped; she'd never seen magic summoned so fast. Barilan left off crying and stared, fascinated. Carlich waved his hand under Barilan's nose, and the baby grabbed at the swarming blue fireflies.

"Carlich!" Voerell pulled Barilan away. His face clouded, until Carlich leaned closer and again passed his hand near his nephew's face. "Be careful! Not to invoke the Holy One at all, not even a quick word…"

"There's nothing to worry about." Twitches of Carlich's fingers turned the sparks red and green and purple in turn.

"Rogelan says it's foolhardy to not at least begin with an incantation. I don't want you flaunting uncontrolled sorcery around my son!" But the fire showed no sign of escaping Carlich's control, and Barilan was so obviously entranced by it that Voerell hesitated.

Maryn edged closer, ready to snatch Barilan if the sparks threatened to harm him. She agreed with Voerell. Blood sorcery was dangerous. The priests constantly stressed how vital it was to always invoke the protection of the Holy One with the full ritual, even for the simple everyday task of cleansing a few accidentally spilled drops.

"Rogelan is a decent enough sorcerer, but he's excessively conservative. Gestures can be just as effective for controlling magic as incantations, if you know what you're doing, and far swifter and stronger. You'd think our family would remember that, considering we only hold the throne because Great-great Grandfather Hoenech was a master of gestural magic." Carlich swirled the flashing sparks, and Barilan watched in fascination.

"I still don't like it," Voerell said, drawing in her breath as a stray spark leaped too close to Barilan's face. "Lord Hoenech's spell escaped his control and killed him. Carlich, stop that."

"If you insist." Carlich made a waving motion with his hand, and the last of the blood's power evaporated in a burst of sparks. Barilan blinked and his face scrunched, until one flailing fist found his mouth and he began to suck industriously. For a few minutes all was quiet.

Voerell shifted her grip on her son. "Should I speak with Marolan?"

Carlich's face darkened, but he kept his tone light. "You might as well not bother. He won't listen."

"Give him a chance, Carlich," Voerell said. "Treaty or not, he will be king someday. You'll be much better off if you get over whatever petty childhood quarrels still bother you, and put some effort into building a better relationship with him."

"Flattering him, you mean. Currying his favor. Come, Voerell, you know me better than that." Carlich gave a mocking little laugh. "I decided long ago I'll never bow to Marolan. The day he becomes king is the day I leave Milecha forever."

"Then I pray the Holy One will grant Father a very long life indeed, and you greater wisdom with the passage of years. For I would grieve to lose my favorite brother to exile."

Voerell tried to catch Carlich's eye, but he turned away from her to gaze into the fire. Maryn was struck by the way the leaping orange light cast deep shadowed lines of pain and anger across his features. They lingered there for only a moment, however, before he composed his expression into its usual lively good humor and turned back to his sister. "Never fear. None of us knows what the future will bring. The Holy One may yet send some unexpected twist of fate to disrupt all our neatly laid plans."

Voerell gave a little shudder mixed with laughter. "I will accept whatever he may ordain, as long as my family is safe." She ran a finger through Barilan's hair.

"Here, let me hold him again while he's content. I'll promise to be quieter with him this time." Carlich reached for Barilan.

"All right. Just no magic!"

Carlich cradled his nephew against his chest. Barilan snuggled there, peacefully alert. Carlich teased Barilan's fist with a finger; the baby's hand stretched open and wrapped around the offered digit, grasping tightly.

"Feel that grip! You're a strong one. Uncle Carlich will teach you to wield a sword whenever you're ready."

Whirter and Carlich fell into a long rambling conversation reminiscing about their own earliest experiences with training in the arts of war. Barilan dragged Carlich's finger to his mouth and sucked on it for a while before drifting off to sleep. Maryn stood and waited on their pleasure, her muscles aching and her eyelids drooping as the hour grew late.

Finally Barilan woke with a sudden cry. Carlich started. Voerell blinked. "I'm sorry, Carlich, I didn't mean to leave you stuck holding him so long. Give him back to the nurse and let her take him to bed."

"I don't mind. It was a pleasure." Carlich shifted Barilan to his shoulder as he rose. The baby's cheek was marked with impressions of the embroidery on Carlich's jerkin. "We heirs to the throne of Milecha have to stick together."

Carlich carried Barilan over to Maryn. "You might want to check his diaper."

"Yes, your Highness." Maryn flushed, deeply embarrassed that the prince would speak to her about such an indelicate part of her job, and offended at the implication that she might not tend to such a basic matter without his prompting. "I'll be changing him as soon as we return to the nursery."

"Good." Carlich passed Barilan into her arms. "I can see you take excellent care of my nephew. Keep up the good work."

Maryn blushed even hotter and ducked her head. "Yes, sir. Your Highness." He grinned in amusement at her flustered manner as she backed hastily away and fled the room.

Eight

Maryn watched with growing impatience as Voerell leaned over the bed and fussed with the dozens of tiny jeweled buttons running down the front of Barilan's long gold brocade gown. The princess had gotten one into the wrong buttonhole, but not realized her mistake until she reached the end of the row. Now she was obligated to unfasten them all back to the place where the error had occurred and redo them. Barilan wriggled and grabbed for one of the trailing pearl ornaments that dangled from her ear. He succeeded in snagging it, and tugged. Voerell yelped and tried vainly to disentangle his fingers.

"Here, your Highness, let me," Maryn begged, pushing in to rescue the princess. She grabbed Barilan's wrist and managed to pry his hand from the earring with no damage done either to it or to Voerell's earlobe. "You can let your ladies touch up your hair while I finish getting the prince dressed."

"If you think that's best." Voerell stepped back and let Maryn take over. Several of her ladies-in-waiting came to fuss over the strands of hair that had worked loose from her elaborate braided coiffure. She scowled as she watched Maryn's quick sure fingers sort all the buttons into their proper places, but

Maryn was accustomed enough to the princess's moods after three months in her service to ignore her. "Be sure you don't forget the shoes. They were made for Father, and Marolan and Carlich both wore them at their heirship ceremonies."

"Yes, your Highness." The shoes were waiting ready in the spot where Maryn had laid them out. She wouldn't have forgotten, but she suppressed her annoyance with Voerell's meddling. The princess was wound tight in nervous anticipation of the day's events. It was the first time her son would be formally presented to Milecha as its newest heir. All the aristocracy of the kingdom would be present, along with envoys from every large or small country with which Milecha maintained diplomatic ties. Little wonder Voerell was fraught to the point where every tiny mishap was magnified into a calamity.

Maryn herself felt an uncomfortable thrill in her gut every time she thought of her own role in the proceedings, holding Barilan before all those watching eyes. Not that they would actually see her. She had grown to appreciate the anonymity her neat blue servant's uniform gave her. She would blend seamlessly into the background, ignored by all the gathered dignitaries, their attention focused solely on the child in her arms.

The shoes were too small. Try as she might, Maryn could not cram Barilan's feet into their narrow confines. She stood staring at one little slipper, heavily encrusted with embroidery in gold thread, while Barilan kicked and babbled loudly, and squirmed toward the edge of the bed.

Madam Semprell stopped him from tumbling to the floor. "He must wear the shoes. It's a matter of tradition. Try again to get them on."

"I can't. They're too small."

"Too small?" Princess Voerell wailed. "I knew I should have had the Royal Tailor bring them sooner. He could have altered them."

The words shook Maryn out of her frozen daze. She turned the slipper inside out. "Here, I can fix this. It won't be pretty, but at least they'll go on his feet. And under the gown no one will be able to tell." She went over to the bedside table and rummaged in a drawer, pulling out scissors and a needle.

She felt as if she were desecrating a national treasure, but she crushed her misgivings and ruthlessly snipped the stitches at the back of the slipper until the soft leather separated. She sat down on the bed beside Barilan and shoved the toe of the slipper over his foot. There was a good inch of separation between the panels behind his heel. Semprell held his leg while Maryn ran a handful of loose, sloppy stitches across the gap in between Barilan's kicks. With great difficulty she managed to tie off the thread. The result looked a dreadful mess, but when she pulled the gown down so nothing but the tips of Barilan's toes were visible it wasn't too bad. Voerell sighed in relief, while Maryn set about adapting the other slipper.

She finished just as the third bell rang. Voerell jerked her head up. "Gallows! We were supposed to be in the garden already. Why did the Wonorans have to arrive today, of all days? Hurry!"

Maryn barely had time to grab her crisp starched headscarf and tie it around her braids. Semprell left off fussing with Barilan's wild tufts of hair, which no amount of water could persuade to lay down flat for more than a few minutes, and thrust him into Maryn's arms. Maryn fell into place immediately behind Voerell, with Semprell and all Voerell's ladies-in-waiting trailing behind them.

Guards waited outside the nursery to escort them down to the garden. Prince Marolan scowled at them as they hurried up. "Where have you been?" he whispered. "The delegation got here a quarter hour ago. I had to keep them waiting! I was about to go on with the greeting without you."

"Sorry, Marolan," Voerell said, contrite. "There was a bit of a problem with Barilan's wardrobe, but we worked it out. You can send for Dolia's party now."

"All right," Marolan said, somewhat mollified, and gestured to one of the guards, who hurried away. Voerell took her place among his entourage, and Maryn stationed herself beside the princess, turning Barilan to face outward so he could be seen and admired. The baby was in a cheerful mood. He always loved walking in the garden, and the late summer morning was pleasantly warm. Maryn was cautiously optimistic that he would remain calm and well behaved.

Duke Whirter put his arm around Voerell and gave a gentle squeeze before returning to formal decorum. Voerell gave her husband a brief smile. Maryn paid close attention as Voerell turned to greet Prince Carlich, where he stood on Marolan's far side, but the two only exchanged polite nods.

Maryn kept her demeanor carefully neutral, but underneath frustration seethed. She had no idea if either Carlich or Voerell had done anything in the past two weeks to address the threat to Barilan posed by the upcoming marriage. She certainly couldn't ask the princess about it. All she could do was watch and wait, and hope that she might catch some stray word, or by chance be present when the matter was discussed. Publicly, preparations for the wedding were proceeding on schedule. A month remained before the ceremony, but the closer it got the more disruptive and scandalous a cancellation would be. Maryn hugged Barilan a little tighter. Maybe Voerell had discovered Carlich was wrong, and there was no danger after all.

Marolan ruffled Barilan's hair, stirring it into wild disorder, completely undoing all Semprell's work. "He looks adorable. That gown is beautiful."

"Yes. Can you believe you were ever small enough to wear it?" Voerell beamed at Barilan proudly.

"Not at all. Clearly impossible." Marolan shot a look at Carlich. "I remember when you wore it, though. Your face was all red, and you cried through the whole ceremony. Mother was so embarrassed."

Voerell laughed. "Marolan, don't expect us to believe you remember that. You weren't even two."

"Maybe it's just the stories I remember," Marolan admitted, shrugging.

"Or maybe it's the stories of your own ceremony you're thinking of." Carlich's voice was light and teasing, but there was an edge underneath it.

"Possibly." Marolan refused to be baited. He fondled the tips of Barilan's toes where they peeked out from under the gown. "And those shoes! Such exquisite workmanship. Let me see—"

Maryn caught her breath, but let it out again in relief when Marolan's examination of the shoes was cut short by the sound of trumpets. He straightened to rigid attention, every sense focused on the far entry to the garden where a line of soldiers wearing the green uniforms of Wonora had begun to enter.

Behind the soldiers came a number of dignitaries

in long, elaborate robes. The most senior of them, a portly man whose breath huffed as he walked, escorted a slim girl with shyly downcast eyes.

Maryn stared curiously at the stranger she'd heard so much about. She knew Dolia was about to turn sixteen, the age when, by Wonoran law, she might legally marry. But she seemed younger. All the Wonorans were somewhat shorter than was average for people of Milecha, and Dolia was a head shorter still than the smallest of the men. Her long black hair hung loose down her back, as no woman in Milecha would wear hers after she turned twelve. But her figure, though slender, had a woman's curves, and she was beautiful, in an exotic, foreign way. Her dusky olive complexion was smooth, and the slanted almond eyes that flicked up to scan the welcoming party were a rich, deep brown. She wore a close-fitting dress in a lustrous fabric heavily decorated with colorful embroidery, which skimmed her body from the high neck all the way down to her toes.

Her escort led Dolia up to meet the delegation assembled to greet her. They stopped a dozen feet away. The herald blew another brief fanfare on his trumpet. Lowering it, he announced in ringing tones, "Ambassador Lord Honro of Wonora. And her Royal Highness Princess Dolia Verimisa Adona Zirwello, Regina of Farleno, Lady of the Fire Isles, only child and heir of King Zirwello of Wonora."

Despite her worries, Maryn couldn't help but be caught up in the excitement of the moment. The colors were so bright, the clear ringing of the trumpet so stirring, the ceremonial phrases so rich with tradition. She still found it incredible that she could be a part, however minor, of such important events. She'd never even seen a Wonoran before she'd come to the palace, and here she was in the presence of their princess.

Marolan bowed deeply to his betrothed, with all of his retinue following suit. Maryn had learned the art of curtsying gracefully with a wiggling baby in her arms. The trick was to stay as vertical as possible and extend the rear foot well back to balance the added weight in front. She had practiced until the movement looked smooth, but it still felt awkward.

The Wonoran delegation returned gracious bows of their own. Dolia sank nearly to the ground in a smooth, sweeping flourish like a move from a dance.

Marolan cleared his throat. "Welcome to Milecha. Our kingdom is honored by your presence, and we offer you our unreserved hospitality. I beg you to pardon the absence of my father, King Froethych. He is indisposed this morning, but he is resting to recover his strength and will join us later at the formal ceremony. I greet you in his name, Ambassador Honro, Princess Dolia."

Maryn was impressed with his ability to deliver the formal phrases steadily, when all the time he couldn't tear his gaze away from Dolia. For Dolia's part, she kept sneaking glances up at him from under demurely lowered lashes.

Next to her, the Ambassador chuckled genially and led her closer to Marolan. "We thank you for your warm greeting, Prince Marolan, and raise our prayers to the Holy One that your father's perfect health be swiftly restored." He spoke flawless Milechan, though flavored with a lilting accent. "Princess Dolia has been anxious to meet her betrothed. I would be pleased to dispense with the full lengthy formalities of welcome in the interest of allowing the two of you more time to converse with each other."

"Thank you, Ambassador." Marolan swallowed, apparently flustered by this deviation from the protocol for which he'd prepared. But he swiftly recovered. "But do let me introduce the rest of my family. Princess Dolia, this is my brother, Prince Carlich."

"I am very pleased to meet you," Dolia said, her voice low and husky. Her Milechan was polished and formal, more heavily accented than the Ambassador's.

Carlich bowed to her with a dramatic flourish. Maryn could detect nothing but courtesy in his manner, whatever private hostility he might harbor toward the Wonoran princess. Rising, he stepped to the side of the path, where a bush laden with delicate pink flowers sent branches arching in every direction. With his jeweled ceremonial knife he cut a long stem bearing a single full dewy blossom and presented it to Dolia. "A rose for you, my future sister-in-law, though its loveliness pales beside your own."

Dolia accepted it graciously. Maryn thought she blushed, although her dark skin made it hard to tell. "I thank you." She studied the flower closely, breathing its scent. "This is a rose? I heard of your roses, though they grow not in Wonora. It is sweet, as the tale-singers claim. I thought they must exaggerate."

"Not at all." Marolan smoothly inserted himself between Carlich and Dolia. He shot a poisonous look at Carlich. "I hope you find everything in Milecha equally pleasing."

"I am certain I will." Dolia twirled the rose between her fingers, eyes fixed on the golden anthers that formed a crown within the soft pink petals.

Maryn looked away, her cheeks hot, and resettled

Barilan against her body. Most likely Carlich's gift was perfectly appropriate, the sort of thing nobles did all the time. But it made her think of his reputation among the servants as a seducer of beautiful women. Surely he couldn't have designs on his brother's betrothed? But Dolia was lovely, and closer to his age than Marolan's. If Carlich wanted to disrupt his brother's wedding, that was certainly one way to go about it.

Marolan gathered his composure and continued with his introductions. "This is my sister, Princess Voerell, and her husband, Duke Whirter Rottolla. And their son, Prince Barilan, the reason for our festivities today."

Voerell took Dolia's hand. Her manner, too, was cordial, betraying no reservations. "I am so pleased to meet my brother's bride. He keeps thanking me for giving birth to Barilan at such an opportune time, to give you a reason to come to Loempno a full month earlier than you might have otherwise."

Dolia looked shyly down. "Ambassador Honro goes to the heirship ceremony. I beg my father to sail with him. Why one ship now, another in one month only? He agreed. I wish time to learn the ways of Milecha, that my home will be. I need also practice with your language. Many years I have studied it, but strange it is to me still."

"Oh, no," Marolan said. "Your Milechan is wonderful. Much better than my own command of Wonoran. Though I have been working on it." He cleared his throat and carefully pronounced a long flowing phrase in the liquid syllables of the Wonoran language.

Dolia smiled and answered in the same tongue. Marolan attempted a reply, but apparently badly botched the grammar, because both he and Dolia broke into laughter, and Ambassador Honro suppressed a smirk. Marolan shook his head. "You see, it is I who need to practice your tongue. I hope to have many opportunities to do so before our wedding." He took Dolia's hand in his and raised the back of it to his lips. Dolia blushed and fluttered her lashes but did not look away.

If Carlich sought to win Dolia's affections away from Marolan, it seemed he would have a difficult task. For Barilan's sake perhaps Maryn should hope for him to succeed. But she found it easy to identify with Dolia, so far from home, little more than a pawn in the games of the powerful. Maryn had been so happy in her own marriage she hated to think others might be less fortunate.

Carlich cleared his throat. Marolan hastily dropped Dolia's hand and stepped back. "In any case, I pray that your early arrival in Milecha will be a joy and a blessing to you."

"And we are richly blessed by the opportunity to become acquainted with you sooner than we might have," Whirter added gallantly.

As if reminded by his voice that other people existed besides her betrothed, Dolia tore her gaze away from Marolan and turned to accept Whirter's greeting. Then she turned to Barilan, as Maryn held him up to her gaze. Dolia's eyes widened. "This is your son? Prince Barilan? But they told me he is three months old only. He is so big!"

Maryn bowed her head modestly, though she let her lips curve up a little. Everyone could see how Barilan thrived on her milk.

"Yes," Voerell said with fond pride. "He takes after my father, I think. Sompirla men tend to the tall and broad. Though both Marolan and Carlich are built more like our mother."

Maryn waited, but Voerell said nothing more. *And he has an excellent wet nurse,* Maryn silently prompted her, although she realized with a sinking heart that the thought would never occur to Voerell. Nor any of the rest. Maryn was invisible to them. Never mind that, whatever his heritage, Barilan could only grow into it because of her constant diligent care.

"Was he so large when he was born?" Dolia asked nervously, twisting the stem of the rose in her fingers, and darting a glance at Marolan's tall form.

Voerell patted her shoulder in understanding. "No, much smaller. He's grown like a young ox. The birth went smoothly. We have the finest midwives in all the kingdoms here in Loempno. I'd be happy to introduce you to Litholl, who attended me. She has a masterful command of all aspects of birthing lore and magic."

Dolia seemed somewhat reassured. "I would like that. Perhaps in a few days, once I have settled—Oh!" She stared at her hand. One of the rose's thorns had pricked the ball of her thumb, and blood welled from the spot.

Carlich stepped in before anyone else could react. "I'm so sorry. I didn't think to warn you about the thorns. Let me get that for you."

He pulled out a lace-edged handkerchief and dabbed at her thumb. A bright red stain spread on the snowy linen. Carlich waved his other hand over the cloth and Dolia's thumb. A shower of blue sparks erupted. Barilan squealed in delight and grabbed for the bright glints; Maryn stepped back to pull his chubby fingers clear.

Dolia jerked away. "You speak not the incantation

to the Holy One when blood magic you work? You use your hands?" She breathed heavily, staring at Carlich with undisguised hostility. "It is unholy. In Wonora such a thing is never done." She seemed far more disturbed than Maryn thought reasonable. Carlich might be careless, but he was a skilled sorcerer.

Carlich released her hand and stepped back, folding the handkerchief into a small, neat square and tucking it into his breast pocket. "It's not? I had no idea. I'm very sorry if I offended you. Here in Milecha verbal magic is preferred also, but I never heard a priest say anything against the use of gestures."

Dolia glared at him, and stepped stiffly closer to Marolan. "Do your priests not know the writings of Bitorlo? He is much honored in Wonora, a disciple of the Holy One. He wrote much of the dangers of blood magic, if constrained not by the words of the sacred language that the Holy One gave to us." She turned a little away. "I should have known such things here I would find. Your people came long ago from Hampsia. It should surprise me not if to their pagan ways you cling, though you have chosen the worship of the Holy One."

So it hadn't been carelessness at all, Maryn realized. Carlich had contrived to offend Dolia. One way or another, he was going to make sure this marriage didn't happen. Maryn just hoped he didn't provoke a war with Wonora in the process.

Marolan took Dolia's arm and tucked it firmly around his. "You must excuse my brother. I assure you he is in no way representative of what you will find in Milecha. Of course our sorcerers always make the proper incantations to the Holy One. I will be happy to introduce you to the Royal Sorcerer,

Rogelan, so that you can discuss the matter." His glance at Carlich was cold and dangerous. "Carlich, I'm sure you must have matters to attend to before the ceremony begins. Perhaps you might go check on Father, and see if he's feeling better."

"I think I shall." Carlich swept a full formal bow in Dolia's direction. "Until later, Princess Dolia." He hurried off.

Voerell beckoned for Maryn. "We should go, also. Prince Barilan needs time to nurse and rest before the ceremony." She nodded to Dolia. "It was lovely to meet you. I wish you and Marolan every happiness. Come, Whirter." She nearly dragged her husband away. Maryn shifted Barilan to her shoulder and followed.

Once out of the garden Voerell's step quickened. "How dare he!" she fumed at Whirter. "On Barilan's special day! Everyone knows gestural magic is forbidden in Wonora. Does he think petty rudeness will be enough to drive Dolia to break the betrothal? He gave her that rose on purpose, hoping for the chance to offend her!"

She stormed through the palace halls, in the direction of the king's chambers. Maryn trailed behind, too wary of the princess's temper to dare ask for permission to take Barilan to the nursery. Whirter hurried after his wife. "Voerell, calm down. You're overreacting."

"You don't know Carlich like I do. This is exactly the sort of thing he always does. If he can't get what he wants in a straightforward manner, he'll connive and scheme until he manages to make things go his way. He hasn't managed to sabotage the treaty any other way, so he's going to try to get her to do it. But it won't work. Dolia's obviously smitten with Marolan."

"Still, if there's a chance he can provoke her enough she goes home, we should support him as we agreed."

"He can do what he likes tomorrow. I'll even help him. But I won't have him disrupting Barilan's ceremony."

Maryn frowned. She agreed with Whirter. If Carlich was right about the treaty, Barilan's life was at stake. What was his heirship ceremony compared to that? Was Voerell discounting the danger because she truly believed it was not that great, or could she just not bear to imagine anything bad happening to her son?

Maryn knew all too well that bad things could and did happen, whether you could bear to imagine them or not.

They arrived at the entrance to the king's suite. Voerell threw open the door and stormed in without even pausing to acknowledge the guards who flanked it. They looked scandalized, but let her pass, Maryn and Whirter behind her.

King Froethych sat on a broad stuffed sofa. Contrary to the report of his ill health, to Maryn he looked robust and vigorous. Carlich sat opposite him. Seeing her brother, Voerell started to speak, but Froethych waved her silent.

The king leaned toward Carlich. "Well? Is she as pretty as all the envoys made her out to be?"

"Oh, yes, Father. If anything, they understated her beauty." Carlich must have hurried to reach Froethych's room before them, but he sat as relaxed as if he'd been there for hours. He wasn't even breathing hard.

Froethych chortled under his breath. "And did she seem pleased with Marolan?"

"Quite, as far as I could tell. Though disappointed you weren't there to welcome them."

Froethych dismissed that with an airy wave. "No, no, the last thing Marolan needs is his father hanging over his shoulder intimidating the poor girl. Much better to let them have a few moments alone to get acquainted. I'm glad you found a reason to excuse yourself."

Voerell executed a sketchy curtsy in the king's direction. "Actually, Father, Marolan dismissed him. He managed to offend Princess Dolia before he had been in her presence five minutes. He went and performed purely gestural magic right in front of her!"

Froethych's bushy eyebrows drew together. "Was that wise, son? I've warned you many times to be careful how you flaunt your ability in that regard."

"Of course, now I realize it was foolish. But she was injured, and I didn't stop to think before I jumped in to help her. I apologized profusely, and I think she accepted it." Carlich spread his hands with an expression of sheepish innocence. Though Maryn was almost certain he was lying, she couldn't detect any insincerity in his voice or manner.

"Oh, that's all right then." Froethych shrugged, dismissing the matter, though Voerell still fumed. He turned toward Barilan in Maryn's arms. "There's my grandson and heir! Come see your grandpa, Barilan." He held out his arms and Maryn passed Barilan to him. The king nuzzled Barilan's neck and made a silly face; Barilan responded with an infectious peal of giggles.

Maryn still felt a little shocked whenever she saw the king abandon all dignity this way in his interactions with Barilan. It was endearing to see

Froethych act like any common doting grandfather, but also a bit alarming to consider that the welfare of all Milecha rested in the hands of the man who at the moment was sticking out his tongue and crossing his eyes.

"I swear, Voerell, he's grown another inch since yesterday. We're going to get you confirmed in your position all nice and official, yes we are, aren't we, Barilan?" Barilan rewarded the king's further efforts at contorting his face with a broad grin, and grabbed at Froethych's full beard.

Froethych disentangled Barilan's fingers and passed him back to Maryn. He turned to Voerell. "Why don't you go make sure he's all ready for the ceremony? It will be starting in less than an hour."

"Father, please tell Carlich to stay away from Dolia and Marolan for the rest of the day."

Froethych frowned at her. "I don't think that will be necessary."

Voerell clenched her fists, but she did not defy the king. "Yes, Father." She whirled and strode from the room. Maryn scurried in her wake.

Whirter caught up to Voerell. "Dear, let it go."

She shook his placating hand from her arm. "I keep getting the feeling he's up to something..." She scowled at her husband. "Don't you have something you need to take care of?"

"No. I'll come with—" Whirter looked at her more closely. "On second thought, I did want to have my boots shined. You go on; I'll meet you in the hall."

"Good." Voerell stalked away and did not turn her head when Whirter stopped and watched her go.

Barilan picked up on his mother's tense mood, and began to fuss. Maryn was glad when they reached the nursery. She settled down immediately into the large soft upholstered chair that was her favorite nursing spot, and put Barilan to her breast. It soothed him as always, and he fell to nursing with gusto.

Voerell stared into the fire for a while, breathing deeply. She ignored her ladies whenever they tried to get her attention. The continued activity around the hearth kept disturbing Barilan, and he would turn his head to look, pulling Maryn's nipple with him and allowing his mouth to slide to a painful position so that she had to detach him and start all over. She would be very glad when this day was over, and Voerell resumed her normal distance from her son's life, leaving the nursery to its regular peaceful routine.

Just as Maryn was beginning to worry that too much time had passed, and they wouldn't be able to make it to the palace's main hall where the ceremony would take place before the bell rang for the fourth hour, Voerell shook herself and came out of her reverie. "We'd better get going."

Maryn pulled Barilan's gown down over his fresh diaper, made one more futile effort to conceal the hasty alteration of his shoes, and fell in behind Voerell as the princess led them through the palace corridors.

Nine

Maryn peeked through the wide open doors of the great hall as Voerell led them to an anteroom. Banners hung from the rafters, and flowers and greenery bedecked every surface. It was packed already; noble guests lined the long tables where the celebration feast would be served following the ceremony. Her pulse pounded in her ears, and she shifted Barilan from hip to hip so she could wipe her clammy palms against her skirt. Though she'd rehearsed every move under the Royal Steward's watchful eyes, she still dreaded making some humiliating mistake. She could imagine the accusing stares and horrified laughter that would follow if she were to trip on her way down the aisle and sprawl with Barilan to the floor.

The fourth bell began to peal from all the churches in the city. The deep clang of the palace chapel's bell resonated behind Maryn's breastbone.

King Froethych waited for them with the rest of his retinue. "Ah, there's the guest of honor. Just in time. Begin the procession."

The Royal Steward nodded acknowledgment and went to signal the musicians in their balcony. The majestic strains of the Sompirla March echoed through the wide spaces of the hall. The members of the royal party crowded out of the anteroom and clustered in the doorway. Maryn hung back, watching the others enter in turn, stirred despite her nervousness by the grandness of the ceremony.

Ambassador Honro escorted Princess Dolia into the hall and down the broad center aisle, the rest of the Wonoran embassage in their wake. Everyone craned to see the foreign woman who would soon marry their prince. She nodded graciously to either side, meeting their eager stares with a pleasant, private smile. The rest of the entourage peeled off, taking their seats in the reserved section at the front of the long tables. Only Honro and Dolia ascended the tall dais at the front of the hall and took places at the high table. The Ambassador sat down, and Dolia followed, sinking into her seat, a few chairs to the left of center.

Carlich strode through the hall, waving and grinning in response to the enthusiastic applause. Normally he would sit at the king's left hand, but the customary order had been shuffled to give Barilan and his parents pride of place. He went to his lower seat on the right with cheerful disregard for his demotion.

Marolan accepted the warm welcome that greeted his entrance as if he considered it his due, looking neither right nor left, but fixing all his attention on the high table where Dolia sat. He took his place next to her and bent his head to murmur in her ear.

Now the Royal Steward nodded at them. Voerell went first, Whirter at her side. Maryn took a deep breath, settled Barilan securely in her arms, and followed.

The crowd erupted into ecstatic noise. It washed over Maryn like a flood. She hoisted Barilan higher and shrank down behind him. It was the prince everyone greeted with such fervor. She was merely the vehicle for his conveyance, as invisible as the horse he would ride when he was grown to manhood and paraded before his adoring subjects. It was galling to be ignored that way, but at the same time Maryn was glad to take refuge from all those eyes in her anonymity.

Barilan stared around him, his body taut. Maryn had been concerned that the noise might frighten him, but he seemed enthralled by the spectacle. Even this early the prince was learning to enjoy being the object of adulation.

They arrived at the front. Maryn placed her feet carefully so she would not stumble as she ascended the steps. She followed Voerell and Whirter around the table. After the princess took her place to the immediate right of the king's chair, Whirter next to her, Maryn transferred Barilan into Voerell's lap. The prince fussed a little and clung to Maryn, but Voerell pried him from her arms and caught his attention with a shiny silver spoon. Mollified, Barilan grabbed it, banged it on the table and waved it about before stuffing it into his mouth. Maryn stepped back and took up her place with the other servants, standing at attention behind the table. She wouldn't get to participate in the feast. Her only duty was to keep a close watch on Barilan and Voerell, helping the princess with her son in any way she might need.

A trumpet fanfare sounded through the hall. As one, everyone rose and faced the rear. Maryn couldn't see well for the line of tall bodies before her, but she leaned to the side until she could peer between Whirter and Carlich. King Froethych paraded down the center aisle, nodding to the assembled nobles, occasionally stopping to take a hand and exchange a few words with a favored guest. It took him a long time to advance all the way through the room to the dais. Maryn wasn't the only one shifting from foot to foot by the time he arrived. Voerell bounced Barilan, trying to keep him happy. At last Froethych squeezed his rotund form around the back of the table and into the grand, ornate chair at the center. As he sat, the music came to an exultant climax and halted. Everyone else sank into their seats.

A new, more reverent piece of music began. A delegation of priests from the cathedral paced slowly down the aisle, chanting a solemn hymn in the ancient tongue. Prelate Kiellan brought up the rear. Maryn recognized him from the times she'd accompanied Voerell and Barilan to Sabbath services. He was an elderly man, but hale, with a full head of thick white hair beneath the red and gold cap of his office. Maryn had always liked the way he laid his gentle hand of blessing on her head as well as Voerell's and Barilan's, his voice the same musical flow of unintelligible words for each of them.

Kiellan led the assembly in a series of prayers and responsive liturgies. For the most part it was the same as any Sabbath service; Maryn echoed the ritual phrases automatically along with everyone else. At one point, while Kiellan read a long passage from the Holy Scriptures regarding the duty a king held toward his people, Barilan seemed about to erupt into loud, disruptive wails. Maryn was ready to swoop in and take him from Voerell to soothe him, but Carlich was quicker. He flicked his knife and waved into existence a fountain of the blue sparks Barilan loved so much, hiding them from the crowd below the edge of the table. Whirter pushed his chair back to allow

Carlich to extend the bright magical display past him. Barilan grabbed at the swarming blue fireflies, completely distracted from whatever discomfort had bothered him. Voerell bit her lip and glanced down the table at the Wonorans on the far side of the king, but didn't protest.

After a very long time the preliminary rituals were complete, and the main portion of the ceremony arrived. Prelate Kiellan summoned the participants forward. Maryn scooted back to let them pass as they made their way around the long table and took up their places immediately in front of it. The Prelate stood in the center, King Froethych on his right, Voerell, with Whirter beside her, holding Barilan on his left.

"We have come today to witness the investiture of Prince Barilan Sompirla-Rottolla as heir to the kingdom of Milecha." Kiellan had to pause to allow the crowd's response to die down.

"By the grace and favor of the Holy One, the magic of the Kingship has endured since it was created by the Blessed Milech, founder and first king of Milecha, by the shedding of his blood. Continually renewed by the blood of those who bear it, the Kingship has passed in an unbroken line from king to king, down through the centuries, until this day. Even when tragedy disrupted the direct line of succession, the Kingship passed safely to those the people of Milecha deemed worthy. Now the current bearer of this sacred trust comes before you to bind the blood of a new generation into the spell."

Once again Kiellan waited for the applause to wane before continuing. "King Froethych, do you acknowledge Barilan as a true-born heir of your body, rightful member of the Sompirla dynasty through your daughter Voerell? Do you purpose to grant him a place in the line of succession to the Kingship of Milecha, after yourself, your son Prince Marolan Sompirla, and your son Prince Carlich Sompirla?"

"I do." The king accompanied his words with a decisive nod.

"And do you, Princess Voerell, speaking for your son Prince Barilan, acknowledge and accept his responsibility to take up the crown of Milecha, should it pass to him in turn?"

"I do."

"And if the crown should come to Prince Barilan before he reaches the age of twenty years, do you, Princess Voerell Sompirla-Rottolla, agree to serve as regent, acting in all respects as his representative, governing Milecha in his name, renewing the Kingship with your blood at the appointed times, and surrendering your position when Barilan comes of age?"

What? Maryn leaned forward to get a better look. During the run-through of the ceremony, Prelate Kiellan had rehearsed the regency portion with Barilan's father. Could the prelate have made a mistake? No, he appeared serene as he waited for an answer.

Voerell looked from Prelate Kiellan to King Froethych, astonished. "Father? I thought Whirter..." She turned to her husband. Whirter grinned and shook his head, gesturing toward the king.

Froethych beamed at his daughter, pleased with the effect of his surprise. He leaned forward. Just loud enough for Maryn to catch above the excited buzz of the crowd, he murmured, "The law might not allow me to make you my heir, but you deserve the honor every bit as much as your brothers. And nothing forbids a female regent. Likely it will only ever be a formality, but I trust you to fulfill the responsibility admirably, if—may the Holy One forbid—the need should ever arise."

The idea of a woman wielding the power of the Kingship, even in her son's name, unsettled Maryn. Queens might occasionally rule foreign lands, but that had never been the case in Milecha. She knew Voerell was strong and intelligent and well versed in the politics of the kingdom, but even so....

Others shared her misgivings, she saw. Throughout the hall, people leaned over to whisper to their neighbors, or studied the tableau on the dais with thoughtful or concerned expressions. At the high table, Marolan and Dolia murmured to each other. When Maryn glanced at Carlich he was sitting up tensely straight, his brows drawn together and his eyes unfocused. But in a moment he shrugged, relaxed, and returned his gaze to his sister, assuming a pleased expression.

Voerell blushed and stammered. "Father, I—I don't know what to say..."

He jerked his head toward Kiellan, smiling. "Answer the Prelate."

Voerell collected herself and drew herself up to her full height. Proudly, her voice ringing through the hall, she proclaimed, "I do."

Kiellan nodded in acknowledgement, smiling a little. With measured, dramatic movements, he withdrew a small gold knife from its sheath at his waist. "Give me your hand, my king. Princess, your hand and your son's."

Froethych extended his hand, palm up. Voerell grabbed Barilan's wrist and placed their hands into her father's. Barilan squirmed and fought her, but she hung on tight and refused to let him wrench his arm free. Barilan began to shriek in protest.

Maryn crossed her arms and pressed them to her breasts as her milk responded to Barilan's cries. She knew this was a vital part of the ceremony, but she still hated it. At least it would be over quickly.

Above the baby's screams, Kiellan's voice rose in the incantation to the Holy One. He didn't rush, but it rolled swiftly from his tongue, and within a few moments he proceeded into the specific part of the spell. His knife flicked, opening a small cut in the king's palm, a matching one in Voerell's, and a tiny prick on Barilan's finger. Maryn winced.

Blue lightning crackled around the three of them, as the buzz of magic vibrated through the hall. A soft halo of light formed around each of their heads. Froethych's glow outlined and illumined the crown on his head, the same that had rested on the head of each of the kings of Milecha since long before the beginning of the Sompirla dynasty. A bright image of that crown shone over Barilan's spiky blond hair. Fainter, but still distinct, another copy appeared above Voerell's head. Barilan's cries, which had spiked loud with the pain of the knife's touch, died away. His eyes and mouth grew round as he gazed at the shining apparitions.

The residual power of the shed blood burned up in a burst of sparkles when Kiellan spoke the concluding words, and the images vanished. Froethych beamed. As Kiellan stepped back, polishing his knife on the soft cloth that hung from his sash, Froethych flung his arms wide and engulfed Voerell and Barilan in a great embrace. Cheers erupted from the watching assembly.

Maryn applauded with the rest. To her surprise,

she found tears stinging her eyes. Froethych's love for his daughter and grandson was so evident. She blinked them away.

At length the commotion died down. Froethych, Whirter, and Voerell came back around the table and resumed their seats. Barilan, tired and hungry and aware once again of the pain in his hand now that the entrancing lights were gone, began to bawl. Voerell passed him with a thankful sigh to Maryn, who stepped back to her place among the other servants and settled him in to nurse. She checked his diaper with a practiced finger. Slightly damp, but not messy; nothing that couldn't wait until later.

A line of dignitaries formed and began to process up the center aisle. Representatives of all the districts and landholdings and towns in Milecha filed to the front of the hall and presented their gifts to the infant heir. A great variety of precious goods and fine workmanship was displayed to the crowd before servants bore them away. Furs and gems, silver and gold. Weapons of every sort: swords, spears, shields, bows and arrows. Examples of every type of craft: wrought metal, carved wood, glass, pottery, embroidery, weaving.

Maryn swallowed and looked away when the delegation from Ralo came forward. She'd tried to prepare herself to face this moment, but still grief welled up, tightening her throat and stinging her eyes. This day should have meant so much for her and Edrich and Frilan. She and her husband had spoken together often of the prince's heirship ceremony, when Edrich's talent would at last be fully recognized, and all their struggles and sacrifices would be richly repaid. She remembered snuggling against Edrich's side in front of their hearth, Frilan on her lap nursing, heads bent close together as they spun out fantasies of what they would buy with all the money that would be theirs once Edrich's tapestries hung in every castle and manor in Milecha.

Though she struggled to keep her emotion hidden, a few tears escaped from the corners of her eyes, and she had to awkwardly support Barilan with one arm while she swiped them away. She scowled at the big swath of fabric the delegation from Ralo proudly unrolled to display to the king. It was a bland, generic tapestry in no way comparable to Edrich's lost masterpiece. The woodland scene and band of hunters pursuing a stag seemed superficially pleasant enough, but Maryn's experienced eye easily picked out the uneven threads, dull colors, and unbalanced composition. It must have been made in a sloppy rush by one of the weavers who resided outside the burned sector where most of the best tapestry artists had lived. Her disdain for the stiff, unnatural position of the stag's legs and the asymmetrical spread of his antlers helped distract her until the worst of the pain passed.

After that it was just a matter of enduring the long, boring procession. Barilan fell asleep. She slipped him off her breast and adjusted her clothing, but Voerell was engaged in animated conversation with the king and her husband, so Maryn continued to hold Barilan. She propped him on her shoulder and swayed back and forth.

Carlich got up and strolled over to stand behind Marolan's chair, where he struck up a conversation with Dolia. There was something strangely taut about the way he held himself, as if poised for action. Remembering her speculation about his plans, Maryn watched him closely. Was he going to flirt with Dolia right in front of the whole court? But no, he kept his attentions well within the bounds of what was appropriate, merely making witty observations about the gathered dignitaries and the offered gifts. Dolia laughed. Marolan looked as if he would like to shove his brother off the dais, but only sat and glowered.

At long last the presentations were complete. Servants cleared away the last of the gifts and began to bring out the first course of the feast. A steward bore tall gold goblets of wine to the high table, served the king first, and moved down the line of dignitaries.

Carlich leaned over and snagged Marolan's cup. He took an exaggerated swig. "Ah, I've been waiting far too long for that." He wiped the back of his hand across his mouth.

"Hey!" Marolan was obviously deeply annoyed, but he forced a genial laugh. "Get your own!" He waved toward Carlich's seat, beyond the king, where Carlich's goblet waited.

"Sorry, brother," Carlich said, with no trace of remorse in his voice. He pulled out his handkerchief and wiped the edge of the goblet with a flourish. "Here. It's a very nice vintage; Father spared no expense for our nephew's feast. Too bad Barilan can't enjoy it."

"I swear, Carlich, someday you're going to learn some manners." Marolan accepted his goblet and took a long draught.

Maryn, watching from behind, noticed something change in the set of Carlich's shoulders, and was puzzled for a moment. But when nothing further happened, she shrugged off her suspicion. Barilan stirred and whimpered, and she shifted her attention to him, swaying and murmuring soothing words to try to lull him into deeper sleep. It worked; he squirmed, resettled his weight, and sank again into stillness.

Carlich returned to his seat. Servants brought in a large, fanciful pastry, a precise replica of the palace baked in savory bread flecked with herbs and stuffed with cheese. The main construction was placed before the king and cut and parceled out among the occupants of the high table; the guests at the long tables each had individual little towers. Maryn's stomach rumbled. She breathed in the warm, salty scent of the cheese longingly. It would be at least an hour yet, probably longer, before she could retire to the nursery and enjoy her own repast. She eyed the remains of the demolished palace, speculating on whether she might be able to sneak a piece unnoticed if she made some pretext to approach Voerell with a question or comment on Barilan's well being.

An odd choking sound cut through the rumble of conversation. Though soft, there was something in the sound that immediately caught the attention. Maryn looked up, seeking its source. She followed the turned heads and shocked eyes of the crowd to the point where they focused. Marolan leaned over his plate, his face deathly pale, retching as if to vomit, but nothing emerged from his open mouth but that soft, strangled cough.

For a shocked instant no one reacted. Then Dolia's scream pierced the stunned silence. Carlich leaped to Marolan's side. "He's choking!" he cried. "Get Rogelan!"

Maryn watched in horror as Carlich whipped out the little jeweled knife he used for sorcery and slashed open his palm. Blood splattered on Marolan. Carlich waved his hands about frantically, and the blood burst into a brilliant display of flashing blue sparks and swirling lights of all colors.

Despite Carlich's efforts, Marolan continued to strangle. His eyes rolled back in his head, and he swayed. Froethych seemed frozen in his chair, staring at his eldest son's distress. But Voerell and Whirter sprang forward. "Stand back!" Voerell cried to the rapidly converging throngs that pushed toward Marolan. "Carlich can help him! Give him space!"

Marolan slumped sideways in his chair. It overturned, spilling him to the floor. His long limbs thrashed about. Carlich crouched over him, never ceasing his urgent gestures.

But it was no use. As the minutes stretched long, Marolan's movements grew slower, and weaker, and ceased altogether. The choking noises faded to a faint rasp, and then nothing.

Maryn stood paralyzed, horrified, staring. She clutched Barilan to her chest, so tight he woke and squirmed in protest.

Rogelan burst through the main doors into the hall and pushed his way through the crowd. "Let me by!" People pressed aside to let him through.

When he reached Marolan, Carlich was hunched over his brother's still form. He raised a pale face to Rogelan. "There was nothing I could do. Something was blocking his lungs, but I couldn't find any food or other obstruction. His throat just swelled shut."

His voice was ragged, distraught, but somehow it seemed off to Maryn, just a little too glib, his words a bit too fast. She wasn't the only one who noticed; Voerell's brow furrowed, and Whirter frowned.

Rogelan looked at King Froethych grimly. "It sounds like poison." He put a hand to Marolan's neck, holding it there for several long moments before shaking his head. His voice was gentle. "I'm afraid he's gone, your Majesty. If Carlich wasn't able to save him, I could not have, either. But if he was poisoned, perhaps I can discover the source. If blood was used to create a magic poison, the traces will remain to be revealed."

Voerell sank to her knees beside Marolan's body, weeping. Dolia sat frozen in her chair, looking back and forth between Marolan's still form and the faces surrounding him, an expression of deep confusion on her face, as if she must strain to understand every word spoken. The Ambassador put his hand on her arm and murmured rapidly in her ear.

Froethych rose to his feet, thunderous anger in every line of his body, his face a dangerous, dispassionate mask. "Do so."

Everyone shrank back, cowed by the king's implacable authority. Maryn backed as far as she could from the still form on the floor, but the wall behind and the press of bodies hemmed her in. She wrapped her arms tight around Barilan, heedless of his flailing arms and kicking legs. Heartbeats hammered in her ears, and she couldn't seem to draw a deep enough breath. She longed to flee, to run until she found some safe dark hiding place where she could cower with her helpless charge, but she was trapped. Guards converged from every direction, their weapons drawn, casting about in confusion for someone to apprehend. But they were no comfort. They had failed to protect one prince; how could she expect them to keep another safe?

Rogelan knelt by Marolan's body. His voice rose in the incantation to the Holy One, shaky at first, but steadying as he fell into the rhythm of the familiar words. He drew his knife and cut the pad of his finger, a generous slice that immediately began to bleed.

Energy buzzed in Maryn's feet and up to her jaw. Blue lightning flashed from Rogelan's hands. Marolan's body began to steam, much as Maryn's milk had when Rogelan tested it. The vapor rose into a cloud, mounting higher and higher toward the ceiling, until it was large enough to be seen by everyone in the hall. Portions thickened, others thinned. The billowing white clouds settled into the distinct shape of a face, the mirror of one that looked up at the mist in horror.

Slanted oval eyes, slim elegant cheekbones, long flowing unbound hair. Dolia's lovely countenance floated over her betrothed's body.

Carlich jumped up, lunging. "You!" he cried, as Whirter grabbed him and held him back. Guards surged in and seized Dolia, wrenching her to her feet, twisting her arms behind her. Ambassador Honro leaped to her assistance, but he, too, was seized.

Carlich continued blurting furious, hoarse accusations. "You used your blood to poison him! You never intended to marry him! Was the betrothal a plot all along, to assassinate him? Or was this the only way you knew to escape an unwanted marriage? Wonora will pay for this in blood! Blood, I swear—"

"Silence." King Froethych's voice was not loud, but it cut off Carlich's tirade in midstream. "Sorcerer. Your spell shows that the princess's blood was found in Prince Marolan's body, yes?"

Rogelan quailed before the king's cold voice. Above him, the last shreds of vapor drifted away. "Yes, your Majesty. And not just any blood; I specifically looked for blood transformed by magic into a poison. Princess Dolia's image could only appear if her blood was what killed the prince."

Froethych nodded. He looked at the captain of the

guards. "You will take the princess to the palace gaol. The Ambassador too, and all their party. Hold them there. In the morning, a trial will be convened, and guilt will be determined. The one responsible for my son's death will face execution."

Dolia remained confused for a moment, until Ambassador Honro spoke urgently to her in Wonoran. She blinked, and her face blanched in horror. "No! No, I kill not Marolan! My betrothed, I love him, hate him not! Why kill him I?"

Carlich growled at her, "Be silent, murderess. Save your lies." His voice rose to a shout as the guards dragged Dolia away. "We'll show your father what he can expect if he tries to tangle with Milecha. There'll be no treaty now to let you steal our crown!"

Voerell, still hunched over Marolan's body, froze. She looked up at Carlich, an expression of profound horror flooding her features. "Carlich," she whispered. "You didn't..."

For a moment Maryn didn't understand. But then cold washed over her, as one by one things she'd seen and heard fell into place.

Voerell looked at Whirter. The same awful realization was dawning in the duke's face. He took a step sideways that placed him between Carlich and the only clear route of escape.

"F-Father." Voerell's voice shook so badly she almost could not form the word. She swallowed and tried again. "Father, I think...Carlich had Dolia's blood, on his handkerchief. I saw it, this morning. She pricked her finger on a rose thorn, he cleansed the blood for her...but maybe not all of it?" She shut her eyes and shook her head, trying to deny the knowledge. "He was so upset about the treaty, so angry that you wouldn't try to change it. He asked for our support, because he was going to try something different..." She blanched. "Carlich, how could you? You—Marolan—our *brother*..."

Carlich slowly swiveled to face her. "Voerell, you're talking nonsense. Of course I would never harm Marolan. Father, she's out of her mind with grief. You can't possibly believe that I—"

Froethych motioned him silent. If it were possible, he had grown even more still. He fixed Voerell with his gaze. His voice was bizarrely gentle, coming from that terrible stern countenance. "Did Carlich have an opportunity to put Dolia's blood in Marolan's food?"

Voerell wrapped her arms around her body and rocked. "I don't know...I don't think so...Wait." She looked up at her father, despair in her eyes. "He did. I saw. He used his handkerchief to wipe—"

"Father, don't listen to her!" Carlich took a step toward Voerell. His hand rose as if to strike her, but he clenched his fist and drew it back down, turning to the king. "I don't know why she's accusing me, but I swear, I did nothing!"

Froethych remained silent. He stared at his son as if his gaze could drill into Carlich's eyes and suck out the truth.

Carlich stepped toward the king, spreading his hands before him. "Believe me, Father, I would never do such a thing." He spoke faster, his voice rising in pitch and volume. "It's true I opposed the treaty. I told Voerell of my fears. Maybe *she* decided to act! Maybe she conspired with Dolia to murder Marolan!"

Voerell scrambled to her feet. "Father, he lies! It had to be him—"

Confusion swept Maryn. She couldn't believe Voerell capable of murder. But it was nearly as difficult to believe it of Carlich. If the princess truly feared for her son's life, what might she do to protect him? Maryn didn't know what to think. She only knew she had to get Barilan away from there.

She tried again to elbow through the throng that packed the narrow space between the table and the back wall, but guards blocked every exit from the dais and refused to let anyone pass. The guards stared back and forth between Carlich and Voerell, poised to seize either or both at the least indication from the king.

Rogelan stepped between Carlich and Voerell, holding up his hands for quiet. "My king, I can settle this matter. Where is the handkerchief in question? I can scry it easily enough and reveal the truth."

Froethych closed his eyes and nodded. "Carlich, give him your handkerchief."

Carlich backed slowly away from Rogelan, edging around Marolan's body. His hand rose toward his breast pocket. "I...I...Of course, Father. Of course I'll give it to him. Only...I must have dropped it..." He groped around the pocket without ever reaching into it. Sweat-darkened strands of hair fell into his eyes.

Voerell pointed. "He's got it right there, Father! Quick, or he'll find a way to destroy it. Whirter!"

Whirter grabbed Carlich from behind, reaching for his pocket. Carlich slammed his elbows into Whirter's ribs and twisted, but Whirter threw a strangling arm around Carlich's neck. Carlich clawed at Whirter's arm. Whirter's free hand plunged into Carlich's pocket and emerged clutching the incriminating bit of fabric. He waved it high. "Here it is, your Majest—"

Carlich snatched his knife from his belt and drove it behind him into Whirter's gut. He tore free as Whirter doubled over and waved the bloody knife in a meaningful gesture. The handkerchief exploded in a burst of blue flames.

Voerell screamed and lunged to her husband's side as Whirter collapsed. Blood poured from his wound and pooled around his body. Voerell tried vainly to staunch the flow.

Guards rushed Carlich. He whirled, brandishing his knife. A wave of lightning poured from the point and swept into the guards, blasting them backwards into the high table. The heavy carved wood teetered and overturned; table and guards together crashed from the dais to the floor below. People shrieked and scattered. Chaos filled the hall as half the assembled guests tried to flee, while the rest surged forward.

Voerell rose from Whirter's side, her face white and terrible. She raised hands scarlet with her husband's blood toward Carlich and began to shout the incantation to the Holy One. Carlich twisted his knife through a complex pattern in the air and sent more crackling blue flames arcing toward his sister.

They crashed into an invisible shield and splashed aside. Voerell fell back, staring without understanding at the sparks flashing inches from her face. Carlich repeated his gesture, stepping toward her, a furious light in his eyes, but the magic only reflected from the impermeable barrier. "What are you doing?" he cried.

Voerell shook her head. Her gaze traveled behind Carlich. He whirled, bloody knife rising before him in defense.

King Froethych stood, blood pouring from a gash across one palm. Blue lightning flickered around him. He moved his arms in a grand, sweeping arc. "You will not...harm...your sister," he gasped, between great indrawn breaths. Blood gushed from his hand, far more than such a small wound should produce.

"You will not...harm...your brother...your blood kin...."

Blood fountained upward, exploding into streamers of blue fire that flashed out, filling the hall, passing through the walls as if they weren't there, arcing up through the ceiling into the sky. Maryn clutched Barilan as the light washed over them. He was screaming, but she could barely hear his wails above the furiously crackling lightning and the intense buzz that felt as if it would shake her bones apart.

For an instant, the scene exactly mirrored Maryn's memory of Edrich's tapestry. King Froethych stood, hands upraised, at the heart of a raging sorcerous maelstrom, looking just like the ancestor whose magic had cured the plague for hundreds of miles around. But that spell had run out of control, and sucked all the blood from Lord Hoenech's body to feed its insatiable appetite...

Froethych staggered, falling to one knee, but his arms never stopped waving. It was as if some outside force had seized control of them, and they moved without his volition. His eyes remained fixed on Carlich and Voerell. Carlich fell back and dropped his arms, watching in horror as more and more of his father's blood gushed forth to blossom into flame. Voerell sank into a huddle between Whirter's body and Marolan's. Writhing blue eddies of light swirled around them both before rushing away to the farthest corners of the hall and beyond.

Froethych slumped toward the ground, but struggled to push himself erect. For a moment he wrenched his hands into a different gesture, and his face twisted into a grimace as he forced a portion of the magic momentarily into a new path. "You are no longer my son, my heir..."

Above Carlich's head a phantom crown appeared. It burst into blue flames and disappeared. Carlich cried out and groped futilely at the place where it had been.

His last strength spent, Froethych fell once again under the power of the spell he'd begun, which rampaged now beyond his control. His arms returned to their possessed waving, and a ragged chant tore from his throat, barely more than a whisper. "Not harm...your kin...no more...no one...never..."

His face was white as bleached linen, white as wool, white as snow-blanketed hills. The last sputtering drops shot from the gash in his hand and exploded into sparks. The buzz reached an unbearable crescendo and died. Froethych's great body crashed to the ground.

Carlich lunged toward Voerell, stabbing at her with his knife, but it was deflected just as his magic had been. His head whipped back and forth, searching for any path of escape. Guards converged on him from every side, wary of his magic but determined.

Maryn hunched over the wailing Barilan, shielding him with her body. A bright blue glow in the shape of a crown appeared over his head, then faded.

For an instant everything else fell silent. The baby's cries were the only sound, cutting harsh and shrill across the huge hall.

Carlich whirled and plunged straight at Maryn.

Ten

Before Maryn could react, Carlich grabbed her and slammed an arm around her throat, choking off her cry of terror. His knife waved wildly, sending blue sparks shooting around them. Servants yelled and scrambled for safety; guards backed hastily away. Maryn fought to keep her grip on Barilan, though she desperately needed to breathe. The baby's howls pierced her ears.

"Barilan!" Voerell screamed. She lurched toward them, her hands still wet with Whirter's blood. She made a flinging gesture, and blue lightning flashed out. Maryn flinched, but the magic splashed harmlessly well away from Carlich, just as his had failed to reach Voerell.

Voerell shrieked as the sorcery consumed the last of her husband's blood and died away. She reached impotently toward her son. Carlich lowered his knife to menace the baby.

No! Maryn's lips formed the word, but she couldn't force the sound past Carlich's grip.

"Stay back or I'll—I'll—" Carlich seemed to be having trouble speaking. His arm around Maryn's throat loosened and she gasped for breath. The knife shook, hovering inches away from the thrashing Barilan as Carlich strained against some unseen force.

To Maryn's shock, Voerell laughed, high and wild. "Father's spell!" she cried. "You can't harm him. Guards, seize Carlich! Barilan is in no danger. He cannot harm his blood kin!"

Hesitant despite Voerell's words, the guards approached. Carlich waved his knife at them, but little blood remained on its blade, and it emitted only a weak sputter of flame. He gripped Maryn with renewed force, dragged her a few steps to the edge of the dais, and wrenched her around. Terror flooded her limbs, weakening them when she most needed strength, for now Barilan hung suspended over the drop, at least ten feet above the hard flagstones below. She closed her eyes and poured all her effort into clutching the baby tight to her body.

"I can harm her!" Carlich's knife pressed cold into Maryn's throat above his strangling arm. Blood rushed in her ears and black clouds gathered at the edges of her vision. "If I kill her, she'll drop him. Are you willing to risk that?"

Voerell threw out her arms to stop the guards' advance. "Wait!" Her face was torn with indecision.

Carlich used the moment of reprieve to slash the back of his hand. His breath rasped hot and loud in Maryn's ear as he wiped the blade in the oozing blood. Then with a shout he whirled, a gesture of his knife sending renewed lightning against the guards, felling many of them, scattering the rest. He dragged her the length of the dais. She nearly fell as he hauled her down the steps, but he jerked her to her feet and propelled her ahead of him toward the door in the back corner of the hall. Servants and nobles alike scattered before the sorcerous power radiating from the bloody knife.

"After him!" Voerell cried. The few guards still

standing bunched together and began a cautious pursuit.

Carlich thrust Maryn through the door and shouldered it shut behind them just as the last of the blood on his knife burned up and his magic waned. He released her, and she fell to her knees, gasping for breath. Carlich waved his knife, cursed when nothing happened, and slashed his palm. The newly shed blood burst into sparks that enveloped the door, fusing the thick oak into the surrounding stone.

Maryn clutched Barilan to her chest, scrambled to her feet, and ran. She only made it a few steps before Carlich caught up and snatched the fabric at the back of her neck, jerking her to a halt. She fought to free herself, but he was far stronger than she, wild with anger and fear, and crackling with the power of the blood that dripped from his hand.

"Be still! Do exactly as I say, or I'll cut your throat and use your blood to bring down death on them all!" Carlich stared at the wailing Barilan in Maryn's arms for a long instant before setting off down the corridor, propelling her before him. "Curse Voerell! She ruined everything. She made Father disinherit me, may the Vulture eat his soul! And that spell—"

Carlich halted, so suddenly Maryn nearly fell. He yanked her around and swung his hand hard toward Barilan's head. It jerked to a halt before it struck the baby. "Gallows!"

He pulled his hand back and slapped Maryn's face. She reeled, her cheek stinging. "Good," Carlich spat. "I am not entirely powerless." He grabbed her upper arm and resumed shoving her down the corridor.

"Please! Please, Prince Carlich," Maryn gasped. "Don't hurt me. I'll do whatever you say. Just please, don't—" Tears blurred her vision and her throat closed with terror. Barilan's cries grated in her ears.

He didn't answer. She stumbled along beside him. His grip cut into her arm, so strong she knew she could never break it. Her thoughts raced in dizzy circles. She had never imagined Carlich capable of such violence. Had he gone mad? Or had his pleasantly affable demeanor been only a ruse all along, a facade concealing a scheming, murderous heart?

The knowledge that she and Barilan were now completely at Carlich's mercy sent her heart racing so wildly she feared she might faint. But she must not allow that to happen, for Barilan was even more helpless than she, and she couldn't leave him without what meager protection she could offer. She sucked in deep breaths and tried to pay attention to where they were going. Maybe the palace guards would yet stop Carlich's flight. He couldn't hope to escape capture for long within the bounds of the palace.

He seemed to have some destination in mind, for he steered her with rapid certainty, choosing their way without hesitation whenever the corridor branched. These were the passages the servants used to bring food up from the kitchen and carry dirty dishes away. Once they came face to face with a group of servants carrying steaming platters of meat. Carlich blasted them with a stream of sparks from his knife; they yelled and scattered back the way they had come, dropping the food. The rich beefy smell enveloped them as Carlich dragged Maryn through the wreckage of broken porcelain and splattered juices.

When they neared the kitchen, Carlich paused at a nondescript door. It was locked, but a quick gesture of his knife and jet of sparks opened it. Inside was a narrow dim corridor, floor thick with dust. Carlich shoved Maryn within and turned to seal the doorway behind them.

Barilan screamed and thrashed in Maryn's arms. Carlich rounded on her. "Shut him up! If he keeps up that racket, they'll be sure to find us."

"Yes, your Highness. Whatever you want." Maryn fumbled blindly with the tie of her shift.

Carlich slapped her again. "Don't call me that! Didn't you hear? My father cast me out of his house! I'm no longer heir, nor prince, nor..." He trailed off, panting.

Maryn cowered away and shifted Barilan into position. It took her a moment of murmuring, her voice strained nearly to breaking, until she could calm him enough to have any interest in her breast. But once she did, he latched on with frantic need, sucking fiercely until her milk let down with a warm rush and he relaxed in her arms. The silence echoed in her ears.

Carlich took a deep breath. "That's better." He stared at Barilan. "You, my nephew, are king now. And your mother is regent, with all the power of the Kingship. Curse her! Everyone believed me until she opened her mouth."

He breathed hard for a few moments. Slowly, his face took on a calculating expression. "Voerell would do anything to get you back, wouldn't she? I can make her pardon me, make her give me safe passage out of Milecha. Or...if I can get rid of her somehow, I can make them give the Kingship to me. Kiellan wouldn't do it, but Vinhor would; he's wanted to be Prelate for years...Father had no right to disinherit me. I should be king now! I am a Sompirla, descended from Lord Hoenech and King Fridollan. The throne of Milecha is my birthright!"

He stepped menacingly toward Maryn. She backed away, terrified of the unreasoning passion in his face, and came up short against the wall of the passage. Carlich loomed over her, putting his hands against the wall on either side of her body, trapping her. "Girl, you will come with me. I need you to take care of Barilan, feed him, keep him quiet. You will do whatever I say. If I catch you disobeying me, or trying to betray me in any way, I'll kill you and find some other nurse for Barilan. Do you understand?"

Maryn gulped and nodded, far too frightened to make any protest. Only Barilan at her breast kept her from collapsing into a weeping huddle.

"Follow me." Carlich set off at a rapid pace. Maryn stumbled after him.

The corridor ended at a tightly spiraling staircase that wound down into the bowels of the palace, lit only by an occasional narrow slit window. Carlich plunged down it; when Maryn hesitated he turned back to her, half raising his hand. She cowered before the threat and set her foot on the first wedge-shaped step. The stone was slick, and only the outermost edge was wide enough that her toes didn't hang off. She had to free a hand to brace herself and support Barilan with only one arm. Even so, she feared she would lose her footing. But Carlich pressed onward, and she had no choice but to follow.

They came to a point where the light from the last window failed and no other appeared. Blackness yawned beneath them like the shaft of a well. Maryn wondered if they had passed underground. Carlich flicked his hand; blue light glowed, illuminating the next turn of the spiral. He rubbed his palm against the shoulder of his elegant jerkin. A smear of light rubbed off and lingered there. "That's enough blood to last a while, I think. If not, between the three of us we have plenty." He gave a little edgy laugh.

Maryn fought to keep from losing control and breaking into sobs. She followed Carlich as he set off again down the stairs. He seemed to feel they had escaped the immediate danger of pursuit, for he slowed to a steady plod. Maryn's fear dulled enough to allow her to realize she was hungry and thirsty and footsore. Barilan had fallen asleep; her arm ached with his weight.

Finally they reached the base of the stair. An arched opening led into a long barrel-shaped vault. Notched shelves lined both walls, empty except for a scattered handful of dark bottles lying on their sides. The air was cool and damp. It looked to Maryn like a wine cellar, but it must have been abandoned long ago, to judge by the thick layer of dust that coated everything.

Carlich headed for the far end, where a portion of the roof and one wall had collapsed inwards. He called up light in his hand and directed it into the corner, where it glinted on shards of broken glass amid the tumbled debris. "Ha! It's still here. Just like I left it." He scrabbled among the stones, dragging several large chunks aside to reveal a long vertical sliver of darkness. He stepped back and pointed into the crack. "You first."

"What?" Maryn couldn't believe he expected her to enter that black crevice. She began to back away, but Carlich raised a threatening hand, blue sparks dancing around his fingers, and she stopped. "You can't be serious. I can't fit in there. Not holding Barilan."

"It opens up after a few feet. I'll be right behind you with the light. You might have to duck, but I could always make it through, and you're not much taller than I was as a page." Carlich gestured again, with the imperious certainty of one who was used to being obeyed. "Now, girl. Unless you want me to kill you after all."

Death seemed almost preferable to that inky nothingness. But Carlich seemed confident, and surely he wouldn't be taking them that way unless he knew it led somewhere. Maryn stroked Barilan's spiky hair for courage, steeled herself, and squeezed sideways into the crack. Cold stone embraced her front and back, but there was just enough room for her to edge deeper. By the time the roof lowered, the walls had widened a bit so she could crouch over Barilan and keep sidling through.

Carlich slipped in after her and called for her to wait. He cut his hand again and spent several minutes piling up stones and fixing them in place. When he finished, they were sealed within the stone as securely as a corpse within a tomb. Maryn swallowed and tried desperately to find some other thought to take her mind away from that image.

Blue light shone past her as Carlich pointed. "Go on."

The crack in the earth extended for several dozen yards, sometimes wider, sometimes narrower, but never quite as tight as the first stretch. It cut back sharply around an outcropping of rock and opened into a much larger space. Maryn couldn't see much in the dim blue glow that emanated from the smear of blood on Carlich's shoulder, but it appeared to be a natural cavern. Spikes of stone hung from the ceiling and lumpy pillars reached up from the floor. Human hands had modified the cave, though. There was a clear path among the rubble on the floor, and occasional mortared stone walls, or archways that showed the marks of tools. She wanted to ask Carlich about the place, but one glance at his face, mouth twisted into a scowl, eyes far away, convinced her that her captor was deeply absorbed in his own bitter thoughts, and any interruption from her would surely be met with fury.

They walked in silence for a long time, through the first cavern and into others. After a while they passed into a section of tunnels that were clearly man-made, for they were straight and level, with smooth, regular walls. Side passages branched off, but Carlich kept them to what seemed the main way.

At length Barilan stirred in Maryn's arms, whining. Her nose told her the nature of the problem, and she tried to quiet him without success. Finally she was forced to choke words out, despite her fear. "I beg your pardon, your Hi—I mean, my lord. We've got to stop. Barilan's diaper is messy. He gets the most awful rash if I don't change him right away. But I don't have any fresh diapers, or anything else I can use." The stiff gold embroidery of Barilan's ceremonial robe chafed Maryn's arms. It was filthy with the dust and grime of the underground passages, and Barilan had lost one of the golden slippers along the way.

Carlich rubbed his forehead. "I don't suppose you do."

Encouraged by his lack of anger at her presumption, Maryn ventured a few more requests. "Please, sir, can we rest a while? I'm hungry, and so thirsty, and my feet hurt. And I need to find someplace I can use…a garderobe, or chamberpot, or something." She ducked her head in shame.

Carlich blinked at her. "Come to think about it, so do I. Here, I think I see a side corridor a little way down. We'll stop there."

When they reached the spot, Maryn sank to her knees. She spread her skirts in front of her so she wouldn't have to set Barilan down on the cold stone. He squirmed restlessly when she pulled his gown up. It was one of his huge, spreading messes, she saw, her heart sinking. The thick yellow liquid had oozed all the way up the back of his diaper, and leaked out around his legs to smear the precious gown.

Carlich gave a little mirthless laugh, watching her. "Disgusting. I always knew I didn't want children."

Maryn dabbed futilely at Barilan's bottom with a corner of the diaper. "There's no water, or anything. I can't..."

She twisted around and ripped a generous strip off her underskirt. She used it to swab at Barilan's buttocks and legs, but accomplished little more than spreading the mess around. She fought to hold back her tears, but it was no use. She wiped her face on her shoulder.

"Oh, gallows, girl. Quit sniveling. This is useless." Carlich rubbed the back of his neck. "You're more trouble than you're worth, nephew. I should have left you at the palace. But then I'd have no hope of ever getting my crown back." He sighed heavily and pulled out his knife. "Get out of the way."

Maryn gasped and hunched protectively over Barilan. Carlich grimaced. "I'm not going to hurt him. Not that I could. I thought you wanted me to clean up his filth?"

Reluctantly, Maryn sat back on her heels. Now that she thought about it, she knew it was true that King Froethych's spell should prevent Carlich from doing Barilan any harm. And in any case Carlich seemed intent on keeping Barilan alive for his own purposes. But she still caught her breath when Carlich crouched over Barilan and added a new cut to the collection of fresh ones that scored his palm.

He winced. "I'll wager Metren never thought I'd put his teachings to this use. Still, it ought to work." He rubbed his hands together, smearing the blood over them, and began to wave them.

Blue lightning built up around his hands. He directed it down onto the fouled diaper and Barilan's messy body. The waste vanished in a burst of blue flame and stinking smoke. Barilan yelped and began to bawl.

Maryn hurled herself forward and gathered the baby up. He was clean, and the diaper as well, only a sulfurous smell lingering. "You did hurt him!"

"Just startled him, I think. Unless we've escaped the effects of Father's spell." Carlich made an abortive strike at Barilan. "No, it's as I guessed. When the magic got out of control, it magnified the effects far beyond what he intended. From what I know of such things, it was probably strong enough to blanket all Milecha, and last for years." He chuckled mirthlessly. "I wonder how it will manifest. Are parents all over Loempno tonight finding they can't beat their unruly brats into submission like usual?"

The thought seemed to amuse him; he laughed a little more as he rose. He swayed before he caught himself with a hand against the stone wall. "Gallows, I've burned a lot of blood today. A few more like that and I won't have enough left to shoo away a fly. You're going to have to take care of him yourself from now on, girl."

Anger boiled up in Maryn, pushing aside her fear. "I'd be glad to, if I had the means. You're the one who dragged us down here. How are you going to provide us water and food? I can only nurse Barilan if I eat and drink myself. He won't be of any use to you if you let us both die."

Carlich raised his hand, and she cowered back. But he let it fall again, and rubbed at his eyes. "You're right. I've got to get us out of here." He rose abruptly to his feet. "Stay put." He headed off down the side corridor, the light from his shoulder vanishing with him.

Maryn fumbled in the darkness to wrap the diaper back around Barilan. She gathered him into her arms. He snuggled against her, babbling softly. Maryn wanted to take him and flee, but blackness surrounded her, far more absolute than the deepest night. She couldn't see even a trace of her fingers when she waved them in front of her nose. She had no idea how to wake her blood into light, not more than the sparks cleansing created, which would fade within seconds. Without Carlich, she would wander lost until they died of thirst and starvation. But she couldn't simply stay, subject to his every volatile whim. She had to find some way to get Barilan safely back to Voerell.

She hadn't yet resolved her debate when Carlich's echoing footsteps heralded his arrival, rendering it moot. Much as she loathed and feared him, still he was another human presence in this miserable place, and her heart leaped at the return of the light.

He gestured down the passage. "Give him to me, and go take care of your business. I left some light so you won't fall down and break your neck."

Maryn hated the thought of entrusting Barilan to Carlich. Would he take the infant king and abandon her? But he did need her, if he wished to keep Barilan alive as a bargaining tool. And if he was right about King Froethych's dying spell, he could not actually harm his nephew. Reluctantly she passed Barilan into

Carlich's arms. Then, because her need was great, she trotted down the corridor. Occasional smudges of blue light on the walls lit her way. At the last light a privy smell told her this was the place Carlich had used for his makeshift garderobe; she followed suit as quickly as she could and retreated back to where he waited.

Carlich handed Barilan back to her. "Come. I think I know where there's water, not too far away."

She nodded and fell in behind him. He led the way for what must have been at least an hour. At last they emerged into another natural cavern. A narrow, water-filled crack wound along the floor. Carlich dropped to his belly and scooped up a double handful. Maryn knelt to drink. The water was icy as snowmelt in spring, clean and sweet tasting.

"Ah. That's what I needed." Carlich sat back on his heels and breathed deeply. "Fill yourself up. We don't have any way to take it with us."

Maryn obeyed, drinking until her stomach sloshed. Carlich drank again. Maryn checked Barilan's diaper, but it remained only slightly damp. After a mess like he'd just made, he might easily go a week before repeating the performance.

Carlich levered himself to his feet. "Come on. We've got to keep going."

Maryn plodded along after him. They wound through endless miles of caverns and corridors. In the unchanging gloom, she lost all sense of time, until the hours stretched like months or years.

After a while, she no longer cared if Carlich hurt her, as long as he let her rest. "Your—my lord, please, I can't go on any further."

His voice sounded almost as weary as she felt. "All right. We should have reached the exit I was thinking of by now, but maybe I took a wrong turn somewhere. Next time we come to a wide place, we'll stop."

He was true to his word. A short while later they came to a small round room with a domed ceiling at the intersection where two passages met. Carlich gestured for Maryn to rest. She collapsed to the ground, too exhausted to care what he might do, as long as she didn't have to move. He circled the room, placing smudges of fresh glowing blood on the walls and making obscure gestures.

When he finished, he put his back against the wall opposite her and slid down. He crossed his arms and studied her. "I've warded us against intruders. It should be safe to sleep. I know it will keep ghouls and specters and rats out. A sorcerer could break it if he used enough blood, but if they were going to find us they would have already."

It was foolish to speak, but Maryn was too weary and sick of fear to be cautious. "I hope they do. I hope Voerell sends the whole army to comb the city until they find you."

Carlich groaned. "Gallows, girl, can't you just cooperate? Do what I tell you and you'll be fine. I'll take care of you. Do you think Voerell will be so generous, if she finds us? You helped me steal her son."

"Not willingly!" But Maryn felt a chill at his words. Would Voerell care that she had been a helpless pawn, or in her rage would she heap punishment on anyone who had been involved?

Carlich's voice softened. "I know my sister. When she's angry she doesn't care who she hurts. It won't matter why you helped me, only that you did."

"I don't believe you! She saw what happened!" But even as Maryn protested, fear churned in the pit of her stomach. Carlich might be right. She'd seen the princess lose her temper with servants several times during her months in the palace. Once Voerell had ordered a maid dismissed for dropping and breaking her favorite vase, even though it was clearly an accident. The girl had been filling the vase with flowers and had been startled by a spider among the leaves. But all her apologies and explanations had not been sufficient to calm Voerell's wrath.

"I hope you don't have the chance to find out." Carlich yawned and slid down to pillow his head with his arms. "Get a little sleep. Don't bother trying to run; you can't pass the wards. And if you're thinking of trying anything, I warded myself, too."

He fell silent. Maryn arranged herself on the cold stone floor, cupping Barilan in the curve of her body. She wished she had the courage to try Carlich's words. Would anything happen if she crept up on him as he slept and cut his throat with his own knife? But if she succeeded, she and Barilan would be alone down here, lost.

Barilan nursed eagerly, latching correctly on the first try. Maryn was grateful for that small blessing. She was so tired she couldn't have faced the usual struggle to get his mouth positioned so it wouldn't hurt her. Now that she thought about it, he'd been latching well all day. Maybe he'd finally learned. After a while his sucking slowed and stopped as he fell into peaceful sleep.

He didn't know or care how much trouble they were in. As long as he had her warm body and sweet milk, he was happy. He didn't miss his mother. As far as he knew Maryn was his mother, the one who held him and tended him and fed him, who changed his diapers and bathed him and slept by his side.

Maryn tried her best not to disturb him as her tears flowed and silent sobs shook her body. She sent up silent hopeless pleas to the Holy One. But who was she, a lowborn servant girl, to attract his attention or concern?

Eventually she slept. She woke often, cold and stiff, and tried vainly to get more comfortable, before sinking into muddled dreams again.

At length a groan from Carlich roused Maryn. He pushed himself up to sit, rubbed at his eyes, and ran his hands through his hair. Catching Maryn watching him, he gave her a wry smile. "Time to get moving."

He broke the wards, burning into nothingness the remains of the blood that had fueled them. They both ventured down a side corridor to relieve themselves. Maryn removed Barilan's wet diaper and replaced it with the torn strip from her petticoat. But there was no food, or water, or any other comfort to ease their waking. Carlich set out without fanfare down one of the passages, and Maryn trudged after.

Eventually they came to a section where the walls were made of brick, with many small rooms and side passages. Carlich brightened and his step quickened. "I think I recognize this place. If I remember right..." He took a few steps down one passage. "No, not this one. Where was it..."

He tried a number of other false starts before he found what he was looking for. "Here it is. We're almost out."

He hurried along a corridor that to Maryn looked just like every other he'd examined. After several turns, they came to a long straight section. Halfway down one wall was a wooden door without latch or handle.

Carlich pressed his ear to the wood. Barilan made

a few cheerful babbles; Carlich gestured urgently at Maryn to keep him quiet. She had little success, for he wasn't interested in her breast at the moment, only wanting to comment happily on his surroundings.

Eventually Carlich straightened. "If no one's heard him by now, I doubt anyone's there." He put his hand on the door, but paused.

He turned to Maryn. "If I'm right, this is the basement of a building near the wall. You could hide there while I scout ahead. But I can't trust you not to give us away."

She would promise him anything if it persuaded him to take her beyond that door, where surely she could find someone to help her. "I swear, I won't. I'll do whatever you say."

She poured all the sincerity she could muster into her voice, but perhaps she overdid it, for Carlich frowned. "You say that now, but what's to keep you from yelling for help from the first person we see? I can't keep a knife on you all the time. No. It's a risky spell, and it will take a lot out of me, but I don't think I have any choice. I should be able to keep it under control." He studied her for a moment, and she gazed back, not understanding what he intended, but sure it was something terrible. He nodded, and sighed. "At least I can use your blood." He extended his palm. "Give me your hand."

"No, my lord, please..." Maryn stumbled back.

Carlich lunged and grabbed her arm, knife poised in his other hand. "Would you rather I cut your face?"

"No!" Maryn ducked her head over Barilan's, pressing a cheek against the softness of his hair. Shaking, she shifted the baby to her hip, freeing the arm Carlich gripped.

He jerked it toward him. A quick flash of his knife

opened a line of pain across the base of her thumb. Her blood welled out, running down toward her wrist. Carlich wiped his hand through the stream and waved it in complex patterns, his brow furrowed in greater effort than she'd yet seen his sorcery require. The blood sparked, and vibrations rattled in the bones of Maryn's skull.

Something happened to her thoughts. She couldn't identify what was different. She was still awake, still aware of everything around her. But she felt oddly numb. She started to wonder what Carlich had done, but the thought faded before it was fully formed. It didn't seem important. Deep down she knew something was wrong, and tried to struggle against it, but she couldn't summon the will to fight.

"There," Carlich said, panting, but satisfied. "Follow me, and do nothing unless I tell you."

"Yes, my lord." Maryn's voice was placid in her ears.

Her palm hurt, but the cut was sealed shut, no further blood escaping. She wrapped both arms around Barilan and followed Carlich. He waved his hand, still sparking with Maryn's blood, to unlatch the door, and they ventured into the room.

It was a storeroom, piled high with boxes and barrels and sacks. Carlich crept down the narrow aisles until he reached a rickety stair. Barilan stared about with interest, and let out a string of inquisitive sounds.

"Silence him!" Carlich hissed.

In automatic obedience, Maryn put her hand over Barilan's mouth, smothering his noises. In the distant corner where she was still herself, she was appalled that she would do such a thing, but she couldn't even muster the strength to figure out why it was wrong. Barilan squirmed vigorously in protest and squawked loudly enough that her smothering hand could not muffle it.

"That's no good." Carlich looked around. Beneath the stair was a small triangular space. "Get under there. Keep him as quiet as you can. Don't move until I come back."

Maryn squeezed into the narrow space, hunching her body over Barilan. He broke into angry cries. Maryn unfastened the tie of her shift and latched him on. His distress made him willing to nurse, and he settled quickly.

Carlich padded up the stairs. Maryn heard the door at the top creak as he pushed it slowly open. His light footsteps slipped through, and it creaked shut again, closing with a bump.

Maryn was alone. She stayed perfectly motionless except when Barilan finished the first side and she transferred him to the other. Eventually he fell asleep. Maryn's back ached from her awkward hunched position, and she was sitting on something hard that pressed into her thigh, but she didn't shift her position. She could tell from the smell that one of the nearby sacks held apples, and her stomach felt like a great hollow drum, but still she didn't move.

After a long time, the door at the top of the stair creaked open. Maryn's heart quickened, but she couldn't budge. Stealthy steps descended above her.

Carlich tossed a bundle of cloth toward her. "Here. Some less conspicuous clothes for the two of you. Get changed. It will be sunrise soon."

Maryn crept stiffly out from under the stair and laid Barilan on the floor at her feet, ignoring his whimpers as the abrupt motion woke him. Ignoring, also, a faint twinge of humiliation, she stripped off her blue uniform bodice and outer skirt, and replaced them with the dull brown ones Carlich had supplied. He hadn't provided a different shift, but hers was nondescript, indistinguishable from what any other woman in Milecha might wear. She knelt to remove Barilan's ceremonial gown and dressed him in a long shirt. It was too large, and kept slipping off his shoulder, but it covered him adequately. There were even three clean diapers in the bundle; she traded one for Barilan's wet one.

"Give me anything identifiable." Carlich spread out her blue skirt and dumped everything else onto it, adding his own richly embroidered jerkin and soft doeskin leggings to the pile. He had changed into a much plainer outfit, Maryn saw. Her thoughts seemed a little clearer now, but she still couldn't muster the initiative to ask him where he had acquired the clothes.

Carlich wrapped her skirt around the bundle and took it back to the door they had entered through, stashing it in the corridor. He regarded Maryn and Barilan. "Very good. No one will give you a second look. Now all we have to do is figure out a way past the wall. I know there must be places thieves and smugglers use. Come, I spotted a fountain where you can get some water."

Maryn, fighting as hard as she could, managed to break through the numbness in her mind and tongue to gasp, "Food."

"Yes, yes, we'll find some food, too. One thing at a time. Just be happy I found a laundry where I could break in and get these clothes. Idiots. They should know if they're too cheap to hire a night watchman they're going to have things stolen."

The struggle wasn't quite so hard this time. "Apples." Maryn jerked her head toward the sack whose tantalizing odors had mocked her for so long.

Carlich blinked. "Oh. If there was food down here, why didn't you just take some? Go ahead, help yourself, and toss me a couple while you're at it."

Released to do what she'd been longing to do, Maryn fumbled with the mouth of the sack until she got the drawstring undone. The apples were dry and shriveled, the last remnants of the previous fall's harvest, but she didn't care. She hurled two toward Carlich to fulfill his command, and sank her teeth deep into the next one. It tasted wonderful, for all that it was mealy and tough.

Carlich rummaged around and found a wheel of cheese. He sliced through the thick rind with his little jeweled knife and cut off a generous piece. He grimaced at the state of the apples, but cut them open anyway and ate the fruit and cheese together. "I don't know how people stand this dreck. That's the blandest cheese I've ever tasted. Here, have some, if you can stomach it." He passed Maryn a slice.

She devoured it, not perceiving anything wrong with the flavor. She felt much restored by the food and far more able to think. She swallowed the last bite of apple, and shifted Barilan to the other arm. Just before she began fighting to force out another unbidden word, she stopped. Her thoughts were as sluggish as flowing honey, but she managed to formulate a dim awareness that perhaps she should conceal the fact that the spell's effects were fading.

"All right. Is that enough? Anything else you want to say?" Carlich eyed her sarcastically.

Maryn shook her head.

"Follow me, then." Not looking to see if she obeyed, he set off up the stairs. Maryn hoisted Barilan to her shoulder and followed.

Eleven

The grey pre-dawn city was nearly deserted. Only an occasional cloaked and hooded form slunk by, intent on some business perhaps even more nefarious than Carlich's. Maryn clutched Barilan close and hurried after Carlich. He led them through the narrow twisting streets, keeping to the deepest shadows, until they reached the large western gate where Maryn had first entered the city. It was closed and barred, even the small side gates shut up tight. A greatly increased number of guards paced back and forth before it.

"Gallows. Voerell's got them on alert. We'll never get through." He stared for another long moment before setting off rapidly in a different direction. "I'll try the north gate, but it's probably the same."

Maryn trotted after him, doing her best not to fall behind. Carlich led her to several more gates, all of which were similarly guarded. As the sun rose and the day brightened the people of Loempno filled the cobblestone streets. Maryn began to see clusters of guards striding by. Whenever one drew near she fought to cry for help, but her lips remained stubbornly closed. She could think much more clearly now, though, which gave her hope Carlich's spell was weakening.

Carlich cursed and grabbed Maryn's arm to pull her into a narrow side alley. She glimpsed a mass of bodies packing the street ahead before the building cut off her view.

"Now they're setting up roadblocks. We'll never get to the docks that way." Carlich scowled and peered down the alley, but it ended in a blank wall only a short distance away. "Come on."

Maryn shifted Barilan to her other hip and plodded after Carlich as he pushed through the crowd back the way they had come. She clung to the hope that they would still be within the city when the spell finally wore off. Carlich couldn't renew it in public without attracting attention. Until then she could only bide her time.

The twisting path Carlich took to avoid the roadblocks eventually led them into a squalid area of ramshackle buildings and muddy streets. Dirty children darted away, and on every corner ragged beggars stretched out eager hands. Maryn hugged Barilan tight and pressed closer to Carlich. He ignored their surroundings, though his step grew less confident with every turn. Maryn couldn't imagine that he'd ever been in this sector of the city before.

A group of women carrying baskets crowded past them. Their clothes, though threadbare, were neatly mended, and the handful of barefoot children among them had clean faces. Maryn caught a whiff of the familiar mingled odors of old sweat and lye soap, and knew the women were taking their laundry down to the river.

One woman in particular caught her eye. Though her basket was piled high with linen cloths that gave off the unmistakable reek of diapers, she walked unencumbered by any baby. Maryn wondered if she'd left her child tucked snugly in bed with its father. She swallowed and tried to blink away the tears that clouded her eyes. She stumbled into one of the women, and Maryn's voice broke when she begged her pardon.

Carlich turned to glare at her. As soon as the women were out of earshot, he hissed, "What's wrong? Everyone's going to stare if you keep blubbering like that."

Maryn would rather have died than reveal her private misery to Carlich, but the spell left her no choice but to answer. "She reminded me of how I left Frilan with Edrich and took my wash down to the river, the day of the fire."

Carlich's brow creased in puzzlement for a moment, before his expression cleared. "That's right. I heard that your baby died. Well, it won't do you any good to cry about it now, so stop."

Anger blazed up in Maryn, fierce and hot. She welcomed the way it pushed aside her grief and cleared the dampness from her eyes. It occurred to her that perhaps this was some action of the spell, allowing her to obey Carlich's order, but she didn't care. She stared at Carlich's back as he turned to resume his progress, imagining her gaze burning into his heart with sorcerous fire.

"Wait." Carlich whirled back to face her, so fast she almost bumped into him. "Down to the river, you said? Do they have a way past the wall?"

Thrown into confusion, Maryn lost the focus of her anger and floundered for a reply. "I...I don't know. Probably. In Ralo there was a little gate the women used. Maybe there's one like it here."

Carlich jumped on her words like a hound on a fresh scent. "Will there be guards?"

"I don't know! I've never been to the one here. But there never were in Ralo."

He eyed her for a moment before turning a speculative gaze on the women hurrying away. Wordlessly he set off after them, beckoning Maryn to follow.

The small postern gate was very similar to the one in Ralo. But this one had a single guard leaning against the post. He unlocked the gate for the women and waved them though.

"Gallows," Carlich muttered. He peered around the corner of the last building and watched as the guard re-locked the gate. "Let me think." He flexed his hand, which was crisscrossed with the many slashes he'd inflicted on it since the ceremony. Then he rolled back his sleeve and set the point of his knife against his inner arm, drawing it across his wrist in a slow, controlled motion. Maryn saw a tracery of similar scars marking his flesh. He swiftly sheathed his knife and gathered the spilling blood in his hand, his fingers making little dancing gestures the whole time. A generous handful of blue lightning built up in his palm.

Still focused on his arm, Carlich leaned toward Maryn, and whispered, "Go, talk to him. Pretend you want to go through."

Maryn fought every step, but it was no use. She approached the guard. "Good morning, sir."

He looked her up and down. "What do you want?"

"Please, I need to go down to the river."

"Why? You've no wash with you. I've got my orders. No one goes in or out without legitimate reason, at least not until the kidnapper's caught." As Maryn tried to think of an answer, his eyes narrowed, and he put his hand on his sword hilt. "Wait a minute, girl. Who are you? What's your baby's name?"

A fierce buzz of magic rang in Maryn's bones. Lightning lanced past her shoulder and into the guard's chest, impaling him. Blue flames erupted from his wide, shocked eyes and open mouth, and he collapsed without uttering another sound.

Maryn couldn't scream. She could only stare in horror, clutching Barilan tight, until Carlich pushed past her, gasping for breath. "Come on." He crouched to unbuckle the guard's belt, then slung it around his own waist, settling the sword at his side. He drew it, made a few cuts at the air, and slid it back into its sheath. After a quick glance up and down the deserted street he pulled the keys from the belt and unlocked the gate.

Carlich waved for Maryn to exit as he pushed the gate open. She edged through, giving the lifeless guard as wide a berth as she could. Carlich grabbed the guard's body under the arms and dragged him into some tall grass just beyond the gate. "With any luck, no one will notice he's missing until he fails to report back after his shift. We'd better be miles away by then." He locked the gate behind them and set off, but turned back impatiently when Maryn did not move. "Follow me."

Numb with horror, Maryn trailed after him. She fought to escape the compulsion to obey, but though the spell had faded enough to free her thoughts it was still too strong for her body to disobey a direct order.

The path slanted across the grassy meadow that extended a bowshot beyond the wall and into a tangle of trees and underbrush. Carlich followed it and Maryn plodded behind. They descended a steep slope. Ahead Maryn glimpsed a sunny break in the trees and heard splashing and cheerful voices.

Carlich held up a hand for Maryn to wait, then slipped from tree to tree until he could see. He backtracked to where Maryn waited. "There's a whole crowd of them down there. Too many to deal with before one manages to raise the alarm." He looked at the thick underbrush. "No help for it." He pushed between two bushes, and Maryn was forced to go along.

Branches tore at her clothing and slapped her face. She nearly turned an ankle when her foot came down on a large stone that shifted beneath her weight. Barilan fussed, and she worked to soothe him. His diaper was soaked, but she dared not ask Carlich to stop.

After a long struggle through the dense growth, they emerged on the riverbank. The river was wide, much wider than the one that circled Ralo. Out in the middle were a few ships. Maryn hoped someone on board might look out and see them, but they were too far away for her to consider that a realistic possibility.

A narrow path ran along the bank a few feet from the edge of the water. Carlich turned onto it and quickened his step. Maryn struggled to keep up.

Before long, though, Maryn noticed that Carlich was dragging, too. His shoulders drooped, and occasionally he stumbled. The city walls still rose beyond the trees to their left and the sun was just reaching its highest point when he turned aside into a small clearing among the trees and called a halt.

Maryn sank gratefully to a seat on a fallen tree trunk. Barilan was bright and happy after their morning's walk, but she was exhausted. Somewhere in there she'd lost a night's sleep, she was fairly sure.

But she must take care of Barilan. At least this time she had water and a fresh diaper to put on him.

While she tended to that duty Carlich warded the clearing. He passed her a few apples and some cheese he'd brought along from the storeroom. "Enjoy. This is the last of it." He rubbed his forehead. "I hope the wards hold. Casual eyes won't see us, but a determined search might. That guard is going to be found sooner or later, and they'll set dogs on our track." He shook his head. "But I've got to get a little sleep. An hour or two at least." He waved a hand at Maryn. "Lie down. Get some rest."

The need to obey was not quite so strong this time. Maryn compliantly lay down on the ground, but she could have resisted for a few moments if she'd tried. Perhaps while Carlich slept the power of his spell would drop off even further, and she could break free.

She clung to that hope when she woke to Barilan's hungry cries. By the sun it was early afternoon. Carlich still slept. Gathering Barilan to her breast, she quieted his wails. Maryn watched Carlich intently and held her breath as she eased to her feet. He hadn't specifically told her to remain in the clearing, and she'd completed his last command to get some rest. It felt like wading through thick mud to step down toward the river path, but she could do it. Once she was well away she'd run. How long would it take to get to the washing place? Would the women still be there?

She hit something that felt like cobwebs across her face. Sticky threads entangled her feet, wrapping tighter the more she struggled. Blue lightning buzzed around her. Carlich jerked awake and leaped to his feet, every muscle tense.

Seeing only Maryn, he relaxed a fraction.

"Thought you'd get away, did you?" He came to her, dissolving the invisible strands with a wave. "We'd better renew the binding right now, before you try anything else foolish."

She cursed herself silently for forgetting about the wards as he cut her arm and used her blood to thrust her again into a dull daze. After, her thoughts were so tightly bound she couldn't even feel miserable.

They spent the rest of the afternoon working their way upriver. Carlich kept eyeing the occasional two- or three-man fishing boats out on the river, but not until the sun was getting low did he act.

"There." Carlich halted so abruptly Maryn nearly collided with him. "Stand back. Stay quiet." He glanced at the sleeping Barilan. "Once we're across the river they'll never find us."

Maryn was just getting enough thought back to know that she should try to cry out and warn the unsuspecting fishers whose boat had strayed so close to the shore. But she couldn't yet even make the attempt. She could only watch, quiet as he had commanded her to be.

Carlich killed the fishermen much the same way he'd killed the guard, except this time the streak of lightning pierced them both in a single flash. The boat began to drift when the man holding the rudder collapsed. Carlich attempted to seize it and draw it closer to shore, but the blood he'd gathered from his arm ran out of power. Cursing, he dove into the river and swam out to the little boat. It nearly capsized as he clambered aboard. Carlich shoved a body aside, unshipped the oars, and stroked the boat into the shore.

There was a rope fastened to the prow; he tossed it to Maryn. "Get that. Tie it around one of those trees."

Maryn obeyed. Carlich rummaged around the bottom of the boat. "They had a decent catch. That will feed us for a while. Here, this should serve." He picked up a wooden bait bucket and dumped its contents overboard. "Put Barilan down somewhere safe and come help me."

Maryn wouldn't have considered anywhere along the riverbank safe enough to leave a baby alone if she'd been making the decision. But the magical compulsion forced her to choose the best spot available. A little grassy hollow well back from the water looked as if it would do. Barilan could roll over, but he hadn't yet begun to crawl, so he wouldn't be able to move far even if he woke. She wished for a blanket to shield him against the damp ground, but she had nothing. She laid him down; he stirred for a moment before sinking back into sleep.

Back at the boat, Carlich summoned her aboard. He hauled at the body of one fisherman. "Grab his feet," he ordered.

Maryn thought she might vomit, but she took up the man's limp legs, and they lifted him onto one of the boards that spanned the boat and served as a seat. Carlich arranged him so his head and torso hung down on one side. "Hold on to him; don't let him slip."

He positioned the empty bucket under the man's neck, and with a quick slash of his knife cut his throat. Blood drained out in a gush. Maryn's head swam, and she had to turn away.

Carlich fussed with the body as the flow slowed to a trickle, raising its limbs so that the force of the stream was increased. When for all his manipulation he could extract no more blood from the body, he spoke sharply to Maryn and she was compelled to help him heave the corpse over the side of the boat into the water.

Dimly Maryn heard Barilan's forlorn cries from the shore. She turned automatically and stepped toward the prow of the boat. Carlich scowled. He looked up and down the empty river and deserted shore. "He'll be fine. Ignore him. You can get him when we're done here."

The spell forced Maryn to turn back and bend to aid Carlich in his work, though her heart felt torn as the miserable wails continued, and a warm rush of milk drenched the front of her shift. They repeated the process of draining blood with the other fisherman. By the time the man's body splashed into the river and sank out of sight, the hour was growing late.

Carlich surveyed the products of their work with satisfaction; the bucket was more than three-quarters full of thick red liquid. "Let Voerell try to catch me now. I could hold off an army with this." He gestured at Maryn. "Get Barilan and bring him aboard. I need to make sure this doesn't turn into a clotted mess, and set wards to keep the specters out. Then we can head across the river."

Maryn had grown increasingly worried about Barilan all during the time Carlich had kept her working. At some point his cries had ceased, and she quaked with fear for what might have befallen him. Now, freed by Carlich's words, she scrambled for the prow and jumped to shore, ignoring the buzz of power behind her.

Barilan had rolled and squirmed a few feet from where she'd left him. His face was red and blotched with grimy tracks of dried tears. He broke into fresh wails as soon as he spotted Maryn and reached for her as she gathered him up. Guilt assailed her at the thought of him crying for her all that long lonely time, until at last he gave up and sank into the despairing misery of the abandoned. She clutched him to her breast. "I'm sorry, little one. I wanted to come, but I couldn't. I'll take care of you, as much as I can, as much as he lets me…"

She thought about attempting again to flee, but the spell was still too strong. She trudged down the bank to the boat.

Carlich looked up from where he was just completing his spell. "Climb in and let's get going." He set the lid firmly on the bucket and stowed it carefully in the stern. As soon as Maryn and Barilan were settled on the rear seat, he untied the prow rope and took up the oars. He grimaced as the many cuts on his left hand contacted the rough wood of the oar. "Tear another bit off your skirt for me."

Maryn perforce complied. He wrapped the long scrap of linen around his palm and tied it, pulling on the free end with his teeth. "That will help a little. I've got to find some healer who's willing to teach me more of the art. They're all so close-mouthed with anyone who's not subject to their oaths and binding spells." He set his hands to the oars and began to pull with powerful strokes toward the middle of the river.

The current pushed them downstream as they cut across the wide expanse. When they veered close to a large trading vessel headed upstream, Carlich paused for a moment to dip a little blood from the bucket and work shielding wards around the boat. Maryn was hungry enough that the mass of fish crowded into the large wooden tank amidships looked appealing, but not yet so hungry she was willing to try how they would taste raw. Barilan kept her busy, his mood by turns irritable and playful.

The pace of Carlich's rowing slowed, and several times he went to the bucket for a dab of blood. He'd wave and mutter, blue sparks would fly, and he'd bend to his task with renewed energy. But each time the effect was shorter-lived.

Near sunset, they reached the far side. Carlich dragged with weariness as he moored the boat at a convenient tree and hauled his precious bucket up the rocky bank. He staggered as he deposited it under a tree. Rubbing at his eyes, he sank to the ground. "Give me Barilan," he ordered hoarsely. "I think it's safe to make a small fire. There must be flint and steel on the boat somewhere. Find it, cook us some of that fish."

Maryn reluctantly surrendered the sleeping Barilan into his arms. Her volition was beginning to trickle back, enough that she could think with sufficient clarity to conceal its return. She set industriously about the tasks Carlich had set her, terrified lest any hesitation on her part warn him that his spell was losing effect. Searching the boat, she discovered a box under the front bench where the fishermen had stowed their gear. In addition to a fire-starting kit she found a filleting knife, a frying pan, and a small flask of oil, along with a flagon of ale.

Maryn eyed the knife thoughtfully and shot a glance over at Carlich. He had his eyes closed, his head leaned back against the tree, while Barilan slumbered in his arms. She tested to see if she might be able to hide the knife away under her skirts. She couldn't quite manage it, but she thought she might be able to soon, if Carlich didn't notice the weapon and order her not to use it.

She spent a long time starting and building up a small fire, and wielded the knife as unobtrusively as possible to clean and gut several of the fish. She rinsed the knife in the river and wiped it on the grass. She still couldn't force her hands to hide it on her person, but she did, with much effort, tuck it under a bush on the far side of the clearing from where Carlich drowsed. She returned to the fire, heated oil in the pan, and put the fish in to fry.

The smell set her mouth watering long before the fish were ready. She burned her fingers and tongue sampling a flaky white bit. Just as she was about to decide they were cooked enough, Carlich stirred and came over to stand beside her, looking down at her handiwork. She gestured to where she'd set the flagon. "I found some ale, my lord. The fish are almost done."

"Excellent." Carlich seated himself cross-legged by the fire and set Barilan in his lap. He uncorked the flagon and took a long swig. "Gallows, I needed that." He thrust the bottle out toward Maryn. "Here, have a drink. You deserve it after your hard work."

She accepted it obediently, though she squirmed within at the warm camaraderie in his tone. She only worked on his behalf because he forced her to. But if he wanted to fool himself into believing she was a willing partner in his flight, let him. It could only make it easier for her to escape. She feigned taking a long, thirsty draught of ale, though in truth she only sipped until she had swallowed the minimum required to fulfill the enforcing magic's idea of "a drink," and the compulsion waned.

Carlich showed no such restraint, drinking heartily and wolfing down the fish. He praised her cookery extravagantly. Gaining the far side of the river seemed to have greatly cheered him.

"Go on, have some more," he urged Maryn, passing her the flagon. She drank and passed it back.

"Tomorrow I'm going to see about stealing a horse or two. It's a long way to Ralo."

He was taking them to Ralo? She'd never expected to return there. The thought of familiar surroundings was comforting in a way. Perhaps she could find someone she knew to beg for help. But what good would it do to see friendly faces, if the spell that kept her in thrall to Carlich prevented her from reaching out to them? And Maryn wondered how she could bear the constant reminders of her former life that were sure to assault her from every side.

Her inner conflict must have shown on her face, because Carlich squinted at her in the firelight. "Something's bothering you. What is it? Tell me."

She had to comply, though she was able to choose her words a bit. "Ralo is my home. I lived there before my husband and child died, and I came to Loempno to be Barilan's nurse."

"Hmm. You'll be glad to return, then."

"I suppose." The magic didn't keep her from formulating a question for him. "Why do you want to go to Ralo?"

He picked up a stick and poked at the fire. "Priest Vinhor has his seat there. He's always been friendly to me. I'm sure I can get him to listen to my story, take my part. Especially if I promise to make him Prelate once I'm king. He's been building his influence for years, trying to maneuver himself into position to succeed Kiellan. With him to bolster my claim to the throne, I can start to build a base of popular support. Also, last I heard the Twenty-ninth Division was stationed at the garrison there. They served under my command three years ago, during the last big conflict on the Hampsia border. They'll follow me sooner than Voerell."

Barilan stirred in Carlich's arms. He passed the baby to Maryn. "He seems to be doing all right. You care for him well." He stared off into the woods. "My nurse's name was Kegill. She always told me being chosen to nurse me was the best thing that ever happened to her. When I turned twelve and became a page Father set her up with a nice house in the best part of the city. I still visit her sometimes, on the Sabbath; she always fixes me a big meal of all my favorites. She won't believe Voerell's lies. She'll know the crown should be mine. When I defeat Voerell and come back to Loempno in triumph, Kegill will be the first to greet me. You wait and see."

Maryn toyed with Barilan's hair as he nursed. The ale must be affecting Carlich, though he was still enunciating his words clearly. He'd drunk nearly the entire flagon. "She must love you very much."

Carlich shrugged. "I suppose. Or maybe she just loved the good pay and easy work. Do you love Barilan the way you loved your own baby?"

Maryn gulped, but the magic was still strong enough to compel her to answer truthfully. "Not...not the same way as Frilan, no. But I do love him," she hastened to add.

He gave a little mirthless laugh. "Of course you do. But not like a mother loves her own child." He was silent for a long time. Maryn thought he was done, and was glad to be through with the awkwardly intimate conversation, but eventually he spoke again. "I barely remember my own mother. I was only four when she died, along with the baby after Voerell. And even when she was alive, I didn't see her very often. I do remember one time, she went walking with Kegill and me in the garden, and told me the names of the flowers. Not much else, though."

He turned his intense gaze on Maryn. "Tell me about your mother."

Maryn wished he would leave off this uncomfortable questioning. He was acting as if she were a person of importance, a friend, whose history and feelings mattered to him, when they both knew that wasn't the case. He would never look twice at her if they hadn't been forced by circumstances into flight together. But the ale had put him into a maudlin mood, and she had no choice but to answer. "She's a serf on Lord Negian's estate. I'm her first child; I have three younger brothers and two sisters. Mother's name is Eryr. She makes the best rye bread of any of Lord Negian's serfs; all our neighbors trade with us for it. And she's a good spinner; she taught me, and Edrich always said my yarn was as fine as any he'd ever worked with. What else do you want to know?"

Carlich shrugged. "I don't know. Anything. Does she love you?"

"Of course." Maryn almost didn't know how to answer that question. Her mother had never been vocal or demonstrative about her love for any of her children, but it had always been there, like the air a bird flew through or the water a fish swam in. It felt strange even to think about whether it existed, as if there were the possibility it might not. "Don't all mothers love their children?"

"Does Voerell love Barilan?" The question darted at her, quick and urgent.

"Yes." Maryn made her voice as strong and certain as she was able. "I know it doesn't always look like it, but Litholl said she loved him so much she had to try to distance herself from him. Because otherwise it hurt too much to have to give him up to someone else." She struggled for a moment with the power of the spell, but Carlich so clearly wanted her to carry on a conversation that she was able to force out even words she was sure he wouldn't want to hear. "She's probably dying inside right now, missing him, worrying whether he's safe."

Carlich jumped to his feet and began to pace beside the fire. "You're wrong. I don't believe you. I mean, I'm sure she cares about him a little. But she's barely seen him since he was born. She'll manage. She's regent, she has all the power of the Kingship now. That's what she wants. She was always angry that she couldn't be one of Father's heirs because she was a girl. I bet she hated it that her son could have what she couldn't. She'd probably be glad for him to be gone forever if it meant she could keep the power for herself."

The spell was weakening with every successful effort Maryn made to defy it. "You don't really believe that."

"What do you know about it?" Carlich took a step toward her, raising his hand. "You're just a hired servant. Nursing a prince doesn't change that. You're only a serf; you know nothing about royalty. We're different from you lowborn scum!"

Maryn cowered away. "Whatever you say, my lord. Of course you're right."

Carlich's arm dropped. "And don't ever forget it!" He stood panting a moment before he waved a dismissive hand around their campsite. "Clean up all this stuff. And put the fire out; we don't want people to see it. Then get some sleep; we're leaving at first light for Ralo."

"Yes, my lord." Maryn held very still as he stormed across the clearing and threw himself to the ground, rolling to face away from her.

Twelve

aryn followed Carlich's orders as slowly and quietly as she could. She disposed of the fish bones in the river and scrubbed the frying pan out carefully. The work was awkward at first with Barilan in her arms, but she found a length of netting in the boat and fashioned a rough sling to tie him to her back. After that her tasks were much easier. But she still dawdled, and the night was well advanced when she finished. She used the empty ale flagon to carry water from the river and quenched the fire in billows of steam.

Carlich didn't stir, even when the roar and hiss of the drowning fire echoed around the clearing. Maryn held her breath and crept close to study him by the pale light of the moon. He seemed to be deeply asleep, even snoring a little in occasional sudden starts. The combination of blood loss, magic, hard physical work, and ale must have drained his reserves and tired him deeply. He had fallen asleep without remembering to set wards or to renew the spell that compelled Maryn's obedience.

She was exhausted herself, but she dared not sleep and miss her chance. She tried to go for the knife again. This time she succeeded by thinking fixedly about how she intended to use it only to gut more fish for breakfast. She tucked it into the waistband of her skirt, where it bumped cold and sharp against her leg.

She glanced over her shoulder. Barilan slept, his body limp against her back, his head lolled to one side. Confident the baby would stay quiet, Maryn went back to Carlich. She could see no sign to indicate his slumber was feigned.

The bucket of blood sat against a tree trunk not far from his feet. The wards around the rim glowed dim blue. If she left the blood, he would have nearly unlimited power to use pursuing her once he woke. If she could dispose of it, at least he would be limited to what he could spare from his own veins. She wished she had the ability to wake power from all that rich crimson fluid, but without knowledge of the proper words or gestures it was useless to her, only a grisly reminder of Carlich's ruthlessness.

She could perform the ritual which would release its potential harmlessly into the air, but that would be noisy and create a great deal of light. Carlich would be sure to wake. Besides, she'd never cleansed even a fraction of the huge amount of blood contained within the bucket. So much power could easily overwhelm her and cause her to lose control of the spell.

She'd dump it into the river. That would put it far beyond Carlich's ability to use. The fresh flowing water would dilute the blood and carry it away. In the unlikely event some ghoul or specter managed to locate and consume enough to pose a threat, it would happen far from here.

She hefted the bucket, its handle digging into her fingers. She had to struggle against the certainty that this was something profoundly against Carlich's wishes, but the spell was quite weak now, and he hadn't thought to specifically forbid this particular action. The magic dragged at her like an extra weight, but she plowed her way through it.

The rocky slope down to the river was difficult to navigate with her burden. Maryn stepped cautiously, testing each foothold before trusting it with her weight. But despite all her care, one flat stone shifted under her foot. She lurched, the unfamiliar weight of Barilan on her back throwing off her balance. Instinctively she flailed her arms. The lid of the bucket came off. Blood slopped against her skirts.

She recoiled, trying to avoid the spilling liquid and right the bucket. Her foot came down on a patch of gravel slick with spilled blood. It skidded forward, and she sat down hard, her rear slamming into a stone. The impact traveled from her tailbone up her spine to her jaw. She flung her hands back to keep from falling on top of Barilan, letting go of the bucket. It capsized in a scarlet flood.

Maryn smothered a cry. Surely Carlich must have heard and would come to recapture her. She hunched forward, fighting tears of anger at her failure and despair that she would ever escape. But when nothing happened after a few moments, she looked over to where Carlich slept. He remained stretched out on the ground. Maryn looked over her shoulder to check on Barilan. He had stirred, but now was still again.

She held her breath and gathered herself, preparing to rise. If she was stealthy enough, could she still creep down to the river and take the boat? At least she had to get away from the dark slick of blood that coated the stones and sank into the earth.

But she was too late. A cold breeze tickled the back of her neck, out of place in the warm summer night. Maryn's heart raced. She jerked around but could see nothing. A chill sank into her ankle, just where it was cool already from the wetness of the drenching blood. This was far icier. She looked down.

An indistinct black shadow hovered over the spilled blood. It was as big as her spread arms, swirling and fluttering, giving an impression of a mass of dark wings beating. As she stared, horrified, it grew more solid, skimming the ground, an ever clearer form against the night. Dark glints like broken fragments of black glass glittered among its folds.

Maryn scrambled backwards. A specter! She'd never actually seen one before, but she'd been warned against them all her life. This one looked very much as Maryn had imagined from the descriptions, though she'd never realized how eerily quiet it would be. Only a faint rustle like wind among grass disturbed the night.

Another dark shape joined the first. Everywhere Maryn looked the night shifted and fluttered as more and more specters arrived, drawn out of the wild forest around them by the scent of spilled blood. A writhing layer of mist blanketed every spot where blood had slopped or spattered. The specters absorbed its power into their bodies, the insubstantial shadows of their wings becoming more real and threatening as they sucked up magical life. Several mobbed Maryn, beating around her drenched skirts. Already they were strong enough she felt the soft impacts of their wings buffeting and light scratches against her legs like the brush of a thorny branch.

Soon they would be solid enough to tear into her skin like razors, freeing her captive blood to feed their hunger. The bucket had contained enough blood to turn a whole flock of them solid. They would go ravening through the night, attacking any who might provide the blood they craved. The city walls would be no barrier to their flight. The slaughter would draw others of their kind to feed, and they would spread in uncontrollable nightmarish horror.

Maryn beat at the creatures, but her fists passed right through them. They felt like frozen slime mixed with shards of ice and glass. When she pulled her hands back her skin was scored with scratches. Not deep enough to bleed yet, but it was only a matter of moments. There was no time to choke out the many words of the cleansing spell or strip off her bloody skirts and run.

She had only one hope. Against this supernatural danger nothing mattered but that he was human and had power to defy the monsters.

Maryn scrambled on hands and knees toward the tree. "Help! Prince Carlich! Specters!"

Carlich woke with a start and rolled up to a crouch. Maryn got her feet under her and ran toward him. Barilan began to shriek, flailing against her back. Carlich took in the spilled blood and the flock of specters with one horrified glance. "Gallows, girl, what have you done?"

He leaped up and pushed past her. A few specters were strong enough now to go on the attack. Sensing a warm body pulsing with blood, they flocked toward him, dark glittering wings thrashing. The rustle of their wings was louder, but still far too muted for such large creatures, no more than the rattle of leaves in a soft breeze. Carlich drew his knife and slashed his arm. He raised his hands, shouted hoarsely, and waved with fierce urgency. Lightning flickered out, striking a specter and hurling it back. It screamed, thin and cold, almost too high-pitched to hear.

Carlich sent more bolts lashing around the

clearing. They damaged the specters they struck, tearing their substance into ragged fluttering tatters, but the creatures kept coming back, shrieking in their eerie piercing voices.

Carlich exhausted the first flow of blood, and beat at his arm to extract more. When it failed him, he cursed and slashed again, opening a wider, deeper gash across his other arm. The blood poured out, and he gathered its power and hurled it against the creatures.

Barilan was wailing. Maryn pulled him around from her back and gathered him in her arms. She huddled behind Carlich. The specters swirled around him, attacking from every direction. One of them came at her, and she beat at it with a clenched fist. This time the scratches it inflicted oozed red.

Carlich managed to shred several specters into small enough tatters that they abandoned the fight and fled into the forest. But a great many remained. Carlich fought his way forward, heedless of the wings that beat around his head and tore deep lacerations on his face, trying to reach the remains of the spilled bucket, over which a thick carpet of specters clustered, feeding.

More flew at Maryn. She pressed close to Carlich. He glanced back and sent a flash of lightning to blast away one hovering around her head. It shook off a shower of shadowy scraps and fled.

Carlich's wound was drying up. He bellowed in rage and slashed himself again. But he was growing pale, his gestures coming with greater effort. How much more blood could he lose, Maryn frantically wondered, before he passed out and left her helpless against the specters?

Carlich drew his lips back in a grimace and

prepared to sink the knife once more into his own flesh. Maryn thrust her arm in front of him. "Use mine!"

He spared her only a single glance before he ripped his knife through her sleeve and skin, opening a long, shallow gash up her arm. Maryn's head swam as the blood poured into his ready hands. Lightning crackled around them, sending specters spinning away on every side.

Twice more Carlich cut her as they fought their way to the rocks and the puddle of spilled blood. Carlich waded in among the feeding specters, ignoring the way their beating wings shredded the legs of his trousers and cut deep abrasions into his calves. Dropping to one knee in their midst, he put his hands down to the blood-soaked dirt. He barked a short incantation.

Blue fire erupted from the ground with a roar. Everywhere the blood had spread it leaped high into the night. Specters blasted upward, shattered into a million fragments. Maryn's bones rattled and her skull shook. She clamped her eyes shut against the fierce glare and hunched over Barilan until the blaze faded and she dared peek out again.

Black shreds of shadow floated down like icy rainfall. Stragglers raced screaming away into the forest, pursued by a few last bursts of power from Carlich's hands.

Carlich sank back to a crouch. He put both hands flat on the ground and dropped his forehead to his upraised knee. Maryn stood panting. Gradually Barilan's wails penetrated her daze, and she automatically positioned him to nurse. She felt too numb to do anything else, though his squirming body dug cruelly against the gashes in her forearms.

As Barilan fell silent, Carlich looked up. His face was pale, streaked with sweat and grime. He shook his head. "Gallows, girl," he whispered.

Then he staggered to his feet, grabbed Maryn's shoulders and shook her, yelling in her face. "By the black beak of the Vulture, do you realize what you could have done? There were enough specters there to devastate all Loempno! The last time an infestation took root it killed thousands before we were able to stop it! What were you thinking?" He slapped her face, a solid crack that sent Maryn's senses spinning, and raised his hand to strike her again.

But he mastered himself and dropped his arm, turning away. "I swear, if it weren't for Barilan I'd kill you right here and now. I should anyway. He'll make it until I find someone else. To pour out two whole bodies' worth of blood, in the middle of wild land… you might as well leave a battlefield uncleansed!"

"It was an accident, I swear!" Maryn shook, her vision a blur of tears. "I didn't mean to spill it!"

"What, you want me to believe you tripped over it in the dark?" Carlich looked pointedly from the sticky patch of residue at their feet to the distant spot under the tree where he'd left the bucket.

Maryn ducked her head over Barilan. "No. I…I meant to dump it in the river."

Carlich stared, uttered a muffled snort, and broke into jagged, crazed laughter. Maryn stared at him. He bent over and braced his hands on his thighs, struggling to get his breath. "In the river. Of course. Because you're not an idiot, just a Vulture-blasted nuisance. Why can't anything be simple and go as I plan? No, even the servants think they can defy me. Gallows, sometimes I wonder why I even bother trying…"

Maryn glared at Carlich. Even after everything that had happened, even after she'd drawn the specters and helped defeat them, he still didn't consider her either an ally or a threat, but only a nuisance, an annoying obstacle between him and his goals. She drew a deep breath. He was exhausted, and weak from loss of blood, and his attention was momentarily turned from her to his bitter musings.

Maryn sidled around Carlich and broke toward the riverbank and the boat. But she'd overestimated Carlich's incapacity. He caught up to her in a few quick strides and grabbed her arm with both hands, dragging her to a halt. To her horror, her grip on Barilan loosened, and he slid from her grasp. Barilan wailed and flung out his arms.

Carlich released her and grabbed his nephew before he struck the ground. Maryn darted toward the boat. She snatched the knife from her waistband and set herself with her back to the river, brandishing it.

Carlich halted when he saw the weapon, and stood holding Barilan. "Go on, then!" he shouted over the baby's cries. "You're more trouble than you're worth! I don't need you! Take the boat, go back, tell them all what happened. I don't care. I'll be far away before they can get here. Leave Barilan with me. He doesn't need you!"

Maryn's heart leaped at her sudden freedom, and the last trace of the compulsion spell responded to Carlich's words, urging her toward the river. But she hesitated. Barilan screamed and twisted in Carlich's grasp, reaching toward Maryn.

Maryn knew she should jump into the boat and go. Surely she could serve Barilan best by alerting Voerell to the direction Carlich had taken him. Carlich would be slowed and hampered by the need to care for the baby or seek out someone else to help him. Maybe an attempt to seize some other woman to nurse Barilan would lead to Carlich's capture. She should grab her chance now, for he'd never allow her another.

But she couldn't do it. Barilan's cries were like a physical force, dragging her back as strongly as Carlich's spell ever had. She couldn't leave him helpless in Carlich's power. Even if Carlich could not act directly to harm Barilan, would Froethych's dying magic prevent Carlich from neglecting the helpless babe? What was to stop him from simply laying Barilan down in some apparently safe spot and walking away? If Barilan died, the biggest obstacle between Carlich and the crown of Milecha would be gone.

She trembled, staring at Carlich. Barilan's sobs were weaker now, but he still stretched imploring arms toward her. Carlich turned his back contemptuously. "Come, Barilan. It's a long way to Ralo." Barilan renewed his shrieks, but Carlich only tightened his grip on the thrashing baby.

Maryn's numb fingers dropped the knife. She stumbled forward and dropped to her knees at Carlich's feet. "Please, my lord. Don't take him from me." She bowed her head, the words pouring forth. "I can't leave him. I can't bear to lose him, too. I'll stay with you, I won't try to escape again. He does need me, he'll starve without me. I won't trouble you any more, I swear, just let me hold him…" She ached to reach for Barilan, but she kept her hands clasped before her. She must show Carlich she was ready to submit to his will.

After a moment, she risked a look upward. Carlich stared down at her, a sneer on his lips. "Why should I believe you, girl? You've been nothing but constant trouble. Why shouldn't I just kill you now and be done with it?"

Maryn couldn't answer. She only ducked her head again and pressed closer to the ground.

The sound of Carlich's knife sliding from its sheath scraped across her ears. She flinched, and momentarily fought the urge to flee after all. But she didn't move.

Carlich gave a deep, gusty sigh. "Hold out your arm."

Without looking at him, Maryn complied.

The cut Carlich inflicted was slow and deep across her already wounded arm, as if he wished to cause pain as much as draw blood. She sank her teeth into her lower lip but didn't cry out. The magic crackled in her ears and buzzed in her jaw.

"Do nothing except what I expressly order you. As soon as you begin to feel the spell begin to weaken even slightly, inform me. I'll renew it every hour, if I must, if that's what it takes to keep you compliant. Now take Barilan and quiet him."

Maryn despaired in the moment before the familiar numbness settled over her thoughts. With these new restrictions, she'd never have another chance to flee. But even under the weight of the spell she knew, as she accepted Barilan into her arms and he clung to her, burying his head against her shoulder, that her choice had been the right one. He needed her, and she needed him.

He was so upset it took a long time to settle him, but at last she managed to persuade him to accept her breast. Carlich examined her bloody skirts and worked the cleansing ritual on the few spots the specters hadn't consumed.

When Barilan came off her breast, she stood motionless until Carlich ordered her to fasten her shift. After that he had to specifically tell her to change Barilan's diaper, and even to go into the trees to relieve herself. She lay down with Barilan in the spot he indicated. Carlich scrupulously warded the clearing, though his hands were shaking by the time he finished. He settled near her, and soon all three of them were asleep.

Thirteen

aryn woke to the pain of Carlich slicing into her arm. She opened her mouth to scream, but he snapped, "Be silent," and the magic forced her to swallow the sound, choking. The numbness that followed the renewed spell did nothing to dull the pain.

Misery and despair overwhelmed the tiny corner of her mind that remained hers even when the spell was strongest. She'd squandered her chance to escape, and now Carlich was on guard against her. There was no point anymore in resisting his control. She sank into a dreamlike daze, barely noticing when her body followed Carlich's orders to nurse Barilan, clear the camp, and follow him through the forest. At some point he placed bread and cheese in her hands, and she ate. She replaced her specter-torn garments with the fresh ones he threw at her feet. After that there was dirt road beneath her trudging feet.

A blast of blue lightning and buzz of power startled her back to awareness. Carlich jumped to grab the reins of a rearing horse as its rider slid lifeless from its back. He turned his sorcery against the rider's companion, and the man slumped across his horse's neck. The spell prevented Maryn from feeling anything but resignation at their deaths, though deep inside a tiny voice was screaming.

At Carlich's word she helped him drag the bodies into the trees beside the road. He lingered wistfully over the last body, fingering the soft skin at the throat, but in the end only cut a shallow gash and used the blood to restore his strength. He ordered Maryn to mount the more docile horse. She sat awkwardly astride, her skirts bunched up around her legs, Barilan in her arms. Carlich swung easily up on the other steed and directed him with expert skill, leading Maryn's mount.

He pressed their pace, forcing the horses to canter until they stumbled, dropping to a walk only as long as it took to keep the beasts from foundering. None of the other travelers on the road spared them more than a brief glance. The miles passed rapidly. Around noon they rode through a small town, and Maryn recognized the inn where she'd spent the night on her journey from Ralo to Loempno. Her stomach rumbled in response to the rich scent of roasting meat coming from its chimney, but Carlich didn't pause.

Perhaps the smell awoke his hunger, too, though. A few miles further on he halted the horses. Maryn looked up from where her head had drooped over the sleeping Barilan. She saw a raggedly dressed boy sitting leaned against a rock not far from the road, scratching the ears of a black and white spotted dog that sprawled at his side. Sheep dotted the rolling green meadow beyond him.

Carlich swung down from his mount and approached the boy. "Do you have any food?"

The boy jumped to his feet, round eyes taking in Carlich's stern features and the sword at his side. He gestured to a leather knapsack lying on the ground. "Just my lunch, sir."

"Good. Give it to me." Carlich gave a sharp nod and held out his hand.

"But sir, it's all I've got. And it's not fit for a lord like yourself." The boy cast a pleading glance at Maryn. His dog crouched, drew back its lips from sharp yellow teeth, and emitted a low snarl.

"Give it to me!" Carlich took a step forward and half drew his sword.

The boy scrambled back with the speed of one practiced in dodging blows. He gave a piercing whistle as he pelted away across the field. The dog barked at Carlich, a few high-pitched yips, before whirling to race after the boy.

The noise woke Barilan, and he wailed. Carlich stooped to pick up the knapsack and rummaged through it. Pulling out a loaf of coarse brown bread, he broke off a chunk and tossed it up to Maryn. "Eat. It's not much, but it will have to do."

Maryn caught the bread and obediently bit into it. Barilan's sobs grated in her ears. Didn't the baby's cries bother Carlich? They tugged at her gut and sent warm waves through her breasts, but she was powerless to respond. She watched Carlich cut slices from an onion to go with his share of the bread, wondering resentfully when he would deign to notice Barilan's distress and speak the words that would allow her to tend him.

Anger at Carlich flooded her. Maryn reveled in the unexpected rush of emotion. Before these last few days she'd never appreciated what a blessing it was just to be able to feel her own feelings, without a smothering blanket of sorcery numbing them. Carlich's spell over her must be weakening again.

No sooner had the thought stolen into her mind, than she blurted, "My lord, the magic you worked on me is beginning to lose its effect."

Carlich's lips stretched in a humorless grin. "It is, is it? Let's correct that."

Maryn hated the smug way he sauntered over to her horse, finishing up the last few bites of his bread. He was so pleased with himself for coming up with this clever twist on the compulsion spell which forced her to be her own jailer. The intensity of her emotions pushed against the weakening effects of the spell. She could clearly picture her foot lashing out to kick the face that looked up at her with such contempt as he drew his knife and held out his hand for her arm. She could imagine the crunch of her shoe smashing his nose, the scarlet of the blood that would pour out. Let him use that, if blood was what he wanted! She longed to act with an ache as sharp as his knife on her skin. But she couldn't move. His magic was still too strong.

The violence of her desire shocked her. Maryn ducked her head over her outstretched arm. She'd never hated anyone before, not like this. She'd never had cause to. Was she really a good person, as she'd always believed herself to be? Or was she as bad as Carlich, willing to hurt her enemies without qualm, if the circumstances demanded it?

She was starting to look like a sorcerer, she thought bitterly, as Carlich's knife cut yet another slice into her arm. If people were to glimpse the crisscrossing lines of healing knife wounds crusted with scabs that scored her forearms and wrists, they would think she was someone who knew how to access power. Someone to be feared, or at least respected. Not the helpless victim she was in truth.

If only she really could learn the spells that would let her turn her blood against Carlich. But such knowledge was not for serfs or servants. Even if she had a sorcerer's spellbook in her hands, she wouldn't be able to read it. The network of old pale scars on Carlich's hands mocked her pretensions as the blue crackles once again sent her into mindlessness.

They rode on, hour after hour, until as twilight neared they came in view of Ralo. Compared to the grandeur of the capital city the town's stone walls looked flimsy, the cluster of buildings within small and insignificant. But Maryn remembered how much the square towers and iron-banded gate had intimidated her the first time she'd seen them, when Edrich brought her here after their wedding. Ralo had seemed huge and crowded to a serf girl who'd never been farther from her father's farm than the village market. The spell had loosened its grip on Maryn's thoughts enough that her throat closed and she had to blink at the memory. Had that really been only the previous summer? Despite all the momentous events of the intervening year, the gate looked the same. She could see no evidence here of the fire that had destroyed so much of the town.

Carlich reined in his horse. The exhausted beast stood with its head hanging, blowing hard, while Carlich surveyed the scene before him.

"Subtle or bold?" he mused aloud. "We can't have beaten Voerell's messengers here. Perhaps it would be wisest to sneak in and talk to Vinhor privately first. But could we do that without getting caught?" He chewed on his lip. "Gallows, I'm sick of hiding and sneaking. I'll be declaring myself eventually; why not now? When have I ever feared the bold stroke?" For another long moment he considered, before setting his jaw and giving a decisive nod. "Very well."

He whirled on Maryn. "You will support me in every way. You will give no indication that you are anything other than freely and willingly cooperative. If questioned, you will corroborate every detail of my story. Tend Barilan as he needs it; speak no more than you must to appear unremarkable. Give me your arm; I'll renew the spell now. At the very earliest moment you feel it weakening, you will seek me out and inform me in some private manner so that I may restore it."

Maryn shifted Barilan into one arm and held out the other. Her emotions were such a turbulent mess, after seeing the place where she had experienced so much joy and grief, it was almost a relief when they subsided under the numbing magic. Once the spell was back in full force Carlich kicked at his weary beast until it stumbled into a heavy trot. Maryn's mount plodded behind.

Carlich rode down the very center of the road, clearly visible to the sentries that flanked both sides of Ralo's main gate. He stood in the stirrups and waved his hands over his head. The guards around the gate stiffened to alert attention, bringing their weapons up to bear on him. As word spread, more soldiers spilled from within the gates and ranged themselves in a defensive barrier.

As soon as he was close enough to be heard, Carlich began to shout. "Hail! Well met, comrades! I rode as hard as I could to get here and request your aid. Milecha is in danger! We are her only hope for salvation. Call Priest Vinhor and Captain Tennelan. I must speak with them!"

The troops around the gate showed signs of

confusion. Some looked questioningly around, seeking orders from their superiors, but others gripped their weapons tighter and glowered. As Carlich led Maryn close to the gate, a tall man in the uniform of an officer pushed through and stepped forward. "I'm in charge here. Halt, and state your business." He faltered, squinting up through the failing light at the mounted figure before him. "Prince Carlich?"

Carlich swung down from his horse and went to greet the officer, arms wide. "Mithoch! Thank the Holy One you're here! I know you'll stand with me and not believe my sister's lies!"

Mithoch hesitated. He jerked his head, and a number of his men came up to form a large circle that encompassed Carlich and the two horses. Drawn swords flashed in the last rays of the setting sun; spear points glittered. Maryn clutched Barilan and watched, unable to feel fear or hope or any other emotion but mild curiosity.

"I'm under orders to arrest you. Princess Voerell has taken control of the government as regent, and has named you an outlaw. She claims you murdered your brother Prince Marolan, and kidnapped her son, who now bears the Kingship." Mithoch's eyes went to Barilan in Maryn's arms, but he didn't make any move in their direction.

He returned his attention to Carlich. "I must follow my orders and take you into custody. But are you saying you dispute her accusations? I was loath to believe it of you, my prince, after you led us so nobly against Hampsia."

Carlich spread his hands. "Of course I wouldn't ask you to disobey your orders. I only seek to speak with Captain Tennelan and Priest Vinhor right away. I have much to tell them, and much to ask of all of you. I swear, what Voerell told you is a lie. She's the one who conspired with Marolan's treacherous Wonoran bride to murder our brother. If not for the spell that took Father's life, I'm sure she would have killed me, too." His voice trembled. Even though she knew the truth, Maryn found his sincerity convincing.

Mithoch looked troubled. He jerked his head, and two soldiers came up to station themselves on either side of Carlich. One looked at the sword and knife at Carlich's belt, and turned to Mithoch. "Should we disarm him and place a binding on him to prevent him working sorcery?"

In the deep part of her mind untouched by the spell's influence, Maryn felt a tiny surge of hope. If they did that, Carlich wouldn't be able to renew the spell when it wore off.

Mithoch stared into Carlich's eyes. He shook his head. "No. But be on the alert. Bring him, and the young king and his nurse as well."

Dull disappointment quenched the briefly kindled flame in Maryn's heart. Other soldiers came up and lifted her down from her mount. She clutched Barilan close, but no one tried to take him from her. She trailed behind Carlich as the soldiers led them toward the church.

They bypassed the sanctuary with its towering stained-glass windows and entered a door to a side wing of the building. Inside, everything was even more ornate and magnificent than in the church proper. Rich burgundy velvet hangings draped the walls, and gilded carvings glittered in the lamplight.

A messenger must have run ahead to warn Priest Vinhor, for he emerged from an inner room dressed in his full priestly vestments. Maryn recognized his lean, ascetic form, long narrow face, and thinning blond hair from the many times she'd seen him at the front of the Sanctuary leading the Sabbath services.

She looked at him closely, remembering Siwell's warning. The midwife had said Vinhor had killed a patient that might have been saved, in order to use her blood to call up the storm that ended the fire. To Maryn he appeared far too noble and pious to be responsible for such an act. The way his sharp gaze took in the waiting group promised that Carlich would not easily deceive him. Maybe Siwell had been mistaken, after all. Maryn found it hard to imagine that an official of the church could put his own ambition before the Holy One's law.

Vinhor hurried forward, his hands outstretched. "Prince Carlich! They tell me you bear portentous news."

Carlich dropped to his knees and bowed his head, then accepted Vinhor's offered hands and rose. "Indeed, your Grace. My heart is heavy with grief over what I must relate, but I trust your wisdom to guide me in the path of the Holy One's will."

Vinhor murmured solicitous words, and led Carlich to an upholstered chair before a wide, inviting hearth. He looked closely at Barilan, who reached toward the jeweled pendant on his chest, before gesturing for Maryn to take up a place standing behind Carlich's chair. He seated himself facing Carlich.

Just then there was a commotion at the door. A burly man wearing the uniform of a high officer in Milecha's army burst in and strode over to them. He had grizzled hair and a puckered scar across one cheek. "What is this?"

Carlich rose to his feet. "Captain Tennelan! How

glad I am to see you! You were ever my strong right arm in our campaign against the Hampsian invaders. If there's anyone I can trust to see the truth and support me in my efforts, it's you. Please, sit down. I was just about to explain everything."

Tennelan accepted Carlich's handclasp, but his brow furrowed and he turned to Vinhor. "Much as I hate to say it of one who always led us ably, this man is accused of committing murder and attempting to usurp the crown. He's implicated in the death of our king. The regent has ordered us to arrest him. Why are you granting him an audience?"

Vinhor waved a placating hand. "Prince Carlich deserves an opportunity to relate his version of events. I am told he brings very troubling accusations against the regent. It's only right we should hear him out before making a judgment in the matter."

Carlich spread his hands wide and gazed earnestly at Tennelan. "Captain, I understand your reluctance. I myself would find it impossible to believe the heinous acts my sister is guilty of if I hadn't seen her commit them with my own eyes. But I swear, when you hear what I have to tell you, you'll be as horrified as I am that she now holds power in Milecha. I know you'll be eager to help me set matters right."

Tennelan only looked more troubled, but he dragged forward a chair and dropped into it. He nodded to Carlich. "Go ahead. I'll listen to your tale."

Barilan whined and rooted against Maryn's shoulder. She stifled a groan as she moved him into position to nurse. She'd been holding him all day without even a moment to set him down, and he seemed to weigh at least twice as much as he had that morning. Her legs trembled. They felt warped out of their normal shape by the long hours of riding, and there were several spots she was sure were rubbed raw. The last thing she wanted was to stand here listening to Carlich's lies. But maybe his blandishments would win them soft beds for the night, at least.

Carlich sat down, but he remained perched on the edge of his seat, leaning intently forward. "My lord, your Grace, you will remember that my brother Marolan, may the Holy One shelter his soul"—He piously made the sign of the noose, and the other two followed suit, Tennelan perfunctorily, Vinhor with a great dramatic sweep—"was betrothed to Princess Dolia of Wonora, and their wedding was set for little more than a month hence."

Vinhor frowned. "I always had my doubts about that match. Though we share a long history of devotion to the Holy One, in recent years the Church in Wonora has come under the influence of highly suspect theology. Prelate Kiellan saw fit to overlook their potential heresies and certify the betrothal, but I wondered if that was a decision made after prayer and in accord with Holy guidance, or if it was unduly influenced by political considerations."

Carlich nodded earnestly. "I, too, had concerns about the marriage." He launched into a long account of his investigation of the marriage treaty, nearly identical to what Maryn had heard him tell Voerell. It had only been a few weeks since that dinner party, but it felt like a lifetime.

Maryn struggled against the spell, trying to think. Now that she knew Carlich so much better some of his assertions rang hollow to her. Was the treaty really that bad, or had Carlich exaggerated a small risk to justify a course of action designed to give him the power he craved?

Vinhor and Tennelan listened attentively. The priest seemed just as persuaded as Voerell had been, but Maryn noticed Tennelan's brow occasionally furrowing. Hope stirred under the spell's oppressive weight. Maybe he would see the truth.

"But Marolan wouldn't listen any more than Father would. He told me to drop the matter." The frustrated innocence in Carlich's voice when he spoke of his brother turned Maryn's stomach.

Tennelan frowned and narrowed his eyes. "What did you do?"

Carlich spread his hands in a gesture of helplessness. "What could I do? I approached Voerell. She and her husband Duke Whirter were more open. She promised to examine the treaty for herself, to see if what I alleged was true. If she agreed, she vowed to give me her support."

His face hardened. "But a few days later she told me that she'd read the treaty and found my worries baseless. I believe now that in fact she was already plotting to seize power for herself. Her son had just been born, and was scheduled to be confirmed as my father's heir, third in line for the throne. She manipulated Father to name her Barilan's regent. Less than an hour after the ceremony fixed those powers on her, events occurred which thrust her into the office. Does it seem likely to you this was mere coincidence?"

Vinhor's eyes narrowed, and his hand drifted up to toy with his chin. "Tell us of those events. We've heard the official account that Princess Voerell circulated, but I take it your version differs?"

"I don't know what she's saying, but I can tell you what I witnessed. The ceremony went off smoothly. Prelate Kiellan sealed Barilan's heirship and Voerell's

Regency with blood. We all sat down to the feast. The first I knew of any trouble was when Marolan began to choke. I rushed to his aid, but it was no use; I was unable to save him. I was shocked, distraught. The Royal Sorcerer Rogelan determined that Marolan had been poisoned, by blood transformed with magic. He worked a spell to reveal the murderer, and everyone present clearly saw Princess Dolia's face appear."

Tennelan nodded. "So far your account agrees with what the regent claims happened."

Barilan released Maryn's breast and whimpered. She shifted him to her shoulder and patted his back. She had to keep him quiet so she could hear what Carlich said. How could he possibly distort the story to make himself look innocent?

Carlich clasped his hands in his lap, twisting them together as he spoke. "Voerell began to shout. At first I was too dazed to register what she was saying. But then I realized she was accusing *me* of the murder! She'd concocted some tale that I'd obtained a sample of Dolia's blood and used it to kill Marolan. I tried to denounce her lies, but it was too late—she'd already convinced Father. Then she attacked me, and I defended myself. Father worked a spell to prevent us from harming each other. I truly believe that if he hadn't, Voerell would have killed me right there. But his magic escaped his control and killed him." Carlich bowed his head, to all appearances deeply stricken by grief.

Vinhor murmured a condolence. Carlich shook his head and held up a hand. Maybe his grief for his father was genuine, after all, Maryn thought. Froethych's death surely hadn't been part of his plan. Barilan rewarded her efforts with a burp, and she shifted him to nurse on the other side.

Tennelan looked away from Carlich, his voice gruff. "We felt when it happened. A wave of blue light washed over the town, all buzzing and crackling with the feel of sorcery. People were terrified. I had to send my men into the streets to prevent riots."

Vinhor nodded grimly. "Shortly thereafter I began receiving panicked pleas for aid from people affected by the strange new magic. Quarreling siblings frozen mid-strike, parents prevented from disciplining their children, that sort of thing. I'd just realized that a blood relationship was the common element in all their stories when your sister's message arrived and confirmed my suspicions."

Carlich sighed. "Father wasn't good enough at gestural magic to constrain his spell. But an incantation would have been too slow to stop Voerell." He clenched his fists. "Gallows, why did he take such a stupid risk?"

"Parents will do irrational things to protect their children." Vinhor patted Carlich's arm. "Thank the Holy One he succeeded in saving your life. Now, please, go on with your account."

Carlich rubbed his forehead. "I suppose you're right." He squared his shoulders and took a deep breath. "Voerell ordered the guards to apprehend me. Just then Barilan's nurse ran to me, begging for help. She said Voerell hated her son and would kill him if she could. I realized Father's spell would prevent Voerell from physically harming Barilan, at least for a while, but I could hardly leave my nephew in the hands of a murderess, could I? So I used sorcery to protect us. We escaped to the cellars, and out through a concealed passage I knew. Isn't that right?" Carlich turned and looked full at Maryn.

Both Priest Vinhor and Captain Tennelan focused

on Maryn, their eyes boring into her. She quailed beneath their stares. But Carlich's spell was still in strong effect, so though she could feel the desire to tell them the truth, she only nodded vigorously. "Yes, your Highness. Everything happened exactly as you described."

Carlich frowned at her for an instant. Maybe he was concerned that her response was too intense, and rang false. She seized on that idea, and tried to push beyond what the spell demanded of her, bobbing her head harder and faster. But neither Captain Tennelan nor Priest Vinhor appeared to notice anything odd about her performance. They both turned back to Carlich, dismissing her as no more than an inconsequential prop in his story.

Carlich shrugged, smoothly assuming again his persona of aggrieved innocence. "We fled, always managing to stay one step ahead of Voerell's pursuit. As soon as we escaped the city, I set my course here. I knew I'd find allies who would listen to the truth and help me restore the rightful ruler to the throne."

Vinhor raised an eyebrow at him. "You mean yourself?"

Carlich ducked his head. "Father disinherited me in the false belief that I murdered Marolan. Though I have no proof, I believe that Voerell actively conspired with Dolia to assassinate him, and therefore should have been the one stripped of her position in the succession. But that's irrelevant now. The Kingship passed to Barilan. I know of no way to transfer the magic to another while Barilan lives. Perhaps you do, Priest Vinhor; I'm sure you're far more versed in the intricacies of inheritance magic than I am. But if there's no way to correct the injustice, I'm content to act in my nephew's behalf. We can remove his mother's malign influence and appoint some more loyal regent in her place."

Tennelan rubbed his jaw, deeply troubled. "You're asking us to commit treason against our lawfully appointed regent by taking your side in this dispute."

Carlich looked shocked. "Not at all! I'm asking you to act against a traitor who has betrayed her family and country and seized power by murder and trickery. I ask only true loyalty to Milecha. Of course, I would warmly remember all who aided the cause of justice, when the crown is once again safely in honorable hands. King Barilan will need trustworthy men in positions of leadership." He turned to Vinhor. "I think it highly likely that Prelate Kiellan was a party to the conspiracy. It was he who sealed the Regency to Voerell. At the very least he allowed her to manipulate him. Milecha would be well served by the appointment of a stronger, more dedicated Prelate, who wouldn't be swayed from the Holy One's service by political concerns."

Vinhor nodded slowly, a look of satisfaction mixed with speculation spreading over his features. "I agree, Prince Carlich. I must say, I find your story most convincing. There were certain matters in the regent's account of events that raised questions in my mind. Questions which you have answered to my full satisfaction. I am tentatively willing to commit myself to your cause. Pending, of course, further investigation on my part into the truth of your statements."

Maryn's stomach lurched. It was true, then. Vinhor was going to accept Carlich's story and support him for his own selfish ends. Under the dampening effects of the spell she despaired. If even the Holy One's servants were corrupt, what was left she could depend on?

Carlich nodded. "Feel free to do whatever scrying you like. I have nothing to hide. But I doubt you will find other witnesses who will be willing to relate the true course of events. Any besides us who were present and near enough to discern what was happening in the confusion have undoubtedly been dealt with by Voerell already."

"I will keep that in mind." Vinhor turned to Tennelan. "What of you and your troops, Captain Tennelan? Without a military component, we will have little hope of overturning Voerell's coup and restoring the true government."

For a moment Tennelan looked torn, gazing back and forth between Vinhor and Carlich. Maryn silently urged him to defy them. Her own thoughts grew stronger every time she made the effort to force them into shape. The spell had weakened quickly this time. Only the fact that Carlich had ordered her to notify him privately kept her from saying so aloud.

Tennelan's face cleared. He rose from his chair and dropped to one knee before Carlich. "I am a simple man, my prince. I have no skill to unravel truth from lies, nor experience in the machinations of the powerful. But I have followed you on the field of battle, and you never led me astray. My sword is yours, and my loyalty, however you choose to direct me."

Carlich rose and placed both hands on Tennelan's head. "I accept the great honor of your service. Together we can save our homeland from the storms that beset it."

Vinhor, too, rose, and signed both of them with a gesture of blessing. "May the grace of the Holy One guide us in all things, and may he bless our endeavor and lead us to victory."

The words of the prayer fell like stones on Maryn's heart. They all believed Carlich. If the Holy One himself blessed Carlich's cause, his triumph was truly inevitable. Her one small voice crying warning would go unheard. His forces would march inexorably forward, and Maryn would be trampled beneath their feet.

Carlich bowed his head. For a moment all were silent. Then Carlich sank back into his seat, rubbing at his brow. "Forgive me. My journey has been long and wearying, and I have been forced to expend much blood along the way. If I might ask you for a place to rest, and accommodations for King Barilan and his nurse, as well…"

"Of course." Vinhor rose and went to the wall where a tasseled cord hung. He pulled it, and Maryn heard a distant chime. Within moments servants appeared, and at Vinhor's low-voiced directions hustled Carlich, Maryn and Barilan off.

Fourteen

The servants led Maryn and Carlich to the church's guesthouse. Maryn had often seen richly dressed people entering and leaving the long low building, but she'd never expected to go inside herself. The lavishly appointed rooms usually housed travelers of sufficient wealth to make generous donations to the Holy One in return for lodging, or of sufficient importance that Priest Vinhor wished to impress them and win their favor. Maryn supposed Carlich and Barilan fell into the latter category. She was just glad to see a wide bed with a deep feather mattress and velvet curtains, and a hearth where the servants kindled a cheerful fire.

Carlich hovered, inquiring whether she had all she needed for Barilan's care and comfort. Maryn felt the urge to tell him his spell was weakening, but as long as the servants were present it was not truly "private," and she could remain silent. Before Carlich could contrive a reason to send them all away that wouldn't seem suspicious, a messenger arrived inviting him to dine with Priest Vinhor in his private chambers. Carlich scowled at Maryn, but she ducked her head subserviently. Apparently concluding the magic remained strong enough, Carlich bid Barilan farewell and left.

Once Barilan was clean and dry, Maryn settled with him in a comfortable upholstered chair. It was such a relief to have a few quiet moments to focus on her charge. Amid the chaos and terror of the past few days there had been no chance for her to simply relax and cuddle him, let alone conduct any "playful interaction" sessions. Although looking back on their journey, Maryn considered it quite an accomplishment that she'd managed to keep him clean and warm and fed the whole time. Even Madam Semprell couldn't fault her for neglecting some of her less urgent duties.

Barilan didn't seem to have suffered for the lack. He always enjoyed the opportunity to see new places and people, if he could observe them from the secure refuge of Maryn's arms. He'd probably considered their whole ordeal a grand adventure.

Barilan gave Maryn a wide toothless grin as he stood in her lap, her hands supporting him under the arms. His feet pushed against her thighs, until abruptly his knees buckled and he sagged. She scrunched up her nose and stuck her tongue out at him, and was rewarded by a peal of laughter. For a while she continued to make faces, his delighted responses driving her to more and more extravagant silliness. When Barilan tired of that and looked away, Maryn laid him down in her lap and covered her face with her hands, peeping around to let him catch glimpses of her eyes. He stared in fascination each time she disappeared and reappeared, as if she were performing magic as wondrous as anything Carlich could conjure.

Barilan's happiness was so infectious that Maryn was able to lose herself for long moments in the pleasure of their games. She lifted him high over her head, his back arched and limbs extended as if he wanted to take flight, then lowered him to eye level and touched their noses together.

Only when the door opened and a servant entered, bearing a laden plate and full goblet, did reality return to the forefront of Maryn's thoughts. Nothing had changed; their situation was just as bleak and hopeless as before. Yet her heart was eased, and hope, irrational as it undoubtedly was, replaced her despair. Somehow she would find a way to save herself and Barilan from Carlich's schemes.

The plate bore a generous serving of roast duck and summer vegetables swathed in a rich sauce. Maryn devoured every bite, though her stomach protested the excess. As she finished, the servant girl returned with a delicate confection of flaky pastry layered with fruit and cream.

"Oh, no," Maryn protested, catching Barilan's hand to keep him from grabbing the plate the girl set before her. "Thank you, it looks delicious, but it's too much."

"We must feed you well, so that your milk may be rich and sweet to nourish our king." The servant gazed at Barilan in wonder. "To think I can say I've served the king! My friends will never believe it. You're so lucky to have the honor of nursing him. Everyone's talking about how brave Prince Carlich was to rescue him. Was it exciting, escaping?"

The girl was so eager to listen. Maryn ached to confess the whole truth to her, but the spell was still too strong. She could only shake her head ruefully. "Frightening. I was terrified the whole time."

The servant squeaked in delicious horror. "Did you really think the princess was going to kill you all?"

The spell bound Maryn's tongue. She pushed

against it with all her might, but it didn't yield. Maryn finally gave up. "I guess. Please, is there a garderobe I might use? I'm so tired."

The servant girl looked disappointed, but she nodded. "Come with me."

Maryn hoisted Barilan to her hip and followed the servant as she pushed through the door. Two guards stood outside. Seeing Maryn, one of them cleared his throat apologetically. "Excuse me, miss, but Captain Tennelan asks that you stay in your room. For your own safety and that of the king, of course."

"Of course," Maryn echoed. For a moment she'd almost forgotten she was still a prisoner. Carlich wasn't taking any chance she might escape.

The servant girl frowned, looking back and forth from the guard to Maryn. "But she just needs to use the garderobe. I'll bring her back in a moment."

"I'm sorry. We have our orders." Neither guard moved, but Maryn was sure they would be quick to stop her if she tried to pass.

"It's all right," she hastened to reassure the disgruntled servant. "I'll just use the chamberpot."

"It's under the bed. I'll come back later and empty it for you." She scowled at the guard, though whether it was for the disregard for Maryn or the increased workload, Maryn wasn't sure. "Don't worry. I'll see you have everything you need."

"Thank you." Maryn watched as she headed off. Neither guard would meet her eyes, instead staring straight ahead. Maryn retreated into her room and shut the door.

She made ready and climbed into bed, snuggling Barilan close. He nursed eagerly and soon fell asleep. But even tired as she was, Maryn's thoughts kept her awake for a long time. Her imagination spun a thousand strategies she might employ either to escape or to get word of Carlich's true guilt to someone who could make use of the knowledge. But each scenario came up short against the reality of the compulsion spell. It imprisoned her far more surely than all the guards Carlich could post. Unless she could find some way to defeat it, any attempt would be doomed to failure.

She woke with a start. The light coming through the diamond panes of the window was the pale grey of dawn. Barilan still slept; she crept from the bed without disturbing him. There was something she had to do; she felt the need as a dragging sensation in her gut. She couldn't think what could be so urgent, but she fumbled at the laces on her bodice in her haste to do them up, and kicked at her skirts in an outpouring of frustration when they twisted around her legs. She finally got them untangled and rushed to the door.

She jerked it open. Two guards stood at attention, different ones than the night before. Startled, they both turned to her.

"Please," she blurted. "I must speak to Prince Carlich. He ordered me to come to him right away." She panted, fighting to contain the desperate compulsion to push past the guards and go in search of Carlich. He'd told her she must seek him out as soon as she felt his spell begin to weaken.

She realized with a wild burst of hope that indeed, the spell was very weak. Over the hours while she slept its power had waned, until now she felt sure she could find a way to defy it. But before she could formulate a plan, one of the guards nodded at her. "I'm sorry, miss, we can't let you leave your room. I'll go tell his Highness you wish to speak to him."

If only she'd managed to figure out what was going on soon enough to hold her tongue! Now it was only a matter of minutes before Carlich arrived to renew the spell. The other guard remained at his station. What could she say to him quickly enough?

She tried hard to speak. She wanted to say, "Prince Carlich is lying. He murdered Prince Marolan, and tried to kill Princess Voerell. I saw him." But the spell was still too strong to allow her to be so direct. She searched her mind for words oblique enough to say despite the remnants of the spell that would still catch the guard's attention.

The guard peered at her. She must look odd, standing there struggling to speak. He was a pudgy young man with a round face and pale blue eyes framed by nearly invisible blond lashes. Something about him struck her as familiar. Surprised out of her train of thought, she looked more closely at him, trying to remember.

"I know you." It was easy enough now to speak, as long as it wasn't in direct defiance of Carlich. "Weren't you the one who escorted us when we went to...to my house, that burned." She swallowed, her thoughts shying away from the horror of that day. But the sympathetic young soldier had helped her, his compassion the one of the few spots of goodness in that miserable time. "The one who kept throwing up. Teor...Tioch..."

"Tior," he supplied. He shuddered, a look of dismay passing over his features. "I remember. You were the last one I took in, before I could finally get away from the bodies, and the ashes, and the stench... Oh, Holy One, you were the one with the baby." He turned away, pale, struggling to swallow.

"Yes." Maryn's voice shook, but she found she

could face the memory. Her current need overshadowed her past grief. "After that I went to Loempno, and was chosen to nurse Prince Barilan. That's why I'm here."

He turned back, face full of sympathy. "I'm so sorry you had to get caught up in this mess, after all you've been through."

Maryn shook her head, impatient. "That's not important right now. But please, can you help me? I need...I need..." Try as she might, however, she couldn't force any indictment of Carlich past her lips, even to this friendly listener.

"What is it? I'd be happy to get you whatever you want, after my watch is over. I'm sure the Captain won't mind. Is there someone I could tell you're here? Your family, maybe? Or that woman who was with you, I think she was your friend?"

Maryn seized on his suggestion. Siwell could help her. She knew about blood magic. Midwives were Healers, and healing was a branch of sorcery. Maybe she could find some way to free Maryn from Carlich's compulsion. "Yes! Please! Her name is Siwell Narila, she's a midwife. She lives in the north quarter of town. Tell her Maryn is here, I have to speak with her. But you can't let P—Pr—anyone know. Can you bring her to me secretly, sometime when you're on guard?"

Tior's brow creased. "I don't know. I mean, of course I'll tell her you're here and want to speak with her, but I don't think I can bring her here. That's against my orders; I'd get in big trouble."

"Please! You have to! You're the only one who can help me! It's important, you don't know—" Footsteps echoed down the corridor. Maryn jerked around to see the other guard lead Carlich around a corner and down the long hall toward her door. Her voice nearly froze, but her need was so urgent she overrode the spell's force. "They're coming! Don't let anyone know you spoke with me! Especially not the Pri—Prin—" She gave him one last, frightened look before ducking back inside her room and shoving the door closed.

She snatched Barilan from the bed and rushed over to the low dresser she'd set up as a place to change his diapers. He squalled in protest at the abrupt waking and kicked mightily, but she had the drenched cloth off him and a fresh one in position before the door opened.

Carlich strode in and murmured a brief word to the guards before shutting the door. She greeted him with a carefully formal nod as her hands stayed busy with Barilan's diaper. "Good morning, my lord. I sent for you as soon as I woke, because I felt your spell weakening."

"Well done," he said magnanimously. "We'll take care of that right away, as soon as you're finished. And you have my permission to call me 'your Highness' from now on."

"Yes, your Highness."

Maryn finished with Barilan's diaper and hoisted him to her hip. Her feet dragged as she approached Carlich. With great reluctance she extended the arm that hurt less. They were both swollen and tender, but none of the cuts had bled further, and they all seemed to be healing cleanly without festering. Still, she grimaced and suppressed a gasp when Carlich took her hand and pushed up the sleeve of her shift.

He frowned. "Someone's going to notice those if we're not careful. Here, I'll be nice to you and use my own blood today; I'm sufficiently recovered." Maryn blinked back tears of relief as Carlich set his knife to his arm and blood gushed forth. The spell was quickly accomplished, and she fell into the familiar dull thoughtlessness.

Carlich pulled his sleeve down. "Stay in your room today unless I summon you. The servants will bring you all you require. Don't speak with anyone beyond a few pleasantries if they should press you. Don't give anyone the slightest reason to suspect you're concealing anything. And remember to notify me when the spell weakens."

"Yes, your Highness." Maryn watched Carlich leave her room. The door swung shut behind him with a solid thunk. She sank into the soft chair by the fire, got Barilan started nursing, and stared at the cold grey ashes in the hearth.

Not long after, the servant girl bustled in bearing a steaming bowl. "I put extra honey in your porridge. Here, don't get up." She dragged a small table over and placed the bowl on it, in easy reach of Maryn's free hand. "There, now you don't need to wait until he's finished filling his belly to fill yours."

"Thank you." Maryn scooped a spoonful of porridge into her mouth.

"Is it to your liking?" The servant girl peered at her anxiously.

"Yes." Maryn struggled to get out a few more words. "It's very good."

The girl smiled, pleased, and perched on a chair facing Maryn. "I can't stay long; I've got to get on with my work. But they won't mind if I keep you company for a few minutes. Now that you're rested, I bet you're just bursting to tell someone about everything that's happened to you."

Indeed, Maryn longed to pour out her heart to the girl, even if she was just trolling for gossip. But the spell forced her to respond with only a noncommittal grunt. She turned away from the puzzled, hurt look in the girl's eyes and shoveled a few more bites of porridge into her mouth.

"I mean, I'd love to hear how you got out of the palace. Are there really secret passages all under the city? I promise, I won't tell anybody if there are."

Maryn shrugged. She ducked her head over Barilan.

"And Prince Carlich is so handsome. I know I wouldn't mind getting lost in the woods with him. Did he ever, you know…" The girl gave a suggestive little wiggle of her shoulder.

Maryn blushed. "No."

"Really, I promise you can trust me. I'd never repeat anything. We servants have to stick together, you know."

Much as she wanted to respond, the spell forced Maryn to look away. "Please go away. I'd like to be alone."

The girl drew back as if Maryn had struck her. "Well! I guess the king's nurse is too important to talk to a mere chambermaid. Don't worry. I won't bother you any more." She snatched up the half-eaten bowl of porridge and flounced from the room.

Maryn closed her eyes against the tears that welled up. She hated the way Carlich's command forced her to treat the girl so rudely. She'd probably lost the chance to befriend one of the few people who might be able to help her. Carlich was isolating her, cutting her off from any contact with others. She was sure he'd keep it up until it was too late for anything she said or did to stop him from claiming the crown.

The morning dragged by. Maryn sang to Barilan, and let him grab at her fingers and hair. She put him down on the floor so he could roll around. She changed his diaper again. She tried to interest him in nursing, but he would have none of it, so she just held him until at length hunger or boredom led him to accept her breast again. A different servant brought her lunch; Maryn didn't speak to him. After he was gone she picked at the food.

Midway through the afternoon, just as she was beginning to feel the spell weaken, Carlich swept into the room. He was cheerful and expansive as he renewed it. "It's been a busy morning. We've sent messengers to all corners of Milecha, calling for people to join us. I have high expectations in that regard. There are a number of divisions of the army who've served with me scattered around the kingdom. Nearly all of them will take our part, I'm sure. Even for the ones who don't know me, the idea of following a woman's orders will rankle. And I have many friends among the lords and nobles. Far more than Voerell, certainly. There are at least a half dozen she rejected when they sought her hand; they'll all rush to my side." He looked Maryn over from head to toe, and nodded, satisfied. "Bring Barilan and come with me. Vinhor asked to examine him."

When they arrived at Vinhor's private office, the priest rose from behind his desk and came to greet them. "Ah, Carlich, the young king is looking well. Have all his accommodations been satisfactory?"

"Oh, yes, just fine." Carlich ran a hand along Barilan's cheek. The baby grabbed at his fingers, and Carlich let him seize them. "You said you could check to see if the Kingship indeed passed to him?"

"Yes, I'll be glad to. Though there's little doubt it did, if the heirship ceremony was completed before Froethych's death. Still, let me take a look." Vinhor brought out a little gold knife and pricked his finger.

He held his hand poised, a single drop of blood balanced on his fingertip, and reached his other arm toward Maryn. "Give the king to me, girl."

"Yes, your Grace." Maryn reluctantly settled Barilan into the crook of Vinhor's elbow. Barilan screwed up his face into a wail and kicked his feet, but Vinhor gripped him firmly and ignored his protests. The priest smudged the blood from his finger on Barilan's forehead, and murmured a long elegant series of incantations. The blood fizzed and sparked.

A soft glow spread from the blood to encompass Barilan's body. He calmed and stared at the light. Slowly the form of Milecha's crown solidified from the misty glow over his shock of hair.

Vinhor nodded, and intoned the syllables that brought the ritual to its conclusion. The last traces of blood on Barilan's forehead flared and vanished. "Yes, it's quite clear. The full powers of the Kingship reside in him. And we must assume that the ceremony was equally successful in establishing the Regency, so his mother will have access to what she needs to defend against our efforts."

Carlich scowled at Barilan. Now the light was gone the baby started to fuss again, and Vinhor passed him back to Maryn. She shifted him to her shoulder and patted his back. Carlich kept his eyes fixed on Barilan until, deep beneath the power of the spell that compelled her, Maryn felt a stirring of apprehension.

Carlich turned to Vinhor. His face paled a bit, and he seemed to speak with effort. "You said there might be some way around this difficulty. That it might be possible to free the Kingship from Barilan. Even vest it in me, as it should be."

Vinhor frowned and drew his brows together. "I did mention that something of the sort might be possible. Though it's not a venture to be lightly undertaken. We are speaking of great mysteries, subjects hidden from all but the most devout students of Holy Scriptures. The secrets concealed within their pages are not for common knowledge. Nor even royalty, but only for those most dedicated to sacred study."

Carlich gave a deferential inclination of his head, his words coming a bit easier. "Surely your Grace is among those to whom all such arcane truth is made plain."

Vinhor smiled a little. Maryn was sure the priest was perfectly aware Carlich was only flattering him, but took pleasure from it anyway. "Perhaps. I do at least know a bit beyond what is commonly available."

"How, then, can we approach this problem?" Carlich leaned forward, intent.

Vinhor sat down behind his desk and motioned for Carlich to take a place in one of the chairs facing it. Neither of them looked at Maryn, so she remained standing, doing her best to quell Barilan's intermittent whimpers before they progressed into full-fledged crying. He probably wanted to nurse again, but she'd rather wait until they returned to their room and she could relax. Now Vinhor had established Barilan was indeed the king, they shouldn't need him for anything else. Hopefully she'd soon be dismissed.

Vinhor leaned back in his chair and steepled his fingers. "What you must understand, your Highness, is that the powers of the Kingship take up residence, not in the body, but in the soul. Are you familiar with the theological truths underlying blood sorcery?"

"Very little, I'm afraid. My studies have focused on practical applications. Please, enlighten me."

Vinhor nodded, and took on a lecturing tone. "Blood is the connection that binds soul and body. Its power comes from the soul; thus human blood is potent, while that of animals is not. The soul inhabits the body, rooted in the blood. When blood is drawn, some of those roots break away and become available for use. And at death, when the soul separates from the body and departs for the courts of the Holy One, it leaves its roots behind in the blood that remains."

"I've heard of such concepts, but never phrased in quite that way." Carlich glanced at Barilan. "Go on, tell me more."

"As your Highness commands." Vinhor lowered his voice until Maryn had to strain to hear. "It is not impossible for the soul to depart the body, and yet the body live on. Cases of such have been recorded. Sometimes it occurs naturally, following some grave injury, particularly to the head. In such instances, the subject can no longer think or speak, or move of his own volition, or respond in any way to what is around him, yet can take food and drink if tended carefully enough, and may live for months or even years in that state."

Carlich frowned. "That wouldn't serve, even if we could bring about such a condition. I need Barilan alive and healthy if I'm to use him to bargain with Voerell. And I must be seen as his protector. I'd lose half my support if it were known he'd come to harm while in my care."

Maryn's face went cold, and she swallowed. Her arms tightened around Barilan, causing him to squirm in protest. She forced her grip to loosen and he calmed, but her legs felt so weak she feared they might refuse to support her. Did Carlich mean he would consider doing that to Barilan?

"No, of course not. But hear me out. Certain sorcerers by magic have induced something similar. A soul can be compelled to depart a living body, if the proper incantations or gestures are employed. It's not a terribly difficult spell to accomplish. Far more delicate is the reverse operation, to call some other soul into the body left unoccupied."

Carlich drew in his breath sharply. "Then such a thing is possible? I'd heard rumors, but I dismissed them as mere superstition."

Trembling, Maryn crept closer, desperate to hear. Though she didn't know what good it would do. If they decided to work some nefarious sorcery on Barilan, she'd be powerless to protect him.

"Oh, no, it's quite real. There are a number of cases well documented in the church's records. We don't share those records often, of course."

"I see." Carlich swallowed. "How is it done?"

"It's a spell like any other, though longer and more complicated than most. Once the body is divested of its native soul, the soul of one recently deceased is enticed to depart the courts of the Holy One and enter the vacant body. As you might imagine, such souls are most reluctant to leave Paradise, yet under certain circumstances they can be persuaded. If they're close kin to the body it's easier, and if they have some pressing desire to return, perhaps to complete unfinished business, or to be with one dear to them."

Carlich nodded slowly. He took a deep breath, and dropped his voice even lower. It seemed a great struggle for him to force the words out. "So if we were to perform this magic on Barilan..."

Vinhor didn't appear in the least shocked, or even

surprised, at the suggestion. "When his soul departed, and flew in joy to the courts of the Holy One, the Kingship would be released. His soul is so young and unformed that no one would mark the difference if it were replaced by another. Preferably one also young and unformed, of a child who died at a similar age. Barilan's body would remain unharmed, and his soul also, in the Holy One's care. But the Kingship would have nowhere to come to rest, since King Froethych sealed no further heirs, and none have ever been sealed to Barilan."

"Could you make me Barilan's heir?" Carlich turned to look speculatively at the baby in Maryn's arms. Maryn forced her expression to remain blank, but she needn't have bothered; Carlich's eyes remained fixed on Barilan.

"I'm afraid, your Highness, that only the one who holds the office of Prelate has the power to seal heirs to the Kingship." Carlich turned back and opened his mouth, but Vinhor held up a hand to silence him. "And only the one who wields the power of the Kingship—at the moment, the regent—can appoint a new Prelate. No, I'm afraid it won't be so easy."

Carlich scowled. "So what would happen? Would the Kingship be lost?"

Vinhor shook his head. "It would be as it was after the passing of King Ettellan and all his heirs during the plague. The Kingship was freed, and became available for your ancestor King Fridollan to take up when the people acclaimed him their leader. In a similar fashion, we could work the spell which would invest it in your soul, correcting your father's error in disinheriting you."

Maryn thought longingly of the door, but the compulsion spell was much too fresh to allow her to even edge in that direction. Even if she were free to run, she'd never get far. Barilan was utterly vulnerable to Vinhor's plan. She'd probably have to watch while they performed the spell.

Carlich breathed hard, in contrast to Vinhor, who remained tranquil. "You're sure this would violate no holy laws?"

Vinhor shifted in his chair and cleared his throat. "That has been a matter of debate for many centuries. Some scholars hold that the spell which frees the soul is equivalent to killing, and subject to all the strictures which bind when such an act is justified, as in war or execution or self-defense, and when it is forbidden as murder. While others hold that as long as the body remains unharmed, no such strictures apply. In my studies I've found no evidence to suggest that the Holy One ever forbade such magic. In fact, one interpretation of the story of the healing of the Basilan demoniac is that He employed just such a spell. It depends on how one translates a certain word in the original...but I see that I've lost you. In any case, although I believe the Holy One would look with favor on this action, I cannot guarantee it. Perhaps it might be safer to entrust the task to another, so that any potential Holy censure would fall on them."

Beads of sweat stood out on Carlich's forehead. "Yes, I think that would be best," he gasped. "I will not do it myself." Immediately he seemed to feel relief, for his panting eased. He wiped his brow. "I think my father's spell must interpret the spell as harm to Barilan, for I can barely manage to speak of the possibility. But another, with no blood ties..." He struggled again, then gave up. "I trust you to take care of the matter as you see fit, your Grace."

Vinhor looked taken aback. "I, your Highness?

Though the risk is slight, I am afraid I cannot take even the smallest chance of sullying my hands with a morally questionable act. But we can have another carry out the task for us. It need not be a sorcerer; anyone could perform the magic with sufficient instruction. I'm sure someone can be found whose loyalty to your Highness is unquestionable."

Carlich looked doubtful. He turned again to Barilan, studying the baby with a troubled frown. Barilan was busy trying to pull a strand of Maryn's hair free of her braids, oblivious to his danger. Carlich focused on Maryn's face. She stiffened at the sudden wild look of speculation that dawned in his eyes.

Carlich rose convulsively to his feet and came to stand before Maryn, staring at her all the time with disconcerting intensity. "You. You had a child, before you came to the Palace. He died. Isn't that what you told me?"

The words forced themselves from Maryn's numb throat. "Yes, your Highness. My son Frilan died in the fire here in Ralo, just before Barilan was born."

"How old was he?" The light in Carlich's eyes was frightening.

"Six weeks, your Highness."

"And Barilan is three months old." He whirled on Vinhor. "That's close enough, surely?"

"I would think so, your Highness."

Carlich turned back to Maryn and took her by the shoulders. He looked directly into her eyes. "Tell me, Maryn, would you like to have your son back? Your own baby's soul, returned to you from the Holy One's courts? Would you like to hold him again, cuddle him to your breast, nurse him?"

It was the thing she had wanted most in all the world since the moment she realized Frilan was lost.

Her heart had not for one minute ceased begging the Holy One to grant her such a miracle. She had grudgingly come to accept how impossible it was, yet some deeply buried corner of her being had never completely given up hope.

No compulsion tore the cry from Maryn's heart, only her own desire. "Yes!"

"What are you willing to do to make that happen?"

Maryn panted. She clutched Barilan protectively close, though she knew she herself was now the greatest threat he faced. She closed her eyes, her voice no more than a whisper. "Anything."

Fifteen

Vinhor looked back and forth from Maryn to Carlich. "Yes, I think she might serve very well. It should be easy for her to call her son's soul back; he'll be eager to come to her and take up the life that was cut short. No one besides the three of us need ever know. And she's not blood-kin to Barilan, so your father's spell won't apply."

Maryn dared not consider what she'd consented to do. Frilan! She must think only of Frilan. This time she wouldn't fail him as she had that awful morning. She would snatch him from death's grasp, no matter what it cost. If she fixed her eyes on Carlich she didn't have to see Barilan looking up at her. The baby's warm body melting against hers, secure in perfect trust, was harder to ignore.

"Yes." Carlich nodded sharply, though he struggled against King Froethych's spell again with his next words. "If you would instruct her in all she needs to know, your Grace, and make sure..." He wheezed to a stop, choking.

"I'll be glad to, your Highness. Rest assured I will leave nothing to chance." Vinhor cocked his head, appearing concerned at Carlich's continued distress. "Perhaps you should absent yourself for the actual enactment of the spell. I'll notify you when it's done."

Carlich nodded wordlessly, and stumbled for the exit. At the threshold, he turned back. Looking straight at Maryn, he forced out between his teeth, "Do whatever he tells you." Then he staggered through the door. It slammed shut behind him.

Vinhor gazed after him for a moment before shaking his head and turning his attention to Maryn. "Come, child, sit down. You're performing a very great service for Prince Carlich and me. Be assured we won't forget it."

"Yes, your Grace," Maryn whispered. She stepped tentatively forward and sank into the chair Carlich had vacated, perching nervously on the edge. Barilan squirmed. She pulled loose the tie of her shift and offered her breast. Luckily, he was willing to nurse. He might fall asleep if she could keep him still long enough.

Vinhor waited until they were both settled. When Maryn looked up at him, he leaned forward, resting his elbows on his desk and interlacing his fingers. "Tell me child, how much do you know of sorcery?"

"Very little, sir," she mumbled. "Only what everyone is taught, how to release power from accidentally shed blood."

Vinhor pursed his lips, but kept his voice gentle. "Then you know the prayer of invocation to the Holy One?"

"Yes, sir."

"The spell I'm going to teach you begins the same way. Let me hear you say it."

Maryn recited the syllables of the ancient tongue. Vinhor winced once or twice. When she finished he went back over the words with her, correcting her pronunciation in several places.

Satisfied at last, he sat back, frowning thoughtfully

at her. "The rest of the spell could be accomplished by incantation also, but it would be very complicated, and it might take days for you to memorize the lengthy stanzas required. I take it you don't read? No, of course not." He sighed. "Let's try something different. Here, can you get one hand free? Good. Do this." He made a graceful gesture with his hand, touching his thumb and forefinger together in a circle and scooping the air with his other fingers spread wide. Maryn copied it as best she could.

"Very good. Yes, this will be much easier. That's the motion which begins all gestural spells. It captures the magic inherent in the blood you'll be using and gathers it ready to be shaped by your will. Gestural magic isn't as exacting as incantational magic. With incantations, the words of the sacred language control the form the power takes. If any words go awry, the only risk is that the spell won't work at all. It's almost impossible for the magic to escape control.

"With gestural magic, it's different. Your will controls the magic. Certain gestures are customarily used, but they're much more fluid; someone with a strong enough will can use almost any motion to direct the spell. As long as you keep your purpose firmly in mind there's little chance your spell will fail completely. But it can easily overwhelm your control, especially if your knowledge of the time-tested gestures is weak, or the amount of blood you're attempting to control is great. Uncontrolled sorcery produces powerful and unpredictable effects, and frequently kills the wielder. That shouldn't be a danger here, however. I'll drill you in the gestures you must use, and the spell will only require a small amount of blood."

So that was what had happened to King Froethych. Maryn shuddered, remembering the eerie way his hands had moved involuntarily, gushing blood, sweeping into ever more extravagant gestures. The thought of falling victim to such wild magic terrified her. She would have much preferred to spend whatever time was necessary to learn the safer method. But the priest had decided, and Carlich's parting order bound her to obey him.

Vinhor proceeded to instruct her in a complex series of gestures. Maryn paid close attention, sweeping her hand through the fluid motions in imitation. As soon as Barilan fell asleep she detached him from her breast and eased him into her lap so she could have both hands free. Vinhor ran her through the series of gestures over and over again, first the sequence that would sever Barilan's soul from his body, then the longer, more intricate sequence that would call Frilan's soul to take its place. Maryn didn't let herself think too deeply about what the motions meant, as her hands darted above Barilan's slumbering form. She only focused on learning as quickly and well as she could.

At last Vinhor sat back. "One more time through the whole set." He watched closely, making no comment, only sitting in silent judgment until Maryn's palms grew sweaty and her mouth dry. But she didn't falter, moving her hands in the graceful dance of the spell.

When she finished, Vinhor nodded slowly. "That should do. You're a surprisingly apt pupil, for a servant and a woman." He rose and came around his desk to stand beside her chair and look down at the sleeping baby in her lap. "Best to do it now, while your memory is fresh."

He drew the little gold knife from its sheath on his belt and laid it on the edge of the desk in front of her. "I shall step out. You may have as long as you need."

He moved toward the door, then paused. "I want you to understand something very clearly. Once this work is done, you must forget all I've taught you. You must never again draw blood to use for magic, nor make use of any blood you might encounter for that purpose. I forbid it, in the name of the Holy One. Do you understand?"

"Yes, your Grace," Maryn whispered. Carlich's spell gave Vinhor's words the force of magical compulsion.

"Very good. Be about your work. Perform the spells, just as I taught you. Restore your son to life. Once you're done, open the door and call, and Prince Carlich and I will return." Vinhor passed over the threshold, easing the heavy wooden door closed behind him.

Maryn was alone with Barilan and the knife. The baby nestled in the valley where her thighs met, relaxed and vulnerable. One arm draped across her knees above his head, and his breath came in little sighs. The heat of his body soaked through her skirts into her legs.

She must not think. If she stopped to think, she knew she wouldn't be able to go through with it. Barilan trusted her, and she was about to betray him. No matter what sophistry Vinhor might weave to justify the act, a voice buried deep in Maryn's heart whispered that it was profoundly wrong to send Barilan's soul off to the Holy One's courts long before its appointed time.

She refused to listen, letting longing swell up to smother all reservations. She *wanted* to work the spell that would bring Frilan back to her. Wanted it so intensely her hands shook and her breath shuddered and she felt as if she would die if she didn't immediately snatch up the knife and jab it into her flesh.

Memories of Frilan overwhelmed her, filling all her senses. His soft dark fuzz tickling her stroking palm. His strident cry waking her from slumber. The milky, musky smell of the top of his head. His warm wet mouth questing for her breast, and the slow, rhythmic sucks when he found it and her milk answered his demands.

She almost reached for the knife, but a splinter of doubt pricked her, and she hesitated. Was she longing for Frilan's soul, or only his body? She wasn't going to get those physical things back. The spell promised something else, something she couldn't touch or taste or smell.

Vinhor thought that no one would be able tell the difference when Frilan's soul replaced Barilan's. That since babies hadn't yet developed the ability to speak or understand or remember, their souls could be freely interchanged without making any real difference. Maryn knew he had to be wrong, but for a moment she couldn't quite articulate why. Would even she, who knew them both better than anyone else, be able recognize Frilan's soul if it lived in Barilan's body?

Yes, she would. The more she thought about it, the more certain she became. Frilan had been so different from Barilan, in ways that had nothing to do with the way they looked or sounded or felt. Frilan had always been easy-going, while Barilan was needy and clingy. Frilan had been happy to go three or four hours between nursings, while Barilan grew restless after no more than two. Barilan had his little way of looking sideways at her, while Frilan had never met her eyes anything but straight on. Frilan had relaxed content in his bath water, even when she poured it over his head to rinse his hair, while Barilan began to scream as soon as wetness touched his skin. Frilan had kicked and protested when she changed his diaper, while Barilan usually lay passive. Barilan was reluctant to spend more than a few minutes in anyone else's arms but hers, even his father's or mother's, while Frilan had scarcely noticed who held him unless he was hungry or sleepy. A thousand little differences, most too small or subtle for her to define and catalogue, but instantly recognizable to her mother's perceptions, that made each of them the unique individual she knew.

Maybe no one else would recognize a change when Frilan's soul came to inhabit Barilan's body, but Maryn would. She was sure of it. She would know her own child's soul, even if a thousand lifetimes separated them, not just the handful of months since Frilan had died.

Her throat grew thick and choked, and her eyes blurred with tears. She could hold Frilan again. She could look into his eyes and see him looking back at her. She could laugh with him and sing to him and whisper to him of her love. Edrich might be lost to her forever, but Frilan wasn't, not anymore. All she had to do was take up the offered knife, and prick her finger to draw forth a little blood, and wave her hands just so...

She ached to reach for the knife, and she felt the pressure of the compulsion spell shoving her hand forward, but something in her still resisted. She interlaced her shaking fingers and stared at them, and past them to where Barilan peacefully sprawled in her lap.

She loved Barilan, too. Not with the intense, overwhelming passion she felt for Frilan, but with a gentle, stubborn affection that had grown almost unnoticed over the months she'd cared for him. He wasn't her blood, but he mattered to her.

Fate had sent Frilan's soul from the world; surely it wasn't right that her action should banish Barilan's. King Froethych's magic obviously considered the spell to be harm to Barilan; Prince Carlich had been restrained by its effects from even talking about it. What other evidence did she need as to how the act would be judged by the Holy One? If they'd told her that in order to get Frilan back she'd have to cut out Barilan's heart, would she do it?

Maryn recoiled from the thought, but at the same time she knew she wouldn't reject the idea completely. So deep was her desire for her lost child, even that prospect would tempt her, however briefly. What they asked of her was so much less, so much easier. Barilan would suffer no discomfort. He would wake to the infinite pleasures of the Holy One's courts, like the blessed souls depicted in the most beautiful of the church's stained glass windows. Their faces shone with radiant joy as they feasted in the midst of ever-blooming flowers.

And Frilan would be in her arms again.

She watched as her fingers loosened and slid apart. Carlich's spell gave Vinhor's words inexorable power, animating her limbs without any volition of her own. *Perform the spells, just as I taught you.* It wasn't her fault she was too weak to resist his magic. It must still be strong enough to force her to comply.

Her left hand turned palm up, ready to receive the

edge of the blade. Her right hand hovered, clenching and unclenching. Beyond it, Barilan slumbered, cheeks flushed a soft pink, chest lifting and falling. Maryn closed her eyes so she wouldn't have to see him.

Instead, she pictured Frilan lying in Edrich's arms. Images that had lurked in the back of her mind ever since that day, horrible pictures she'd never dared fully consider, surged to vivid life in her imagination. She saw flames creeping in around the sleeping baby, licking up from the straw of the mattress to engulf him. Smoke invaded delicate nostrils and slid between bow-shaped lips. Heat shimmered, oven-bright. Tender flesh roasted. Skin blackened and split and peeled away from bones that gleamed white for an instant before they, too, burned. Maryn tasted vomit, burning in the back of her throat. Lidless eyes stared at her, lipless mouth gaping in a piercing scream that echoed, redoubled, from every deepest crevice of her heart.

Restore your son to life.

She had the power to stop the screams. She could quench the fire, as if it had never burned. She could give Frilan a new body, whole and unblemished and free from pain.

Maryn opened her eyes and stared at the knife where it lay on the edge of the desk.

Frilan. Alive. Nothing else mattered.

Maryn grabbed the knife and slashed her palm with a strangled gasp. She raced through the incantation to the Holy One, spitting out the syllables. Dropping the knife, she raised her bloody palm, touched her thumb to her forefinger, and made the scooping gesture Vinhor had taught her.

The blood in her hand crackled into life, blue

sparks spitting and fizzing. Her bones reverberated with the buzzing, much sharper and more intense than cleansing had ever evoked. She forced herself to face, unflinching, the full truth of what she wanted. She willed the magic to sever Barilan's soul from his body, leaving an empty vessel ready for Frilan's soul to fill.

Her hands shaped the necessary gestures. With the final motion, lightning burst from her palm and plunged toward the child in her lap.

An invisible shield blocked the sorcery. Fire splattered harmlessly in all directions and faded. Barilan slept on, undisturbed.

Maryn gaped, uncomprehending. Only slowly did she grasp what had happened. She let her hands drop. The sparks gradually subsided. Not all her shed blood had been consumed by the spell; a drop fell from her hand to the floor.

She'd failed. The spell hadn't worked. Barilan's soul still stubbornly occupied his body. Frilan remained lost. His screams still echoed in her heart, just as they had ever since he died.

She groped for the fallen knife. She must have erred somehow in her gestures. She'd perform the spell again, correctly this time. It would work. It had to.

Her motion disturbed Barilan, and his face screwed up, mouth opening in a wail. The sound was thin and petulant, far different from the agonized screams of her imagination. But she caught her breath, staring at him. Her breasts responded to his cries with a familiar tingling rush. Dizziness swept over her, and confusion, thoughts and feelings tumbling chaotically as Barilan's cries beat on her ears.

Maryn pressed her hand to her mouth, shutting in an answering cry. Dear Holy One, what had she done? She'd nearly *killed* him. If her spell had succeeded, there would be two voices screaming in her heart now, not one.

She snatched Barilan up and pressed him to her chest, burying her face in his hair. She shook as waves of emotion washed over her, tossing her back and forth. "I'm sorry, I'm sorry..." She was, and yet...It wasn't fair. She was supposed to be holding Frilan now. A part of her hated the baby in her arms for not being her son.

But as Barilan squirmed, complaining stridently about the tightness of her grip, horror at what she'd almost done rushed back. She loosened her grip and eased him down to sit in her lap. She reached out to stroke his hair, tears blurring her eyes. "I wouldn't have—" She couldn't complete the lie. "I shouldn't have—"

His face cleared, and he grabbed her hand, pulling it to his mouth. He gummed her finger vigorously, cheerful again, momentary displeasure forgotten. His bright eyes sought Maryn's.

She met them, swallowing, her stomach cold and hollow. If the spell had worked, how would it have felt to look into those eyes and know Barilan's soul was no longer behind them? Could even the joy of meeting Frilan's gaze have countered the horror of knowing that she had put out the light of Barilan's eyes forever?

She stared at Barilan until he looked away. The sickening truth crept over her until she could deny it no longer. It wouldn't have. The spell's failure had saved her from doing something terrible, something she would have regretted for the rest of her life. No matter how much she longed for Frilan, it had been wrong, horribly wrong, to try to sacrifice Barilan in order to bring him back.

Again she wrapped her arms around Barilan and buried her face in his hair. For a while all she could do was shake.

At length she took a deep, shuddering breath and resettled Barilan in her lap. She tried to think what she must do next. Carlich and Vinhor would wonder why it was taking her so long if she didn't call them soon. She'd have to admit she'd proven incompetent after all and failed to work the spell correctly.

Maryn frowned. She was nearly certain she'd made all the gestures just as Vinhor had taught her. And the magic had responded. Though she could hardly bear to think of that moment, she clearly remembered the blue lightning plunging toward Barilan. Something had blocked it, the same way Carlich and Voerell's magic had been blocked when they attacked each other.

Could King Froethych's spell have protected Barilan from her attempt to harm him, just as it had shielded him from Carlich? But why would it? The spell shouldn't apply to her; she wasn't Barilan's blood kin.

Maybe they'd all been mistaken about the sorcery the dying king had worked. Perhaps he had simply protected his own kin against all harm. But no, she'd heard his words, and that wasn't what he'd said. Carlich had not been protected against the specters. And Vinhor had told Carlich that in Ralo, and presumably throughout Milecha, the action of the spell had been evident, shielding even serfs and commoners against harm by their own family members.

No, somehow the spell must consider her Barilan's kin. As she was, of course, though not by blood. Hadn't Coewyn made a huge effort to ensure that no other living person had tasted her milk? If they had, they would be legally kin to Barilan. Magic, too, must consider milk-ties valid. She was Barilan's milk-mother, bound by kinship ties as strong as those forged by blood.

What had Siwell said? White blood. Some people called milk white blood.

Barilan grabbed at her face, and his fingers found a purchase on her lip. They didn't pinch, though. Of course. He couldn't hurt her, either. That's why his nursing had never once caused her pain since the light of King Froethych's spell washed over them both, no matter how careless she'd been getting him latched. She should have realized that long since.

Maryn noticed blood from her cut palm smeared on the shoulder of Barilan's gown and splattered on the floor. She muttered the spell of cleansing. She didn't have to rush past the Holy One's name this time as she had before. She'd known in her heart it was sacrilege to ask his blessing on a sinful act. When the cleansing was done, she kept her eyes closed a moment longer in prayer. "Thank you," she whispered. "Forgive me…"

A small creak from the direction of the door jerked her eyes open again, and she froze. But when a few moments passed with no further sound, she relaxed a fraction, though her heart still raced. She had to think. How would Carlich and Vinhor react, when they found out she'd failed? It wasn't her fault the spell hadn't been successful; she'd tried her best to obey. They'd understand that King Froethych's spell bound her as much as Carlich. Probably they wouldn't punish her. They'd just find some other way to go forward with their plan.

New horror flooded Maryn, and she slumped back in her chair, despairing. King Froethych's spell hadn't saved Barilan after all, not for long. Carlich would recruit someone else to perform the soul transfer. Vinhor might even overcome his scruples enough to do it himself. Nothing Maryn could do would stop them. Despite this reprieve, Barilan's soul would perish anyway, and his body would become a vessel for some other child's soul.

She froze, her breath coming fast and shallow. If she begged, would they still allow her to perform the second half of the spell? If she couldn't save Barilan, at least she could still have Frilan back. That wouldn't be wrong, surely? There would be no virtue in refusing to call Frilan's soul into the body left vacant, if Barilan's soul was doomed whatever she did.

She wouldn't have to do anything to make it happen. Just tell the truth when Carlich asked. She was still the obvious choice to finish the spell; most likely he'd order her to do it. She could go passively along, not attempting resistance that would only prove useless, and her heart's desire could still be hers.

She wanted it, just as much as before. The faint echo of imagined screams rang in her ears, ready to overwhelm her again if she let them. But she was wiser now than she'd been a few minutes ago. She was glad King Froethych's spell had stopped her. Much as she still longed for Frilan, she could no longer honestly say she was willing to do anything to get him back. Barilan's life was too high a price to pay.

She stared at the baby in her lap, determination

flooding her heart. She had to save him, somehow. She had to find a way. *Dear Holy One, please make it possible, please show me what I must do. I'm sorry, forgive me, I'll never think of breaking your law again, I swear. Just let me save Barilan from Carlich, please, oh please...*

She struggled to think of some way, willing some glorious divine revelation to burst into her mind. But only one possibility presented itself, and Maryn was miserably certain it would never work.

She would have to lie. She couldn't let Carlich and Vinhor suspect that her spell had failed. Instead, she'd have to fool them into believing she'd completed the soul transfer as ordered, and keep up the ruse as long as she and Barilan remained captives. Though she didn't see how she could maintain the deception. Surely the first thing Vinhor would do would be to repeat the scrying spell. When the glowing crown appeared over Barilan's head her lie would be exposed.

Setting aside that worry for the moment, she considered other practicalities. Had the compulsion spell weakened sufficiently to allow her to lie? She thought it had. Vinhor had spent a long time instructing her; it was at least four or five hours since the spell's last renewal. That was usually about the time she could begin to defy it, if her need was great. She'd held back from following Vinhor's orders right away.

At that thought, Maryn felt a stirring of the urge to seek out Carlich and inform him. Her mouth twisted in a grim smile. That was a sure sign that defiance was now possible.

Maybe she could use her new knowledge of sorcery to improvise something to interfere with Vinhor's scrying. He'd said any gesture could be used—

Carlich's voice came from outside the door, muffled but comprehensible. "What's taking her so long?"

"Patience, my prince. Give her time. We wouldn't wish to interrupt her."

"She's had plenty of time. One more minute, and then I'm going in."

It was too late to try anything. Barilan wiggled, and Maryn scooped him into her arms. She tried to imagine how she would feel if the spell had gone forward as planned. Guilty, but burying it deep. Happy, joyful even. She gazed into Barilan's face, imagining Frilan's soul behind his dark blue eyes. For a moment the pretense was so vivid she almost believed it, and she gasped with the tearing shudder of elation that ran through her. She shook, and wept, and pulled aside her shift to bring the baby to her breast. Barilan, puzzled but willing, latched on and sucked enthusiastically.

The door swung open and Carlich strode in, Vinhor close at his heels. "Well, girl?" Carlich demanded. "Did it work?"

"Yes," Maryn whispered, forcing the word out past the compulsion spell. Then, louder, "Yes. I...I can hardly believe it. But this...this is Frilan...."

She ducked her head over the baby, hoping that the strain in her words would be attributed to emotion, rather than the difficulty of fighting the spell.

After a moment of silence, she heard Carlich's elated voice. "She did it! The Kingship is free! Voerell won't have access to the powers of the Regency, and you can crown me king!"

"Not so hasty, my prince." Vinhor held up a hand. "Before we proceed, I want to repeat the scrying, and confirm that the Kingship is indeed no longer bound."

"Do we have to bother?" Carlich stepped toward Maryn, his hand lifting. "One good slap—"

Maryn cringed and hunched her shoulders over the happily nursing baby. She hadn't thought of that. Was her deception going to be exposed so quickly? As soon as Carlich realized he still couldn't harm Barilan, he would know.

Vinhor scowled. "Crude violence will tell us nothing. It's still Barilan's body; I doubt your father's spell is sophisticated enough to differentiate. I would expect it to operate just as before. Only scrying will give us the truth."

For a moment Carlich hesitated. Then his hand lashed out, too quick for Maryn to react. It glanced off the air inches away from Barilan.

Maryn twisted Barilan away and glared at Carlich. The motion jerked Barilan off her breast. He gave a cry of protest and groped until his mouth once again found her nipple.

Carlich shrugged, and crossed his arms on his chest. "Very well, your Grace, you've proved your point. Get on with the scrying, then."

Vinhor shot Carlich a dark look, then turned to Maryn. "Give him to me, girl." He reached for his knife.

Maryn clutched Barilan tighter, rising shakily to her feet. "But—he tried to hit Frilan!"

"Your son is unharmed." Vinhor beckoned sharply to her. "And will remain so as long as you continue to cooperate with us. Now give him to me."

"Of—of course, your Grace." Maryn's pulse hammered in her ears. Frantically trying to think of some way to stop Vinhor, she made as long and slow a production as she could of detaching Barilan from her breast and adjusting her clothing. Just as she could delay no longer, inspiration struck. "Um, your Grace, I hope this won't take long. See how he's kicking like that?" She gestured at a random motion of Barilan's legs. "Frilan always used to do that right before he made a big mess in his diaper. I'd hate for any to leak out and spoil your beautiful robes."

Vinhor drew back. "Ah. No." He lowered the knife that had been about to prick his finger. "Perhaps it might be wiser to wait until after that's done and you've cleaned him up."

Carlich laughed. "Good move, your Grace. I promise, you don't want anything to do with that one's messes."

"Are you sure?" Maryn held Barilan out toward Vinhor. "It will probably be a few minutes. If you're lucky."

The priest made no move to take the baby. "There's no rush. Take him back to your room. I'll summon you in the morning."

Heart racing at the nearness of the escape, Maryn stepped toward the door. She suppressed a wild urge to giggle. Men might be able to face all manner of blood and gore without a qualm, but the prospect of a little harmless baby mess turned them into squeamish cowards.

Carlich put a hand on the doorframe to block her and turned to Vinhor. "I was hoping we could perform the ceremony to invest me with the Kingship tonight."

Vinhor shook his head. "It's not so simple, my prince. We can begin making arrangements, but it will take time to bring about the necessary circumstances. When the Kingship is freed, with no heir to settle in, not just anyone can claim it. You must first win the acclaim of the people. A large enough group of Milechans must publicly demand you assume the Kingship for me to be able to work the magic that will bring it home to you."

Carlich scowled, but after a moment's thought his face relaxed into better humor. "That should be easy enough. Voerell won't have much luck winning them over without the Regency bolstering her. You said our supporters have already begun to arrive?"

"They have, your Highness. We should meet with them tonight to begin forming our plans. Lord Negian is here with his men, and several other of the local lords. Messengers have arrived from those farther away, promising their allegiance. By the end of the week there will be enough to begin your move on Loempno, and more will join us along the way. You should have enough to challenge the forces who stand with Voerell."

"Good. We can depart after the Sabbath." Carlich threw an arm around Maryn's shoulders. "My great thanks for what you've done. I know no reward can be greater than what you've received already. Yet even so, be assured I'll remember your service generously when I'm king." He looked down at the baby. "It's perfect. No one will ever be able to tell the difference. My congratulations on your reunion with your son."

"Thank you, your Highness," Maryn murmured. A wave of grief for what could never be swept over her. She kept her eyes downcast, but forced a tremulous smile to her lips.

"I'll escort you to your room. I'm sure you'll appreciate some privacy to get reacquainted." Carlich looked again at Barilan in wonder, and shook his head. "To think, his soul was with the Holy One just a few minutes ago. What could you tell us, little one, if you could speak! Though I suppose by the time you learn, you won't remember, any more than any child does." There was something almost wistful in his gaze as he reached out and let Barilan grasp his finger.

"It is indeed a holy wonder, my prince," Vinhor said, taking Carlich by the elbow and drawing him away. Carlich shook his head, gathered his composure, and strode down the hall. Maryn followed him.

Sixteen

They arrived back at her room just as the guard shift was changing. Maryn's heart leapt when she saw that Tior was on duty again. He tried to catch her eye and convey some message by his expression, but his wagging eyebrows and contorted grimaces were so exaggerated she turned away lest Carlich notice him and become suspicious.

As soon as the door closed behind them, Carlich cut his arm and began the compulsion spell. She worried in the moments before it took effect that she might be forced to reveal her secret. Thankfully, he seemed in a hurry, for he didn't question her, only reminded her not to tell anyone of his control over her.

Maryn nodded mutely, and Carlich swept out, shutting her in. She collapsed with Barilan into her chair by the fire. There was no point trying to fight the fresh spell, but she didn't care. It was a relief to be able to rest from all the emotional and magical turmoil of the last few hours.

A servant brought her supper, more of the rich, delicious food she was quickly becoming accustomed to. She ate, and changed Barilan's diaper, and played with him, and sang a lullaby, and nursed him until he dropped off to sleep. She was trying to summon the initiative to rise and ready herself for bed when the door creaked open. Tior's anxious voice called quietly, "Miss Maryn?"

She slid Barilan to the seat of the chair without waking him and went to the door. The initial heavy dullness of the spell was just beginning to wane a bit, but she could muster none of the pleasure or enthusiasm she should have felt. "Yes?"

"I brought Madam Siwell, just like you asked. Go on in, quick. Kempich will be back soon. I'll tap when I manage to get rid of him again."

A cloaked and hooded figure slipped in. Tior eased the door shut, and the figure threw back its hood to reveal Siwell's angular features. "Dear Maryn, I came as soon as I heard. Are you all right?"

She threw her arms around Maryn in a fierce embrace. Maryn could only stand, unresponsive.

"Maryn? What's the matter? They haven't hurt you, have they? Tior said you were terribly upset; that you could barely manage to ask for help..." Siwell held Maryn out at arm's length, and looked closely at her face. "What's Carlich done to you?"

The compulsion spell forced Maryn to shake off her grip. "I'm sorry. You must be mistaken. I'm fine. There's nothing wrong." She turned toward the fire. Underneath she fought with all her strength to say something, anything, that would give Siwell a hint of the real situation. But it was still too soon for her efforts to prevail against the power of the magic.

"You're sure? Carlich hasn't harmed you?"

"Prince Carlich has been very kind to me. Now, please, go."

"If you're really all right..." Siwell took a step back. Then her voice hardened. "Wait. There's something wrong here. He's worked some spell on you, hasn't he?"

Maryn shook her head, miserable inside. How could she let Siwell know her suspicions were correct? She kept shaking her head, unable to do anything else. The spell even prevented tears from forming in her eyes.

Siwell cocked her head, studying Maryn with a worried frown. Hope stirred in Maryn's heart. Siwell knew Maryn. She must realize Maryn's response was not at all what she would expect from the girl she'd helped give birth.

Maryn whipped her head from side to side so hard she felt dizzy. She'd tried this tactic before, with Vinhor and Tennelan, only they hadn't been paying attention. But surely Siwell would notice.

"Prince Carlich would never put a spell on me. Never, never, never!" Maryn threw all her passion into her voice. Nothing in the compulsion spell or Carlich's orders prevented her from defending the prince, or praising him, even in wildly over-enthusiastic tones. "He's a great sorcerer! He's going to become king of Milecha, and I'm going to help him. I totally and completely and fully and utterly without reservation support him. I don't need help, from you or anyone else. Go away and leave me alone!" Maryn panted, staring at Siwell, willing her to understand.

The midwife stared back, her mouth open in shock at Maryn's performance, her forehead drawn into baffled creases. "What in the world?" She blinked a few times, then her eyes widened. "Oh, dear Holy One, that's just what he's done. He's ensorcelled you to speak only good of him. I'd heard he'd studied Hampsian gestural magic, I knew it was capable of some nasty stuff, but this…"

It was a joy to speak words that flowed easily

within the spell's constraints, knowing Siwell would realize what she meant. "He has not! He has not used gestural magic to put me under a spell. He has not compelled me to do exactly what he says. He has not renewed it every few hours since we left Loempno. He did not kidnap Barilan and me!"

As Maryn spoke, comprehension flooded Siwell's expression. She gave Maryn a wry smile of approval, though her eyes remained clouded with concern. "So that's how it is. I understand. Now, can I counteract it? He's very good; I doubt I'll be able to undo his spell completely. But it can't be that strong, or how did you manage to ask Tior to fetch me? Ah, it must fade over time—every few hours, you said?"

The portion of Maryn's mind controlled by the spell felt confused and panicked. An urge began to grow to seek out Carlich and warn him that the spell was not working as it should. She might not be able to keep tricking the magic much longer. "No! There is no spell! I don't know what you're talking about!"

Tior cracked the door open and stuck his head in. "Quiet!" he hissed. "Kempich's coming down the hall. He'll hear you if you keep shouting like that!" The door closed.

Maryn resisted the growing impulse to rush out and call for Carlich, but she feared it would soon overwhelm her. She kept her voice low. "Siwell, you have to go away. Please, hurry…"

Siwell set her mouth. "We'll get you free of it in just a moment, my dear. I don't have much training in blood work besides healing and cleansing, but I'll see what I can do." She unsheathed her small steel sorcery knife and sliced into her finger.

Her voice rose in an incantation. It took all Maryn's strength to remain still and not flee to fetch Carlich.

The blood sparked in Siwell's hands. The midwife turned her palms outward, and a burst of light washed over Maryn. Energy poured into her mind and muscles. She stood up straighter, lifting her chin and putting back shoulders she hadn't realized were hunched. It felt as if the crushing weight she'd been carrying had suddenly become much lighter. No, she'd become stronger, able to lift with casual ease the burden that used to bow her down. She felt powerful, competent, able to accomplish any task, no matter how challenging. The contrast with the helpless terror of her captivity was so great it made her giddy.

Siwell dropped her hands as she spoke the last words of the spell, the sparks fading. "Better?"

"Yes!" Maryn threw her arms around Siwell. "Oh, thank you!" The midwife returned her fierce embrace. Maryn stepped back, drawing a deep breath and evaluating the state of her mind. The desire to run to Carlich was still there, but reduced to no more than a nagging itch, easily ignored. She could think and speak as freely as when the spell was nearly gone. "What did you do?"

"Just a little spell to strengthen your courage and resolve. I use it when women are worn out by a long difficult labor. So you were under a spell?"

"Yes. I can fight it off, now. Prince Carlich's been using sorcery on me all this time to make me do what he tells me."

Siwell's eyes narrowed. "Why?"

"Because I know the truth! Because I saw him kill Prince Marolan, and try to kill Princess Voerell, and kidnap Barilan. He'll do anything to make himself king. Just now he tried to make me—" Her throat closed on the horror, and she couldn't finish.

"Oh, my dear." Siwell put an arm around her

shoulder. "I feared as much. We've got to get you away from him. I know people who'll listen to your story and be able to spread the word that Carlich's lying. But we have to make sure you're safe first."

Maryn leaned against Siwell's strong support. As the first flush of exuberance at her new freedom waned, the reality of her situation reasserted itself. Even without the compulsion spell, Carlich still had tremendous power over her. "How? I'm always guarded. They say it's for Barilan's protection, but it's really to keep me from escaping."

"That could be difficult." Siwell paced to the hearth, gazing at Barilan where he slumbered in the chair. "There are guards all around the building. Tior got me past them by saying one of the guests summoned a midwife to deal with her female troubles. I have to be seen leaving alone, or they'll start asking questions."

Maryn fought panic at the thought of Siwell leaving her behind, still a prisoner. "Maybe Tior will be able to figure out some way to get Barilan and me out. I can tell him everything, now. Once he knows about Carlich, surely he'll help us escape."

"I hope he can, but we have to face the possibility he won't be able to. Even at best it might take him several days to arrange something." Siwell came back over to Maryn and put a hand on her arm. "You'll need to remain fortified against Carlich's compulsion until then. I can teach you the spell I used; it's not difficult." She led Maryn to the seating area by the hearth.

Maryn checked Barilan; he was still deeply asleep, nestled against the chair's padded arm. Siwell took a seat on the settee and drew Maryn down beside her. Maryn listened intently as the midwife recited the incantation, elated to think that she would finally have a tool that could free her from Carlich's control. She repeated back the syllables, throwing all her energy into committing them to memory. Over and over Siwell drilled her in the stanzas of the spell.

Eventually Siwell sat back, satisfied. "You have it. Just don't forget. This spell fades over time, the same way the compulsion spell does. Whenever you feel Carlich's spell weakening and know it's close to time for him to renew it, work this magic. Do you have a knife, or something sharp?"

"No, but I can get one, or make something." Maryn thought of the fine silver utensils the servants always brought with her meal.

"Good. And if it comes down to it, you can always use your teeth or fingernails. This spell only requires a drop or two to work, so don't go draining yourself to no purpose. And be sure to make the cut somewhere Carlich won't easily see it."

"All right." Maryn's head spun with all she needed to remember.

"Be patient. Pretend Carlich's spell is still in effect. Once Tior gets you out, come to my home. I'll leave the back unlocked so even if I'm not there you can go in and hide while you wait for me. We'll get you out of the city and Barilan back to his mother. The poor princess; she must be worried sick about him."

"I suppose." Maryn was sure Voerell was, at least in an abstract way. But the princess had always been so careful to keep an emotional distance between herself and her son. She'd often gone a week between visits to the nursery; the few days Barilan had been gone weren't that different. His absence couldn't be as hard on Voerell as it would have been on Maryn.

Maryn looked over at Barilan, sprawled on the other chair. "There's something else." She swallowed.

Much as she hated to admit what she'd almost done, Siwell was the only one who might be able to help her. "Prince Carlich and Priest Vinhor tried to have me work magic on Barilan." Stammering, she explained about the soul exchange.

Siwell sat up straighter, eyes blazing. "How dare that man call himself a priest!" She shook her head, her expression softening. "My dear Maryn, what a cruel thing to ask of you. What happened?"

Maryn dropped her gaze. "I agreed to do the magic. I mean, I wanted it so much, to have Frilan alive again." She glanced up. Siwell's expression held only compassion, but Maryn could all too easily imagine it changing to cold judgment. She looked down again. "But then...when it came to the point, I just...couldn't."

It wasn't exactly a lie. Maryn rushed on. "I told them I'd done it. I'm sure they believed me. Even so, they were going to check him for the Kingship again to be certain. I managed to put them off. But in the morning I won't be able to stop them, and the crown will appear just like it did last time, and they'll know I lied to them. Prince Carlich will be so angry..." Maryn faltered as she imagined his rage. "There's got to be some way, some magic you can do to interfere with their scrying and make it look like it really is Frilan's soul in Barilan's body."

Siwell frowned. "Theoretically it should be possible, but I'm afraid I don't know any spell that might serve. That has to do with illusions, and inheritance magic, and that's far outside my training. You're sure you can't stall again?"

Despite her disappointment and fear, Maryn smiled wanly. "I'll try, but they won't be scared off by fear of a messy diaper forever."

Siwell chuckled, and rubbed at her eyes. "I don't know...I'll check with the sorcerers I know, but it will be hard to inquire without alerting them to why. There are a couple I think I can trust not to report me to Carlich. I'll get word to you if I find out anything. Tior could carry a message...but you don't read, do you? He could bring me back here..." But she sounded doubtful. "Until then, you'll just have to do your best. Maybe they'll be careless enough to forget, or lazy enough not to expend the effort."

Carlich was neither careless nor lazy, Maryn knew, or at least not enough to let such an important matter pass. But if Siwell couldn't help her, she'd just have to keep improvising ways to distract him until Tior found a way for them to escape.

A quiet rap sounded at the door. Maryn sprang to her feet. Siwell rose more slowly. "I'll do what I can," she told Maryn. "I just hope it's enough. If Carlich were to discover your deception...you've been in his company for a good while now. Do you think he might have enough feeling for you to spare you?"

Maryn swallowed. Carlich did sometimes talk to her as if he considered her a companion, a confidant. But surely he was much too practical to let so tentative a connection interfere with his ambition. "No. I'm nothing to him. He'd kill me without a thought." She shuddered. "He killed his own brother. Now that we're in the town, he'd easily be able to find another woman to nurse Barilan. So he doesn't even need me anymore."

For that matter, why hadn't Carlich killed her as soon as they reached Ralo? Wouldn't he prefer to replace her with some woman who didn't know about his crimes and didn't have to be controlled by sorcery? He must consider keeping her available to confirm his story and bolster his claim that he'd rescued her and Barilan from Voerell valuable enough to justify whatever effort it took to control her.

Of course, now he thought she'd willingly gone over to his side, and had her own reason to keep his secrets. "As long as he believes I really did switch Barilan's soul for Frilan's, I should be safe. He promised to reward me." She felt nauseated at the thought of accepting Carlich's blood money. She'd do it, though, and pretend to be delighted, if that was the only way to protect herself and Barilan. "I just have to get away before he learns the truth."

Siwell bit her lip, her face drawn. "All right. Only be careful. Don't put yourself in danger."

"I won't." Maryn's promise wasn't entirely sincere. She wasn't brave enough to try anything really risky, but she would dare a lot more than Siwell would approve of to escape Carlich.

"Maybe Tior will know an easy way for you to get out." Siwell's tone was encouraging, but it lacked conviction. She went to the door and opened it for Tior.

He slipped in. "What took so long? I told Kempich I wouldn't report him if he snuck off to get us some ale, but he'll be back soon."

Siwell held up a hand. "Wait. Maryn has something she needs to tell you first."

Tior turned to Maryn with a puzzled frown. Maryn gulped, not knowing where to begin. "You've got to help me, Tior. Everything Prince Carlich is saying is a lie. I saw what really happened." She poured out the whole story as tersely as she could.

Tior's eyes got rounder and rounder as she spoke. Maryn searched his face for signs of outrage or anger, but all she saw were pale cheeks and a pinched mouth. She put all the desperation she could into her voice. "Please, Tior, you've got to help us. Barilan and I have to get away."

Even before she finished speaking, Tior started shaking his head. "I can't. There's no way. Captain Tennelan has guards stationed at every door of this building. They check everyone going in or out. Most of them served with Carlich in Hampsia, back before I joined. They'll never believe you."

"You believe me, don't you Tior?" Maryn tried to convey the truth of her words with her gaze, but Tior wouldn't quite meet her eyes.

"I don't know. I don't think you're lying, exactly, but Prince Carlich...all the other soldiers love him. Are you really sure what you saw, what you heard? Maybe it's all just a misunderstanding." He twisted his hands together. "You don't know what you're asking. I'm sworn to obey my commander. If I tried to help you escape they'd catch us, I know they would. I'd be strung up for treason. And you'd be right back in here. No, you've got to be wrong. I can't believe Prince Carlich would really harm a woman and a baby. If you cooperate with him, you'll be fine."

"Not if he finds out I lied to him!" Maryn's eyes blurred with tears, and her throat was so tight she could barely force the words out. "I know what I saw. Carlich is a murderer, and if you don't help us he's going to succeed in putting himself on the throne. Don't you even care?"

"That's not—Look, I'm just doing my job. It's not my place to question my orders." A quaver in Tior's voice betrayed his unhappiness. "I'm sorry, but I'm not...I'm not the kind of person who...who gets involved in this sort of thing. I wish I could help you, but I can't."

He finally looked at Maryn, eyes pleading for

understanding. She turned away. "You are involved, whether you want to be or not. But I guess you're too much of a coward to admit it."

Tior drew in his breath. Siwell put a hand on Maryn's shoulder. "It's all right, Maryn. We'll find some other way. You'll just have to continue coming up with excuses to prevent them from scrying Barilan, and bide your time until you get a chance to slip away."

Maryn turned her back on both of them. "Unless Tior thinks it's his duty to go to Carlich and tell him everything."

She could tell her words had stung by his hurt tone. "I wouldn't do that. I won't tell anyone what you said, or what you're planning. I really do want to help you, Maryn."

"As long as it doesn't cost you anything." He started to protest, but she cut him off. "Never mind. Siwell, I'll manage somehow. I'll keep working your spell, and keep looking for a chance to get away. Without help." She glared at Tior, then turned and embraced the midwife. "Thank you for everything you've done. I'll never be able to repay you."

Siwell hugged her back fiercely. "If what you know can help save Milecha from a civil war, that will be more than thanks enough. But remember, take care. You can't help Barilan or anyone else if you get yourself killed."

"I know. I'll be careful."

Tior tugged at Siwell's sleeve. "Kempich can't stay gone much longer. You've got to go."

Siwell gave Maryn one last hug and hurried away.

Seventeen

Maryn was exhausted. Disappointment over Tior's refusal to help drained all the joyful energy she'd felt on first learning Siwell's spell. Though the spell gave her the strength to resist Carlich's compulsion, fighting it still took effort. Her arms felt leaden as she undressed and gathered Barilan up to carry him to the bed. She crawled in and settled him beside her. The disturbance roused him, and he cried a little, but nursing soon soothed him back into slumber.

But Maryn couldn't sleep. Her mind was too busy with all that had happened. She went over and over the incantation Siwell had taught her. She would have to work it first thing in the morning, then call for Carlich to come renew his spell so he wouldn't suspect anything. She fretted, wondering what opportunity might come for her to flee with Barilan. Carlich hardly ever let her out of her room. Would she have to wait until he set out on the planned march to Loempno? Would he even take Barilan and Maryn with him? Surely he would, for Barilan was still his best bargaining tool against Voerell.

She tried not to think of those moments alone in Vinhor's office, when she had moved her hands in the gestures that, if they'd succeeded, would have sent

Barilan's soul to the Holy One's courts. How much of that had been her own choice, and how much Carlich's compulsion? The question burned in her heart, but she couldn't answer it.

She thought back over all Vinhor had taught her concerning sorcery. She'd never given much thought to magic before. She'd certainly never dreamed she'd be able to learn more than the basic cleansing spell. Greater magic was for priests and sorcerers and healers, not ordinary folk.

But when she had spoken the incantation and made the proper gestures, the magic had answered her. It had sprung to life in her hand as crackling bright as it ever had in Carlich's. If not for the interference of King Froethych's spell, she was sure it would have worked just as it was supposed to. She ran her thumb along the aching cut in her palm in wonder.

Before Carlich and Vinhor had interrupted her, she'd considered improvising some sort of magic to block their scrying. Maybe she should take advantage of her privacy to try now. She concentrated, calling up Vinhor's exact words. *Someone with a strong enough will can use almost any motion to direct the spell.* She'd never considered her will to be particularly strong. But she had Siwell's spell to bolster it, and surely anyone's will was strongest when their need was great.

The idea frightened her, but she couldn't put it from her mind. Finally she pushed the blankets down and sat up. She parted the bed's curtains so that a bit of moonlight could stream in. Arranging herself cross-legged, she gazed down at Barilan's sleeping form.

Just a tiny bit of blood. She didn't want her experiment to make much light or noise, or risk escaping her very uncertain control. She gnawed at the corner of one fingernail until she had bitten through the layers of dead skin to the living cuticle beneath. Blood seeped out, black in the moonlight. She rubbed it between her thumb and forefinger, then pressed on the little wound until the bleeding stopped.

In a whisper she chanted the incantation to the Holy One, adding a fervent unspoken plea for him to guard her from danger. Finished, she held her blood-smeared fingers over Barilan. She hesitated, but then drew a deep breath and pressed her thumb and forefinger together into a ring and swept them down and up again, the other three fingers on that hand spread wide.

The magic woke instantly. Brilliant blue sparks shot from between her pinching fingers. Her throat felt full of buzzing bees.

For a moment she panicked, not knowing what to do. She almost blurted out the words of the cleansing spell. But she stopped herself and gathered all her courage. Almost any gesture would do. She parted her fingers, sending blue sparks showering, and waved her hand, palm down, in a circle over Barilan. She fixed in her mind a vivid image of the ghostly crown of the scrying spell and pictured it fading to invisibility, still there, but unobservable. She drove all her might into the mental image and swept her hand around faster and faster.

It was working; she felt it. Blue fire rained down over Barilan, haloing him with light in which no faintest image of a crown appeared. She pushed harder, exultant that her idea had succeeded.

A sharp pain stabbed into the corner of her nail where she had bitten it. She tried to slow her hand

and pull it back to look at the spot, but she couldn't. Some outside force had taken control of her arm and kept it relentlessly circling. The pain quickly grew to a fierce dragging ache. All the other half-healed cuts on her hands and arms throbbed in response. Horrified, she saw a tiny new stream of blood break free from her finger and fly to join the flood of magic, bursting into a shower of blue sparks.

Faster and faster her hand flew. She couldn't stop it. Suction dragged her veins toward the spell's vortex. The trickle of blood increased to a stream. The fresh scab on her palm bulged and started to crack. Magic flared higher, brilliant blue flames leaping toward the bed's canopy, bright as lightning.

Terror lent her strength. With a tremendous effort, Maryn wrenched her hand back. She made a sharp cutting gesture, and cried the closing words of the cleansing spell. The blue fire subsided, and the controlling force released her arm. She fell back and stuck her burning finger in her mouth. The metallic tang of blood bathed her tongue as she sucked at the wound.

Barilan woke with a wail. Outside the bed's shrouding curtains she heard the door open. Tior's voice called, "What's wrong? We felt magic; are you all right?"

Maryn pulled her finger from her mouth and pressed her thumb to the wound. "I'm fine." Her voice trembled on the edge of a sob. "I, um…Barilan bit me, is all. I had to clean up the blood. I'm sorry I disturbed you." She scrambled to gather Barilan up and get him latched on to her breast. His cries cut off as he began to suck.

"Oh. You're sure you don't need any help? You yelled." Tior sounded concerned.

"No. It just startled me. Woke me up." Maryn forced a little laugh. "Everything's fine."

"Well, good-night, then." The other guard's voice rose in a question, though Maryn couldn't make out the words, and Tior murmured to him as the door closed.

Maryn bowed her head over Barilan and took deep, shuddering breaths. At length she lay down and curled her body around the baby as he continued to nurse. Violent shivers wracked her body.

She had very nearly suffered the same fate as King Froethych. The forces unleashed by that tiny smear of blood and a few waves of her hand had been almost enough to destroy her. If she hadn't managed to break away, the magic would have continued until it sucked her dry of blood and discarded her like an empty husk.

Such forces were far beyond anything an ignorant girl like herself should dare meddle with. It was worse than a toddler jabbing a poker into a blazing fireplace. Silently she vowed never again to play with magic she didn't understand. Only then did her trembling subside enough for exhaustion to drag her into sleep.

Maryn was almost too afraid to work Siwell's spell the next morning. But the thought of falling under Carlich's mind-numbing control once again frightened her even more, so she steeled herself and pried away the scab from the corner of her fingernail until the blood flowed anew. She kept her hands scrupulously still and concentrated on everything Vinhor and Siwell had taught her about the proper pronunciation of the words. The spell worked flawlessly. As the blue lightning subsided and the buzzing in her teeth faded away, she felt a wonderful flush of confidence.

After breakfast, Maryn went to the door and opened it. Both guards were strangers. She looked back and forth between them before dropping her gaze, surprised how disappointed she felt that Tior was not there. Angry as she was with him, still he was the closest thing she had to a friend here. He'd brought Siwell to her; she owed him a great debt for that. With him gone she felt more alone than ever.

She glanced up at one of the strange guards and down again quickly. "Please, I must speak to Prince Carlich. He'll want to know."

The soldier nodded. "We have our orders." He gestured to the other, who hurried away.

Carlich looked red-eyed and disheveled. Maryn suspected he hadn't slept much, if at all. He went though the motions of the spell swiftly and efficiently. She watched his curt gestures with new interest. The scooping gesture at the beginning was quite plain now that she knew what to look for, and here and there through the sequence she recognized other motions Vinhor had taught her.

As soon as he finished, he beckoned to her. "Get Barilan and come with me."

"But your Highness, I haven't even changed his diaper yet." As soon as she'd spoken, Maryn realized her mistake. Normally she wouldn't be able to contradict Carlich's wishes, even in so minor a way, immediately after he worked the compulsion spell. She made an effort to let her reinforced will sink into abeyance and allow the compulsion to come to the front of her mind. "But of course I'll be happy to do whatever you command."

Carlich's eyes narrowed. "Did it take him so long to produce the mess you were worried about?"

Maryn hurried to the bed and scooped Barilan up.

"Oh, no, your Highness. That happened last night, just as I expected." She carried the baby to the changing table and rushed to remove his soaked cloth and replace it with clean one. "It got all over everything, too, the way I knew it would. But that's all cleaned up. He's just wet now." Her fingers fumbled in her nervousness, but a quick glance over her shoulder showed her that Carlich had apparently accepted her story and lost interest. He stared at nothing and tapped his foot in an irregular rhythm until she was finished.

Maryn fastened the last tiny button on Barilan's gown and hoisted him to her shoulder. He was cranky this morning, not outright crying, but seeming constantly on the verge. She bounced him a little to try and settle him. It hardly ever worked, but she always tried. She carried him to Carlich, who nodded and led her out.

Carlich strode without a word through the corridors to Vinhor's office. He held the door for Maryn to precede him, and slammed it behind them. "Here he is. Go ahead with your scrying."

"Thank you, your Highness." Vinhor gestured for Maryn to pass Barilan to him. She complied, though her heart raced and she felt cold all over. Could her clumsily improvised attempt at a spell prevail against such a powerful and skilled sorcerer? It had seemed like it was working. By the time she'd managed to break off the uncontrolled magic a great deal of blood had gone into it. That surely must count for something.

Vinhor nicked his finger and moved smoothly through the words of the incantation. A halo of light glowed around Barilan. Vinhor bent close to examine his head, but the space above his spiky blond hair shone as limpidly clear as sunlit well-water. Vinhor nodded and slowly straightened, his voice bringing the spell to a murmured conclusion. The last of his excess blood sparked away.

Maryn closed her eyes against stinging tears of relief. Her magic had worked. They were safe. Even if she couldn't find a way to escape, even if Carlich succeeded in defeating Voerell and making himself king, all she had to do was play along until afterwards. She could swear she'd never tell what she'd seen, and he'd believe her, because he'd think she was concealing her own guilt as well as his. She would still try to get away, so that she could help rally Carlich's enemies and save Milecha from falling under his control, but if she failed at least she would survive.

Carlich couldn't contain his triumph. "See, the girl really did it! Everything is going as we planned."

Vinhor inclined his head. "Now there's no doubt. Send them back to their quarters and let us proceed with our work. If you still intend to launch our venture to Loempno immediately after next Sabbath, I'm afraid you'll suffer many more sleepless nights in preparation."

"Whatever it takes." Carlich pushed his stringy hair back from his eyes. "We can't give Voerell time to bring in troops from Wonora. I'm sure she's got messengers on the way already. The first ships full of soldiers could be here in another week."

"Very well. We will do as your Highness wishes."

Maryn hoped Carlich might order her alone back to her room, but he called a guard and told him to escort her. She didn't think he doubted the potency of his spell to make her obey, but perhaps he feared some supporter of Voerell might sneak into the building and make an attempt to seize Barilan. In any case, she had no opportunity to slip away before she was once again immured in her pleasant prison.

Nor did any chance arise over the next several days. She was hardly ever allowed to leave her room. Carlich seemed to nearly forget her existence, and that of the baby he believed was no longer truly his nephew. He only made brief appearances each morning, afternoon, and evening to renew the spell of compulsion. Maryn became comfortable working the spell Siwell had taught her and skilled in dissembling the proper subservient attitude. She continued to wait and watch, despite the boredom of long empty days and fear that her patience might prove fruitless. She never knew when her chance might come; she had to be ready to seize it.

Eighteen

On the Sabbath servants brought a fine gown for Barilan, almost as richly decorated as the one he'd worn to his heirship ceremony, and crisp fresh servant's garments for Maryn. Guards escorted them to the church sanctuary. Maryn watched for any chance to slip away, but the guards were alert, and Tior wasn't among them. Carlich had appropriated the elevated box at the side front where the town council usually sat. He gestured for Maryn to take a seat in one of the ornate high-backed chairs. She sighed. No escape would be possible from up here, where all eyes could focus on the infant king she held.

Before the service began Carlich introduced Barilan to a group of nobles, all of whom had assembled in support of Carlich's endeavor. They bowed to Barilan and listened approvingly to Carlich's account of how he had rescued the young king from his deranged mother. Maryn forced her expression to remain approving. Within she writhed, torn between disgust at Carlich's blatant falsehoods and laughter at how ridiculous his story had become. He'd twisted it until it bore little resemblance to the events she'd witnessed. Instead it was a stirring tale of adventure, featuring Carlich in the role of the valiant hero who had single-handedly saved Milecha from foreign conquest.

None of his listeners showed any sign of doubting his account. They listened attentively and made noises of outrage or pleasure in all the right spots. Carlich was an excellent storyteller. Maryn admired his eloquence and animated delivery even as she despised his lies.

The beginning of the Sabbath service interrupted Carlich and sent the nobles back to their places in the lower section. Maryn sat demurely beside Carlich and tried to keep Barilan quiet. At first it was difficult, for the baby was happy and inquisitive, babbling in excitement as he gazed about. Jewel-colored light streamed through the towering windows, and the rich vestments of the celebrants shone and sparkled as they processed up the aisle. But the haunting chants of the brothers and sisters quieted him as they echoed around the cavernous space. Melody and counterpoint twined around each other, the syllables of the ancient language as mysterious to Maryn's ears as to Barilan's. By the time Priest Vinhor read from the Holy Scriptures and launched into his homily, Maryn managed to get Barilan to nurse, and he quickly drifted off to sleep.

The scripture Vinhor expounded told the story of a corrupt king and the prophet who defied him. Maryn had heard the text before, and enjoyed it for it was a stirring tale. But this time Vinhor twisted the interpretation until, without actually naming any names, he as much as asserted that the Holy One squarely supported Carlich's cause against Voerell.

Murmur of approval rose from the assembled worshippers. The sanctuary was as packed as Maryn had ever seen it, even on Holy Days. The only empty places were those around Carlich and her in the box. People filled every seat in the section reserved for the nobility and the wealthy, and crammed shoulder to shoulder in the area where the commoners stood. Many of those standing were men wearing the livery of various lords.

Vinhor concluded his message with an impassioned prayer to the Holy One, entreating his blessing on the next day's venture. A long tedious liturgy followed. Maryn let the responses she had been repeating every Sabbath since her childhood roll automatically from her tongue while her mind wandered. She jerked back to awareness when it was time to rise and follow Carlich forward to the rail to receive the ritual sanctification of the Holy One's dying Breath. At least her status as a mere servant meant one of the junior priests administered it; she wasn't sure she could have borne it if Vinhor had been the one to breathe the gentle gust over her head and hands. Of course Vinhor ministered to Carlich, and made the sign of the noose over Barilan as he slept in her arms.

They filed back to their seats to wait for all the other attendees to come forward and receive the Breath from the priests. Maryn drowsed, lulled by the sound of shuffling feet, the quiet murmur of priests' voices, and the soft chanting of the brothers and sisters. She shifted Barilan to the side and propped one elbow on the arm of her chair to cradle her head.

She was nearly asleep when she heard Vinhor's voice, very soft. "What troubles you, my prince?"

She cracked her eyelids open just enough to glimpse Carlich raise his head slowly from where it had been bent in prayer, resting on his clasped hands. She pressed her eyes back shut tight, though Carlich didn't even glance at her. "Nothing, your Grace. Shouldn't you be at the altar still?"

Maryn heard the sound of rustling vestments as Vinhor settled into a chair. "All those of note have been served already. The other priests can take care of the rest. I thought it more important to counsel you in your distress. Don't try to convince me I'm wrong, my prince. I've been a priest too long not to recognize the signs of a man laying his heart bare to the Holy One."

Carlich remained silent for a long time. Maryn was wide awake now, but she continued to feign sleep. At last Carlich spoke, his voice barely more than a whisper. "I just want to be sure I'm doing the right thing. I want to know that the blessings of the Holy One go with me."

"I've invoked them for you, have I not?"

"Yes, and I value that. But...You and I both know that everything I've done has been for the good of Milecha. All we're planning is justified for my kingdom's sake. But there's so much others would see as crimes. Sins. So much we must keep secret. I was asking the Holy One for reassurance that any who would think so are wrong, and ignorant, and my course is truly good in his eyes."

"Is not my assurance enough?"

"It is. And most of the time I feel the truth of it in my bones. But every once in a while, I doubt."

"Doubts are the whispers of the Vulture, to tempt the Holy One's followers from His true path."

"I know. I don't regret anything I've done. I just wonder...Are you sure everything we've planned is completely necessary? It seems we might show a little restraint. I know my sister must...must...well, you know. But what about the child? He's an innocent. Surely nothing would be lost if we allow him to live."

It was all Maryn could do not to cry out. Instead she froze, trying to avoid even the slightest movement that might alert Carlich or Vinhor to her awareness.

"My prince, he would always be a threat to you. Your enemies could use him as a rallying point and say the throne should be his. You cannot take that risk."

"He's not royalty any more."

"That can never become known. He must be dealt with, my prince. There is no other choice."

"Mm." Carlich was silent for several long moments. Maryn had to fight the impulse to clutch Barilan close.

"What about the nurse?" There was a mulish quality to Carlich's voice, like a petulant child arguing with a parent. "We could spare her, at least. She cooperated with us; she can't betray us without revealing her own role. And in any case I have her well controlled."

"Hush, your Highness. You shouldn't be speaking of such things where others might hear. The girl is right there."

"She's asleep. You worry too much." Maryn heard a rustle as he turned toward her. "Sleep. Forget anything we say that you've heard or might hear."

The command triggered the compulsion spell, sending a wave of drowsiness washing over Maryn's mind, but Siwell's spell made it easy to resist. She couldn't forget these words; they burned in her ears and twisted in her gut.

"There." Carlich sighed. "I suppose I know what you're going to tell me."

"I'm sure you do, your Highness." Vinhor's voice dropped even lower. "She knows far too much. No matter how completely you control her, you cannot be sure your control will never slip. Your enemies would be willing enough to overlook her guilt in exchange for the information she could give them. As soon as we no longer need her to keep up the impression that you rescued her and she affirms your version of events, you must remove the threat. Such an action is fully approved by the Holy One. One need only look at the story of—"

"Yes, I know, I know. I've already listened to one of your sermons today; spare me another."

"We serve the Holy One's purpose in this world, my prince. Do not allow your resolve to weaken."

"I won't." He sighed again. "If it must be done, I won't hesitate."

"It must. Now don't risk speaking this way again." The chair creaked as Vinhor rose. "It looks as if they're nearly finished. I'll go now to lead the benediction. You still intend to join me for dinner?"

"Yes."

"Good. I'll see you then."

Maryn didn't stir, even long after she was sure Vinhor was gone. She made Carlich shake her shoulder after the last notes of the recessional music died away. "Wake up. It's time to leave."

Maryn made a great show of rousing groggily. "Wha—Oh. Yes, your Highness." She gathered the slumbering Barilan close. Her shoulder was damp where he'd drooled as he slept. She stumbled to her feet, praying that her numb shock and horror looked like the aftereffects of an interrupted nap.

Carlich didn't look at her, only snapped, "Come with me," and strode away. She followed him until he turned her over to a guard who escorted her back to her room.

Maryn managed to contain herself until the door

closed behind her. She eased Barilan down on the bed
without waking him. Then she threw herself into the
chair by the hearth and gave in to shaking and sobs.

The magic she'd counted on to save her, that she'd
nearly died to perform, was worthless. Carlich was
going to kill her anyway. Surprisingly he seemed a bit
reluctant, but Vinhor would push him to carry
through, and Carlich would go along. She knew
Carlich was a liar. Why did it shock her so deeply that
he'd lied about rewarding her, too? Was this always
the reward he'd had in mind?

She had to get away. It was more urgent now than
ever. And she had to take Barilan with her, for Carlich
planned to kill him, too.

But what if she didn't get the chance? What if
Carlich was careful enough to leave her no
opportunity to escape before his confrontation with
Voerell? If he was successful in defeating the regent,
Maryn would surely have no opportunity to get away
afterward.

Barilan was safer than she was, for Carlich couldn't
himself harm his nephew, at least not until the effects
of Froethych's spell faded. That could well be years.
The spell even seemed to prevent him from ordering
anyone else to harm Barilan. But if he wished it to
happen, surely someone who wasn't kin to Barilan
would contrive to carry out the actual murder.

Nothing, however, prevented him from slaying
Maryn with his own hand. If only the milk-ties that
bound her to Barilan extended also to Barilan's kin!
But that didn't seem to be the case. Carlich had hurt
her many times since the spell took effect without any
sign of difficulty.

A thought struck Maryn, and she froze. Not only
infants could be bound with milk ties. Siwell had

asked whether any man had ever tasted her milk, and was relieved when she assured her that only her husband ever had. Because he was dead, just as Frilan was, and couldn't impose an unwelcome bond on the new prince. And when Rogelan had scried her milk for kinship ties, Edrich's face had appeared alongside Frilan's.

Maryn buried her face in her hands, shaking as she remembered the sensual pleasure of Edrich's mouth on her breast. He'd taken such enjoyment in the abundance of her body to nurture their child and the cozy intimacy of being allowed to share in it. Siwell had said that some women didn't like their husbands to touch their milk-filled breasts, but Maryn had never minded, and she and Edrich had continued to enjoy her breasts as part of their lovemaking after Frilan's birth much as they had before.

Could she seduce Carlich? She nearly gagged at the thought, but she forced herself to consider it. Would she be able to fake interest in him enough to persuade him to dally with her? And would he be thoughtless enough about the ramifications to allow her milk to touch his tongue?

No. There was no chance. She might be able approach him subtly enough he wouldn't realize she was immune to the compulsion spell. She might be able to overcome her horror at committing such a grave sin. But she could never act well enough to conceal her disgust at his touch. Besides, even if she could, he'd never look at her. She was far beneath him. Palace gossip held that Prince Carlich had his pick of all the most beautiful and high-ranking women in the kingdom, and he was rumored to be very discerning in his tastes. He certainly wasn't among those nobles who were known to take their pleasures with any servant who caught their eye. He'd had plenty of opportunity to take advantage of her during their flight to Ralo, and he'd hardly seemed aware of her as a fellow human, let alone a woman worthy of his interest.

Maryn breathed a little easier. But there might still be merit in her idea. Surely she could figure out some way to sneak a little of her milk into Carlich's food or drink.

Jumping up, Maryn began to scour the room for any container she might use. The water pitcher and basin were much too big and bulky. She could offer Carlich a drink of water when he came to her room, but she'd never done anything like that before, and he might grow suspicious. And he might taste something strange about water with milk in it; better to add a few drops to something strong or sweet flavored. She needed a small, sealed container she could fill with her milk and keep concealed on her person, ready to pour a little into Carlich's plate or cup whenever the chance arose.

Nothing in her room fit that description. She hesitated. It had been two days since the last time she'd seen Tior on duty. He usually stood a shift every other day, so chances were good he was outside her door right now. She'd been too upset when she was brought back from the church to notice.

The door creaked when she eased it open. Both guards twisted to stare at her. "Yes, Miss?" one asked. "Do you need something?"

He was a stranger, but Tior stood on the other side of the door, his mild eyes anxious. Maryn gave him a quick, pleading glance, before she turned back to the other. "No. I'm fine. I was just wondering when my meal would come."

"I'm sure it's on its way." The guard scowled at her.

Maryn bobbed her head. "Of course. I'll try to be patient." She shot Tior one last impassioned look before ducking back into the room and closing the door.

Soon the servant did arrive with dinner, meat and vegetables in a creamy sauce so richly spiced Maryn was sure it must be the same Priest Vinhor was serving the guests at his high table. Carlich would never notice a few drops of her milk mixed into something like this. Maryn pulled down her shift and squirted a little onto her plate to make sure. She swirled the thin white liquid into the thick sauce and tasted it. No, she could detect nothing suspicious. Her plan might work, if she could pull it off.

Barilan woke before she was done eating. She finished her meal supporting him in one arm and nursing him while she plied the spoon with her other hand. The silver plate was empty and she was contemplating licking the last traces of the delicious sauce from its surface when the door creaked open. Tior hissed at her. "What do you want? I've only got a moment before he comes back."

Maryn set her plate down and rose, supporting Barilan with both arms. He was getting so heavy that carrying him around while he nursed was growing harder. "Can you get me a small container? It needs to be watertight, and sealable. A little flask, perhaps, or a small bottle of some sort? Like an apothecary would use."

Tior frowned, puzzled. "Whatever do you need that for?"

"I can't tell you. But please, it's important. Just something I can carry a bit of liquid in."

He shrugged. "All right. That shouldn't be too hard."

Maryn fidgeted with a fold of Barilan's gown. "Can you bring it soon? Later today? I know Prince Carlich plans to leave tomorrow, so you might not get another chance."

"I can't go running off to the apothecary during my shift! And I'm not allowed in here when I'm not standing duty." But at her stricken expression Tior's tone softened. "I'll do what I can. But Captain Tennelan ordered us all to pack our gear, so I expect we're going with you. Hopefully they'll keep assigning me to guard you. It's a dull job nobody wants. They think I'm lazy because I keep volunteering, but they're happy enough to let me have it."

Maryn swallowed. "I truly appreciate it, Tior. You don't know how much…"

"It's nothing. I told you, I want to help you." Tior started and glanced over his shoulder. "He's coming. I'll bring you something as soon as I can."

He nodded to her and closed the door. Maryn worried that he might not be able to find what she needed, or get it to her in time if he did, but she had to be content. She retreated to her chair by the hearth and switched Barilan over to the other side. The steady rhythm of his mouth on her breast helped lull her to calm and push to the back of her mind the knowledge that if she didn't manage to accomplish her plan, Carlich would surely kill them both.

Nineteen

Tior didn't come back all that day. At last, late into the dark hours, Maryn gave up her vigil and crawled into bed.

At first light, just as the church bells pealed the beginning of the day's work, fists pounded on her door. "Wake up!" a guard's voice called. "Prince Carlich orders that you prepare the king to depart in one hour!"

Maryn scrambled out of bed and flung on her clothes. She was only half dressed when the door swung open and the servant girl hurried in with breakfast. "Do you have everything you need to care for the king on the journey?"

Maryn eyed the pile of clean cloths. "More diapers, I think. And I'll need something to pack them in. Do you know how long Prince Carlich plans to have us on the road?"

"Only as long as it takes to reach Loempno, if all goes well." The girl lowered her voice. "I heard he plans to challenge Princess Voerell as soon as he gets to the gates! They say Barilan didn't inherit the Kingship after all. Do you know anything about it?"

Maryn quickly tried to think what answer might best serve Voerell and hinder Carlich. Maybe she could sow doubts about Carlich's story. She glanced at the door and stepped closer to the servant, lowering her voice. "Don't let anyone know I told you, but Priest Vinhor did some sort of spell on Barilan. I saw Barilan light up all over, and it looked like a crown was floating over his head. But then Priest Vinhor kept chanting and waved his hands around, and the crown faded until I couldn't see it any more."

The servant girl's eyes grew big and round. "Ooh! Does that mean Barilan really is king, and they hid it?"

"I don't know." Maryn didn't want to appear too certain for fear the girl would get suspicious. "They didn't say what they were doing. But that's what it looked like to me."

The servant nodded, eyes unfocused as she digested this piece of gossip. Suddenly her eyebrows shot up. "Or maybe the *princess* put an illusion on him, and they got rid of it!"

Could what she'd said be interpreted that way? Maryn thought back over her words and realized they could. It was too late to change her story, though, so she just shrugged, trying to look like she didn't care one way or the other. "I don't know. Maybe." She bit her lip. "Please don't tell anyone else. Prince Carlich would be angry at me if he found out I told you about it."

"Oh, I won't. I swear." But Maryn was certain the servant girl would begin spreading the rumor as soon as she left the room. She had a sinking feeling she had inadvertently helped Carlich instead of undermining him.

Maryn snatched bites of porridge between tending a fussy Barilan and speaking with the servants who were constantly in and out of her room. A man brought a small trunk and began loading all Barilan's belongings into it. Another brought a leather pack into which Maryn stuffed her spare set of clothes. The need to call Carlich nagged at the back of her mind. She worried she wouldn't have a chance to work Siwell's fortifying spell before he came. But she snatched a moment when her room was empty to bite her finger and race through the words of the spell, barely finishing before another servant arrived to clear away her dirty bowl.

Eventually Carlich appeared and sent everyone else from the room. For the first time since they arrived in Ralo, he made her bare her arm so he could cut her. "I need to save all my strength," he said. "I can't afford to be low on blood when I face my sister. You'll have to provide until this is over."

Maryn suppressed a wince. Her arms were just starting to recover from the cuts he'd inflicted on their way here. Only in the past couple of days had she been free of a constant dull throb in her forearms. Now this fresh wound would start the healing process all over again.

When he finished the spell, Carlich beckoned to her. "Get Barilan and come with me. The servants will bring the gear."

She obediently gathered up Barilan and followed him from the room and down the corridor, though her heart quailed. Tior hadn't come through for her. How would she ever find the means or opportunity to spike Carlich's food with her milk while they were traveling?

Outside the guesthouse, in the courtyard that surrounded the Church's buildings, a huge gathering of men and horses milled about. Brightly colored banners snapped in the breeze; shouts and the stamping and snorting of beasts filled the air. Large groups of heavily armed men arrived, received orders, and departed, to be replaced by others wearing different livery. Carlich must have gained the support of every lord within a hundred miles to command so many.

Servants brought a tall, fiery warhorse for Carlich, and a placid palfrey on a lead rein for Maryn. Carlich held Barilan while Maryn mounted and settled into the sidesaddle, then passed him up to her. She wrapped her arms firmly around the baby. Barilan stared, captivated, at the activity around them, but his tense body told Maryn he was close to being overwhelmed by the noise and excitement.

Carlich swung up onto his mount. He made the beast rear and pivot, both of them restless with impatience. Captain Tennelan hailed him from across the courtyard; Carlich rode over to consult with him. The mounted guard leading Maryn's horse guided it to one side, out of the way.

They waited for a short while before Priest Vinhor appeared, wearing plain travel vestments. Servants helped him onto a glossy bay horse with an elegantly arched neck.

Carlich sidled his mount next to the priest. "What took you so long? Is everything ready?"

"Yes, your Highness. The last of the messengers has gone out. We may depart."

"It's about time!" Carlich wheeled his horse around and cantered toward the gate. Captain Tennelan joined him, and a number of soldiers formed an escort around them. The guard leading Maryn's mount clucked to his horse; Maryn tightened her knee around the pommel as the palfrey swayed into motion. Priest Vinhor fell into place, and all the rest of the company followed.

Their procession wound through streets lined with cheering and waving townspeople. The main gates swung open to let them pass. From the fields surrounding the town, great masses of mounted men and foot soldiers converged to join the throng. Every time Maryn twisted around to look, the line stretched farther behind them. Once she spotted Lord Negian's banner and wondered if her father or her brothers were among the levies he'd raised to march in Carlich's train.

Throughout the day's ride more troops flocked to their side. Every time a new band joined them, the leader would report to Carlich and Captain Tennelan, and Priest Vinhor would check off another name on his list. Carlich's eyes flashed brighter and his hands moved in ever more expansive gestures as the number of those prepared to fight for him against Voerell grew.

Because of the size of their company and the large proportion of foot soldiers, their pace was slow, and sunset overtook them less than halfway to Loempno. They made camp in a large wheat field, trampling golden stalks only a few weeks from harvest.

Maryn's legs nearly crumpled beneath her as she slid down from her mount. Her thighs and buttocks throbbed where the saddle had rubbed sores. Her arms ached from supporting Barilan all day and shook when Carlich passed the sleeping baby back to her. The motion roused him, and he screwed up his face and emitted a thin wail. Maryn closed her eyes and groaned, leaning against the solid side of her horse. Barilan had cried for most of the afternoon, resisting all her efforts to comfort him. She'd finally managed to lull him to sleep only a short time before they stopped. Now, robbed of a full nap, he'd be cranky all evening.

"As soon as my tent's ready, report to me there," Carlich ordered, fingering his sorcery knife and glancing at her arm.

Rage bubbled up within Maryn. She longed to spit a refusal in Carlich's face, jab a knee into his groin, and bolt. She didn't care that they were surrounded by thousands of Carlich's supporters and miles from any place she might find refuge. She just wanted the satisfaction of seeing the shock on his face when he realized he no longer controlled her.

It took all her strength to master her reaction and feign the proper meekness. "Yes, your Highness." She'd renewed Siwell's spell the last time they'd let her duck behind a bush to relieve herself. She could endure the pain of one more cut, and one more, as many as it took until the right time came to act. As she bowed her head and followed the servant Carlich indicated, she sent up a passionate prayer to the Holy One that the time might come soon.

She and Barilan were given a tent to themselves. It wasn't large, but it was well appointed with carpets and lamps and a spacious cot. They were confined to it, of course, with the usual guards at the entrance. But at least it was quiet and private. After a guard returned her from the requisite trip to Carlich's tent, Maryn was finally able to relax. She devoured slices of meat from one of the bullocks that had been commandeered from a nearby farm, slaughtered, and roasted over great fires to feed the prince and his retinue.

She moved slowly to put the dirty tin plate by the flap of the tent. It wasn't yet full dark, and Barilan was far too wound up to settle, but she longed to fall into bed and flee into sleep. Her anger had faded as quickly as it had come, leaving only despair. If Carlich guarded her like this all the way to Loempno, how could she ever slip away? She sat down on the cot and propped Barilan on her shoulder, rocking him and patting his back despite his vigorous protests.

So many people supported Carlich. Would he be able to prevail against Voerell, even though she was still regent? Maryn didn't know what mysterious magical power the Kingship was supposed to offer, only that Carlich and Vinhor feared facing Voerell while she wielded it. But she doubted any magic, no matter how strong, could stand against the sheer overwhelming size of the army Carlich had gathered.

Barilan's cries finally lost their angry edge and took on the pleading tone that told her he'd be receptive to nursing. She lay down on the cot and snuggled him to her breast. He sucked for a very long time, through many switches from one breast to the other, fighting every effort Maryn made to soothe him enough for exhaustion to overcome his resistance.

Even after he finally surrendered to sleep, Maryn lay awake, unable to quiet her circling thoughts. When Carlich won, when Princess Voerell was captured or dead and Carlich sat upon the throne of Milecha, Maryn would be doomed. He would kill her as soon as he had the chance. Barilan, too, when he contrived a way to get someone to do the deed for him. He'd have to make their deaths look accidental, but that wouldn't be difficult.

And their personal fates would be only the beginning. Her homeland would be left under the control of a usurper and murderer. Wonora would be furious about the broken treaty and his accusation of Princess Dolia. Carlich would call on his friends in Hampsia for help. How long before her small country was crushed in the conflict between the two great powers?

A strident whisper roused Maryn. "Miss Maryn! Quick, I only have a moment!"

Maryn slipped her breast free of Barilan's slack mouth and adjusted her clothing as she hurried to the tent flap. Her heart leapt when the stout figure ducked through. "Tior!"

He pulled a small object from under his jerkin. "Will this work?"

It was a glass bottle typical of those used to store perfume. The mouth was small, which would be a challenge, but it had a tight-fitting wax stopper. When she pried it open, a sweet floral scent wafted out. "It should do just fine. Where did you get it?"

Tior's round face reddened. "I found it in a trash pile," he mumbled.

Maryn was fairly sure he wasn't telling the truth. No one would throw away such a pretty and well-made bottle. Not that she cared. "I can't thank you enough." She threw her arms around him in a quick hug.

Blushing even deeper, Tior muttered, "It was nothing." He backed toward the tent flap, but then hesitated. "Actually...the perfume was mine. I keep it for when I have to deal with garbage, or bodies, that sort of thing. You know how I get queasy. After I helped clean up from the fire, I discovered that a little perfume on a handkerchief helps a lot. I just can't let any of the other soldiers find out; they think I've managed to get over it. That bottle was nearly empty, anyway."

The image of a rough soldier pressing a perfumed cloth to his face like a delicate lady struck Maryn as ridiculous, but she swallowed her laugh. She'd hate for Tior to think she was mocking him. "That's a clever solution."

Tior shrugged. "Yes, well, it works." He looked at

her earnestly. "I hope you manage to pull off whatever you're planning. If you need anything else, just ask. I'm willing to help." He ducked his head and studied the toe of his boot. "I've been thinking...You were right to call me a coward. I've been acting like one. I should have tried to smuggle you out of the Church guesthouse after all; it would have been easier there than here. We're right in the middle of the camp, with the army all around. But if you want, I can try. "

Maryn's throat tightened. "I'm sorry, Tior. I don't think you're a coward any more." She fingered the bottle. "I mean, you brought me this, just like you promised. Because of it, I've got a chance, now."

Heart pounding, she pulled the tent flap open a crack and peered out. Soldiers and servants bustled everywhere. As far as she could see campfires dotted the fields, their soft orange glow illuminating rows of low tents. Reluctantly, she let the flap fall. "You're right; it's too much of a risk to try escaping right now. With any luck I can make my idea work, and I'll be safe, at least for a little while. But could you please keep checking back with me as often as you can?" Her voice shook. "You're the only one here I can trust."

"I will. And I'll keep my eyes open for anything I can do." Tior bobbed his head at her. "I'd better go, before the other guard gets back from the latrine." He backed out of the tent.

Maryn stared after him, clutching the little bottle in her hand, struggling to cope with the rush of suddenly reawakened hope and all its accompanying fear. She half-wished she could stay resigned to despair; it would be easier than this constant rise and plunge of emotions. There was so little possibility her plan could actually work. But she pushed the thought away. A small chance had to be better than no chance at all.

She opened the perfume bottle and rinsed it with water from her washbasin until she could no longer taste any trace of the bitter flavor of the perfume. She tried to express a little milk into it, but had no luck. Both her breasts were thoroughly drained by Barilan's long nursing session, and she could get only a few meager drops. At last she gave up in frustration. She could try again in the morning; her milk was always most plentiful when she first rose from bed. She'd be sure to wake early enough, before the servants brought breakfast or Carlich called her to renew his spell. Barilan usually roused to nurse at least an hour before the sun rose; she'd do it then.

But Barilan chose that night to sleep through until dawn. Maryn was so worn out by the journey that she slept deeply also. She woke to the shouts of officers rousing their troops and the bustle of servants distributing breakfast.

She had to risk working Siwell's spell under her covers, using Barilan's eager nursing as an excuse not to rise while servants hustled about her tent, packing all the furnishings into neat bundles and bearing them out to the waiting wagons and pack mules. She finished barely in time. The guard who came to escort her to Carlich's tent was forced to wait, tapping his foot, while she pulled her skirt and bodice over her shift.

Carlich's tent was much larger and more elaborate than hers. The prince sat at a small table, picking at a bowl of porridge. He dropped his spoon and came to stand before her, gesturing for the guard to leave them alone.

Maryn's eyes darted past Carlich to where a lazy curl of steam rose from his bowl. She forced her gaze away. If only she'd been able get milk into the bottle!

She could feel the hard lump between her breasts where she'd tucked it down the front of her shift. She couldn't imagine that Carlich would leave her alone in his tent long enough for her to squirt in a little directly from the source. Although maybe, if Barilan was nursing, she could pop him off for just long enough. She shifted the baby in her arms, wondering how he would react to an offer of another nursing so soon after the last.

But she could do nothing while Carlich's eyes were on her. He drew his knife and beckoned for her arm. She balled her hand into a fist as she held it out to conceal the scabs that studded the corners of her fingernails. She hoped it looked as if she were merely prone to biting her nails. Who wouldn't be, after all she'd been through? But she didn't want to give Carlich any chance to become suspicious.

She should be used to the stroke of his knife by now, but if anything, each time hurt worse than the one before. Maybe it was the anticipation of pain that made her clench all her muscles, try as she might to relax them. Carlich completed his spell with precise efficiency.

He pointed to the tent flap. "Go on. The guard will escort you back to your tent. Get ready; we'll be riding within the hour."

Maryn risked a question. "Will we reach Loempno today, your Highness?"

He frowned, but answered. "No, that's not my intent. We'll camp tonight a short distance from the city and come to the gates at midmorning tomorrow."

Maryn fought to keep her shoulders from slumping in relief. She would have one more day and night to try and establish the milk-ties that would keep Carlich from killing her.

Several times that day she tried to snatch a few minutes alone to express milk into the little bottle, but it was impossible. The only times she wasn't closely guarded were when she was allowed a moment of privacy to take care of her bodily needs. She had to use that time to renew Siwell's strengthening spell, lest her will weaken and allow her to fall under Carlich's control.

Barilan was especially clingy and needy, wanting to spend many hours nursing. Her breasts labored to keep up with his demand, let alone produce extra. She thought he must be having one of those periodic growth spurts babies were prone to, when all they wanted to do for several days was nurse and sleep, and came out the other side an inch longer and a few pounds heavier than they'd been before.

She didn't get an opportunity to express milk all that day, and that evening she had as little success as the night before. But this time her determination and fear won out over her exhaustion. Even though Barilan again slept through the night, Maryn roused a full hour before sunrise and crawled from the cot.

Her breasts were full and heavy, and her milk flowed easily in response to her coaxing. Many full streams squirted out. Though much milk missed the narrow opening of the bottle, soaking the lap of her shift and spraying the rug around her folding stool, she managed to fill the bottle well before the rest of the camp began to stir.

She stoppered it, triumphant. Now the only thing that remained was to get access to something Carlich would eat or drink. If he followed the same pattern as the day before and summoned her to his tent, with any luck his breakfast porridge would again be there. She'd have to distract him long enough to pour a bit in. She pondered various schemes, trying to decide which Carlich would find least suspicious.

The damp folds of her shift clung to her legs. Siwell had said milk didn't attract specters the way blood did, but the memory of those horrors made Maryn loath to take any chances. She murmured the words of the cleansing spell. Showers of blue sparks exploded from her shift and the ground around her. Vibrations buzzed up her spine and into her teeth.

Maryn looked at the sparks and wondered. Maybe she could have used the power stored in the milk to fuel Siwell's spell instead of having to chew yet another painful sore on her finger. She'd never heard of milk being used that way. But if it released that much power when cleansed, it stood to reason she should be able to harness it instead of only burning it up.

It was too late to try this time. She went ahead with the familiar process of drawing a few drops of blood and worked Siwell's spell.

Maryn hoped Tior would be the one to escort her to Carlich's tent, but the guard was another stranger. Her heart fell when she saw him. The best plan she'd come up with involved Tior creating some sort of commotion that would draw Carlich from the tent. Now she'd have to use a different ploy, one she feared would be less likely to succeed.

As soon as she stepped inside the tent, her eyes went to the table. A bowl of porridge rested there, just as she'd hoped. It looked as if Carlich hadn't touched it yet. Far across the tent, he peered into a small polished bronze mirror, adjusting the way his richly embroidered surcoat fell over his chain mail tunic.

A servant stood beside him, holding a long scarlet cape trimmed with gold. At Carlich's curt gesture, he helped fasten it to the prince's shoulders. Finished, the servant stepped back and inclined his head. "Now, your Highness, you must eat. Priest Vinhor bade me remind you that you'll need all your strength today."

Carlich waved him away with a snarl. "I'm not hungry. Leave it there; maybe I'll manage to choke down a little later." He turned, the cape swirling around him, and looked over his shoulder into the mirror. "That will have to do. Leave us."

"Yes, your Highness." The servant bowed and brushed past Maryn out of the tent.

A few quick strides carried Carlich to Maryn. He held out his hand. Maryn's heart pounded in her ears. She made her voice strained, as if she were fighting the dregs of his spell. "A—a moment, your Highness, please?"

"What?" He scowled at her.

She didn't dare meet his eyes. "Please, your Highness, would you look at Fril—I mean, Barilan, for me? He seems so different since we worked the spell to bring Frilan's soul back. I can't believe Princess Voerell won't notice right away. What if she realizes we've done something to him? I'm afraid she'll try to hurt him."

"I won't let her do that." But Carlich accepted Barilan when she held him out.

"Just take him over there, and I'll go over here where he can't see me." Maryn walked across the tent, stopping next to the table. "See if anything about the way he acts seems strange to you. If you can't tell it's really Frilan, I'm sure Voerell won't be able to either."

"I don't have time for this." But Carlich stepped to the far side of the tent and held up Barilan at arm's length. The baby laughed as Carlich swooped him from side to side. "Well, little one? Will your mother—your other mother—be able to tell you're not really hers any more? I need her to believe you are, at least for a short time. I can win the day by force if I must, but it will be far better if she surrenders without a fight."

As soon as he turned his back, Maryn snatched the little bottle of milk from her bodice. She fumbled the stopper free. Only a few drops, or Carlich might taste the difference. She dribbled milk into the bowl; more than she intended sloshed out, puddling on the surface. Maryn corked the bottle and shoved it back into its hiding place, then grabbed the spoon and gave a few quick stirs. It seemed the milk would never incorporate into the thick porridge, and she despaired that she had used too much, but just in time she became satisfied that it was mixed in enough to be undetectable.

She stepped away and put her hands behind her back as Carlich gave Barilan a final bounce. The baby squealed in pleasure. Carlich turned back toward Maryn. "No, I can't see anything odd. Voerell should be fooled without any problem."

Maryn hurried across the tent, speaking rapidly the first words that came into her head to keep Carlich's attention away from the bowl. "Are you sure Frilan has to be there when you confront Princess Voerell?" She reached to take the baby back, and wrapped her arms around him. "What if she resists, and there's a battle? I'm so afraid he's going to get hurt. Couldn't you leave us behind in the camp where it's safe?"

To Maryn's surprise, Carlich tilted his head to one side and narrowed his eyes as if he was actually considering her proposal. She scrambled to think of more arguments. If she could persuade him, surely she could find an opportunity to slip away with Barilan while he and all his men were engaged in the conflict. "I don't see what good it will do you to have him there. It will just give the princess a chance to figure out what we've done."

Carlich's expression hardened. "No. She'll insist on seeing him. She'll never believe I haven't harmed him, otherwise. And they must see for themselves that he does not hold the Kingship."

"Couldn't you—I don't know, make an illusion, or something? Make it look like we're there, when we're not? You're a great sorcerer, I'm sure it would be easy for you." Maryn hoped she wasn't overdoing the flattery.

Carlich snorted. "I can only dream of such skill. I've never heard of sorcery strong enough to create such an illusion out of nothing. It would have to be real both to sight and touch, and last for hours, moving and speaking. Utterly impossible." His eyes went unfocused. "Now, if I started with some other woman and child, so that I only had to alter their appearance…That would be fairly simple. Maybe that would have been a better plan from the beginning…" He shook his head. "It's too late to consider anything like that now. You and Frilan will be safe, I promise. If it comes to a fight, I'll make sure you're protected."

Oh, well. She hadn't really expected it to work. The distraction had accomplished its main purpose; Carlich hadn't even glanced at the bowl of porridge. "If that's what you think best, your Highness. Thank you." She wasn't sure if she should continue, but she had to know for sure what he intended. "And…after it's all over, when you're king and Princess Voerell is no longer a danger to you, you'll let Frilan and me go? I swear, I'll never breathe a word of anything I saw. I know you only did what you had to, just as I did. You'll always have my full support, even long after your spell wears off. It's not necessary anymore. Not since you gave Frilan back to me."

As soon as she started speaking Carlich opened his mouth, his expression falsely bright. But as her words poured out he shut it again and listened, his brows drawing together. When she fell silent, he gave her a long, searching look. "You really mean that, don't you? Tell me the truth. The spell's still strong enough you have to obey me. Have you truly given me your loyalty? Do you want me to become king?"

Maryn forced herself to meet Carlich's eyes, her expression as open and guileless as she could make it. "I do, your Highness." She ignored the twist in her gut the lie provoked and tried to make herself believe the words as she spoke them, so Carlich would read sincerity in her face and voice. "I've seen enough to know you're far stronger than Voerell. Milecha will be safe in your hands."

Carlich rubbed his chin, staring at her. Maryn returned his gaze for as long as she could bear, but when his silence stretched long she dropped her eyes to Barilan and fussed with untangling his fingers from the tie of her shift.

Abruptly Carlich stepped toward her and gripped her upper arms. She smelled the metal and leather of his mail mingled with his masculine scent. "I'm going to be honest with you, Maryn. Vinhor wants me to get rid of you and Frilan after we don't need you anymore. He's sure you'd go to my enemies and they'd use you against me."

Maryn trembled, fighting the urge to wrench herself from his grasp. "I wouldn't. I swear."

"I believe you. I don't care what Vinhor says; I'll

protect you and your son. I'll see you settled safe somewhere far away, with new identities and enough money you'll never want. All I ask is that you stand beside me and support me in my bid for the Kingship."

"Of course I will, your Highness." Maryn's voice was so ragged she was sure Carlich would perceive her deception, but his gaze never wavered. "I'll do whatever you ask. But I don't see how anything I can do will make a difference."

"There's one thing." Carlich released her arms and stepped back. Maryn felt limp with relief, and her breath came more easily. "When the time comes for me to claim the Kingship, I'll need the whole crowd shouting that they want me as their king. Vinhor says the magic will be most potent if the cry arises spontaneously from the common people, rather than me asking for it. I was going to have Tennelan or one of his soldiers get it started, but I think it will work even better coming from you. Everyone will see that your motives are pure. Why else would Barilan's nurse acclaim me as King, except that you believe I'm the best ruler for Milecha?"

Maryn swallowed, her mind racing. There was no reason she shouldn't shout for Carlich to become King. As long as Barilan safely held the Kingship, it wouldn't accomplish anything. And her cooperation would prove to Carlich that he could trust her. If he managed to win after all, he'd remember. She was almost certain he was sincere in his promise to spare her. Maybe she really could save herself and Barilan.

She inclined her head. "I would be honored, your Highness."

"Good." Carlich grinned. "When I give you the signal, shout as loud as you can, 'King Carlich!'"

"King Carlich!" Maryn echoed, putting all the enthusiasm she could muster into her voice. Fed by her new hope, the cry rang out clear and strong.

Carlich nodded approval. For a moment his eyes were far away, and his hands sketched a few motions in the air. Maryn thought he must be listening to the crowd's acclaim in his imagination and practicing the gestures that would bring him his greatest desire.

Would he be willing to forgo the compulsion spell if she asked? It was possible, but she didn't want to risk him changing his mind later. If he was going to cut her, she had to make sure he did it before he tasted her milk. If the magic worked as she hoped, he wouldn't be able to afterward. She still wanted that protection. There was always the chance Carlich's new resolve would falter under Vinhor's persuasion.

She gave a little cough to draw his attention back to the present. Shifting Barilan to one arm, she thrust the other toward Carlich. "I'm ready, your Highness." The spell would last half a day. Carlich planned to meet Voerell outside the city gates at midmorning. Before the time came to renew the magic, it would all be over, one way or another.

Carlich drew his knife and took her wrist in his hand. He paused, the tip of the knife poised over her flesh. "I'm sorry. I still must do this. Vinhor would never let me hear the end of it if I didn't."

"I understand, your Highness." Maryn kept her voice level. "It's not so bad, not when I want to obey anyway. Only—if I might be allowed to think for myself…"

"I can do that." Carlich moved with his usual surety to open a neat slice in her skin and wave his hands through the familiar motions of the spell. "There. Do what I tell you as usual, but you may think whatever you wish, and speak freely to me when no one else can hear."

Even under the effects of Siwell's spell Maryn could feel the difference. The effort of fighting his magic for control of her mind vanished. She felt more clear-headed than she had since Carlich first cast his spell. She didn't have to fake the relief in her voice. "Thank you, your Highness."

Carlich regarded her with a little half-smile. "Go on now. Get Frilan—I mean Barilan, of course—ready to show Voerell. We ride in an hour."

"Yes, your Highness. I'll be ready to act at your command. And I'll pray to the Holy One for your success." Maryn curtseyed deeply and turned to go. Carlich strode back to the mirror and scowled into it.

Maryn hesitated. She hated to leave without knowing whether Carlich would ever eat the porridge. From what he'd said, he probably wouldn't. Since he'd given her permission to speak, maybe she could risk giving him a nudge in that direction without rousing his suspicion. "Aren't you going to eat your breakfast now, your Highness? As your servant said, you need all your strength today." She picked up the bowl and carried it to him. "Nothing must interfere with your ability to stand against Princess Voerell and work the magic you plan."

He grimaced. "I never have any appetite before a battle." But he accepted the bowl, though he only poked at the porridge with the spoon.

Maryn gave her voice the warmly affectionate scolding tone her mother had always used on her. "Do you think you can breathe in sustenance with the air? The Holy One has given us the great blessing of his bounty; we shouldn't let it go to waste. Eat!"

Carlich grinned crookedly at her. "You remind me

of my nurse." He scooped up a small blob, stuck it in his mouth, and made an exaggerated swallowing motion. "There. Happy now?"

Maryn wanted to break into a broad grin, but she contented herself with a little severe smile. "Very good, your Highness. Now take another bite."

Carlich waved the spoon at her. "Stop it. You sound exactly like Kegill." He shot her a teasing smirk. "Do all wet nurses receive the same training in bullying their charges?" He scooped one more spoonful into his mouth before setting the bowl down on a nearby chair. "Go on, go on. I promise I'll be a good boy." He shooed her away, chuckling, until Maryn couldn't help but grin in return.

As soon as the tent flap closed behind her, the smile fell from Maryn's face, and she gave her head a hard shake. Sometimes Carlich acted so charming she doubted herself. It was easy to see why people liked and trusted him, and why so many were willing to answer when he called.

Could she be wrong? Maybe Carlich really would rule Milecha better than Voerell. Kings had to be ruthless, didn't they? They couldn't always abide by the rules that governed ordinary folk, not when the fate of their kingdom was at stake.

Maybe she could go along with his plan. If she demonstrated her loyalty in a convincing enough fashion, Carlich would defy Vinhor and keep his promise to protect her. She and Barilan would be safe. She tightened her arms around the baby. She'd never have to give him back to his mother. She'd never again risk being dismissed from her position as his nurse. Barilan would be hers for good. Maybe he'd be happier growing up as her son, never knowing who he really was, far away from the dangers and burdens of the Kingship. Why not let Carlich take those on himself if he wanted them so much?

The waiting guard escorted Maryn back to her tent. Everywhere she looked she saw soldiers strapping on armor, stringing bows, and sharpening blades. Carlich's army blanketed the fields all the way to the horizon.

Maryn set about changing Barilan into his most ornate gown. She considered her options. When Carlich signaled her, she could do as he'd asked and raise the shout of acclaim. It wouldn't bring him the Kingship, but with the people's support he might very well defeat Voerell by force of arms anyway. Perhaps she could risk working another illusion spell and make the crown appear over Carlich's head, so he wouldn't discover her deception. Carlich would believe her loyal to him and provide for her as he'd promised.

Or, when the time came, she could instead denounce Carlich as loudly and forcefully as she could. Maybe enough people would hear and believe her to make a difference, before Carlich silenced her. If her ploy was successful, King Froethych's spell would protect her from him. Maybe it would buy her a few more minutes to declare the truth. Maybe she could sway the balance and Voerell could triumph.

But if Voerell failed, and Carlich won the day despite Maryn's best efforts, he would know she'd betrayed him. Then nothing could save her and Barilan from his fury. It would be easy enough for Vinhor or someone else to kill them, even if Carlich couldn't give the order.

Was she willing to risk herself and Barilan for such a small chance of saving Milecha from Carlich? Or would she take the safer route and sacrifice her homeland?

Maryn gathered Barilan in her arms and pressed her face into the top of his head. Would it really be that bad if Carlich became king? Could she honestly condemn his actions, or would she have done much the same in his place? Maryn, too, had been tempted to kill. She knew what it felt like to want something so badly all other considerations faded away. She'd surrendered to that temptation, at least a little, at least enough to weaken her resolve to fight the compulsion spell. Maybe everyone could be bought, if the price was high enough. Maybe Carlich was no worse than anyone else.

No. Somewhere Carlich had crossed a line most people didn't. Maryn thought of him crouched over his brother as Marolan choked out his life. She remembered the rage in his eyes as he'd threatened her and the speed of his hand striking toward Barilan. She recalled the eagerness in his voice as he'd offered her Frilan's soul in exchange for Barilan's.

How could she support that, even if she was just as guilty? How could she help him take power, even if she could buy her own safety and Barilan's by doing so?

She couldn't. She would have to take the riskier path and pray that Voerell was strong enough to defeat her brother.

Maryn was only a servant, only a woman, weak and insignificant. It was ridiculous presumption for her to think anything she could do would hinder a powerful man like Carlich. The chances were vanishingly small that her attempt would work.

But her resolve was clear. If she could stop him, she would.

Twenty

aryn caught sight of a cloud of dust on the road ahead. She straightened in her saddle, watching. As the cloud drew closer, she made out a cantering horse with a fluttering white banner streaming over its back.

Carlich shaded his eyes against the glare of the early morning sun and studied the approaching rider. He turned to Tennelan. "Voerell's sent a herald to answer me. Give the men a rest break while I confer with him."

Tennelan saluted and wheeled his horse. He rode back toward the ranks of troops, calling orders. Men thronged the road as far as Maryn could see, professional soldiers in disciplined straight lines interspersed with peasant levies in ragged blocks. There had to be thousands of them.

Carlich kicked his steed into a trot, and the rest of his immediate company followed. Maryn clutched Barilan and clung to the pommel of her saddle as her palfrey stretched its legs to keep up with her guard's mount.

The herald reined in his horse as Carlich drew close. "Your Highness!" he called. "Regent Voerell has sent me to inform you that she accepts your request for a parley." He dismounted and dropped to one knee.

Maryn's horse slowed to a walk and halted close behind the prince's steed. Carlich swung down and took the roll of parchment the herald offered, gesturing for the man to rise. Maryn strained to hear what they said. The more she knew of what would happen when they reached Loempno, the better prepared she'd be.

Carlich unrolled the parchment and scanned it. "Hmm. Looks like she's offering the standard terms. I wouldn't have thought my little sister familiar enough with military matters to know what they were."

The herald ignored the insult to his mistress. "Your Highness, the regent instructed me to emphasize that she will only consent to meet if King Barilan accompanies you, alive and unharmed."

Carlich waved expansively toward Maryn. "There he is. I'm happy to agree to her demand. You can tell her you saw Barilan yourself, fat and happy."

The herald walked toward Maryn's horse. Maryn held Barilan up. He was in a good mood, waving his arms around and making cheerful noises. The jewels on his gown sparkled in the sunlight.

The herald studied him gravely for a long moment before nodding. "I will convey your agreement to the regent."

Carlich held up a hand. "Wait. This section is not acceptable." He jabbed a finger at the parchment. "My men must be able to see me and hear what I say. There's no need for a bowshot of clear space around us. I'll ward the area against weapons, and Voerell can have Rogelan do the same. That was always standard practice when we met with the Hampsians."

The herald inclined his head. "The regent agreed to negotiate any terms save the one I specified."

"And here. What's she thinking, putting us down in a hollow? There's a nice little hill about a quarter mile from the gates. From there we can each address our troops. Vinhor, fetch your clerk so he can write all this down."

Vinhor came forward with his brown-robed clerk, who set to work transcribing Carlich's counter-proposal. Vinhor leaned close to Carlich and murmured in his ear too quietly for Maryn to hear. Carlich listened, then nodded. "Good point." He turned back to the herald. "I require at least ten guards be allowed to accompany me inside the wards. Of course I'll agree to Voerell bringing a similar number if she wishes..."

Maryn shifted in the saddle. The negotiations over minor details seemed likely to go on for some time. She cleared her throat to get the attention of the guard holding her mount's lead rein. "Excuse me, but Barilan's diaper needs changing. May I dismount so I can take care of it?"

The guard looked at Carlich, who remained deep in conversation with Vinhor and the herald. "I suppose," he said, scowling. Though Maryn had done her best to make friendly overtures, the man had remained curt and hostile during the whole journey. He displayed greater impatience every time he was required to keep watch over Maryn as she tended Barilan's needs. Maryn hadn't even been able to learn his name.

The guard glanced around. Suddenly his scowl was replaced by a broad grin. "Hey, Tior! Get over here. I've got a job for you."

Tior bounced up on the back of a horse as short and round as he was. "Yes, sir?"

"Take the nurse over there and help her with the

king's diaper." He sniggered, then opened his eyes wide and gave his voice a broadly exaggerated tone of solicitude. "Oh, dear. I forgot all about your little— *problem*. A stinky diaper might make you lose your breakfast. Should I get someone else to do it?"

Tior kept his face and voice expressionless, though Maryn saw his fingers tighten on the reins. "No, sir."

"Get to it, then." The guard settled back in his saddle, a mocking smile returning to his features.

Tior swung down from his horse and tossed the reins to the guard. He held Barilan while Maryn dismounted and grabbed her saddlebag. Together they hurried off the road. Maryn went as far as she dared, aware of the guard's watchful eyes on her back. She found a level patch of grass and kicked at it to make sure no rocks or sticks lurked, then knelt, spread out her skirts, and laid Barilan down on them.

Tior cleared his throat. "Should I get out my handkerchief?" He nearly succeeded in keeping his voice light.

"No, he's not messy, just wet." Maryn busied herself unfastening the cloth and digging in her bag for a clean one. She spoke quietly. "Any chance to run, do you think?" If she could bring Barilan to Voerell and let the princess know he still held the Kingship, she could weaken Carlich and gain a refuge for herself and Barilan at the same time.

Tior looked across the rolling fields to where the rooftops of Loempno were visible in the distance. "We'd never get there before they caught us, even if I could get my horse. He's slow."

"I didn't think so." Maryn's voice shook. "I guess I'll just have to go through with my plan. Listen, Tior. I need you to help me. I'm going to denounce Carlich, as loud as I can. When I do, he'll try to stop me. I worked magic so he can't hurt me himself, but Vinhor can, or anyone else. If you could stop them, if you get the chance, or at least slow them down..." She swallowed.

"Of course," he assured her. "I'll be ready. Whatever you need."

"Thank you. I don't know what I'd do without you." Maryn bent to her task.

Tior scuffed at the dirt with his foot as Maryn finished fastening Barilan's diaper. She scooped the baby up and straightened. Before she could head back, Tior put out a hand and touched her arm. "Maryn...Did you really tell me the whole truth? Because everyone around camp is saying you saw Priest Vinhor work a spell to remove an illusion from Barilan. That he never inherited the Kingship after all, and it was all a trick by Princess Voerell. I wouldn't blame you if you didn't trust me. If you thought you had to lie to get my cooperation. But I can help you better if I know the truth."

Maryn grabbed his hand. "Of course I told you the truth." She couldn't help but respond to the lost, hurt look in his eyes with compassion. But at the same time, impatience flared. How many times was she going to have to coddle him through another crisis of confidence? He was her only ally; she had no choice but to depend on him. But what if he lost heart at a crucial moment?

She shook her head and pulled her hand free to rub her temple. "I tried to start a rumor that Vinhor had created an illusion to hide Barilan's Kingship, but that stupid girl got it all wrong. Everybody's saying it? That means they'll all be ready to believe Carlich when he tells them Barilan isn't really king." She fought back tears. "What if I can't stop them, Tior?

What if no matter what I say, they acclaim Carlich anyway? Will they even realize when Vinhor's spell doesn't work to give Carlich the Kingship? It won't take a glowing crown over his head to make them willing to fight for him. It will be all my fault when he defeats Voerell."

Tior stared at her. "Wait—you think Carlich's going to try to take the Kingship for himself, by acclaim?"

"I'm sure of it. He told me so himself. He wants me to start the shouting when it's time." Maryn shuddered. "He promised to protect me and Barilan, if I do. But I won't! Even if I can't stop him, I won't help him!

"But Barilan is really still king, right?"

"Of course. Carlich thinks he's not, because he believes I worked the magic to switch his soul for Frilan's. I did magic to hide the crown when they scried for it. But the Kingship is still his."

Maryn didn't understand the excitement that lit Tior's face. "But that's perfect!"

"What?"

"Don't you know? If Carlich tries to make himself king while Barilan still holds the Kingship, the magic—it will kill him." Fearful awe tinged Tior's words.

Maryn gaped at him. "Kill him? How? Are you sure?"

"That's part of the magic of the Kingship. It protects itself from being stolen. They taught the recruits all about it when I joined the army."

"Carlich knows?" Even as she asked, Maryn realized that he must. That was why he and Vinhor had been so determined to make sure Barilan was no longer king before setting their plans in motion.

"He would have to. So all we need to do is keep

quiet. Or you can even start the shouting, just like he wants. Then when he tries to take the crown—"

Maryn's breath quickened. "He'll die."

Tior nodded.

Maryn pressed her face into Barilan's hair, breathing deeply, trying to come to terms with the rush of conflicting emotions this new information triggered. Carlich would fail. She wouldn't have to do anything else, persuade anyone to believe her, work any more magic. What she'd already accomplished was enough. One cry of "King Carlich," and she and Barilan would be safe. Milecha would be saved. She had worked so hard and so long for that—could it really be so easy?

She should be overjoyed, and joy was certainly a part of what she was feeling. But she'd never dreamed, when she'd worked the magic to hide Barilan's Kingship, that her actions would result in Carlich's death. She'd never imagined that she would be in a position to kill anyone. Even Carlich. Especially Carlich. Even if he deserved it, even if it was his own greedy ambition that would doom him, not her choice. Could she begin the shout that would invoke that magic, knowing what it would do?

She'd have to. This was the opportunity she'd prayed for. "Come on." Maryn set off back toward the cluster of horses and people. "It's more important than ever that we don't do anything to arouse suspicion. Can you stay close?"

"That's what I've been trying to do." Tior trotted to keep up with her. "I'll ask to guard Carlich during the negotiations. Everybody will want to be picked for that, but Captain Tennelan is good about rewarding people who've been willing to take the dull jobs."

"Good." Maryn glanced at him, doing her best to smile, though it was shaky. "Thank the Holy One you told me. I was determined to do whatever I could to *stop* people from acclaiming him."

"I didn't realize you didn't know, or I would have told you before."

"Anything else I should know?" Maryn shivered to think that everything might turn on some bit of information about magic or the Kingship that she'd never had the chance to learn.

Tior shrugged. "Not that I can think of. It's not like I know much either. I'd never heard of most of the history they taught the recruits. There's not much chance for a merchant's youngest son to learn those things."

"Even less for a serf's daughter." If somehow she lived through this, that would change, Maryn promised herself. It was too dangerous to live among the powerful without arming herself with all the information she could.

They arrived just as Carlich was concluding the negotiations. The herald saluted and cantered off toward the city. Tior helped Maryn mount. He shot her an anxious look as he swung back onto his steed and went to join the other guards.

The sun had risen halfway up the sky when they arrived at the appointed place outside the walls of the city. Voerell's troops blanketed the surrounding countryside, their indigo uniforms bright as bluebells against the golden fields. Archers crowded the tops of the walls, and spears bristled among the ranks on the ground. They appeared more disciplined than the majority of Carlich's forces, but even Maryn could tell there were fewer of them.

The hill Carlich had chosen as the meeting place

rose not far from the road, a smooth green swell broken only by a few outcroppings of rock, bare of any trees or bushes, its peak flat. Four white flags marked off a large square area at the top. Voerell's forces thronged the far side, crowding right up to the foot of the rise, but the open meadow away from the city was empty, awaiting Carlich's troops.

Maryn fretted while the preparations went forward. It took at least an hour for Carlich to get everyone in place to his satisfaction. Maryn watched him surreptitiously as she waited with her guard off to one side, trying to keep Barilan quiet. Carlich rode back and forth, erect in the saddle, arms waving in grand dramatic gestures as he called directions to the various officers. He never lost his patience, even when many of the peasant levies wandered into the wrong places or ignored their superiors' orders while they gaped at the soaring walls of the city and the towers within. Instead, he kept after them with the skill and persistence of a dog herding sheep, until they covered the fields like a great patched quilt. At last he nodded his approval and sent a herald to notify Voerell that he was ready.

The delegation gathered at the base of the hill. Carlich called Maryn to stand next to him. Vinhor waited on his other side. Captain Tennelan set his ten chosen soldiers in order. Maryn scanned them. Yes, there was Tior. He flashed a grin at Maryn as he unbuckled his sword and laid it in a pile with all the others. Maryn managed a wan smile back. Her heart was beating so hard she could scarcely breathe.

Carlich led them up the hill. Just outside the square of flags, Carlich stopped. For a moment he studied the area. Two heralds, one of Carlich's and one of Voerell's, faced each other motionless in the center, long trumpets at their sides. Carlich turned in a slow circle, taking in the troops gathered all around like an audience awaiting a traveling players' show.

He gave a sharp nod, then turned to Maryn. "Stay close to me, and be ready to present Barilan when I call for him." Carlich stared searchingly into Maryn's eyes as she nodded obedience to his order. He must have been satisfied by what he saw, for he squared his shoulders and strode between the flags. Maryn clutched Barilan and followed, the others crowding close behind.

Princess Voerell and her retinue entered the square from the far side. Voerell, in the lead, was dressed in a regal scarlet robe, heavy with gold embroidery, over ornate skirts. She wore a smaller, less elaborate copy of the crown of Milecha. Maryn saw her head move restlessly back and forth, scanning Carlich's group, until her eyes found the baby in Maryn's arms. Voerell froze, staring at Barilan.

Maryn hoisted Barilan high so the princess could see him clearly. Barilan kicked his feet and babbled, his eyes tracking a bird that broke from the cover of the grass at their feet and soared skyward. Maryn tried to catch Voerell's gaze. *See, I kept your son safe for you. I've made it so Carlich can't take his crown, so he'll die trying. I'm on your side; you can trust me.*

But Voerell never spared so much as a glance for Maryn. Even the sight of her son didn't lighten the grim stoniness of her face nor soften the harsh lines that hadn't been there the last time Maryn had seen her.

Prelate Kiellan laid a hand on the princess's arm and murmured to her. Voerell shook herself and proceeded forward, but her eyes kept going back to Barilan as she took her place. Kiellan and Rogelan took up stations on either side, and her guards arranged themselves in a semicircle behind her.

Carlich positioned himself facing Voerell, a few feet away. He beckoned Maryn to stand beside him. Vinhor and Tennelan stood on his far side, and the guards spread out behind. Maryn couldn't tell where in the arc Tior was stationed, and she didn't dare look around to see.

The two heralds raised their trumpets to their lips. In unison a bright fanfare rang out. At the first blast Barilan jerked and screeched in protest. Maryn cupped her hand over one of his ears and pressed the other to her chest to muffle the sound, but he wailed in strident discord with the music while the heralds completed their tune. In the quiet that followed, his cries continued. Maryn fumbled with her shift. The heralds snapped their trumpets down, bowed to the delegation on each side, and turned on their heels to exit on opposite sides of the square. Maryn ducked her head over Barilan, her face hot, certain everyone was looking at her, until finally she managed to get Barilan latched on and his shrieks abruptly cut off. A hush fell over the square.

Rogelan cleared his throat and stepped forward. "As was agreed, the square will now be warded. No one may enter nor exit until the parley is over and the wards are broken. All weapons will be excluded, save that each side may choose two who may retain their sorcery knives. I will be performing the magic for the regent. I will keep one knife, as will Prelate Kiellan. Who will do so for you, Prince Carlich?"

Carlich nodded to him. "I'll perform the spell myself, Rogelan. Priest Vinhor and I will retain our knives. Come, let us begin." He moved to the left edge of the square, midway between the two corner flags. Rogelan glanced at Voerell, and at her nod he stepped to stand beside Carlich. In unison the two sorcerers drew their knives, pricked their fingers, and spoke the opening words of the spell. Maryn noticed that Carlich performed this spell verbally, speaking the ancient language with just as much skill and confidence as Rogelan. They moved apart, each circling behind the other's delegation, stooping every few steps to smudge a bit of blood on the ground. Where they passed, a subtle blue shimmer hazed the air, growing until it walled in the entire square and arched overhead. When they met at the far side they spoke the closing words together, then each returned to his place. A murmur rose from the observing armies on both sides of the hill. Maryn could hear it clearly, though the ward spell blurred her view so that colors ran together as if viewed through thick glass.

The voices fell silent as Prelate Kiellan stepped forward. "As was further agreed, I will conduct a ritual of blessing before we begin the negotiations, that the Holy One may guide us in all our dealings today. Would Priest Vinhor like to assist me?" His voice was cordial, betraying no hint of displeasure at finding his rival among the enemy's close associates.

Vinhor was somewhat less adroit at concealing his hostility, though it manifested only as excessive precision in his motions and an exaggerated clarity in the way he enunciated his words. "I would." He stepped forward. The two clergymen inclined their heads to each other and in unison began to chant the invocation to the Holy One. The ritual proceeded in perfect harmony, the two men's voices blending pleasantly, the blue sparks of their blood fountaining upward from their open palms. Maryn closed her eyes and added her own silent pleas for the Holy

One's guidance. When Vinhor and Kiellan finished, they bowed to each other and stepped back to join their respective parties.

Voerell stepped forward into the clear space vacated by Priest and Prelate. Tearing her eyes away from the nursing Barilan, she fixed a fierce glare on Carlich. Everyone hushed to hear what she would say.

Her voice rang out harsh and clear in the silence. "My brother, I have agreed to meet with you only so that I may tell you directly what I think of your actions. How dare you raise an army against your lawful sovereign? You have incited those who follow you into treason against their sworn king and his regent. You have kidnapped my son, the rightful king of Milecha. For these crimes, along with the foul murders of our brother Prince Marolan and my husband Duke Whirter, you have earned the most severe penalty." Voerell's voice betrayed her strain, but she managed to get the words out without breaking her smooth rhythm. "But if you surrender immediately and unconditionally, and dismiss all your followers back to their homes, I may be persuaded to show mercy. I will not hold them culpable for consenting to follow you as long as they all depart at once, for I know you to be most persuasive. But I will accept nothing less from you than your surrender to royal justice, and the return of King Barilan to me unharmed."

Carlich listened to Voerell's speech with a slight, amused smile. When she finished, he nodded graciously. "Thank you for your welcome, my sister. If you show somewhat less warmth than I might desire, I'm willing to let that pass. You misunderstand my purpose here. Treason? I assure you, nothing is farther from my intent. I wish only the good of Milecha, and to see our land's rule restored to its true king. Will you allow me to put forth my case?"

Voerell's lips twisted into a snarl, but her voice remained controlled. "Speak your piece."

Carlich inclined his head. "In our distress following our brother's death, we both seem to have made a number of false assumptions. You jumped to the conclusion that I had murdered Marolan, while I assumed that you had conspired with Dolia of Wonora to carry it out. I now believe we were both wrong, and that Dolia committed the deed herself, perhaps with the aid of the Wonoran ambassador. In our haste to accuse each other, we each made grave mistakes. In the struggle I slew your husband, for which transgression I deeply apologize." He bowed low to her, though Voerell's expression didn't soften from its hard scowl. "And you persuaded our father to disinherit me. When his spell ran out of control and killed him, there was no opportunity for him to correct that error, and the Kingship did not pass to me upon his death as it should have."

"I made no mistake." Voerell started to step forward, but Prelate Kiellan restrained her with a light touch to her arm. She balled her hands into fists. "We all saw you destroy the evidence that would have proven your guilt."

Carlich waved dismissively. "Because I feared Dolia—or you, though as I said I no longer suspect that—had contaminated it so I would be falsely convicted. But that's irrelevant."

Voerell began a hot retort, but Carlich held up a hand and raised his voice to drown her out. "We both assumed that the Kingship had settled on Barilan. Yet now I know that was not the case. Perhaps the heirship ceremony was not performed properly, or maybe my unjust disinheritance disrupted the magic. But whatever the reason, Priest Vinhor and I have examined Prince Barilan, and the Kingship does not presently reside in his soul."

A murmur of surprise ran through all those assembled on both sides of the hill. As heralds transmitted Carlich's words throughout both waiting armies, a clamor arose. Carlich let it run for a few minutes. Voerell turned and spoke with quiet urgency to Prelate Kiellan and Sorcerer Rogelan, who drew close and murmured in reply. At length Carlich raised his hand again, and the outburst gradually faded.

"I don't expect you to believe me without proof. Therefore, my sister, I'm willing to allow whichever priest or sorcerer you choose to examine Barilan right now, here in full view of everyone, and ascertain that what I say is true."

Voerell consulted with her advisors again. After they spoke for a moment, she faced Carlich and raised her voice. "You're right, brother. I don't believe you. I will certainly examine Barilan. But first, let us say that you are correct, and Barilan does not hold the Kingship, and therefore I do not hold the Regency. What do you propose should then be done?"

Carlich spread his hands. "Why, in that case, my sister, the Kingship will be unclaimed, available to whoever wins the support of the people. All I ask is that it be returned to the one our father chose as his heir, in the proper line of succession, before the chaos surrounding his death disrupted it." He turned to face his assembled troops. "Who will you acclaim as your king?" he shouted.

"Carlich!" came the return shout. As word of his

question spread to those who were too far away to have heard it, more and more joined in, until the rhythmic chant thundered across the plain. "Carlich! Carlich! Carlich!"

Maryn couldn't be sure, but she thought that even some among Voerell's troops on the far side of the hill took up the cry. Voerell listened with a white face and lips pinched into a thin line.

Carlich basked in the adulation for a few minutes, then made a great show of waving his hands, attempting to subdue the chanting. After a long time it quieted, though occasional cries of "Carlich!" still broke out. Maryn gulped, recognizing how cleverly Carlich had prepared the crowd. One shout from her, and they all would erupt again into their ardent demand.

He turned to Voerell with a triumphant expression just short of a smirk. "Well, my sister?"

Voerell met Carlich's eyes, bitter loathing in her gaze. She raised her voice until Maryn was sure it would carry to the farthest reaches of the crowd. "I still believe you guilty of our brother's murder. Father was right to disinherit you. Even if you're correct and the Kingship has not yet transferred successfully to Barilan, I will never accede to your claim. The Kingship will not settle on a usurper!"

A roar of approval rose from her troops. Briefly a chant of "Barilan! Barilan! Barilan!" sounded from a few scattered places, but it soon died. Voerell waved behind her without looking, and her forces quieted. Kiellan whispered in her ear; she listened stony-faced.

Carlich didn't appear worried by her rejection. Maybe Tior was wrong, Maryn thought, a sick feeling in her stomach. Maybe it wouldn't matter that Barilan still held the Kingship. Maybe if enough of the assembled masses wanted Carlich to be king, their desire would tear the magic free from Barilan's soul and transfer it to Carlich's without harming him. How could a construction of a few drops of blood and some ancient words prevail, set against the power of so many people's will? Maybe she should speak out to stop Carlich from making the attempt, after all.

No, she had to believe the magic would perform as it had been designed and act to destroy the usurper. Barilan was the rightful king, and nothing short of death, of either body or soul, could change that. All she had to do was bide her time. Her spell would continue to conceal the truth from Carlich along with everyone else. Voerell wouldn't be able to stop Carlich from asserting his right to the crown. He would give the signal, Vinhor would work the spell, and Maryn would cry the words that would set the fatal magic in motion.

Barilan's nursing had slowed to an occasional fluttering suck; he didn't complain when she slipped her finger into the corner of his mouth and detached him. She adjusted her clothes and shifted him to her shoulder, running her fingers through his silky hair. What if her spell had faded by now? Could even the copious amount of blood the runaway magic had torn from her be enough to conceal Barilan's Kingship for so long? Or would the phantom crown once again appear over the baby's head, proving to Carlich that she'd deceived him?

Prelate Kiellan stepped forward. "I am quite sure Barilan's Heirship ceremony was complete and successful. Let us examine him and resolve this dispute."

Voerell jumped on his words. "If in fact Barilan

holds the Kingship, are you willing to give up this nonsense and accept my rule in his name?"

Carlich hesitated only an instant, his eyes flicking to Barilan, before smoothly inclining his head. "Of course, sister. I've never wanted anything but what's right for Milecha."

He gestured to Maryn. Prelate Kiellan held out his arms. Maryn reluctantly surrendered Barilan into them. A wave of excited murmurs washed over the gathered troops. Barilan fussed a little, reaching for Maryn, but quieted in Kiellan's firm, gentle grip. Voerell watched them, her hands clenched at her sides. Maryn moved back to her place beside Carlich. Gradually the noise of the crowd faded into an expectant hush.

Kiellan nodded to Rogelan. "Would you? Your expertise in scrying exceeds my own."

"Of course, your Holiness." Rogelan moved to join the Prelate. He drew his knife and cut his finger, then extended his bloody hand over Barilan, intoning the incantation in his rich melodic voice.

Maryn peered at the light that grew into a halo around Barilan's small form. Was that a trace of brighter mist over his head? No, it was only her imagination. The light over his spiky blond hair remained clear.

Voerell raised shocked eyes to Kiellan, her face white. The Prelate frowned at her, then turned back to study the baby in his arms, his brows drawing together in bafflement.

"Look deeper, Rogelan," Voerell ordered, hoarse. "This has got to be some sort of trick!"

Beside Maryn, Carlich stepped back and leaned toward Vinhor. "Prepare to begin the spell as soon as I give the word."

Vinhor inclined his head. "Yes, your Highness." He drew the knife from his belt. Keeping his hands low, he quietly cut a slash across his palm and cupped his fingers to conceal the welling blood.

Carlich caught Maryn's eye. "Hold..." he murmured, his hand cocked in a stilling gesture, low at his side.

Maryn swallowed and nodded. Just a moment more, and she would call down Carlich's destruction. She couldn't understand why that thought distressed her so much. He'd captured her, kidnapped her, threatened her, hurt both her body and her soul. Didn't he deserve whatever judgment the Holy One visited upon him? Didn't she want to see him meet justice for his many crimes?

She did, and yet she writhed inside at the image of him falling lifeless at her feet, burning with the same blue fire that had consumed his victims. How could she do that to him?

Rogelan broke off his chant, though the light continued to glow around Barilan. "I'm sorry, Princess. It seems he's right."

"No! Keep looking!" Voerell stared at her son as if her will alone could strip away any illusion.

"If you insist." Rogelan raised his voice again. Outside the wards the crowd stirred, and a restive buzz started. With each passing moment it increased in agitation.

"Now!" Carlich jerked his hand down, pointing at Maryn.

Maryn crushed her doubts, focusing only on her purpose. Carlich must be stopped, no matter what it cost her. She sucked in her breath and opened her mouth, her tongue pressed to the roof of her mouth, ready to explode into sound.

Nothing emerged. She struggled to force the words out, but her tongue and breath would not obey her will. She couldn't utter so much as a whisper.

Was she so weak after all, so much of a coward, that she couldn't follow through on her resolve? But certainty blazed within her. She was willing to take the responsibility for killing Carlich, if that was the only way to stop him. No conflict remained in her heart. So what was silencing her voice?

King Froethych's spell! She'd made Carlich her kin to protect herself, but now it was working in reverse, preventing her from harming him.

Carlich glared and motioned urgently at her. When she didn't respond, she thought for an instant she saw disappointment in his eyes. His lips curled into a sneer of disgust. Whirling, he hissed, "Tennelan, quick—"

"Look!" Rogelan cried.

Maryn snapped her head around. The royal sorcerer stood over Barilan, one hand upraised, staring hard at the light haloing the baby's head. "Look," he repeated. "There's something here. Some sort of illusion. It's strong. I almost didn't see it, but there's a bit of roughness around the edges."

"Can you break it?" Kiellan asked.

"I think so. It will take time, and much blood." Rogelan glanced at Carlich.

Carlich strode forward and stared at Barilan. He traced the edge of the glow around Barilan's head with one finger. "You're right." Breathing hard, he shot a glance at Vinhor, than back at Rogelan. "I don't know how it got there."

Voerell took a step toward him, her hands rising. "You hid it! You worked a spell to conceal the crown from us!" She faltered. "What did you think to gain?

Hidden or not, if Barilan holds the Kingship, you couldn't take it. You wouldn't be stupid enough to try; you know what would happen…" She stared at Carlich for a moment, then whirled back to study Barilan again.

Maryn saw the realization of just how close he had come to death sweep over Carlich. His cheeks blanched, then flushed red. His fists clenched at his sides. Slowly, slowly, he began to swivel toward Maryn.

Her guts roiled and her knees quivered. She had to get away from him. But there was nowhere to run in the warded space. Would Voerell's guards protect her if she flung herself among them?

A sharp gasp jerked Carlich's attention back to Voerell. She looked up, her gaze going back and forth between Carlich and Rogelan. "Is this really Barilan at all?" Her voice was barely more than a whisper. "Did you spell some other child to look like him? Is he hidden away somewhere?" Her voice rose to a shriek. "Or did you kill him, after all, to free the Kingship? Did you think to foist a substitute on me—"

Carlich's sharp laugh cut her off. "I couldn't harm him, even if I wanted to. You saw Father's spell stop me."

He breathed hard for a moment, staring at Barilan. Rogelan held his hands out over the baby, murmuring rapidly. Barilan's face crumpled; Kiellan stroked his hair and he relaxed.

Carlich's lips twisted into a bitter parody of a smile. "And I know better than to try to deceive you that way, Voerell. I could never fool you by substituting some other child for Barilan. You're his mother. You'd know the difference."

Voerell glared at her brother. Fury shone from her

eyes, but Maryn read crippling doubt there as well. No, she wouldn't know the difference, and Maryn could see that she knew it. If that really had been Frilan, or some other child, Voerell didn't know her own son well enough to tell them apart.

Suddenly Carlich's eyes narrowed. "Maybe you're more right than you know, Voerell. Maybe someone did work an illusion on another baby to make him look like Barilan. Maybe the real one is hidden away safe somewhere…"

He whirled on Maryn. Grabbing her by the shoulders, he bent close, his breath hot in her face. "That's what you did, isn't it? To protect your son. What I said gave you the idea. I understand why you'd want to. It can all still work out, as long as the Kingship is free. Just tell me the truth!" He shook her.

"Yes!" Maryn gasped. He'd have to believe her; he still thought her bound by his spell to obey him. "That's what I did. Frilan is back in Ralo, safe. I used what Priest Vinhor taught me to make up a spell and worked it on a child I—" She couldn't think up a plausible lie quickly enough.

Carlich's brow furrowed. "But we told you no magic. How—"

He broke off as Rogelan swore. Barilan twisted in Kiellan's arms and broke into a wail. Rogelan shook his head, sucking in a deep breath. "Gallows, this is strong magic. It must have just about killed whoever worked it. A novice spell gone out of control is my best guess." He drew his knife and pushed up his sleeve to cut a long gash in his arm. "I'll break it, Princess. It will just take a moment."

New sparks burst from the fresh gush of blood. Barilan quit crying and grabbed for them. Voerell

looked at him, then back at Carlich. Her eyes went to
Maryn, deeply confused. "Nurse? You—"

Maryn wrenched free from Carlich and stumbled
toward Voerell. "I did, your Highness. I can explain—"

Carlich shouted over her, drowning her out. "She
wanted Barilan for herself! She knew I'd give him
back to you, so she hid him away and spelled some
other child. I had no part in it." He grabbed Maryn
and dragged her back. "Tell her I'm right!"

Maryn poured out words as fast as she could
before Carlich could silence her. "No! That's Barilan,
he's still king, I hid the crown—"

Carlich clapped his hand over her mouth, but it
slid away. Tight as he gripped her, his fingers stopped
short of digging into her flesh. Maryn twisted free.
Voerell didn't know what to believe, she saw. The
princess looked from Maryn to Carlich to Barilan,
mouth moving soundlessly.

"Guards, seize her!" Carlich cried.

Maryn flung herself at Voerell. "Princess, help me!"

Voerell's face hardened. She gestured curtly to her
guards. "Protect her."

Her guards surged forward to grapple with
Carlich's. Voerell grabbed Maryn's wrist. "Don't lie to
me! Is that my son?"

"It is! I'll prove it!" Maryn's free hand flew to her
mouth and she sank her teeth into her finger. Blood
welled out, hot and salty on her tongue. Maryn spit it
into her palm and scooped her hand through the
motion Vinhor had taught her. The blood burst into
flames. A surge of power shook her, but this time she
held on and it didn't quite escape her control. She
flung the crackling fire at Barilan, willing with all her
might for her spell to end and the crown to appear in
its full glory over Barilan's head.

Her power joined Rogelan's. Together they flared around Barilan, bright as lightning. The light over Barilan's head collapsed inward to form the glowing shape of a crown.

All around, guards fought, punching and kicking and grabbing. Voerell dragged Maryn close to Rogelan and Kiellan. "Is it real?" she demanded of the sorcerer. "Or another illusion?"

Rogelan studied the glowing crown, and nodded sharply. "It's real."

"You!" Carlich shoved between the wrestling guards, staring at the shining crown over Barilan's head. He whirled toward Maryn, whipped out his knife, and slashed his palm. Lightning poured from his thrusting hand, lashing directly at Maryn. Her eyes clamped shut and she cowered away from the surging blaze.

She felt nothing, not even the buzz of power in her bones and teeth. Opening her eyes, she saw Carlich's lightning splash harmlessly around the bubble of air that surrounded her with its protection.

"How are you stopping it?" Carlich screamed in frustration. He lunged at her, pouring more fire from his hands, but he couldn't touch her.

Rogelan rushed to her, raising bloody hands, but she waved away his help. She laughed, filled with wild exultation. "He can't harm me. I put my milk in his food. We're kin now!"

Carlich's face turned red and purple as he understood. With a convulsive movement, he sent the lightning shooting toward Rogelan. Rogelan's own fire met it, blocking it in a burst of showering sparks.

"Vinhor! Someone! Get—" The magic choked off Carlich's words.

Vinhor stepped to Carlich's side. Coolly, as if he stood at his own altar and not in the midst of chaos, he scooped his bloody hand through the air. A fountain of sparks erupted. At first Maryn thought he intended to attack her. But shock coursed through her as she recognized the first familiar gesture his hands traced and saw his gaze fixed on the child in Kiellan's arms.

"Stop him!" Maryn cried, throwing herself at the prelate. "He's going to sever Barilan's soul. Just like they tried to make me do—"

Kiellan's eyes went wide in horrified understanding. He reached for his knife, but Barilan lunged for Maryn, arms outstretched. His kicking foot knocked the blade from Kiellan's grasp and sent it spinning to the earth. Kiellan clutched the squirming baby and stooped after the knife. Vinhor's hands swept farther into the sequence that would leave Barilan a soulless husk and free the Kingship for Carlich to claim.

Maryn jerked her hands up. Nothing prevented her from harming Vinhor. The blood she'd drawn earlier was gone, consumed by her magic, so she raised her finger to her mouth. She must bite deep and draw enough blood to prevail against any spell the priest might cast at her.

Blue light washed over her. She bit savagely into her finger, bracing herself for the anticipated pain, but none came. Her skin felt like tough leather between her teeth. She gnawed frantically, but was unable to make even a scratch on flesh suddenly as impervious as iron.

Her eyes traced the sorcerous fire to its source in Carlich's hands. He laughed at her, harsh and bitter. "Father's magic can't stop this spell. I didn't harm you, I kept you from harming yourself!"

Maryn lunged at Vinhor, but Carlich twisted his hands and a wave of blue fire shoved her away. Voerell flung herself at her brother, but Carlich's magic beat her back, too. Ropes of lightning writhed from his fingers, twining around both of them, and Rogelan and Kiellan as well. Barilan wailed. Vinhor's hands shaped gestures Maryn recognized as the final few motions of the spell.

Behind Vinhor, a pudgy figure broke free of the guard who held him. He charged Vinhor and tackled him around the waist. Together they sprawled to the ground. Tior scrambled atop Vinhor and drove a knee into his back, grabbing for the priest's hands.

At a shouted command from Voerell, the guard who'd been holding Tior jumped to help him restrain Vinhor. Carlich looked wildly about him. Maryn saw that none of his guards were free to come to his aid, either subdued by Voerell's guards or still struggling for dominance. The blue fire pouring from his hands momentarily sputtered, but he slashed his arm and renewed its force. It swirled around her, pressing her into a tight cluster with Voerell, Rogelan, Kiellan, and Barilan.

Outside the shimmering wards, men from both sides beat against the magical wall but couldn't penetrate it. Shouts and clashing weapons echoed over Barilan's cries, as all along the border where the two armies met skirmishes broke out between Voerell's troops and Carlich's.

"Rogelan, Kiellan," Voerell said, low and urgent. "Is there anything you can do?"

Rogelan shook his head, driving the tip of his knife against his arm. It dented the skin but didn't break it. "He got me before I could block it."

"All of us, I think." Kiellan held out his hand,

which also proved invulnerable to Rogelan's knife. A quick test on Voerell gave the same result.

Kiellan grasped Barilan's hand and held it up. Ignoring cries of protest from both Maryn and Voerell, Rogelan applied his knife, at first delicately, then with more force. Barilan shrieked and twisted to get free, but no blood emerged. Rogelan and Kiellan exchanged grim looks.

Kiellan stepped to Maryn and pressed the screaming Barilan into her arms. "I think the young king will be happiest with you."

Maryn wrapped her arms around the baby. He clung to her, quieting. She pressed her face into the top of his head and breathed deep. Voerell reached toward her son, but let her hand drop, turning away.

Carlich diverted a thread of blue flame away from their cage, sending it against a guard who held the struggling Tennelan captive with an arm around his throat. The man's grip loosened. Tennelan twisted away and drove a fist into the guard's jaw. The guard crumpled.

"I'll hold them here." Carlich jerked his head toward Maryn and the other captives. His voice was strained. "We have the bigger army. I'll let you through the wards so you can take charge of the attack. Time enough to sort things out once we hold the city."

"As you wish, my prince." Tennelan inclined his head.

"But first deal with the traitor who attacked Vinhor." Carlich glowered at Tior. The pudgy soldier straddled Vinhor's back, pressing the priest's outstretched hands into the ground, while Voerell's guard pinned Vinhor's legs. At Carlich's words Vinhor thrashed, and both men struggled to hold him.

Tennelan edged closer. "Tior, let him go. That's an order!"

"No, sir," Tior gasped between jerks as Vinhor yanked him from side to side. "You saw the crown over Barilan's head. He was trying to kill the king."

Tennelan hesitated. Carlich scowled. "Ignore him. Get Vinhor free! Then we'll settle the matter for good."

When Tennelan still didn't respond, Carlich's lips twisted into a snarl. He looked down at the sparks raining from his hands. They were subsiding once again. He pulled back one hand and went for his knife. The other kept the magic swirling around Maryn and the others.

Maryn took a step toward Carlich, but the magic shoved her back. "No!" She couldn't let him hurt Tior. And she couldn't let Vinhor get free to renew his attack against Barilan. But she was helpless, her body imprisoned by Carlich's sorcery, her blood locked away where she couldn't reach it. She turned an imploring gaze on the others, but they were as trapped as she. Rogelan and Kiellan were speaking together in urgent low voices. Voerell stared at Carlich with loathing, her fists clenched before her.

"Tennelan, listen to me!" Maryn cried. "He's been lying to you all along!" The captain glanced at her, eyebrows shooting up in surprise. His brow furrowed, and she caught her breath in hope. "Leave Tior alone! Stop Carlich!"

"Don't listen to her, Tennelan!" Carlich waved his knife in a threatening gesture. "Free Vinhor!"

Voerell pushed as far forward as the restraining magic would let her. "Captain Tennelan, I order you to apprehend my brother. Your treachery in following him can be forgiven if you act now!"

Tennelan shook his head and backed away, face torn with indecision. Carlich snarled, taking a step after him, but the fountain of sparks from his hand sank lower every moment. "Fine! I'll do it myself!" He whirled back to his captives, driving his knife into his arm. "Filthy serf girl! I should have let those specters drink your blood. You'll pay for defying me. I'll—" His voice choked to silence as King Froethych's spell prevented him from voicing the threat.

Maryn shrank away from the hatred in his eyes. Despite everything, Carlich was going to triumph, and there was nothing she could do to stop him. She clawed at her arms until her fingernails bent and broke without effect. She sank her teeth into her tongue, but it remained unharmed.

Blood poured from Carlich's arm, and he dropped his knife to catch it. For a moment the magic swirling around Maryn flickered and Carlich's face went pale.

Had he misjudged, and spilled too much blood? Maryn shoved against the imprisoning wall. The others did the same. She was sure she felt it yielding.

Carlich swayed, but caught himself. Panting, he bent over. Blood spattered from his hand as he braced it against his thigh. His upraised hand shook, blood flowing from the new cut, but blue fire continued to pour from it. He sucked in deep shuddering breaths. With every gasp more color returned to his cheeks. The barrier firmed under Maryn's thrusting hand and forced her back. Carlich slowly straightened.

Maryn closed her eyes in despair. She clutched Barilan so hard he struggled in her grip and wailed. Her body responded to his cry, sending a hot tingling rush through her breasts. It wasn't fair. She'd failed Barilan after all. She would gladly give all her blood to save him, but it wasn't enough. Did she have time to put him to her breast, so at least he would have the comfort of her milk in the last moments before Vinhor tore his soul from his body?

Milk...

Barilan's body pressed against a small hard lump between her breasts.

White blood...

Maryn whirled and thrust Barilan into Voerell's arms. The princess gaped at her, almost dropping him, but tightened her arms around him as he shrieked in protest and grabbed for Maryn. "Please," Maryn gasped, "distract Carlich. Just for a moment. I have an idea."

Voerell's face registered only blank confusion, but Kiellan understood. The prelate leaned against the sorcerous barrier. "Prince Carlich," he called. "Listen to me. You don't want to do this. It's not too late. The Holy One can forgive any sin, if only you're willing to repent."

Carlich paused, his hand poised to gather new blood from his wound. He sneered at Kiellan. "You're quick to speak of forgiveness when I have you at my mercy. Don't think I'll fall for your tricks. You're trying to weaken my resolve by making me feel guilty. It won't work. I've done nothing wrong."

Maryn edged to the back of the closely packed group so the others' bodies shielded her from Carlich's view. She snatched the little perfume bottle from its hiding place in her bodice.

Kiellan's voice was gentle. "Is that truly what you believe, my prince? Or have you allowed your own desires to drown out the Holy One's voice in your heart? Do you think he condones betrayal and murder?"

Maryn worked the stopper free from the bottle's mouth and poured the milk into her hand. It dripped between her fingers and splashed on the ground. Dropping the bottle, she rubbed her palms together, frantically thinking. King Froethych's spell wouldn't let her harm Carlich. What could she do that wouldn't hurt him, but would stop him from killing Tior and freeing Vinhor?

Carlich's hand jerked. A tendril of fire slashed Kiellan's face. "Be silent! I know the Holy One is with me!"

Kiellan staggered. Rogelan supported him. The sorcerer glared at Carlich. "You know he speaks the truth. Let us go, and give up this nonsense."

Voerell clutched the writhing, sobbing Barilan. "The Holy One will feed your soul piece by piece to the Vulture for your sins!"

Carlich snarled at her. He swept his hand up the bloody wound on his arm and rubbed his palms together. Fresh sparks blazed skyward. "It's your own sins you should worry about, Voerell!"

Maryn stared at the blood-fueled fire blazing in Carlich's hands. Of course. She knew one spell she could use. She'd seen him shape the necessary gestures dozens of times.

Curling her fingers into the proper position, she raised her hands and scooped the magic up. The milk burst into blue lightning in her palms.

Kiellan held up a hand. Carlich's attack had left a charred track across his cheeks; he spoke through blistered lips. "Prince, stop. Let this conflict be settled by honorable combat, not the slaughter of innocents. Keep me as a hostage if you must. But let the women and children go, at least. Your sister, and Barilan, and his nurse—"

Maryn's hands flew through the spell. Magic crackled around her, buzzing in her spine and skull. She didn't remember every nuance of the motions, but her will was strong and her purpose blazed in her heart.

Carlich laughed, high and wild. "And lose my chance at the Kingship? Never! It will be mine, and nothing you can say will stop me!"

He whirled. A spear of fire blazed from his hand, piercing the guard who held Vinhor's legs. He slumped, and Vinhor kicked him away. Carlich turned on Tior.

Maryn elbowed between Voerell and Rogelan, her hands never pausing in their motions, sparks shooting out in all directions. She shouted, "Carlich!"

He spun to face her. Shock widened his eyes and stilled his hands for an instant. He recovered and twisted his hands into a motion that would send his magic to block hers, but it was too late. A wave of sparks poured from her hands and engulfed him.

The magic swelled huge and untamable, wrenching away from Maryn's control and taking over her arms, driving them to ever more frantic motion, but she didn't care. She focused all the strength she had on her desire. Carlich stared at her, fear in his eyes, and took a step backwards.

She crowed in triumph, over the roar of the magic. "Stop!" she cried. "Don't hurt Tior! Let us go!"

Carlich's arms shook as he fought to resist her order and keep them raised. He was strong, much stronger than she'd ever been. Maryn threw herself with renewed effort into the magic. It carried her along, sucking at her with the same ferocious power that had torn King Froethych's life from his veins and had nearly killed her once before. She surrendered to its force. Let it burn all her blood into blue fire, if that's what it took to force Carlich to obey her.

Carlich's eyes went blank and empty, just as hers must have all those times. The fire of his sorcery died. His hands fell to his sides, unconsumed blood dripping from his fingertips. The wall of flame that confined Maryn and the others flickered and vanished.

Kiellan and Rogelan rushed to Carlich and grabbed his arms. Voerell backed away from Maryn, clutching the wailing Barilan to her chest. "What's happening?" she cried. "What are you doing?

The magic had Maryn in its claws, drawing her life into its sucking vortex. She couldn't stop it. Any moment now her skin would split open and the spell would drain the blood from her body. She'd never have the chance to tell Voerell everything that had happened, all the secrets she longed to make known.

Behind Carlich, Tennelan backed toward the shimmering wards. "Men!" he shouted. "Forward! Herald, sound the advance!" Maryn heard the blare of a trumpet, and caught a blurry glimpse of masses of men surging forward, past the hill, toward the city.

No! She had to do something, fast, before the spell overcame her and she could no longer command Carlich. What could she make him do that would end his threat forever?

Carlich stared at her with dull eyes, ready to obey. Maryn's arms thrashed. Her skin throbbed in time with the pulse hammering in her ears. The earth tilted under her feet. Blackness crowed the edges of her vision.

Maryn wrenched every scrap of will she possessed into one final effort. "Tell them the truth!" she cried. "All of it! Tell them how you murdered your brother, and kidnapped me and Barilan, and tried to make me destroy his soul!"

Lightning burst in a fountain from her chest. It felt like her heart exploding from her body. Hot liquid poured from her, fueling the flames of her sorcery into a blazing inferno.

Dimly over the roar in her teeth and bones and skull, she heard Carlich's voice, dull and emotionless. "I killed Marolan. I gave Dolia the rose hoping she'd prick herself. When she did, I captured a few drops of her blood on my handkerchief. I'd prepared it with a little of my own so I could make a show of cleansing it..."

Maryn sagged to her knees, unable to hear any more, but it didn't matter. She'd done it. No one would ever acclaim Carlich king now. Voerell would have all the evidence she needed to arrest and imprison him. Tennelan would hear and call off the army. Milecha would be safe from Carlich's malice.

Soft grass pillowed her head. A sharp rock pressed into her cheek, but her skin was still impervious to harm. Night swam up to claim her, quiet and peaceful.

Regret stabbed though the calm. Barilan would cry for her. She wished she could be there to comfort him.

But Edrich and Frilan would be waiting for her in the courts of the Holy One. She took the joy of that thought with her into the darkness.

Twenty-one

An arm slid under Maryn's shoulders and lifted them. A hard surface pressed into her lips. "Here, drink a little. It will help you recover your strength."

Warm, salty broth sloshed into Maryn's mouth. She spluttered and coughed, spraying the liquid all over whoever had been holding the cup. She heard an exclamation of surprise, and the arm dropped her abruptly. Maryn fell back, tensing for impact, but the surface she struck was soft and yielding. A bed, she realized.

Blankets covered her, pinning her arms. She pulled her hands free and rubbed at dry, sandy eyes, blinking until tears cleared away the blur of sleep. Overhead, a canopy stretched, woven with a familiar pattern of twining vines and flowers. For a moment she couldn't remember where she'd seen it before, but then she placed it. She was back in the royal nursery, in the bed she had shared with Barilan.

"She's waking up." Maryn turned her head and saw Litholl, Voerell's midwife, sitting beside the bed. She was twisted toward the open door, speaking to someone in the next room. "Send for the princess."

Maryn struggled to sit up. "What's going on?

Where's Barilan? Is Carlich—What happened?" She faltered, swallowing. "I thought I was dead."

Litholl smoothed tendrils of hair back from Maryn's face. "No, dear. You're fine."

Maryn tried to sort out her confused memories of the moments before everything had gone black. "The spell got out of control. I was sure it would suck all the blood from my body—"

"Ah." Litholl took Maryn's hands in hers. "But you didn't use blood to work your magic. You used your milk. Your spell did run out of control, and used up all your strength until you fell unconscious, and sucked all the milk from your breasts. But of course that didn't kill you." She smiled. "Rogelan and Kiellan keep arguing whether a spell worked with milk couldn't draw on blood for power, or whether Carlich's spell still prevented your skin from breaking open and letting your blood out. But in any case, none of your blood went into the spell, so you'll be fine. You've only been unconscious a few hours. Princess Voerell had you brought here to recover and summoned me to tend you."

Maryn blinked. She raised her hands to her breasts. "All my milk...Does that mean I can't nurse Barilan any more? Where is he?"

The midwife patted Maryn's shoulder. "He's in the next room, with Semprell. She's quite annoyed, you know, that he missed two whole weeks of exercises and language lessons. As to your milk...We can't know for certain until you try, but I strongly suspect there won't be a problem. As I always tell new mothers, your breasts are never truly empty. They're always making more. Your spell took all there was at the moment, but they've been busy ever since to replace it. If anything, your supply will be increased because of the great demand. That could be convenient, if you have any plans to study magic and become a great sorceress."

Maryn shuddered at the thought, crossing her arms over her breasts. "Oh, no. I've had more than enough of magic to last me for a lifetime."

"Are you sure? Rogelan is wild to speak with you and find out exactly how you did it. He's never heard of anyone using milk to fuel a spell before." Litholl snorted. "Of course, most sorcerers are men. Midwives have always known milk had power, but the sorcerers considered it a trivial thing. Of concern only to women and children, not worthy of study." She shook her head. "Never mind. Right now you need to rest and recover from your efforts."

Maryn nodded and slid back down to lie flat, closing her eyes. Maybe she shouldn't be so quick to dismiss the idea of learning more about sorcery. She couldn't help but tremble when she remembered the wild destructive fury of the forces she'd unleashed. But it had been her ignorance that had made her bumbling attempts to use magic so dangerous. Surely it would be better to learn at least a little about the proper ways to harness it, even if she never intended to make use of that knowledge. Her blood and her milk did have power. If she was better prepared, she could use them to protect herself and Barilan should their lives ever again be in jeopardy.

If she was still able to be Barilan's nurse. She couldn't rest until she knew for sure. She rolled to face Litholl, pushing herself up on her elbow. "Please, bring Barilan to me," she begged. "I have to see…"

Litholl started to deny her, but stopped and looked more closely into her face. Her expression softened, and she went to the doorway. "Semprell, he's had enough for one day. You're not going to be able to make up for all the time you lost. Let Maryn take him for a while."

Semprell wore a scowl when she came through the door, but Barilan reached for Maryn as soon as he saw her. She hurried to sit up, and Litholl helped arrange the pillows behind her back. Maryn accepted Barilan into her arms. His warm heavy body felt infinitely precious, as if it had been days since she'd held him, not merely a few hours. She hugged him tight, breathing in his milky, musky scent, then slid him down into position and pulled loose the ties of her shift. He latched on and began nursing with great vigor. Maryn watched him anxiously, sure he'd soon pull back in offended frustration at finding nothing there.

But after a minute or so of frantic sucking, Maryn felt the blessedly familiar warm rush, and Barilan's sucks changed to long, slow draws punctuated by swallows. The angle of his jaw by his ear flexed in and out. Maryn kept her head ducked over him until she mastered the tears that threatened to overwhelm her. At last she could look up and found Litholl beaming at her. She returned a tremulous smile.

"See?" Litholl said. "I told you there'd be no problem. Look at him. I've seldom seen such a content—"

The door opened. Litholl broke off as two guards entered and stationed themselves at either side of the door. Voerell passed between them, her steps heavy, her shoulders slumped in weariness.

Maryn bowed her head over Barilan, watching the princess from the corner of her eye. She didn't know what to expect. The final confrontation with Carlich had been so confusing, with so much happening so quickly, so many lies mixed with the truth. She hoped Voerell understood enough to realize that Maryn had always been on her side and had done her best to protect Barilan and work against Carlich. But she feared Voerell might dismiss her efforts as inadequate. The princess might allow her anger with her brother to expand to include everyone associated with him.

Voerell brightened a little as she saw Maryn with Barilan at her breast. The princess gestured to the guards, and they left the room to take up positions outside the door. "Litholl, is everything all right?"

"Yes, your Highness. Maryn seems to be well on her way to recovery, and Barilan's just shown us that her milk remains plentiful."

"Thank the Holy One." A weight seemed to lift from Voerell's shoulders. Only one burden of many, Maryn knew, but not insubstantial. She approached Maryn's bed. Litholl rose and offered her chair to Voerell. "Your Highness, would you like me to leave you three alone?"

"Yes, please, Litholl. Thank you." Voerell pressed her hand and gave her a grateful smile. Litholl slipped from the room and closed the door.

Maryn didn't know what to say. She'd never been alone with the princess before. Voerell didn't look at her at first, only gazed at Barilan as he busily nursed.

At length Voerell sighed and raised her eyes to meet Maryn's. "I don't know how to begin to thank you. I owe you so much. You kept Barilan safe, you managed to get the better of my brother..." She trailed off, her gaze sliding past Maryn to stare unseeing into the distance.

The silence stretched long, until Maryn had to say something to break it. "It was nothing, your

Highness. I only did what I had to do. Anyone would have done the same."

Voerell focused again on Maryn. "I greatly doubt that." She leaned forward, her eyes dropping to Barilan, her voice rough. "When Carlich seized you and Barilan, and dragged you away...I knew I'd never see my son alive again. Yet here he is." She reached a tentative finger to stroke Barilan's hair.

Maryn blushed and looked away. She knew she didn't deserve such praise, but she couldn't contradict Voerell.

The princess went on. "From what Carlich says he did to you, it must have been a struggle just to survive with your mind intact, let alone discover a way to defeat him. The spell he used on you, that you turned against him—he must have learned it from that Hampsian sorcerer, for surely no follower of the Holy One would condone it."

"I'm not in trouble for using it, am I?" Maryn blanched at this new worry. "I wouldn't have, but I didn't see any other way—"

"No, no. Under the circumstances it was perfectly acceptable." Voerell patted Maryn's hand.

Her reaction gave Maryn the courage to ask the question that troubled her. "Did it work? Did Carlich tell you everything he did?"

"My dear, Carlich hasn't been able to leave off confessing." Voerell gave a short laugh. "Once he recited the whole sorry tale, he started over at the beginning, in greater detail. Every wicked thought he ever had, every wicked deed—and there were many. It was quite a shock. I thought I knew my brother, but it seems he had me fooled as much as everyone else. He's in the gaol now, and as far as I know is still regaling his guards with the litany of his sins."

"Oh, no." Maryn struggled to swing her legs over the edge of the bed. "I never meant for that to happen." The continuing strength of her magic both awed and appalled her. She wished, now that the crisis was safely over, that the lingering effects would go away before they drew far too much embarrassing attention to her. And she felt ashamed of the rush of vindictive pleasure that swept her when she pictured Carlich's plight. She knew how cruel such compulsion was, no matter how richly Carlich deserved it. "I can try to cancel the spell, though I don't know how."

Voerell gave her a stern look and put a quelling hand on her arm. "You stay right there. It will do my brother good to dwell on his misdeeds for a while. If the spell hasn't worn off after a few days, I'll have Rogelan see to it. Don't you waste another thought on Carlich."

Maryn sank back into the bed, but she couldn't leave the matter entirely. "What will happen to him?"

Voerell bit her lip. "He will be brought to trial. The evidence from his own lips will be ample to convict him. He should be—" She swallowed, shaking her head. "What he's done is worthy of—"

Her lips moved soundlessly. Maryn winced in sympathy, remembering the choking sensation when King Froethych's spell had prevented her from speaking. Voerell made a few more abortive attempts before finding words she could force out. "The—the usual punishment for treason is death."

Voerell breathed deeply for a moment, then went on, still with difficulty, but clearly. "Father's spell prevents me from ordering his execution. As a prince of Milecha, he cannot be put to death on any lesser authority. So I have little choice but to keep him confined in the Royal Gaol for the foreseeable future, under sufficient wards to prevent him from using magic to escape. At some point the effects of Father's spell will fade, though Rogelan and Kiellan tell me it might be years." Beads of sweat had formed on her brow; she wiped them away and gave Maryn a crooked smile. "I suppose it's just as well. There are worse things than dwelling in a land where no one can cause harm to their blood kin. Perhaps by the time that changes, Carlich will have come to repent his crimes."

That didn't seem very likely to Maryn. But not impossible, either. "What about those who followed him?"

Voerell scowled. "The lords who answered his call will pay heavy fines. It's not enough, but I can't imprison half my nobility, not with Wonora and Hampsia both making threats. Their men will be pardoned. Kiellan is convening an ecclesiastical court to strip Vinhor of his priesthood. Captain Tennelan will be court-martialed." Her face went hard and cold. "Nothing prevents me from executing *them*."

"Oh." Maryn gulped and looked away.

Barilan came off her breast and began to cry; Maryn propped him on her shoulder. After a bit of patting he released a loud burp. Relieved of his discomfort, he began to root at her shoulder. Maryn shifted him to her other breast and he resumed nursing happily.

Voerell watched all this business silently, an expression of both hunger and pleasure on her face. She waited until Barilan had been settled for several minutes to speak. "Carlich told us about his plan to remove Barilan's soul from his body, and how he offered you the chance to replace it with your own lost child's soul."

Maryn couldn't respond. She ducked her head, staring down at Barilan.

Voerell went on, her voice very soft, almost a whisper. "I don't see how any mother could have refused that offer. Had it been me, I think I would have worked the spell. I am eternally in your debt that you chose not to, that you chose to sacrifice your own son for Barilan's sake."

Maryn didn't want to speak, but she couldn't let Voerell continue under such a terribly false impression. She turned her head away, and forced the words past numb lips. "Actually...actually, I did...try to work the spell. Carlich...he had his compulsion spell on me, that was part of it, but it was weak enough by then I could have fought it." The words came easier and faster as she went along, until they tumbled out in a headlong rush. "But I didn't want to. I wanted Frilan back, more than anything. So I let myself give in, and made the gestures. And the magic would have worked, except King Froethych's spell stopped it. I'm Barilan's milk-mother, you see; we're kin. That's how I knew the same thing would work with Carlich. I'm not as good as you think I am. You shouldn't trust me with Barilan anymore, because I didn't protect him. I would have killed him..." Maryn drew Barilan as close as she could without disrupting his nursing, tears clouding her eyes.

Voerell said nothing for a long time. When Maryn finally steeled herself to look up at her face, she found the princess gazing off into the distance.

Noticing Maryn's eyes on her, Voerell shook her head and focused on her son. Her voice was rough. "If I can't trust you, who can I trust? Didn't I just say I would have made the same choice in your place? My father's spell protects us all, from ourselves as much as from each other."

Maryn could hardly believe it. Voerell had heard the worst there was of her, and yet was willing to overlook it. "You mean—you still want me to nurse Barilan? You won't find someone else?"

Voerell took a deep breath and met Maryn's eyes squarely. "Of course I still want you to nurse Barilan. Coewyn tells me the character of the wet nurse is imparted to the child through her milk. If that's true, I couldn't ask for a better nurse than you. If Barilan receives even a tenth of your honesty, your resourcefulness, your courage, he'll be well served."

Maryn blushed and looked down. There was nothing she could say to that.

Voerell was content to sit beside her in silence. Nothing further was said until after Barilan drifted off to sleep. Maryn eased her nipple out of his mouth and pulled up her shift. Voerell hesitated a moment, then reached for her son. "May I?"

Maryn wanted to refuse, but she couldn't deny the princess. She gathered Barilan carefully, and they managed to transfer him into Voerell's arms without waking him. Voerell settled back into the chair, cuddled Barilan to her shoulder, and rested her cheek on his head. She closed her eyes. Maryn looked away, not wishing to intrude on their intimacy. "If you don't mind, your Highness, I'd like to get up and get dressed. I feel much better."

"Go ahead. Speak with Litholl and let her check you over." Voerell kept her voice quiet so she wouldn't wake Barilan.

Maryn scooted to the far side of the bed and climbed out. At first her legs felt rubbery and blood rushed in her ears, but after a moment those sensations passed. Maryn went to the wardrobe and pulled on a fresh servant's uniform as quietly as she could. Voerell didn't stir or open her eyes when Maryn passed her on her way to the door. She pushed it open and slipped through.

Litholl was sitting by the hearth with Semprell. She rose and came to take Maryn's hands. "You look much better. How do you feel?"

"Fine. Hungry. The princess said you should check me over."

"I'll do that." Litholl spent a few minutes examining Maryn, looking into her eyes and mouth, smelling her breath, feeling her pulse, and questioning her further about her condition. At length she nodded. "I'd say you're well recovered from the aftereffects of your spell. Sit down. Semprell, could you have the servants bring her a bite to eat?"

"Thank you." Maryn was glad to sit down in the chair Semprell quickly vacated. Her legs were still a bit weak. But she couldn't fully relax until she knew more. "Litholl, there's a soldier from the garrison in Ralo. His name is Tior. He stopped Priest Vinhor from hurting Barilan; Princess Voerell saw. Do you know what's happened to him?"

"No, but I'll ask her." Litholl rose and went to the bedroom door. She stuck her head inside for a few minutes, speaking with Voerell in a voice too low for Maryn to understand. When she emerged she spoke quietly with one of the guards, who nodded and left the nursery. She returned to the hearth and sat down next to Maryn. "He's being held until the princess can speak with him. Carlich could tell her nothing of his involvement, so she thought it best to wait until you could give the full story."

Maryn jumped to her feet. "I couldn't have done

anything without Tior's help! I've got to tell the princess—"

"They're bringing him here." Litholl beckoned to the servant who arrived at the door with a tray. "Sit down and eat first."

Reluctant as she was to delay, Maryn devoured the bread and cheese gratefully. A full stomach dispelled the last of her shakiness. As she finished, the guard arrived back, accompanied by two others who flanked the bedraggled Tior. A rip in the shoulder of his uniform flapped open, a bruise spread across one cheek, and he walked with a limp. But he brightened when he saw Maryn and hurried to her side. "You're all right!"

She rose and threw her arms around him in a quick embrace. "Oh, Tior. How can I ever thank you enough?"

He shrugged and pulled away, blushing. "It was nothing. But you—that was amazing! It was like you were on fire with magic. I've never seen anything like it!"

It was Maryn's turn to blush. "I'm lucky it didn't kill me." She grabbed his hand and dragged him toward the bedroom door. "Come on. I've got to tell the princess everything you did."

She ignored his protests. The guards nodded and let her open the door. Maryn held up a hand to warn Tior to be quiet, and he stilled as she led him into the bedroom. Princess Voerell hadn't moved since Maryn had left; her eyes were closed, her head bowed over Barilan. Maryn worried that the princess had fallen asleep and dithered over whether to wake her, but Voerell raised her head. Her eyebrows rose when her gaze fell on Maryn's companion.

"Excuse me for disturbing you, your Highness,

but this is Tior. You saw how he stopped Priest Vinhor. And before that, in Ralo, he helped me so much."

Voerell edged her body around to face them, careful not to wake Barilan. "Ah, yes. Go on, tell me more."

Maryn poured out an account of all that Tior had done. Tior hung back so she couldn't see his face, but she was sure it must be bright red. Voerell paid close attention, but Maryn couldn't tell from her expression what she was thinking.

When Maryn finished detailing how Tior had interrupted Vinhor's spell just before he finished it, Voerell nodded. "Come here, Tior."

Tior stumbled forward and fell to his knees before her chair.

"So, has Madame Maryn given an accurate account of your actions?"

Tior squirmed and sank into a deeper obeisance. "Close enough."

"You're one of Captain Tennelan's men?"

"Yes, your Highness." Tior turned pleading eyes up to Voerell. "Please forgive me, your Highness. I should never have followed Captain Tennelan when he turned against you. I deserve to be punished. And I broke my oath and disobeyed a direct order—" He stopped and looked at the floor.

Voerell freed one hand from its hold on Barilan and waved expansively. "All is pardoned. Rise."

Tior obediently climbed to his feet, raising questioning eyes to Voerell.

"I saw how you nobly and courageously defended my son. Such devoted service deserves to be recognized. I wish to offer you a position on King Barilan's personal guard. I plan to assemble a division of the finest soldiers in Milecha to be responsible for his protection; I want you to be among them."

Tior stared at her, his face pale. Maryn wondered if his weak stomach could stand the shock. He took a deep breath, and swallowed. "Your Highness, I'm not worthy of such an honor. Surely others—"

"I disagree. Your actions have proven you more than worthy. I know of no other I would trust as much with my son's welfare. Will you accept the appointment?"

Maryn was unhappily certain that Tior would refuse, but he surprised her. He glanced at Barilan, gulped, took a deep breath, and drew his stout body to its full modest height. "Your Highness, I would be most honored to accept."

"Excellent. I'll inform the Captain of the Palace Guard. You can begin your duties tomorrow." Voerell tilted her head, regarding Maryn and Tior. "I'd like to invite both of you to dine with me in my private quarters this evening. I think it would be wise for me to become personally acquainted with those to whom I trust my son's safety."

The prospect dismayed Maryn. She would have much preferred a quiet evening with Barilan to collect herself after all the chaos. But she dared not refuse the princess. And she was glad for the honor to Tior. "As you wish, your Highness."

Tior brushed at his torn and dirty uniform. "I'm afraid I'm not in any fit state to dine with Milecha's regent."

"That can be taken care of." Voerell gestured at the door. "Have the guards escort you to the garrison so you can get cleaned up and properly outfitted."

Tior bowed to her and turned to leave. He gave Maryn a crooked grin as he passed. But he carried himself with a tentative assurance that made Maryn confident he'd rise to his new position admirably.

Maryn curtsied to Voerell. "Thank you, your Highness. I know you won't be sorry."

"I have every confidence in Tior." She sighed. "I'll spend a few more minutes with Barilan, and then I must leave."

Maryn nodded and slipped through the bedroom door. Tior was following a guard toward the main entrance of the nursery suite. Maryn hurried over to him and clasped his hand. "Thank you again, Tior. I'm so glad we'll be serving Barilan together. I promise, the worst you're likely to encounter in this duty is a few smelly diapers. And they're not even that bad. Though after he starts eating solid food they'll get much worse."

He grinned at her. "Well, I know how to deal with that." He mimed putting a perfumed cloth to his face and inhaling. Maryn giggled.

Tior stepped back and saluted her formally. "I welcome the opportunity to protect my king and his nurse." He turned on his heel to follow the guard out. But at the last moment he spoiled his official facade by glancing back and winking at her.

Maryn smiled to herself as she returned to her seat by the fire. She spoke quietly with Litholl for a while, expecting Voerell to emerge from the bedroom at any moment. But more than half an hour passed, and the princess remained within.

Litholl rose from her seat. "I must be going. I have several mothers I promised to check on today before Voerell called me. I think you should be fine, but if you have any difficulties, don't hesitate to call me."

"I won't." Maryn walked with her to the door.

After Litholl left, the nursery was quiet. Maryn

stood for a moment, uncertain, looking at the bedroom door flanked by its silent guards. Finally she took a deep breath and nodded at them as she went to open it. "Your Highness?" she called softly. "Are you ready to leave?"

"No," Voerell said. Maryn was about to withdraw, but the princess continued. "I must, though. I have official business to tend to that I've put off too long already."

Maryn entered the bedroom and went to stand beside Voerell. Barilan was still deeply asleep, his head lolling on his mother's shoulder. Maryn held out her arms, but Voerell made no move to surrender him. Maryn dropped her hands.

After a moment Voerell spoke. "Is there anything else you need, Maryn? Anything else I can do for you?"

Give me Barilan and go away. But Maryn certainly couldn't say that. Instead, she thought for a moment. "The midwife in Ralo, Siwell Narila—I mentioned her when I was telling you about Tior. She risked a lot to help me. She's the one who taught me to fight off the compulsion spell. If you could find a way to reward her…"

"It will be done. Do you wish me to bring her to Loempno to attend you?"

"Oh, no. Not unless that's what she wants. I'll be fine with Litholl if I need any help of that sort." Not that she'd need a midwife's expertise any time soon, Maryn reflected sadly. If a second marriage and more children awaited her somewhere in the future, it wouldn't be for a long time yet.

Perhaps a similar thought passed through Voerell's mind, for her face was pensive for a moment. Sighing, she rose to her feet. She stroked

Barilan's head, then extended him toward Maryn. "I must be going. But I look forward to seeing you in my quarters at suppertime."

Maryn wasn't looking forward to it. She was afraid the meal would be terribly stiff and awkward. What right had a simple servant like herself to socialize with the princess and regent of Milecha?

After she transferred Barilan into Maryn's arms, Voerell paused, looking at the two of them. "Be sure to bring Barilan with you, of course. I want to spend more time getting to know him. My duties will never allow me the kind of relationship with him that you have. I accept that. I'm tremendously glad he has someone who can give him the love and attention he deserves. But I want to be closer to him than my father ever was to me, to any of us. Maybe if he'd spent a little more time with us, Carlich wouldn't...or maybe not." She shook her head, a quick, convulsive movement. "In any case, I'd like to make it a custom to share supper with you and Barilan whenever my duties permit."

Maryn ducked her head. "Whatever you wish, your Highness."

Maryn thought that was the end of the conversation. She expected Voerell to turn and go, but the regent just stood looking at her. Maryn shifted her feet. "Your Highness?"

Voerell reached out and put her hand on Maryn's arm. "Would you...would you call me Voerell, please? When we're in private?"

Maryn stared at her, scandalized. Voerell hesitated, then rushed on. "My family is gone. My husband, my father, both my brothers...I'm alone now. There's no one I can relax with and be myself, not the princess or the regent. I know you lost your family, too, your husband and your child...Neither of us can make up for what the other has lost, but maybe, if you're willing, we could try to be friends. We both love Barilan; that's a place to start."

The hurt and loneliness in Voerell's words and voice resonated strongly in Maryn's heart. But she resisted it and turned away, a bitter lump in her throat. "I'm your servant. Do I have any choice?"

"You do." Voerell's voice was fierce. "It's not as princess or regent I ask this; only as another woman who's suffered some of the same sorrows you have. You are free to refuse, if that's your wish."

Voerell took a step back. Curtains began to veil again the openness and vulnerability that had shone momentarily from her eyes. Maryn felt a pang of regret to see the offered hand withdrawn, stung by her rejection. She found, suddenly, that she believed Voerell. The princess really did want to try to be a friend. To reach out, perhaps for the first time in her life, to another person based not on rank or status or wealth, but only on what their hearts shared.

Would the princess really be able to put those things aside? Maybe not, but Maryn realized she was willing to take that risk.

Maryn put out her hand. Voerell's eyes widened, and she slowly reached to grasp it. Maryn drew a deep breath. "I think...I think I'd like to be your friend—Voerell. I'll be happy to join you for supper, tonight and every night you're able. I think Barilan will benefit greatly from spending as much time as possible with you."

Voerell broke into an uncertain, uncharacteristically shy smile. "Well, in that case...I'll see you then." She gave Maryn's hand a brief squeeze, released it, and strode quickly from the bedroom. Maryn trailed after her into the nursery. The guards converged on Voerell and ushered her into the hall. The door shut behind them, and all was quiet.

Barilan stirred in Maryn's arms. He opened his eyes and began to fuss, chewing on one fist. Maryn hugged him close. "Hungry again already? Are you trying to grow as big as your grandfather before you're a year old? Just because you're the king now doesn't mean you have to fill his shoes for quite a few years yet. Your mother will do that very capably until you're ready."

The infant king squirmed in her arms, showing her in every way he knew how that he was hungry, and thirsty, and needed the closeness and comfort of her breast. Maryn didn't mind. Barilan would have to grow up far too soon, with far too many responsibilities thrust upon him at a very young age.

Who would he become, as the years passed? Would he grow to be as strong as his mother? Or might he choose to follow the same corrupt path as his uncle?

Maryn didn't know. Nor did she know if anything she or Voerell could do would alter that outcome.

Only one thing was within her power. She could give Barilan the love and care that would form the foundation on which he would build his life, for good or ill.

Maryn sank into the large soft chair by the hearth, pulled down her shift, and settled Barilan in to nurse.

Author's Note

Although *White Blood* is fantasy, a number of elements in the story are drawn from history. The idea that children who breastfeed from the same women become siblings has been held by various cultures. The upper classes of many times and places employed wet nurses to care for their children. The mirror test that Coewyn gives Maryn's milk is based on a real practice. And the phrase "white blood" has been used to describe breastmilk because of the multitude of living cells, enzymes, and active immune factors it contains. If you'd like to learn more about this fascinating subject, visit my website at www.angelaholder.com.

Acknowledgements

Thanks to all the women online and in real life who taught me about breastfeeding, helped me breastfeed my own children, and let me help them learn to breastfeed their babies. Special thanks to all the past and present Leaders of La Leche League, who built and continue to run an international organization while always putting family first, and who tirelessly champion the power of breastfeeding in a world where people all too often consider it a trivial thing, not worthy of study, of interest only to women and children.

Thanks to the women of YAAPS who have supported me in my parenting journey, and whose generosity in sharing their lives and emotions over the past fifteen years have opened my eyes to worlds beyond my own. Anyone who doubts that real community can exist on the Internet need look no further than this very special website for proof that it can.

Thanks to the people of TORC who helped reawaken my passion for writing, and the people of Henneth Annun, TheForce.net and Fanfiction.com who encouraged it.

Thanks to the people of Nanowrimo who helped me make the leap from fanfiction to original works, and taught me how to get the stories in my head onto paper (pixels) in a timely fashion.

Thanks to the people of CritiqueCircle.com who helped me turn a rough draft into a polished book.

Thanks to ShadeyBabey at deviantART for the image I used as the background of the cover.

Thanks to my husband Anthony for his unwavering support, and to my children, Rachel, Bethany, and Gareth, for being my first and most enthusiastic audience and my best proofreaders.

About the Author

Angela Holder lives in Houston, Texas, with her husband and two younger children; the oldest is grown, married, and out on her own. She spends a lot of time in Starbucks, drinking skinny vanilla lattes and telling stories about her imaginary friends. She enjoys dabbling in many hobbies, including spinning, knitting, weaving, costuming, hot air ballooning, singing in her church choir, and performing in amateur musicals. She's been a volunteer breastfeeding counselor for over twelve years. This is her first published book. For news about future releases, visit her website at www.angelaholder.com or like her Facebook page at www.facebook.com/angelaholderauthor.